QUICK OFF THE MARK

An Alex Quick Mystery

Susan Moody

This first world edition published 2016
in Great Britain and the USA by
SEVERN HOUSE PUBLISHERS LTD of
19 Cedar Road, Sutton, Surrey, England, SM2 5DA

Trade paperback edition first published 2017
In Great Britain and the USA by
SEVERN HOUSE PUBLISHERS LTD
Eardley House, 4 Uxbridge Street, London W8 7SY

British Library Cataloguing in Publication Data
A CIP catalogue record for this title is available from the British Library.

ISBN-13: 978-0-7278-8658-3 (cased)
ISBN-13: 978-1-84751-760-9 (trade paper)
ISBN-13: 978-1-78010-826-1 (e-book)

PROLOGUE

By now the pain had been ratcheted up to such an extreme that he was jolting in and out of consciousness, head filled with a black blur of agony, edged with the crimson of blood which had seeped from the places where slices of his flesh had been removed. A brutal blow to his hammer-shattered knee sent him into another abyss of excruciating pain. His lips pulled back from what were left of his teeth. Blood dripped heavily into his mouth from his ruined nose.

And all the time, the voice – real or imagined? – intoned, 'This is what it feels like.'

This was not interrogation, but punishment, pure and simple. He wondered at its extreme ferocity. What had he done? Did he deserve this? Some might say he did, but he'd been no worse than hundreds of others. So why him? Why now? OK, so he had sometimes been careless. Dangerously so. *Criminally* so, though it had not always been his fault. Not entirely. This level of brutality was not something he had ever encountered before. Never even come close to. Not personally. Not in Afghanistan or Somalia. Not in Kyoto. Not even in Hong Kong.

A sledgehammer smashed into his chest. Bones cracked. 'This is what it feels like.' He tried to scream, but he had howled so much over the past few hours that his lungs no longer had the capacity to fill with air and his throat was little more than a torn and ragged wound.

Pale images drifted. The decorated bone handle of the knife he'd once used to slit a man's throat. A length of butterfly-embroidered brocade. His unknown father. Alex Quick's fox-red hair. A girl he'd once had in Kabul, all milk-chocolate skin and terrified eyes.

He registered the noise of something mechanical being switched on. By now he was beyond fear, just abandoned to pain. He cringed at the racking torment as the electric drill bit into his hip bone. 'This is what it feels like.'

Despite the clouds of agony, he was able to wonder if it had all been worth it. Able to decide that it probably had.

It had certainly meant a lot to him. Everything, really. Those who had it would never understand the hunger for money of those who did not have it, but wanted it. Poor Mother. He'd hated to see her weeping over the household bills when he and Dim were small. Now the money was so well concealed that they would probably never find it. His lips moved faintly. What irony. What a waste.

Death reappeared somewhere close. It was the drill again. The voice again. 'This is what it . . .' The pain was so excruciating that, as darkness gathered, as his eyes melted and bled tears, as his heart wavered, he was in no doubt that it was the last sensation he would ever feel.

ONE

'Come along, Marlowe, stop bloody mucking about, will you!'

Major Norman Horrocks stared round his garden. Where had the wretched animal got to now? He'd never been a dog-lover in the first place, certainly not the sort who cootchy-cootchy-cooed with them ('*Oh, isn't he* sweet?') or kissed them on the lips. Disgusting when you thought about where and what they licked and sniffed. Kissed? *Kicked* would be nearer the mark, long as nobody else was around. Mind you, he'd once owned a gun dog, best there ever was, pure-bred setter, called him Leo, not his pedigree name, of course, which was as long as your arm. But this ruddy little centipede . . .

He didn't normally use such coarse language, especially when his next-door neighbour – Marlowe's mistress – was at home, but she wasn't today. Nor, sadly, would she ever be.

'Marlowe!' he shouted militarily. 'Get yourself out here, sir. Quick, now. On the double.' He slashed at some nettles by the garden gate with his walking stick (a present for his retirement from the regiment; nice gold band round the ferrule with his dates of service inscribed on it), and speared an empty crisp packet which had drifted down from the rubbish bin at the top of the lane. Bloody litter-louts, he thought sourly, sourness tending increasingly to be his default position. Bloody Marlowe. Marlowe, forsooth! All Nell Roscoe's dogs had preposterous names: give him a Rex or a Towser any day. Still, Marlowe was better than her last one, unfortunately run over in the lane by an anonymous van. Never knew who, though Nell had her suspicions. Called it Dashiell, if you please. Dashiell . . . I ask you.

Nell Roscoe, rightful owner of the dog. Only had to go and get herself taken to the General Hospital a couple of months ago, didn't she? Suppurating ulcers on her legs or some such, really didn't need to know the details, thank you. Which had left Marlowe to be cared for by himself until such time as they brought her back home. At the time, God alone had known when that was likely to be, the way they were running hospitals these days, lying on a gurney the first three weeks, like as not, nobody helping the poor old girl to the WC. Didn't bear thinking about.

He paused. And now she never would be coming home. Just as well, really. Frankly, she'd never been the same since Lil did away with herself, after the child's unexpected death. Upshot was, he'd done what he could to help out, which recently had included taking the dog Marlowe for its daily craps. And now . . . Hells bells.

'Marlowe!' he called, his voice gentler than before because when all was said and done, Nell had been a nice old biddy, always ready with the gin bottle and a Findus Shepherd's Pie, and so what if half of it was horse meat? Nobody's dropped dead from eating horse so far, don't know why the newspapers got their knickers in such a twist about it. Even Princess Anne getting in on the act, pointing out the bloody Frogs do it all the time, and look at *them*, if you could bear to, all black berets and garlic, and anyway, he'd eaten far worse during his life in the military. 'Marlowe,' he called again. 'Let's be having you. Come on, boy. Look lively. Quick march!'

Marlowe emerged backwards from a bush which the Major was trying unsuccessfully to train into a facsimile of a peacock. When he'd moved into Rattrays (Rattrays? What kind of a name was that for a country cottage? Nell's place next door was called Metcalfe . . . I ask you!) ten years ago, and absorbed its acre of unkempt grass and shapeless box hedges, he'd had a vision of exquisitely laid-out knot-gardens with orderly growths of herbs and aromatic plants, a water-garden, maybe a maze, and topiary which would astound and delight passers-by. Not just balls, cones and spirals but cats and cockerels, rabbits, tortoises. He'd seen a full size elephant-family once, on the lawn of a stately home he'd visited with his wife. Dragons, he'd seen elsewhere. A pop group, complete with guitars and drums. Huge cats. All made out of bushes of box.

'Man's ingenuity never ceases to amaze me,' he'd said to Esther at the time. 'You what?' she'd responded. But his own topiarial efforts had been, he had to admit, something of a failure. One straggling ball, one tottery cone, and a peacock that might just as well have been a newspaper for all the resemblance it bore to a bird of any kind.

He walked along the lane, remembering other visions he'd had at the time they'd moved down here from Catterick. Esther in a longish sort of dirndl skirt, putting up preserves from garden produce, and gathering blackberries for jam. Himself breeding sheep, or maybe goats, keeping bees at the end of the garden, rows of little white hives, hat with a veil on it, Esther raising Buff Orpingtons, hatching eggs between her substantial breasts (a mental picture which never failed to rouse him, even now). Himself in a cherry-coloured waistcoat over a tattersall shirt, waxed jacket hanging on a hook behind the door, except Esther had told him he looked like a right ponce when he came down one morning in the waistcoat and shirt, and he hadn't worn it since, not even after she passed away from stomach cancer. A sad end, really. She'd been a helluva girl when he married her, Anglo-Indian blood she'd told him at the time, beautiful as sin, all black eyes and crimson mouth, not to mention that waterfall of ebony hair halfway down her white back. Gorgeous.

'These are moments of pure magnificence,' he'd said to her once, looking at the knobs of her spine, the cataract of her hair, feeling something transcendent, far more uplifting than mere sexual desire.

'You been at the whisky, Norm?' she'd said.

That'd been years ago. To be honest, the years had not been kind to her.

Marlowe snuffled along beside him. Marlowe only came up to the Major's ankle, step on the bloody animal if you weren't careful, a bundle of ginger and white fur, always looked in need of a good barber. 'Wouldn't get away with that hairstyle in the Army,' he said now, feeling something close to friendship with the little animal. 'It'd be short back and sides before you could say clippers.' After all these enforced days together, it was only to be expected. He had devised a way of smuggling the tiny creature into the hospital when he went to visit Nell, used to cheer the old girl up no end. A small bottle from the fridge, cunningly disguised as orange juice, although it was at least fifty per cent Gordons, used to cheer her up even more than the dog. All over now, of course, since she'd finally shuffled off this mortal whatsit.

Feeling melancholy, he started to sing. '*Goodby-ee, goodby-ee,*' he carolled, slashing at the blackthorn on either side of the lane. '*Wipe the tear, baby dear, from—*' Around him, all nature cowered breathlessly, stunned by the sound.

Coming towards him along the lane was a horse, Charabanc III (by *Coach-Party* out of *Off To The Races*), with a chignon-netted, black-helmeted woman up (the Major, an infantry officer who'd never been nearer a horse than a Dick Francis novel, loved using this kind of equine jargon).

'Oh, it's you, Major, making that infernal din,' she said, leaning down and tapping him on the shoulder with her crop. 'Charry nearly threw me when you started up.'

'*—your eye-ee,*' sang the Major firmly, tipping the brim of his hat, or at least raising his finger to where the brim would have been had he been wearing a hat, wishing Charabanc III had had the guts to go through with it. He wasn't going to let the likes of Maggie Double-Barrel boss him around. If he wanted to sing, then he would jolly well sing.

'I hear the Head of Music at the girls' grammar school takes private pupils,' Maggie said, bearing her yellow teeth in a grin that would have startled Charry even more than the Major's singing. 'I'm sure he'd take you on, he likes a challenge.'

Oh, piss orf, you old cow, thought the Major. 'How're the grandchildren?' he asked. The two of them proceeded to exchange anecdotes about their grandchildren, all of them designed to indicate how clever, gifted, gorgeous and kind their own were, while Charabanc III gnawed at the grassy verge, occasionally showing the whites of his eyes or producing whiffling snorts.

Honour satisfied (the Major definitely the winner on points), the two of them parted. Where the lane forked, he took the lower road, which went past fields to the road leading onwards to the town and the sea, and paused to lean in a bucolic kind of way on a five-barred gate in order to gaze at the view. Had there been a grass-stem at hand for him to chew on, he might have picked one, but even if there had been, the Council had recently sprayed both sides of the road, and the Major had no wish to come down with some toxic disease; eyeballs turning yellow, like as not, tongue gone black, giant pustules starting up all over his body, nose falling off. He'd seen enough of that when he was growing up in Edmonton, thank you (Just kidding, of course). It was on service in the tropics – Senegal, Morocco – that he had indeed seen men with ghastly diseases; beriberi, dysentery, dengue fever and the like, great big swollen legs, family jewels so enlarged they needed a wheelbarrow to carry them around in, poor chaps, eyes swivelling like ping-pong balls. Horrible.

'Ah,' thought the Major. 'This is the life.' He took in a deep breath of sun-warmed country air, and wrinkled his nose. What the hell was that stink? Didn't smell like manure. Nor dog poo. Marlowe was going bonkers inside the field on the other side of the hedge, whining and scrabbling and he yelled at him to shut up, not that the dog took a blind bit of notice. A black cloud of flies suddenly took to the air, buzzing like helicopters. The Major breathed in again, and bit his lip. The smell was all too familiar, a smell he'd experienced time and again during his army career. The stench of death.

He lifted the rectangular metal thingy which kept the gate shut, and trod over the deep ruts which criss-crossed the muddy entrance to the field (dried up now, of course, hadn't been a drop of rain for weeks), until he could see down the line of the hedge to where Marlowe was barking, lifting a paw as he did so, then moving round the object of his attention, barking and lifting again. Even from this distance, the Major could tell that it was a body. He'd seen plenty of death in Africa, and later in Afghanistan (bloodthirsty little devils they were, too) and it was never a good experience, though death comes to us all, as Esther had told him when he stood teary-eyed beside her hospital bed, ('*and don't you forget it, Norm, could be you next.*').

Not so bad when the person had died relatively peacefully, or even like one of his superior officers, shot neatly through the head at his own desk, brains all over the wall behind him, gun tidily on the surface in front of him. Never did find out who was responsible, not that the investigating officers tried too hard, because the man was such an arrogant, self-righteous bastard, that the entire regiment had a motive, the general feeling being let sleeping colonels die.

As he approached closer, it became apparent that this corpse had been horribly mutilated before death. It lay on the rough grass at the edge of the plough, hidden from the road by the blackthorn hedge. It was semi-naked, cigarette burns everywhere, looked as though someone had carved it up like a Sunday joint, trousers pulled down to the knees (good-quality cavalry twill, the Major couldn't help noticing) to display the fact that where there had once been a – ahem – penis, there was now merely a hole full of jellified black blood and flies. Coming nearer, the Major saw that the gashes in the chest had been carefully cleaned so that it was possible to make out that they actually spelled the word *cheat.*

Gawd help us, he thought, and what kind of cheat would that be? Hardly a game of Scrabble or Bridge, though possibly a poker game might rouse anger enough to lead to murder (chairs pushed back, guns drawn, "*Why, ya lousy stinkin' cheat, take that!*"). What about adultery? Or a drug deal gone wrong? Lies told, money embezzled, or – the Major's imagination surged wildly – a vendetta?

Not killed here, though, he thought. There was no blood on the grassy edge of the field, so the dirty deed must have taken place elsewhere. Would have to have been somewhere isolated so you couldn't hear the screams – an empty barn, perhaps, or that derelict warehouse sort of place more or less hidden in the woods alongside the Longbury Road. Then loaded into a van, brought here and tossed over the hedge, maybe even two of them in on it, work of a minute, no CCTV cameras either, not out here, so no danger of identification, then back behind the wheel and away, no one the wiser. Not a dignified death, in any sense of the word.

A soldier he might once have been, but he didn't like bloodshed. He'd seen enough of both while on active service, as well as with poor Esther's long-drawn-out submission to the Grim Reaper.

He grabbed Marlowe's collar, attached the lead, set off at a fair old pace back to Rattrays, in order to call the police. His son had given him one of those mobile things with a miniature screen, but he couldn't be doing with it, and though the grandchildren were always urging him to get with the programme, Grandpa, babbling on about tweets and twitters and such like ('*sounds like a blasted aviary*'), he'd never managed to come to terms with the Internet. Load of old cobblers, in the Major's opinion. Who needed to be in constant twenty-four-a-day touch with their nearest and dearest? Certainly not him.

Behind his house, the trees in the little copse which bordered the canal were tossing about in the rising wind, a few early leaves swirling off their branches to spin in the turbulent air. The skies were darkening, too.

'Rain at last,' the Major said to the nearest box-tree, as he passed it. 'And it looks like it's going to bloody pour.'

Having called the police, he opened a tin of some revolting meaty mess (unwashed pigs' bums, diseased cows' lips, all ground up, ugh!) and turned it out into Marlowe's dish. There were some boiled carrots left from last night's supper and the Major mixed them in while Marlowe looked at him as if he were mad. *Carrots?* his expression said. *Dogs don't eat vegetables, you dick.*

Leaving Marlowe to his meal, the Major donned his best thorn-proof tweed jacket and marched smartly back down the lane to the field where he (or rather the dog, Marlowe) had found the body, narrowly avoiding being run down by a group of men bent over the handlebars of their racing bikes. Bloody cyclists! Looked like bloody wasps in those poncey yellow outfits.

Though the rain was holding off, the lane was already clotted with police cars, burly men in hi-vis jackets, other people shuffling about in white coveralls that made them look like they'd just landed on the moon, some kind of white tent erected to hide the body from the elements and the gathering gawpers.

'Stand back, if you please, sir,' some police jobsworth ordered, and the Major said importantly, 'Look here, sonny, it was me who found the body. I'm the one who called the police.'

'Right.' The cop walked over to a sandy sort of bloke in suit and tie, conferred with him and then came back. 'Inspector Garside will be with you in a moment, if you wouldn't mind waiting. Behind the barrier, if you please.'

'Don't want to contaminate the scene of the crime any further, eh?' The Major tapped the side of his nose, feeling like something out of a gangster movie. Maybe tomorrow he'd break out the cherry waistcoat and the Tattersall-checked shirt (if the moths hadn't got to it first), now there was no Esther around to pass remarks. The thought brought him up short. Over the years, she'd turned hypochondria into a fine art, although no doctor worthy of his salt was going to sympathize with her catalogue of illnesses, which were mainly of a sort that prevented her from doing anything useful round the house. She'd been a gifted self-diagnostician, suffering – if you believed her – from every ailment going, especially if she read about it in the *Daily Mail*, though until it was far too late, she'd failed to spot the stomach cancer which eventually took her off. But he missed her, missed her voice yacking on from the kitchen about her sciatica or her swollen ankles and her latest carcinogenic scare ('*I'm not being funny, Norm, but I'm sure I've got cancer of the fingernails*'). Would he ever find another woman to love as he had loved her? Sadly, he thought not.

The sandy man arrived. 'So what can you tell us, Captain—'

'Major,' corrected the Major.

'—Major . . . um . . . Horrocks?'

The Major told his tale. Mentioned the possibility that there could have been two perps, pointed out the number of flies. 'Body must have been there a while.'

'And did you touch anything, Major Horrocks? Disturb the scene of crime?'

'Not bloody likely.'

'Recognize the victim?'

'As you may have noticed, Inspector, not a lot of the face was left, so no, I didn't. Though I can't,' he added, 'speak for Marlowe.'

'Marlowe?'

'The dog, Marlowe. Named after some American Private

Eye, I believe, Philip Marlowe, played on the silver screen by Humphrey Bogart and Robert Mitchum, among others.'

The Inspector didn't think this was as interesting as the Major did. 'Did the animal interfere with the scene in any way?'

'He got there before I did, so I can't say. But I don't think so. All he interfered with was the flies, basically.'

'I see.'

Depressing sort of chap, the Major thought. Some people have no sense of humour. He'd learned from long experience that a little light-heartedness helped things along, especially in a situation as wretched as this one. Anyway, sad though it was, *tragic* for some poor soul, he certainly had something to keep his mates at the pub going when he got down there later.

Nell would have been sorry to miss all this, she liked a nice murder, did Nell – house full of old crime novels, always watching stuff on the TV, especially those stern Nordic ones, not his cup of tea at all. He decided he would shortly walk into town, get his shopping done, stop in for half a pint at the Fox and Hounds on his way home, calm his nerves after the excitement of the morning.

All in all, and bodies notwithstanding – we've all got to go sometime, one way or another – a good sort of day, really. Well, good was perhaps the wrong word given the corpse along the lane, but out of the ordinary, certainly.

As he walked back to his cottage, it started to rain.

TWO

I was lingering over a cup of tea at the breakfast table. Contemplating my current unattached status. Wondering if I minded being on my own. Knowing that deep down, whatever I might pretend, I did.

Over the years since my former husband, Jack the Love Rat, had left, I'd more or less recovered physically from the loss of my unborn child, though in my darkest moments the sheer emotional agony of the miscarriage, the sense of loss and terminal despair, flooded back as if it had occurred only that morning. I doubted if I would fully recover psychologically for years to come, if ever. Since those black days, there had been plenty of opportunity for new relationships, if that's what you wanted to call them. Nothing serious, on either side. Nothing more than phantoms of possibilities, serving to remind me that at least I was in some measure still desirable. Or, at its lowest, still female. Some guys didn't even make it to a first date, let alone anything else. For example, I'd encountered Michael McLellan, a visiting history prof, at a party up On The Hill, as we liked to call our higher education college.

'So, pretty lady, what do you do for a living?' he'd said. Definitely not my preferred pick-up line. Especially from someone who couldn't care less what I did out of bed. He'd leaned an arm against the wall beside me, blocking my means of escape. I'd heard of him from a friend who worked in the college library: his easy ways, his film-star looks – brown hair flopping over his forehead, intensely grey eyes, a ready smile. His ways were a bit *too* easy, in my opinion, since I knew he had a wife and two small children at home.

'Brainy, as well as beautiful,' he commented, when I told him I was a picture anthologist. Condescending prick. Probably didn't even know what that meant. And certainly wasn't interested in finding out. 'So how about meeting me for a drink tomorrow evening? Or dinner. Or . . . whatever?' The final word loaded with cheap sexual significance, backed up by some active eyebrow work.

'Lovely,' I said, slipping out from under his arm. 'Would this proposed meeting be before or after you've kissed your kids goodnight?'

He stared at me, non, as the saying goes, plussed. 'Bitch!' he said finally. He tossed back his hair. Showing me what I was missing?

I flipped him the finger. 'Take a hike, Mike,' I said, and moved off, something I'm sure he wasn't used to women doing.

So much for Michael McLellan.

Dr Milton Novak was a different story. Small, energetic, a

serious man with a serious mission, seconded from his hospital in Charlottesville, USA, to spend a sabbatical in England. Not the philandering sort. Definitely not another McLellan. I had felt a real kinship with him, especially when I discovered that he knew everything there was to know about the films of the Coen brothers. He was divorced, he told me, and lonely. We had sat over food, or drink, or both, for hours discussing the merits of *No Country for Old Men* as against *Fargo,* Frances McDormand's performance in *Fargo* against *Raising Arizona.* I went to bed with him and found his energy was as much sexual as intellectual.

One cold midwinter morning we were in bed together in my flat when the phone rang. I reached out a sleepy hand and picked it up. 'Yes?'

'I'd like to speak to Milt,' a voice drawled in a Katherine Hepburn kind of accent. 'It's his wife.'

Wordlessly, I handed him the phone, listened to the first two sentences of his conversation, got out of bed, poured the contents of a flower-vase over his clothes lying on the floor, then opened the window of my bedroom and threw them as far as I could. In the bathroom, I ran the cold tap, filled a tooth mug and tipped it over his chest.

'*C'mon*, baby,' he protested angrily, the phone call now over, still stark naked as he got out of bed and tried to wipe himself dry with one of my silk scarves which was lying across a chair. He glanced from the window to where his clothes lay scattered on the frosty grass below, calculating whether he had time to get to them from the front door of my block and clamber into his, by now (with any luck), stiffly frozen trousers before some startled citizen passed by.

'You told me you were divorced, you bastard,' I said, surprised at how calm I sounded.

'So I am.'

'You said you were lonely.'

'I'm in England, honey, of course I'm lonely.'

'Don't call me honey,' I said. 'And how come you didn't mention that you'd married again?'

His voice hardened. 'What did you think? I'm thirty-seven, I'm a doctor in the States, so apart from Donald Trump, one of the biggest catches on the planet, I was temporarily single . . . naturally the gals came flocking.'

'Not this one,' I spat. 'Not any more. Now get out!'

Opening my front door, I watched him start off down the passage towards the lift, butt-naked, buttocks jiggling together in a manner I had to admit was dead sexy, then screamed, at the top of my voice, 'Help! Somebody help me! Help!'

The sound of doors opening up and down the building, voices exclaiming – I could distinctly make out the fluting voice of Miss Gardiner from the ground floor – was almost satisfaction enough, though once I'd watched him through the window as he shivered into his ice-stiffened clothes, explained himself to an inquisitive policeman, then driven off in his BMW, I found myself in tears. I was an educated, independent, energetic woman of ideas. The world – so the careers mistress at school had told me several times – stood at my feet. If only I didn't sometimes feel like I was falling off the edge of it.

On the other hand . . . a friend, Charlotte Plimpton, who worked in the college library, had recently persuaded me to join a drama group up on the hill. 'You need to get out more, Alex,' she'd said. 'Meet some new people. Take an interest in something different. They're very nice – at least most of them are, though there are some sizeable egos as well. I'm sure you'll enjoy it.'

She had been right. At first I did. Especially after coming across the fanciable dude who ran it. He was called Milo Stanton. Dark, brooding. The Heathcliff type. Very much on my wavelength, and a pretty good amateur actor. He taught Drama and Eng Lit and, at first sight, seemed to be a Good Thing. A bit too much up himself, if truth be told, but definitely promising.

All at once, there was a frenzied banging at my door. A finger pressed to the doorbell. More banging. It didn't take too much detective work to realize that someone wanted to speak to me. I stood up, went into the hall, opened my front door.

'Dim!' I exclaimed. 'What're you—'

Dimsie Drayton pushed past me. 'Oh God, Alex!' She moved rapidly into my sitting room and collapsed on to the sofa. 'Alex. Oh *God*!' She bent her head into her hands and began sobbing.

'What?' I sat down beside her and put an arm across her shoulders, drawing her closer. Perhaps unkindly, I wondered what had set her off this time. A drama queen to the core, Dimsie was given to copious weeping over things like dead birds and squashed beetles. I wasn't. Not that I didn't feel vaguely sorry that they died, but at least it was quick and I certainly didn't take it to heart. 'What's happened, Dim?'

'It's Tristan,' she said.

'Tristan?' I could feel my heart drop inside my chest. This didn't sound like dead birds. This sounded serious. Tristan was her brother. A man with whom I had dallied when we were both in our early twenties, though Dimsie didn't know that. 'What's he done? Drink? Gambling? Gun-running? People-smuggling?' I laughed. Nervously. I loved Tris dearly, but I could easily believe him capable of any, or all, of the misdemeanours I'd mentioned.

'He's *dead*.' Dimsie clutched at my shirt. 'Someone *killed* him, Alex.' Her voice rose to a shriek. 'My darling brother. Oh *Alex* . . .'

'Tristan? Dead?' Two words it was almost impossible to connect. I got up and poured her a glass of Armagnac. 'Drink that,' I ordered. 'Then tell me what's happened.' I gave myself a nip, too, despite the early hour. Tristan murdered simply didn't compute.

She gulped at the brandy, tears pouring down her face, coughing as the spirit caught at her throat. Through sobs and hiccups, she managed to explain that a dog-walker had found Tristan's body dumped in a field along a little-used lane on the outskirts of town. 'He'd been . . . he'd been *tortured*, Alex. They'd smashed his knees, his chest. Cut . . . cut bits off him with knives. *Castrated* him! My poor brother. But why, Alex? What has he ever done?'

'I don't know.' I couldn't think of an answer. On the surface, Tristan Huber really was the most harmless of men. I always thought of him as a Scarlet Pimpernel, a languorous fop on the surface, a man of steel beneath. Rosy cheeks. Hair slicked back. Languid in a particularly English way. The Bertie

Wooster *de nos jours*. The sort of guy you see in the background of ads for waxed jackets or green wellies, carrying a broken gun in the crook of an arm. It was difficult to imagine him getting on the wrong side of somebody to the extent that they would use knives on him.

'Oh, Tristan . . .' Dimsie moaned. Her shoulders shook. I put my arms around her and held her close. She smelled of thrice-milled soap, something French and expensive.

'Do you know who the dog-walker was?'

'A man called Major Something. Hassock? Hollick? Some name like that.' She bent over herself, tears dropping from her eyes.

'Horrocks. I know him.' Norman Horrocks ran the Poppy Day collections once a year for the British Legion, close to November Eleventh – the *Royal* British Legion, if you wanted to be pedantic about it, which the Major usually did – and I always volunteered, standing outside Sainsbury's with my collecting tin and tray of papery poppies.

'You used to be a policeman, Alex.' She hiccupped. 'A police *officer*.'

'This is true.' In fact, I'd been the youngest Detective Chief Inspector in the country, at one time. Passed out second highest in my class at Hendon Police College, then moved rapidly from uniform to plainclothes. (Just saying).

'So you'd be able to talk to the local bobbies, find out what they know.'

'I could try. Better still, I could go and talk to the Major myself. It might be more productive.'

'And then you'll tell me?'

'Of course I will.'

'Because, Alex, when I find who did it, I will personally kill them.'

She spoke through gritted teeth, sounding so like her ferocious mother that I involuntarily cringed. 'Good idea, Dim.'

'I *mean* it.' She gazed at me with tear-flooded eyes. 'Tristan never did anyone any harm. He was the sweetest, kindest . . .' She pressed at her face with the sheet torn from the roll of kitchen towel I'd handed her.

I wondered how well she really knew her brother. Sweet

and kind, sure. But also a man with a deep well of hard ruthlessness into which he dipped when he needed to. I'd once watched him see off three shaven-headed yobs menacing a couple of Asian girls with nothing more lethal than his hands. Mind you, a properly executed karate chop could be as dangerous as a gun, I had thought, as two of them fell howling to the ground and were scooped up by the police, while the third legged it round the corner, only to be returned to join his mates by a cold-eyed Tristan.

'Why do you want me involved?' I asked. 'Why not leave it up to the police? All I'd be able to do would be to duplicate what they'll already have done.'

'Yes, but to them, he's just another c-corpse.' Her voice trembled. 'Whereas to you, it's m-more personal. You *know* him. Besides, I just know they won't k-keep me in the frame. Not like you will.' Her chin trembled too. Her little hand clutched at my sleeve. A maiden truly in distress. 'Alex, you can't possibly refuse to help me.'

Of course I couldn't. It was blackmail of the crudest kind. But Dimsie was one of those women with lashings of what my uncle up in Scotland, Sir Aylward de Cuik, called Winning Ways. In other words, a quivering lip, a tear falling from one of those velvety purple eyes, a blush-mantled cheek. Most people gave up the fight and did whatever she asked them to. So I agreed to do my very best to find out what the cops knew and then to pass it on to her. It was another half hour before she left, refusing my offer to drive her home. I promised to get in touch as soon as I knew anything more. I walked her downstairs to the parking area. I watched her steer her racy little late-model Porsche 911 up the drive which led from my block of flats to the main road and across it, the promenade and the sea.

My heart was bruised by the news she'd brought. I'd known Dimsie and Tristan for most of my life. Their mother, the fearsome Dorcas Huber-Drayton, was a good friend and contemporary of my own parents, Edred and Mary Quick. When we were about eight years old, I asked Dimsie where her father was and – obviously coached by her mother – she said he was circumnavigating the globe, which I thought sounded very grand and mysterious. It wasn't until I was fifteen or so that it occurred to me that he was taking a heck of a long time about it. In fact, I'd never heard another word about him.

My father calls the Huber-Draytons 'the People of the Mislaid Spouses'. Like Tristan, Dimsie had been married – or so she said – but there were no marital encumbrances hanging round either of them. Nor any offspring. Nor had any of us been invited to attend either wedding. The siblings were very close, in age, in outlook and in ambition, not to mention hearts, and I knew Dimsie would find the loss of her brother a terrible blow. She travelled through life on a series of roller coaster ups and downs, a gifted manic-depressive – or bipolar, as it's now called – since childhood. Luckily her depressive stages had been short-lived and her manic ones benign. So far, at least. But I could easily imagine her trying to avenge her brother. And succeeding.

Tristan was tall and strapping, unlike his tiny fawn-like sister. Despite his distinguished school career – prizes for classical studies, prizes for history, prizes for French and Spanish, top marks in the public exams for Russian, cricket captain – he had wanted to go to art school but was dissuaded by a battery of military Huber-Drayton uncles ('*never earn a decent whack out of painting pretty pictures, boy*') and the fact that his mother, Dorcas, had no money for fees. I know he was bitter about it. By the time he was twenty, he had done nothing in particular: odd jobs here and there, a stint with an architectural firm, a short course in EFL (which he hated).

'I don't want to go into the Army,' he told me once. 'But my mother can't afford to subsidize me – nor would I expect her to. I had a privileged education, I know that, but it was mainly because the uncles didn't want a Huber-Drayton attending a comprehensive.'

Eventually, to placate them, he signed on with some elite regiment, reached an impressive rank or other, was posted to various danger-spots and then two or three years later, resigned.

On his twenty-seventh birthday, he took me out for dinner. The next morning, he inexplicably vanished without saying a word to anyone. Just up and left with little more than a toothbrush, a passport and a clean pair of knickers – and about the latter I'm only guessing. Where did he go? What did he do? He'd never talked about it, though he did once tell me that he'd gone through some life-changing experiences. That was all he ever said.

'I think he's finding himself,' Dimsie told me once, thereby conjuring up images of gurus in saffron robes, begging bowls, wailing sitars. We all assumed he had been killed. Until he returned one day, two years or so later, looking much the same as when he disappeared. Leaner, perhaps, and harder, with a scar extending from his right temple down to his jaw. I never knew if he'd found himself, or someone else altogether. After reverting to his first love, art, he took a diploma course at the RCA, then set up a highly successful business with his sister, both keeping their independence as separate companies, but usually working alongside each other: Huber Associates and The Dimsie Drayton Studios. There was a pleasing piquancy between his athletic physique, his Army career and his somewhat effete (come on, be honest) occupation, which sometimes took him away from home for weeks at a time.

Although at first sight, nothing could seem more unlikely, Dimsie was in fact a clone of her terrifying mother. Despite the golden hair and the big violet eyes, she possessed a business brain like a steel trap, with a soul to match. Hence her huge success in the interior design world. Her car alone must have set her back a cool £75,000 and counting. Equally, Tristan was constantly in demand all over Europe, particularly in the Gulf States and, surprisingly, in France. The former were looking for the Stately Home look, which always seemed odd to me, given the whole architectural and interior design ethos of the region, *white founts falling in the courts of the sun*, black shadows shed on alabaster tiles, minarets and domes and all that, while the latter wanted country *chateaux* or their *apartements* in the best *quartiers* done up in *le style anglais*. Lucrative on either count. Given my artistic credentials, even I had sometimes been roped in to work for them under the banner of Artistic Director. And a very useful source of extra income it was.

My brain whirred. Why anyone would want to torture someone like Tristan I couldn't imagine. Let alone kill him. What could they possibly have against him? What information did he possess that they wanted? Or was it a case of a jealous competitor, a disgruntled employee given the sack for whatever reason, a client who didn't like the way he had redecorated their home? Or was it something further back in his life: the Army, or those two missing years. All highly unlikely, in my opinion. I concentrated on not thinking about it until I knew more.

I pressed a number into my phone. 'Hey, Fliss,' I said, when the phone was answered. 'Quick here.'

'I know why you're calling,' Fliss said. 'It's about that body in Honeypot Lane, isn't it?'

'What are you, psychic or something?'

'No. I just know you and your Pinocchio nose.'

'Are you saying I've got a long nose?'

'Perhaps I mean Cyrano de Bergerac, not Pinocchio . . . or am I thinking of Gérard Depardieu?'

'Fliss, I have no idea what the hell you're thinking about.'

'OK, Quick, how can I help?'

Detective Chief Inspector Felicity Fairlight was one of my best mates, and had been a close colleague before I resigned from the force after my husband had left me to live with his long-term mistress. 'Tell me where the police are up to on this murder . . . it *is* murder, isn't it?'

'I should say so. The guy was cut to ribbons with a knife, joints broken, johnson sliced off by some bloodthirsty maniac. Then his body dumped in a field. Been there two or three days at least.'

'In this heat . . .' I murmured.

'Precisely. His wallet was left untouched in a back pocket of his trousers, so no problem identifying him. Said wallet stuffed with cash, just to inform interested parties like us that this wasn't a vicious mugging for money, but something much more.'

'Bizarre.'

'Murder's always bizarre. One way or another. You of all people should know that, Quick.'

And of course I did.

She coughed. 'And Quick . . .'

'What?'

'He wasn't dead when he was dumped.'

Oh, Tristan . . . 'Crap,' I said. We were both silent, thinking that one through. Finally, I said, 'What was the actual cause of death?'

'Basically, he bled out. Plus his heart gave way, I think. Some of the wounds should have been fatal. He must have been a pretty tough cookie to have lasted as long as our guys say he did.'

'Double crap. And no idea who could have wanted him dead?'

'Not a clue. Other than what we can get from the sister and the mother, we don't know anything about the man, apart from his client list. Not yet, anyway.' She filled in some more detail, most of which I really didn't want to hear.

'He was a good friend,' I said, voice wobbling a little. 'Him and h-his sister. W-we grew up together.'

'So this is a bit of a blow.'

'You could say that. Except that it's more than a "bit". I loved him. Most people did. He was lovable.'

'Any offspring?' Fliss herself was resolutely gay, with absolutely no ambitions to be a parent.

'None that I ever heard of. He was married at one point,' I said. 'They split up maybe four or five years ago. His sister can tell you more.'

'Thanks, Quick. In case they haven't already found that out, I'll pass it on.'

'Aren't you in charge on this one?'

'Unfortunately not. I got in after the body had been called in yesterday morning, so someone else got the job.'

I groaned. 'Please don't tell me it's Alan Garside again.' Inspector Garside and I went back several years, all of them acrimonious. Added to which, he'd been best mates with Jack the Love Rat, my former husband.

'Afraid so.'

'You will keep me up to speed, won't you?' I said. 'Like I said, I've known Tristan most of my life. My parents will be devastated at this news. I'll have to drive over to offer aid and comfort.'

Just as I was about to end the call, Fliss said, 'Quick . . .'

'Yes?'

'Your ears only . . . he had a word carved across his chest.'

'What word?'

'*Cheat.*'

THREE

Drowning in misery during the days after I was sent home from hospital following my miscarriage, I had found myself obsessively walking. Round the town, along the towpath, across the business school campus, down narrow streets I had never noticed before. One morning of aimless wandering, I'd found myself at the top of Honeypot Lane, the rural road where Tristan's body had been found. Fields on one side, woods on the other.

Now, I parked my car and walked slowly down the incline towards where I knew the Major lived. As I went, my eye followed the line of the hedge where what was left of poor Tristan had been dumped. As far as could be calculated – so Fliss had told me – his corpse had lain there in the blazing heat for two or three days, unnoticed by any passers-by, concealed from the road by the hawthorn hedge bounding the field, plus rough grass and thick overhangs of hazel growth and elder. The flat plates of white elder blossom of spring and early summer had given way by now to hard bunches of green berries turning dark purple. My mother liked to make a lethal elderberry wine called Mary's Malbec, bottles of which were left for three years in their cellar before drinking. They shared a shelf with the remaining bottles of their potato vodka, the rest having exploded.

I went through the gate and walked along the edge of the plough on the other side of the hedge, parallel to the road. From here, it was fairly obvious where the body had been found, since there was still a flutter of police tape hanging from the bushes, plus a marked car parked opposite the site, although currently there was no one sitting inside. A few gawpers had gathered, and further down, a couple of inquisitive cows leaned over a gate.

I knew that Major Horrocks lived in one of the only houses along the lane, two conjoined brick-and-flint cottages, with slate roofs and gingerbread eaves. As I walked back up the lane, emerging from one of them was a man with a dog on a red lead. A sign saying Rattrays was fixed to the gate. I quickened my pace.

'Excuse me,' I called.

The dog walker turned. He touched his hand to his forehead in an old-fashioned gesture.

'Major Horrocks?' I held out my hand. 'We have met. My name's Quick . . . Alexandra Quick.'

'Of course it is, my dear.' He was a tall man, with an erect carriage and a solid body. Despite his age, a good man to have around if trouble broke out, I would suspect. 'I remember you well.'

'You're the one who found poor Tristan Huber – his body, that is.'

'I'm very sorry,' he said. 'I didn't know him at all, but everything I've heard since points to him having been a good sort of chap. What a way to go, really doesn't bear thinking about.'

'You're obviously walking your dog,' I said, indicating the tiny hairy animal which danced and jittered on the end of its lead. 'I'll walk with you.'

'He's not exactly mine.' The Major made a face. 'Though I suppose he is now . . . used to belong to my neighbour but I've had to take possession.'

'Perhaps you would be kind enough to talk me through exactly how you came across the body.'

He stopped. 'Are you sure you want to do that?'

'Tristan Huber and his sister, Dimsie Drayton, have always been close friends,' I said. 'Dimsie is well aware that the police are doing everything they can. But she has also asked me to look into things, where possible, if only to collect the kind of detail the police might not bother to pass on to her. So I'd really like to see the site.' Although I'd just looked at it, roping in an on-the-spot witness is always a good scheme. 'And to hear anything else you'd care to tell me,' I added.

'No objections on my side.' We walked on until the Major stopped again. 'It was right behind that stretch of hedge,' he said. 'I let the dog, Marlowe, off his lead and leaned on that gate, as one does in the country, to survey the terrain, breathe in that good old country air, and then realized it wasn't all that good, if you know what I mean. At the same time, young Marlowe here was in the field and had started going barmy, barking and whining, and when I leaned forward to see what was upsetting him, looked along the hedge . . .' He indicated the prickly length of hawthorn which separated the field from the road, '. . . I could see what was obviously a body lying there . . . seen enough of those in my time, I can tell you.'

'What did the corpse look like?'

'It was bare-chested, trousers pulled down so you could see that he'd been . . .' The Major shuffled a bit, '. . . emasculated. Cuts all over the body, word carved on the chest . . . it really doesn't bear thinking about. Haven't felt the same about walking Marlowe down here since. Used to be nice, but looks like a war zone now.'

The grass along the hedge was crushed, the undergrowth trampled flat, thanks to the emergency services. It was horribly easy to see how Tristan's body had lain hidden for several days from passing cars and probably even from the occasional joggers for several days.

'Apart from myself, very few people walk along here,' the Major explained, as though following my thought processes. 'And as it happens, I'd gone away for five days, to stay with my son and his family – took the dog with me – or the . . . uh . . . body might have been found sooner.'

'So you wouldn't have heard or seen anything?'

''fraid not.'

My throat was thick with grief. Tristan had still been alive when he was dumped here like a sack of garbage. Still alive . . . desperately hurt, hoping, praying someone would help him, knowing both mother and sister, not to mention me, were so near. If someone had come across him sooner, he might have been saved. Even with the loss of blood. Even with the mutilation. I couldn't bear to think of his final moments, hoped he'd been unconscious by then.

The Major coughed. 'This may sound disrespectful, but it was Marlowe here who really did the finding. What a bastard the chap responsible must be, eh? Excuse my French. Do we even know if the police have produced a time of death?'

'They said that despite his wounds, he wasn't dead when he was thrown down behind that hedge.' I made a choking sound, somewhere between sorrow and rage. How frail the human body is, I thought. How susceptible to violence and disease. How easily dispatched.

'Bastard!' the Major repeated. He yanked at the dog's leash. 'Come along, sir. Chop, chop.' He looked at me sideways, and I sensed he was trying to do something to lighten my mood. 'All Nell Roscoe's dogs have had these preposterous names, d'you see? Still, Marlowe is far better than her last one.'

'What was *he* called?' I asked.

'Called it Dashiell, if you please. Dashiell . . . I ask you.'

'She was a detective fiction buff, then.'

'I'll say.' He turned back towards his house. Looked at his watch. Said, 'Could I tempt you in for a cup of coffee? Or tea?'

Why not? I thought. *Nothing now can come to any good* . . . 'That would be kind of you.'

The Major's cottage was neat, and surprisingly cosy for a single man, a military one at that. Evidence of time spent in the Far East was everywhere. Brass-topped tables, fretted mirrors, copper bowls, all highly-polished. Horse-brasses winked above a blackened oak mantel. Oriental vases stood here and there, or did service as the bases for lamps. He bustled about in the kitchen, while I did a swift inquisitive prowl of his sitting room, looking at the photographs displayed on most surfaces. Family groups. Ancient relatives from bygone eras. A couple of teenagers, one boy, one girl, the Major standing proudly behind with his hands on their shoulder. The same children, now grown up, on their various wedding days. An exotic-looking female in a fringed shawl, displaying rather more bosom than was advisable. Several of the Major in different ranks of military uniform, or uneasily holding babies. Another of him in a white judogi with a black belt.

I had picked one up which showed an elderly woman with her arm round a pale-faced younger one, when the Major brought in a tray with tea things. There were biscuits on a willow-patterned plate, and milk in a one-handled jug embossed with silver filigree over painted china flowers. He nodded at the photo in my hand.

'That's my neighbour,' he said. 'Nell Roscoe. My *former* neighbour, I should say. With her niece, Lilian Harkness. There's a very tragic story there.'

'What was that – if you don't mind telling me?' It was a good idea for me to remember that Dimsie's (or Tristan's) was not the only tragedy.

The Major poured milk and added tea. 'Try these biscuits,' he said, handing me a plate. 'Made them myself.'

I took one. 'Delicious!' I took another one.

'I enjoy cooking. Didn't have much choice really. It was that, or starve to death, my poor wife being a bit lacking in the culinary arts department.'

'Like my mother,' I said. 'And why do you have your neighbour's picture on your mantelpiece?'

'Least I could do, really. Poor old girl finally succumbed to years of – not to put too fine a point on it – gin and crime novels. Not,' he added, staring nervously around, as though Val McDermid or Lee Child might lurking behind the sofa, 'that crime novels are necessarily likely to cause death. Anyway, I got a letter from some solicitor chappie a few days after her death, informing me that, if you can believe it, she'd left me her house – that's Metcalfe, the cottage next door – and all its contents. On condition I gave Marlowe a good home. Could have knocked me down with a feather, as they say.'

'How very kind of her.'

'I'll say. Can't get over it, really. Mind you, she didn't have anyone else to leave things to, I suppose, what with one thing and another. Adopting Marlowe was a small price to pay for her generosity. Went out and bought the creature a new leather lead and collar especially for the interment, bright scarlet, to cheer things up.'

'I think I read about her death in the local paper. Wasn't she once the Head of English at the High School?'

'That's right. Sad, really. There were only five mourners, me and that woman from the shoe shop – Mrs Drummond, a former pupil, I believe – and Mr Vine, the man from the wine shop, who came every now and then to deliver the booze she ordered from him and to have a cup of tea and chat with her. Plus a couple of teachers from the school. And, of course, the dog Marlowe.' He held up a hand. 'No, tell a lie: there was someone else, came late and left early, the sister of – gawd, at the time, I never gave it a second thought! – the poor man who was murdered.'

'Why would she have come to Ms Roscoe's funeral?'

'Mark of respect, I suppose. Nell had one of them – can't remember if it was the brother or the sister – in to do up her sitting room. The former owners had made a right dog's dinner of it, ruined the spirit of the place, if you know what I mean.'

I didn't, but nodded anyway.

'Just going into that room before they got to work was enough to give me nightmares for a week. Don't know how she stood it for so long. No wonder she drank a bit more than was good for her. Anyway, I thought more of her former pupils might attend, but it's been a long time since Nell's schoolmistress days, and I suppose generations of girls have passed through the school since then. *Sic transit gloria mundi* and all that . . .' The Major seemed downcast.

'I expect you'll miss her.'

'Indeed I will. Not that I'll have much of a chance, with Marlowe to look after.' He drank some of his tea. 'Can't help feeling that Lil's husband could have made an effort to attend, considering how often his wife had come to stay with Nell, and how Nell had looked after her in her hours of grief.'

'Lil?'

'The one in the photo. Lilian Harkness. Nell's niece. Such a nice person, she was, though I couldn't say the same about the husband. Only seen him a couple of times in the distance, mind you, helping his wife into the car to take her back home. Surly sort of fellow, dirty great black beard, made him look like Captain Haddock or something. Dear Lil, I got to know her well over the years, felt really sorry for her. Nell told me she wasn't very keen on her husband, his attitude to her, the way he kept her on a tight rein, didn't like her doing things without him. It's a miracle that he ever allowed her to come to stay with Nell from time to time, if you ask me.'

'But he didn't come to see Nell off?'

'Disgraceful. No manners. You'd have thought he'd have learned some in the Service, if nowhere else.'

'So what's the story with Lilian?'

'Apparently she and the husband had been trying for years to have children. He's completely obsessed with having an heir to hand on the family business to, him being the fourth generation to run it. Or so I gather.'

'And what's the family business?'

'Mobile phones? Furniture? Disposable nappies? I can't remember exactly which.'

'What's it called?'

'Harkness & Company, I believe. Saw an ad for it once in some magazine or other. *Practical Mechanics* or some such.'

'So probably not disposable nappies, then!'

'Doesn't sound likely, does it?' The Major guffawed.

'And where's that located?'

'Cambridge? Bedford? Somewhere round there. I believe he even has a warehouse somewhere local. Anyway, poor Lil kept having miscarriages. And then a few years ago – five, six? – she managed to produce a little boy. A bit sickly, in and out of hospital quite a lot, but all right. And then about eight months ago, the poor kid was rushed to the emergency ward here in town and died of meningitis or sepsis – something horrible, anyway. Lilian was at his bedside for days on end, not sleeping, not eating. And shortly after the poor kid had finally died, she goes back home to wherever it is they live, and kills herself. Drinks down a bottle of Drano, if you please. What a way to go. Doesn't bear thinking about, does it?'

'How absolutely terrible,' I said.

'Nell was pretty cut up about it. Blamed the husband. So do I. Poor Lil couldn't stand the pressure, according to Nell. One pregnancy after another. Getting her hopes up each time, only for them to be dashed again. The husband – what was his name? Brian? Peter? I'm not sure what – refused to adopt, wanted to try again, and after losing the boy, I imagine she'd just had enough.'

'That's so sad.' I wasn't about to launch into the story of my own miscarriage: the Major would have been mortified at his lack of tact, not that he could have known. 'It must have been a terrible shock for you, too.' Did this tale have any bearing at all on the death of Tristan Huber? It seemed unlikely.

'You can say that again. Spent my working life in the Army, theatres of war and all that, but it doesn't make death – especially violent death – any easier to cope with.'

Changing the subject, I nodded at the photo of him in his black-belted kimono. 'I see you're a judoku.'

'Fourth dan. Army champion in my day, my dear. Don't keep it up nowadays, of course, though it does give me an incentive to maintain my fitness levels.'

'Major Horrocks, is there anything further you can tell me about your discovery of the body?'

He frowned. Shook his head. Chewed at his moustache. 'Nothing, my dear. I've been over and over it in my head, and absolutely nothing springs to mind. I'm sorry, Alex.'

'Well, if anything comes up later . . .'

'You'll be the first to know.'

'Thank you.' As I stood up, I added, 'Your lemon cookies are totally delicious. You'll have to give me the recipe.'

No amount of lemon cookies was going to dispel my sadness at the loss of lovely Tristan Huber.

Back home, I went on to the Internet and typed in Harkness & Company, near Bedford. It didn't seem likely that the husband of the Major's next-door neighbour's niece could be connected to Tristan, as yet, but too much information is way better than too little. I learned almost nothing about either the company or the managing director, apart from the fact that he was called Brian Roger Harkness.

FOUR

Back in town, I parked outside Dimsie's shop and went in. The receptionist, a bimbo who looked as though she might score forty-five per cent if she was asked to fill in her name, told me Dimsie was out to lunch. The receptionist looked pretty much out to lunch herself. 'I'll come back,' I said.

On my way home, I drove past Sam's bookshop and saw him staring out of the window. I turned the next corner, parked against the pavement on double yellow lines, and thumbed in his number on my mobile. 'I really need to talk to you,' I said. I could feel grim tears at the back of my throat, a torrent of them, and I wanted to shed every last one of them.

'What's up?' he asked gently.

'Nothing.' I half-laughed. 'Everything.'

'I'm in the bookshop.'

'I saw you.'

'Park in the space behind my garden and come through the back gate. How long before you get here?'

'Four minutes max.'

'I'll be waiting.'

Four minutes later, I was stumbling out of my car. I walked up the weed-filled alley which ran along the backs of the High Street shops and houses. I lifted the latch of the gate set into the shabby overlap fence panelling which marked the boundary of Sam's garden. Inside, a path led to the back door of the bookshop. Through a screen of flowering shrubs – viburnum, philadelphus, spirea – planted against the wooden boundary between Sam's garden and that of the wine shop next door, I could see the peaked roof of a small conservatory attached to the rear of the Vine house.

Sam was waiting for me at his back door. Despite Milo Stanton, my heart gave an involuntary flip at the sight of his kind face. Why? He was a big man with a gentle soul. And a good friend. But he was most definitely not *that* sort of a friend. Not that Milo was, either. Not yet. If ever. He held out his arms and I moved into them.

'Oh Sam,' I said. My voice was full of tears. My whole *body* was full of tears. I told him about Tristan's hideous death. Even if he had already heard, he was kind enough to let me repeat the ugly facts. 'It's so cruel, so horribly sad,' I said. 'Why? How can anyone do that to a fellow human being?'

'Man's inhumanity to man,' Sam said softly against my hair. 'It never ends. It never will.'

For a moment they passed before me: a vile nightmarish procession of the tortured, the torturers, the starving and mistreated, bewildered children hurt and abused, neglected, vulnerable, trafficked women, the fraudulent and the defrauded, cheaters and cheated, the lost and the persecuted, pain, misery and needless pitiless deaths.

Who would be a human? And where did the idea of an all-merciful Supreme Being come from? After a while, he patted me gently on the back and indicated the garden next door. 'Why don't you go round to Edward's place? He invited me to join him for a post-work drink anyway. Let me lock up here and I'll be with you both.'

I did as he suggested. Edward Vine had been a good friend during my married days. When the Love Rat took off, he remained one. He was also Sam's closest friend, which said a lot. Edward was clever, with a starred First from Cambridge, and a wide-ranging intellect. I knew he'd been offered a Fellowship at his college and I never understood why he had preferred to run an off-licence in some seaside town, miles from dreaming spires and gothic towers. He kissed me on both cheeks and ushered me to a garden bench beside a tiny lily pond with a fountain burbling gently into it before leaving to return to his wine shop. I sat in the green peace, waiting for him to come back, and felt an easing, however temporary it might prove, of my grief over Tristan's death.

Edward came back with an opened bottle of wine, and three glasses.

'Sam told me recently that the wine shop's lease is coming up shortly for renewal,' I said.

'That's right.'

'At which time you're going to hang up your corkscrew.'

'That's the idea.'

'So if you go, where are we going to buy our wine?'

'Haven't you noticed that new boutique wine shop, *Grand Cru*, just off the High Street?'

'No.'

'They're good. Really know their stuff,' Edward said. 'If I wasn't going, that might have become a problem. Despite the uni students, there's too much competition these days for a smallish town like this. It's certainly one of the reasons for my decision to retire from the wine trade. Plus, of course, my political ambitions. I come up before the committee for selection as a prospective parliamentary candidate in a couple of weeks' time.'

'It'll be a shoe-in,' I said. 'You've worked so hard for the community. Been on the council for years. Served as the town Mayor three times. No hint of scandal. No dodgy bottles on your shelves.'

'I should hope not.'

'You'll be selected without any problem.'

'Not necessarily. I'm not the only person wanting to be chosen, by any means,' Edward said cautiously. 'If there are two candidates with equally good CVs, then the slightest thing can sway the balance one way or another.' He clenched his fists together. 'God, how I long to be where the real political power is. Where I can really do some good, make a difference.'

'Isn't that what they all say, when they first go into politics? And don't they all find that the only way to get anything done is to make compromises? Shave their principles here and there?'

'Inevitably there'd be a bit of that. You wouldn't believe some of the inducements I was offered when I was on the Council. I managed to maintain my integrity, but I made some enemies.'

Looking back into the shop, I could see three or four customers scanning the shelves, picking up bottles and examining their labels, checking out prices. 'I'd better go,' Edward said. 'Help yourself. I'll be back shortly.'

When he'd gone, I read the label on the bottle he'd brought out. Something rather special, I fancied. Lovely. I poured myself just a minuscule refill and leaned back in my chair.

Edward's garden was charming, leafy and overgrown. Water trickled. Birds chirruped. Sylvan was the word which sprang to mind. Had it not been for the distant sound of traffic, you might have expected a deer to leap from a clearing, or a fox to peer through the carefully maintained undergrowth. There was a gate set into the rustic fence between Sam's property and Edward's, and over the past year, Sam had spoken of expanding the bookshop by buying the lease to Edward's place when it came up for grabs. It would be very easy to knock down the fence and amalgamate the two gardens. I envisaged small round tables, checked tablecloths, thin white china, summer sunlight dappling the scene, people reading as they munched home-made cakes and scones. Sam's notion of a teashop-cum-bookstore could be a winner. Presumably they'd have to buy the book first, in case of buttery fingers on the covers or crumbs between the pages.

Eventually, business over for the day, Sam joined me. Then Edward reappeared, though since off-licences didn't keep normal business hours, he continued to keep one ear out for the sound of new customers.

'Now, Alexandra,' he said, leaning a little towards me. 'What is this terrible news I've been hearing about with regard to my good friend Tristan Huber?'

The concern in his voice brought my tears back again. I let them fall. I gave him a quick rundown on the facts as I knew them, while he nodded sympathetically. 'And the worst of it is,' I hiccuped, 'that he was still alive when he was dumped in that field. If there'd been someone to help him, he needn't have died.'

'Effing bastards.' Edward took a hard swallow of his wine.

'You're friendly with the ex-wife, aren't you, Edward?' Sam said.

I knew from Dimsie that Tristan's wife, Christie, had parted from him fairly acrimoniously, and had married some kind of Spanish nobleman and wine grower. 'She's got about a dozen names now,' Dimsie had told me. 'Condesa of this and Duquesa of that, plus God knows how many other honorifics and titles belonging to the new husband.'

Edward nodded. 'We're in the same line of business now, so yes, I know her. She comes over to England two or three times a year to see family and hype her husband's products.'

'Are they any good?'

'Getting better all the time. And definitely not appreciated enough. They need to launch a really eye-catching campaign, raise awareness. Trouble is, some of the wines currently being produced in the south Mediterranean are superb, but because we associate them with cheap and cheerful, student parties and the like, people simply aren't prepared to pay a proper price for them. So she's had a hard time breaking into the market here, despite a heavy advertising budget.'

Sam refilled our glasses. Something chirped from a bush. A ladybug landed on my arm. 'Nothing to do with what we've been talking about, but I'm seriously thinking of taking a few months off,' he said. 'My brother's been suggesting for some time that I visit him in New Zealand.'

'What about the shop?' asked Edward. 'The expanded shop, that is, if you're still on to buy my place?'

'I could supervise the necessary building works needed to turn the two places into one. Or even appoint a manager to oversee the project while I was gone. Knocking through and so on, fitting the new place out, buying the necessary equipment.'

'I like your idea of adding a café,' I said. 'I really enjoy those places where they provide the daily papers for you to read.'

'Me too,' said Edward.

'Shelves all round the walls to create a bookish sort of ambience,' Sam said, eyes dreamy. 'The bookshop's crammed with second-hand books I could fill them with.'

'I've got a bust of Shakespeare you can have,' I said.

'Well, that's certainly a start.'

'And I've got one of Plato,' added Edward. 'Used to be my mother's until she threw it out. I rescued it literally from the recycling box, felt the old boy didn't deserve such ignominy.'

'Will you chuck it in with the shop, or do I have to buy it from you?' asked Sam.

'I'll make you a gift.'

'Or I could wait until I've got the place up and running, then appoint a manager. My assistant would love to take it on, so I could easily take some weeks off. Fly to New Zealand. Visit some of the places I've never been. Spend time with brother Harry and his brood. I haven't seen them for ages.' Sam looked across at me. 'Want to come along, Alex?'

My world had recently been much churned up by hurt and death, and I sometimes wondered if I would be staying in the town for much longer. I would come back eventually, but I needed fresh breezes to blow about my head. I needed to get away from a place where so much loss had occurred. Losses now added to by Tristan's death. Sam's question chimed exactly with my thoughts.

'Hmm.' Fresh breezes was one thing, New Zealand quite another. Did I know Sam well enough to want to go to the other side of the world with him? Did I *want* to know him well enough?

Inside the house, the telephone pealed. At the same time, Edward's cell phone buzzed on the garden bench beside him. He picked it up. 'Please God that's not my dreadful Ma,' he said. 'Or my poor sister, currently putting up with the old dragon's tyranny in Canada.' He pressed it to his ear and said, 'Vine here.' On the other end of the line someone talked for a few minutes. I saw his face collapse. 'What?' he said. 'What? But that's terrible, that's . . .' He pressed a hand against his mouth. 'I simply can't believe it. Are you sure?'

Whoever was on the other end seemed absolutely sure.

'Well, thank you for telling me.' Edward looked grim as he closed his phone.

'Bad news?' I asked.

'As bad as yours about Tristan Huber.' He drank the contents of his wine glass and refilled it with a hand that shook. 'That was the president of the chess club, saying that my friend, Kevin Fuller, a research fellow up at the college, he's . . .' His voice died away.

'He's what?' I asked. It was unlike Edward to be inarticulate.

'I can't take it in . . . Kevin's dead. I just can't . . .' He dropped his head in his hands and stared at the grass.

'How, Edward? Where? And when?'

He groaned. 'A week ago. I wondered why I hadn't heard from him. Apparently he was found at the foot of Nelson Point. He'd gone . . . I can hardly believe it . . . over the edge of the cliff.' He swallowed. 'What's worse, it seems the poor boy survived for two or three days.'

Just like Tristan, I thought.

Nelson Point was a grassy headland a couple of miles around the coast from Longbury, where a white cliff fell down to a pebbly little beach strewn with big chunks of chalk. It had been commandeered years ago by the Army and never formally reassigned, so the undercliff was usually deserted except for a range of seabirds – terns, gulls, cormorants – and the very occasional seal which had lost its way from the treacherous sandbanks on the horizon. The cliff itself was hazardous: bits of it were always detaching themselves without warning and plunging to the beach below. It was a place best avoided.

'Oh God . . .' Edward lamented. 'Is there anything sadder than a promising life cut short?'

Many, many things, I thought. 'Did he have a heart attack or something? Was it one of those cliff-falls?'

'He was fucking murdered. By some *fucking* bastard.' Tears began to fall down Edward's cheeks. His eyes were full of pain.

'How do you know?'

'Because his hands were taped behind his back and his ankles were taped together. Somebody deliberately threw him off.'

I hated to think what the poor guy must have been feeling as he plunged to the beach below.

Edward shook his head. 'How could this have happened? He was working towards a PhD in Mathematics. He'd already got a Masters from some American university, he had a great future in front of him. And he wasn't just a brilliant man, he was nice as well.' When he looked at me his expression was one of appeal, as though he thought I might be able to change things, bring Kevin Fuller back to life.

I didn't ask if he had any further details, for fear of hearing of more unspeakable atrocities. But two murders in three weeks, in a town where there was little more violence than the odd random stabbing or fist fight outside the pub on a Saturday night, seemed excessive. A thought flew into my head – and swiftly out again. Could there be a connection between this man's death, and Tristan's? At first sight, of course there couldn't. Indeed, why should there be?

'I'm so, so sorry, Edward,' I said.

He nodded, acknowledging my concern. 'It's his poor parents I'm worrying about. They doted on him.'

'Are they local?'

He shook his head. 'Family runs a dry-cleaning business at Borton, on the Rochester road. They'll be devastated.'

Eventually Sam and I said our goodbyes, made our way to the end of the garden between tree and overhanging bush, and out into the area outside the gate. I started to head towards my car as Sam said, 'I've never seen Edward in such a state.'

'Nor me.' I stopped suddenly. I couldn't rid myself of the notion that there must be some connection between Kevin Fuller's death and Tristan's. 'Sam, I know this is a heck of a stretch but do you think . . . is it possible that there's a link between the deaths of this Kevin Fuller and Tristan Huber?'

'Highly unlikely, I would have thought. What did they have in common, as far as we know?'

'Their cruel deaths, for a start. And also . . .' I was remembering that last year, Huber Associates had been commissioned to refurbish and upgrade some of the student common rooms up at the uni. It was quite feasible that a senior graduate of Kevin's status might have been on the student committee keeping an eye on the work as it progressed.

'Nonetheless,' I said. I checked my watch. It was still relatively early. If I drove fast, I should get to Borton before closing time. I stood for a moment, car keys in hand. Looked at the traffic passing the end of the little back alley without seeing it. Heard a blackbird singing from a chimney pot. Kissed

Sam's cheek, got into my car and set off towards the motorway which would take me most of the twenty-five-mile journey to Borton.

Why? What did I think I'd obtain? Well, information, first and foremost. And I also had some vague notion of bonding with the parents, assuring them that time doesn't heal – how can it? – but that some kind of inner peace will be achieved if you can only survive the first agonies of loss. Looking back, this seems pompous and patronizing in the extreme. I can only say that at the time I meant well.

As I drove out into the country towards Borton, my speed dropped. First a flock of sheep was herded from a field on one side of the road to one opposite, a black sheepdog steering them in a crouching run, barking if one of them got out of line. Then a tractor with a trailer piled high with hay lumbered out of another field and down the road, bits of grass flying from the top-heavy load into my windscreen like demented stick insects, while I uttered a few swear words. The clock was ticking, and I realized that if I didn't get a move on, by the time I reached Borton, the dry-cleaners would almost certainly be closed.

But no. As I parked in front of its steamed-up windows, I could see that all the lights were still on. As I pushed open the door, the place was like any other such premises: stacks of plastic bags full of bundled clothes, stainless steel machines churning at the far end, the astringent smell of chemicals, dozens of dry-cleaned garments and laundry shrouded in film-wrap, hanging off racks suspended from the ceiling like so many empty carcasses.

A man was at the far end of the shop, stuffing laundry into the maw of an industrial-sized stainless steel washing machine, moving stiffly, as though every movement was an effort. He came over to the counter, shoulders hunched, lines on his face that I guessed had not been there a few days ago.

'Mr Fuller?' I asked.

He nodded.

I explained who I was, that I had heard about the death of his son, that I had no clear reason for coming, that I simply wanted him to know how much I felt for him, and to offer what tiny spark of comfort I could. And as an afterthought, ask him a couple of questions.

He stared at me without speaking for an unnerving length of time. Then he lifted the flap which separated the business end of the place from the customer. 'The kettle's boiling. Come on into the back,' he said.

Five minutes later, I was sitting across from him at a tiny round table, drinking instant coffee from a thick blue mug. 'The wife and me, we love all our sons the same,' he said, after some time had elapsed. 'I wouldn't want anyone to think different, least of all Francis and Michael, Kevin's brothers. But Kevin was special, always was, right from a little boy. Wanted to do things, wanted to be the best at everything, wanted to go places. That's why he put in for that scholarship and went off to college in America for two years. Got involved in everything going out there: mountain-climbing, scuba-diving, working with indigenous peoples in Peru, volunteering on some of those programmes they have in America for deprived kids. And the same when he came back here for his PhD at the university. Joined in all the student activities – chess, drama, sport of different kinds. Helping out with literacy programmes, reading to the kids in the hospital, even learned how to manipulate those puppets on strings – marionettes I think they call them – to amuse them.'

'He sounds like a son you can be proud of.'

'He's that all right. He *was* . . .' he amended carefully. His eyes welled with tears. 'His mother and I, we loved him so much. He was such a . . . such a bright star. Something bright and shining's been taken from our lives. Only someone who's been through it could possibly begin to understand how we feel.'

My own eyes began to fill. 'I guess, Mr Fuller, the main reason I came to see you was because we need to find out who was responsible for his death.'

'We?'

'The police,' I amended.

'They've already been here, asking their questions, wanting to know if we can think of anyone who might have had it in for Kevin, which of course we couldn't. What had he ever done?'

'They'll find the killer, Mr Fuller, I assure you. And when they do, it will make a difference to you, I promise. It's like having an abscess lanced: a lot of the pain and poison will drain away. It won't bring Kevin back, but knowing is so much better than not knowing.'

But I could feel him thinking that whatever I said wasn't going to make a blind bit of difference to him or to his family. Not at the moment, in the new rawness of their grief. Unfortunately, he was probably right.

There was a long silence. Then Fuller said, 'Thank you.' He clenched his fists on the table. 'Though I tell you, if I came face to face with the bastard responsible right now, I would murder him with my own hands. No compunction, no mercy, no more than he showed my boy any mercy. Cutting Kev with a knife. Treating him like a human ashtray. Trussing him up like a . . . like a carcass in a butcher's shop.'

It sounded exactly like the MO in Tristan's death.

He waved his hand vaguely, indicating some direction outside the shop. 'They threw him off the cliff like a . . . like a sack of garbage.' His voice rose, lifted by the sobs which fell from his mouth. He sobbed a couple of times, his throat sounding hoarse and overused. 'My Kevin.'

'Was there anything – the cuts on his body . . . did they by any chance spell out a word?' Seeing his look of dawning outrage, I quickly explained about Dimsie asking me to look into the murder of her brother.

'Well, yes,' he said eventually. 'The police think there was an attempt to . . . uh . . . write something, but they only got as far as an L and an I. The bastard must have been interrupted.'

If I wanted any further proof of a connection between the two murders, this clinched it. *Liar*, I thought. Who had Kevin lied to? And what about?

Again, there was silence between us. In the shop the machines whirred and swooshed, endlessly turning the clothes they contained. Then suddenly, as if the words had been wrenched out of him, he blurted out, 'We didn't mind that he was queer, you know. It didn't make a ha'p'orth of difference to either of us, we just felt about him exactly as we always had. Sad that there'd be no grandchildren, of course, but there are the other two to provide us with those, so no, we accepted him exactly as he was.'

'Kevin was gay?'

He gave a mirthless chuckle. 'That's what they call it nowadays. No reason why you should know that about him, of course. And he didn't exactly take out full-page ads in the newspaper. But yes, he "came out" as they say . . .' His mouth twisted wryly. 'When he first went off to America. We'd wondered why there weren't any girlfriends but we put it down to him concentrating on his school work.'

I couldn't think of anything to say.

'His mother took it a bit hard, but I pointed out to her that Kevin had so much else to offer the world and it wasn't for us to judge him.'

'Very true. Now, I have another question, a very important one. Did you ever hear Kevin talk about someone called Tristan Huber?'

'Do you mean that chappie from the decorator's?'

Not exactly how Tristan would have described himself, I thought, but near enough. 'Yes, I think so.'

'Kev was on some kind of committee,' Fuller said. 'Voting on colour schemes and the like. You can't beat Magnolia, I used to say, but they go in for much fancier stuff these days.'

'Do you know if your son and Mr Huber ever got together at any point? Over a pint or two, something like that?'

'I don't know. The wife might, but she's not really . . . not at the moment.'

'I understand.'

'You should try the university. They're bound to know.'

'You're right. I'll try that. It might give us a lead as to what happened.'

He stared at me. He had very round blue eyes. 'Oh, Kev,' he said. The pain in his face felt like a knife in my own heart. He mopped at his eyes with a handkerchief he took from his pocket, sniffed a couple of times, stood. 'It's been very good of you to come,' he said formally, holding out his hand. 'And I very much appreciate the trouble you've taken.'

I stood too, shook his hand and left. I looked back and saw him with his head on the table, his shoulders shaking with sobs.

On the drive back to Longbury, I wondered if Inspector Garside was linking Kevin Fuller's murder to Tristan's. Did he also know that Kevin was gay and, whether he did or not, what difference could it make to the CID investigation now going on? Presumably the information might give them another lead to follow in the hunt for Kevin's killer.

Back in my flat, I telephoned Sam. 'I'm back and I'm sad,' I said. 'I could do with some company.'

'I'll be with you in ten minutes.'

And he was. In my flat, we drank a little wine and chatted about nothing for an hour or so. Closing my eyes, I leaned against his shoulder, taking comfort from the steady beat of his heart before he left. Alone again, I switched on the TV, needing voices and movement, anything not to be on my own. The offerings were meagre. Football. A quiz show. Some mindless sitcom about a chicken farm, starring a 'personality' I knew far more about than I wanted to, since he'd recently been giving interviews all over the place to promote his next series, which sounded even more crappy than this one. Some woman with large hair brightly flogged jewellery or cosmetics. More football.

I switched off. Not for the first time, it struck me that the set wasn't worth the licence fee, let alone the initial cost. I went to bed.

FIVE

The air smelled of wind and freshly landed mackerel as I walked along the High Street, past the greengrocer, and the gift shop selling objects decorated with kitsch slogans like *Keep Calm and pass the Whisky,* or cushions embroidered with *For the Best Mum In the World.* Past the café where the playschool mums gathered before they congregated at the school gates. I might have been one myself, if only . . . I forced myself not to go there. I don't do *if onlys.*

In the windows of the British Heart Foundation's charity shop I stopped to look at the flyers for coming events. A classical concert at the Open Space; a day-long book-fest; a concert at the Assembly Rooms; an early warning of the panto over in Margate, *Aladdin*, starring Chris Kearns as Widow Twankey; a Craft Fayre in the Town Hall.

I was heading towards the Fox and Hounds since I knew that Major Horrocks favoured the place for a mid-morning pint and, if he was there, it would be quicker than driving out of town towards his house and finding him absent. And there he was ahead of me, right on cue, coming out of Marks & Spencer. I saw him stumble on an uneven paving stone and nearly fall. I ran forwards.

'Easy, dad.' A passer-by caught him by the arm and kept him upright.

The Major pulled away. For some reason, he was wearing a red woollen waistcoat and a long-sleeved flannel shirt on a hot day in August. It was easy to see he was regretting it. 'As far as I'm aware,' he was saying crossly, 'I'm not your father, and even if I was, I should certainly not allow you to address me as Dad.'

'No offense, dude.' The stranger looked around and saw me grinning. He smiled back. American, I thought immediately. With teeth that perfect, he had to be. Unless he was wearing dentures, which I was prepared to bet he wasn't.

'Nor dude,' said the Major. Then remembering his manners, added, 'But thank you anyway.'

'My pleasure. Your shopping, sir.' With a small bow, the stranger handed over a green plastic bag which had fallen to the pavement. 'Is that tonight's dinner?'

'Well, yes, since you mention it . . .' The Major was obviously trying not to look pathetic. 'Pretty much on my own these days, you see, and though I enjoy the art of the cuisine, I get rather fed up cooking for myself night after night.'

'Know how you feel.' Again the stranger smiled at me, by now standing beside him.

'And you can get some really good ready-made dishes these days,' the Major continued.

'Hear what you're saying, man.'

'Major Norman Horrocks.' The Major looked at his watch, and held out his hand.

The other guy took it. 'Todd DuBois. The Third.'

Something about his delivery of the name lacked the ring of truth. Did he think none of us had heard of *A Streetcar Named Desire*?

'Why don't you let me buy you a beer,' suggested the Major, 'seeing as how you saved me from a nasty tumble?'

'A splendid idea.' His voice orotund, DuBois briefly made a very successful stab at sounding like an upper-class Englishman. Why would he do that, when a minute ago he'd sounded like a character from a Tennessee Williams play? Getting his roles mixed, or what?

'There's the Fox and Hounds just up the street,' the Major said. 'Or the White Swan Hotel further on. Does a nice drop of beer.'

DuBois launched a mega-watt smile, the sort guaranteed to melt the heart of a grand inquisitor, had there been one present. 'I agree about the beer. I'm staying there for a couple of nights. It's never going win prizes for its décor, mind you, let alone its mattresses. I may even have to move if I stay any longer – I really don't want to do my back in again.'

'We'll go to the Fox and Hounds. I can tell by your accent you're a visitor to our shores.' The Major could swap clichés with the best of them and indeed, frequently did. 'Divided by a common language and all that, ha ha.'

'Major,' I said. 'Might I ask you something?'

'Of course, m'dear.'

'Better still, why don't you join us?' said DuBois, as I had mentally laid odds that he would.

'That would be very . . .'

We pushed our way through the lunchtime throng in the saloon bar of the Fox and Hounds.

'I'll have a tomato juice,' I said firmly.

'Right you are.'

'Not so much a visitor . . .' DuBois picked up on the

conversation when the three of us were seated on an oak settle and a three-legged stool such as a milkmaid might have used in days gone by. 'More like an immigrant.'

I could see by the expression on the Major's face that the word suggested hollow-eyed children carrying indeterminate bags and men in ratty cloth caps being processed on Ellis Island, before spending a lifetime of grinding poverty and discrimination in the slums of the bigger cities of America. Or some refugee from Africa. Or even hefty young men with iPhones and leather jackets. These days, immigrants were just as likely to be terrorists posing as asylum-seekers from dictator-run countries. In fact, the word had taken on a whole new meaning as the diaspora of hundreds of thousands of people from war-torn countries trekked westwards in search of a safer life or a better economic future.

Either way, this soi-disant Todd, smartly dressed, silk socks (I would bet that the Major always noticed men's socks), nice bit of barbering, couldn't be further from the popular image of a refugee. 'Immigrant?' the Major echoed faintly.

'Wrong word, perhaps. Back home in Louisiana,' said Todd, 'my family's a long way from being immigrants.'

'Is that so?'

'Sure is.' Todd pointed at his cream linen shirt. 'Fact is, this kid is descended from a long line of plantation owners, some of whom joined with John Paul Jones to fight the English over the emancipation issue.'

'And stayed on?' I said. I was trying very hard to keep the cynicism out of my voice. I'd run across a number of conmen in my time on the force and was pretty sure I was talking to a prime example of the breed right that minute.

'You got it. Mint juleps on the verandah, gambling on the riverboats which ply their trade up and down the Mississippi, fireflies and hominy grits, Tom Sawyer and Huck Finn, all that southern jazz.' Todd looked regretful. 'Unfortunately, over the years there was rather too much of the juleps and the gaming tables, and by the time my daddy inherited, the land had mostly been sold off and the plantation acres reduced to a small farm which produced little more than dust and weeds.'

'Good heavens!' exclaimed the Major.

'Mind you, far as my daddy's concerned, the DuBois are still way at the top of the social tree. And I gotta say my parents made a handsome couple, driving off to parties and balls in their well-worn finery and their ancient Lagonda. But there was no way Poppa was ever going to dirty his hands with Lousiana mud, and since he couldn't afford to employ anyone efficient enough to turn the farm into a going concern, the two of them just mouldered gently on in that big old tumbledown house of ours.'

'It's like a film,' said the Major. '*Gone With the Wind,* or something. Vivien Leigh, Atlanta in flames, exciting stuff. Or that other one, with a lot of dust in it, something to do with grapes. Talking of which . . .' He drained his glass and signalled for refills for the three of us.

'You know what my daddy used to tell me?' said Todd.

Major Horrocks shook his head. 'No idea.'

'Used to say "*Son, ah hev a dream*". He has this real hokey fried-chicken-and-Spanish-moss accent, and what he never realized was he was exactly repeating Martin Luther King's words from back in the Sixties.'

'Right.' The Major nodded sagely. 'Martin Luther King.'

'And the ironic thing about it was,' Todd wagged a finger at us both. 'Mah Daddy would *never* have said such a thing, if he'd realized, King being a man of colour, know what Ah'm sayin'?'

'And did your da— father's dream come true?' I asked.

'I was never quite sure what the dream was, to be honest with you. Restoration of the ancestral lands, I should think. But in the end, he had to sell off what was left of our acreage, and the two of them relocated to a smaller (only seven bedrooms! What a come-down!) house outside Baton Rouge, living on nostalgia for the good old days.'

'So what about you.'

'Hey, I hightailed it out of Louisiana soon as I could. No way I was ever going to restore the family fortunes. "*Ah'm lookin' to you, son . . .*" my daddy would say, and I'd think, *You'll have to look elsewhere, Poppa, 'cause this mother's son won't be back any time soon.*' Over the rim of his glass,

Todd looked at Major Horrocks. 'So, Major, what's your story?' he asked.

'My story? Well . . .' The Major shook out the flannel sleeves of his Tattersall shirt, obviously feeling a trifle warmer than he would have liked. 'Regular army for thirty years, got a job as bursar and sports master at one of the local private schools, so me and the wife moved down from Catterick and bought a house here.'

'Why here?' I asked.

'Mostly because of the job. But I always fancied the place because my grandmother came from these parts, and I'd spent holidays with her when I was a boy. Seemed a logical move at the time, though looking back, perhaps it wasn't. My wife never really settled, she wasn't one for the WI and the—'

'WI?' Todd's brow creased.

'Womens' Institute. Jam-making, knitting and so forth, not her thing at all. Though she did do the church flowers from time to time, thanks to our next-door neighbour.'

'Church flowers?' Todd seemed bewildered. *Chu'ch flahs* . . . I was still trying hard to see him as genuine.

'Oh, you know. Teams of ladies taking it in turns to decorate the church on Sundays. My poor Esther could just about tell a rose from a daisy, but that was as far as it went. Flower-wise, I mean. But she enjoyed the company.'

'Guess she had other talents,' Todd said.

'If she did, I never found out what they were, in forty years of marriage.' The Major produced a snorting laugh. 'I even went to a couple of basic cookery courses, took over the cooking, just to make sure she didn't poison us both.' He looked uneasy, as though long-gone Esther might be about to launch a lightning bolt from the realms of bliss.

'Sounds like my *petite maman* back in Louisiana,' Todd said. 'Never lifted a finger about the house. In fact, I'm not sure she even knew where the kitchen was.'

'A large staff, I suppose.' The Major was clearly chuffed at being on a par with the DuBois *materfamilias.* He adopted a knowing expression, as one used to cooks and parlourmaids, footmen and tweenies, though in fact once he left the Army,

I doubt if he and Esther had employed anything more than a weekly cleaner.

'Twenty in the house alone,' said Todd. He grinned his all-American grin at me again. My sceptic's antennae jiggled about as though they were caught in a high wind.

'Goodness.'

'Of course, they ran the place. More or less told my parents what to do and how to do it.'

'Sounds very democratic,' I said. Did Todd realize I was not being pulled into the golden bubble he was so effortlessly creating?

'I guess it was.'

'So what is a gentleman like yourself doing in these parts?' asked the Major.

'I had some unfinished business,' Todd said. Evasively.

'Finished it yet?' I asked, wanting to know what his connection to this seaside town was. Whether he had any kind of link to Tristan Huber, though there no reason at this point to think that he might have. Or exactly what his unfinished business was.

'More or less.' Todd picked up his beer glass and tossed back a couple of swallows. 'Slightly delayed by the absence of the other party involved.' He quaffed his beer. 'Say, I read about this murder you've just had here . . .' Todd let the sentence trail, guessing the Major would pick it up.

'Indeed, sir. Met the victim a couple of times when he was doing up my neighbour's place. Nice fellow. The poor young man's body was abandoned behind a hedge just down the lane from my house. Doesn't bear thinking about.'

'It was the Major who found him,' I said to Todd.

'Is that so?' Todd stared at me over the rim of his glass. 'Hey, they mentioned the guy's sister in the papers this morning. Dimsie. What's that short for?'

'I don't think it's short for anything, actually,' I said. 'What's Todd short for?'

'Search me.'

'I read somewhere that it means a fox. Wily. Devious,' said the Major.

'That's me, boy. Wily and devious.' Todd laughed, revealing

once again his perfect teeth, of which he seemed to have at least twice as many as the average man on the street.

'I'll just bet you are,' I said.

'It said that this dead guy was only thirty-eight. That's awful young to die.' He pronounced it '*dah*'.

'Did you by any chance know him?' I asked.

He thought about it, then shook his head. 'Not's far as I know. By the way, where does this Dimsie dame hang out?'

'Why?' I asked, wondering why he was so interested.

'Why not? Put it down to my chivalrous southern upbringing, wanting to offer aid and comfort to the bereaved.'

'How kind.' In my opinion, the soi-disant Todd DuBois had slightly overreached himself by asking about Dimsie, a woman supposedly of whom he knew nothing. 'I'll tell her.'

'So what's next?' The Major sucked at his pint of bitter, looking at Todd. 'For you, I mean.'

'I'm not exactly sure.' Todd did the grin thing again.

'World your oyster, eh?' said the Major.

'Maybe.' Todd picked up his second half. He shrugged. 'Who knows? Maybe I'll try France. I have French blood in me, after all. Most everyone in Louisiana does.'

'France? Wine, cheese and sun. Wonderful country. My late wife and I spent many a happy holiday there. You could become a cheese maker. Or buy a vineyard and start producing wine.' Major Horrocks stared wistfully into his glass. 'Matter of fact, it's always been a dream of mine to—'

'Whoa! Not another one with a dream!' Todd broke in. 'On the other hand . . . a vineyard, hmm, sounds good.'

'I'll say.' Major Horrocks was obviously picturing himself, straw hat on head to protect himself from the fierce Charentais, or it might be, Burgundian sun, walking between the rows of vines, holding the ripening bunches in his hand to test their weight (rather like checking his balls for that telltale prostate tumour, I should imagine), sniffing at the grapes and nodding wisely, Todd perhaps in the neighbouring row, ('*Going to be great harvest this year, Todd.*' '*You just betcha, Norm*') 'I mean, how hard can it be?'

'Pretty darned hard, since you ask,' Todd said. 'I spent a summer vacation in the Napa Valley one year, picking grapes for the harvest, and believe me, it's back-breaking work. Returned for six months after I graduated from college, learned quite a bit about the whole process, too.'

'There you are!' The Major beamed at me as though I was responsible, patted Todd's arm. 'We're already halfway there. Don't know about you, old son, but I've got no ties here anymore, could be on my way tomorrow.'

'I say, steady on, dude. It takes years to build up a vineyard. And without wishing to be offensive, you're not exactly in the first flush of youth. Say you bought a vineyard tomorrow – day after, perhaps, give you a chance to unpack your bags – when would you anticipate tasting the first glass of wine from your own vines?'

'Good point. Unless we could buy a going concern.' Major Horrocks heaved a sigh and ordered another half. 'And anyway, I suppose Chateau Horrocks doesn't quite have the ring. Oh well, another one bites the dust.'

'Tell you what though, I've always rather fancied going into catering of some kind,' Todd said, after a short silence, leaning his elbows on the small round table between us. 'Can't you just see it? The little village restaurant, checked tablecloths, *confit de canard*, grape arbours, freshly made lemon mayonnaise, *pichets* of the local wines, wonderful country *potages.*'

'Homemade patés,' added the Major. 'Ducks flapping about, lavender fields, garlic all over the show. I could help with waiting tables, stacking the dishwasher – done quite a bit of that in my time – opening bottles, that sort of thing. Not to mention the actual cooking, too. Tell you what, as well the basic stuff, I also took a course in French cuisine once. My *boeuf bourguignon* has to be tasted to be believed.'

'Sounds good,' I said.

Horrocks leaned towards Todd and me confidentially. 'Know what my secret is?'

We both shook our heads.

'Guinness!'

'Guinness?' I said. 'My goodness.'

'Sounds unusual,' said Todd.

'Cooked with two tablespoons of cocoa powder and then,

just before serving, a couple of squares of bitter chocolate added to the sauce.' The Major sounded triumphant. 'Absolutely bloody delicious, if I say so myself. It'll go down a storm in France.'

'Aren't we getting slightly ahead of ourselves here?' Todd smiled at the older man. 'I only met you half an hour ago. You don't know anything about me. I could be a . . . well, for instance, a confidence trickster, for all you know. Take your life's savings and do a runner.'

'I can well believe it,' I said.

'Nonsense.' The Major tapped the side of his nose. 'Wouldn't have got where I am today without being a good judge of character. I know an honest man when I see one.'

Call me prejudiced, but I couldn't help thinking he was way off beam here. If the so-called Todd DuBois was an honest man, I was a Rolling Stone. The man was as phoney as a five-legged hedgehog.

Horrocks's benign expression changed. 'Truth to tell, I'd be glad to get out of this place for a while. Haunted by it all, you see. Well, I mean to say, how often do you stumble over a body all gashed about, carved *up*, if you please?' He elaborated on the details of his recent early morning walk with the dog Marlowe: the hedge, the flies, the body. '*Cheat*,' he said. 'Clear as dammit, engraved, as it were, right into the poor chappie's chest.'

Todd opened his guileless eyes wide. 'That's . . . that's *terrible*.'

'I can't get it out of my mind.'

'I'm not surprised, sir. What a truly dreadful experience. What do the police think?'

'As always, a useless bunch of tossers, if you'll pardon the expression.' He cut his eyes at me and then back away. 'Not all of them, obviously. Trying to blame it all on a passing psychopath. My Aunt Fanny! Psychopaths don't do a lot of passing, in my opinion. They're more like mosquitoes: see a tasty meal and dive straight in. No, I reckon it was someone with a grudge. Ice cream salesmen, bloodthirsty lot, always at each other's throats, brandishing stilettos and the like.'

'This dead guy sold *ice* cream?' Todd was looking confused, as well he might. 'They didn't mention that in the papers. And the cops have gone into the victim's background, all that?'

'I imagine so.' The Major blew froth off his moustache and shuddered. 'I'll tell you, Brad—'

'Todd.'

'—Todd, I've spent my life in theatres of war, but finding that body was one of the most unnerving events of my life.'

'I can well believe it, sir.'

'And setting up a catering business in France with Todd would help you get over it, do you think?' I asked.

Horrocks nodded. 'Could well be. And why not? Why the hell not?'

'Hear, hear,' said Todd. 'Especially as you obviously know something about cooking and the gastronomic arts.'

'Just call me Escoffier!' The Major chuckled at his own wit.

'A small café restaurant,' Todd said wistfully. 'I can see it so clearly.'

'Well, if you've got the cash, son, I've got the time.' The Major drank deep and thoughtfully. 'Matter of fact, if you've got the time, I've got the cash.'

There was a very faint frisson in Todd's expression. 'Really?'

'Just been left a few quid by my neighbour, d'you see?' And Esther, my wife, might have been a dead loss around the house, but she turned out to have a pretty hefty bank account.' He coughed. 'Never wanted to dig too deeply into how she'd obtained the money.'

Todd was looking thoughtful. 'We could go down there, look at it as a reconnoître,' he said. The word seemed to fall on the Major's ears like a sonata. (*Reconnoître* . . . how many times had he set up a recce, in those far-off days of service?) 'Suss the place out, see what's what.'

'Which area are you thinking about?'

'Somewhere with decent vineyards where property doesn't cost the farm. Bordeaux, St Emilion, Cahors.'

'Are you serious?'

'You bet I am. Are you?'

'Most definitely.' The Major held out his hand ('*put it there, pardner*!') and the two men shook.

'And how long do you have in mind for this preliminary recce?' I asked. I felt I ought to take the Major on one side and tell him to keep his eyes open. I didn't like the way Todd's face had changed at the mention of cash.

'What do you think, Maje? A week? A month?'

'Two weeks minimum. A month might be better.'

'OK, we'll look into it.'

'Draw up our . . . uh . . . battle plans.'

'Battle plans, right. Do you have wheels?'

'If you mean a car, of course I have.'

'Maybe we could drive down, take our time, scout out the area. Not just for wines, but for suitable buildings we could convert.'

'Excellent.' The Major was obviously a happy man, hardly able to believe his luck. He looked refreshed. Invigorated. Happy at the thought that the days ahead already seemed filled with wine and sunshine. And purpose.

'OK, but I still have things to do elsewhere. I'll come when I'm done and get in touch.' When Todd finally pushed back from our table, I got up too.

Once out of earshot, I said, 'How about a coffee, Mr DuBois? Unless you're pressed for time.'

He laughed. 'Honey, I'm not pressed for anything right now.'

Across the road was Willoughbys Bookshop. Sam Willoughby was staring out of the window as Todd and I walked along the pavement. Seeing me and Todd together, he looked like a man whose crest had just fallen. For a moment I considered going in with Todd and having coffee in the bookshop, but Sam might have felt even worse if I'd sat laughing and joking with someone who wasn't him. He had the hots for me in a big way. Sadly, I didn't feel the same about him. Anyway, what I did was my concern, not his. He didn't own me, for heaven's sake. So why did I feel so mean? I pretended I hadn't seen him.

I turned into the Coffee Bean, further along the street. We ordered lattes, mine with a splash of hazelnut syrup, Todd's straight up. We sat down opposite each other in a booth near the back.

'So,' I said. 'Tell me why you're here. It's rather off the beaten track for tourists.'

'I already said: unfinished business.'

'Which you've now concluded?'

'Indeed.'

'Any chance of telling me what it was?'

'None whatsoever.' He was no longer smiling.

The two of us stared at each other. Got the measure of each other. Recognized that we were cut from the same fabric. Weapons drawn. Swords unsheathed. Showing the steel beneath the smooth façade. 'So how much longer shall you be staying here?' I said.

He shrugged. 'I'll be hightailing out of town this afternoon, as it happens. People to see, places to go, you know how it is. But if the Major's really serious about this possible place in France . . .'

'The Major is a very good friend of mine,' I said. Not really a warning. Merely something for his files.

'I'm just thrilled to hear it.'

I stuck out my chin. 'Mess with the Major and you mess with me.'

'Oh jeez. I'm trembling so hard I'm gonna shake the hair right off of my scalp.'

'I believe you said you didn't know Tristan Huber.'

'That's right. So I got no motive for doing the guy in, if that's what you're trying to imply.'

'I'm not trying to imply anything.' I sipped from my mug of coffee, thinking he was pretty quick to recognize the name from nothing more than a newspaper report.

'Wouldn't mind saying Hi to Miss Dimsie before I leave.'

'Walk along the High Street, turn left at the traffic lights, and go into the fifth shop along on the right. Drayton Studios. Whether she'd be there is another matter. She's often not.'

'It's worth a try.' He grinned his grin.

The trouble with Todd DuBois was that he was immensely likeable. That boyish smile. That cowlick of hair. Those clear blue eyes. But likeability is the first prerequisite for a conman – if that's what he was.

'Why don't we do dinner sometime soon?' he said.

I thought rapidly. Saw no objections. Unless underneath the charm he was a psychopath about to dive straight in, rather than passing, as the Major had already asserted. But it was a risk I was prepared to take, since I might just find out a little bit more from the guy. 'OK. You're on.'

'How about next week? I'm kinda tied up for the next few days.'

'It's a deal.'

'I'll find you.' He winked. Grinned. Bussed my cheek. And very nice too. I watched him walk away, feet striking the pavement with an almost audible jingle of non-existent spurs, thighs wide, like a cowboy. Or a gunslinger.

SIX

Who doesn't have regrets? About love. Loss. About things done. Things not done. In my case, my most profound regrets were about the things which could not *be* done. Such as me becoming an artist. A painter. Trouble was, I had absolutely no talent. I could see pictures so clearly in my head, but somewhere between brain and paper aptitude failed. I was like someone who had always wanted to become a singer but was thwarted by the inability to hold a tune. Or even to find one in the first place. Such as poor Sam Willoughby, who longed to be a C&W star but had no singing voice.

I understood his frustration. I was lucky in that a love of art in general and a supportive art teacher at school had led me to take a degree in art history, and after six years in the police, and by now armed with a certain amount of knowledge, to turn it into a means of making a living of sorts. Which I was trying to do at this very moment. After the loss of my collaborator and close friend, Dr Helena Drummond, I still had contracts which would carry me through the next two or three years, if I was careful. But the work no longer seemed as compelling. I'd lost the exciting frisson of discovery which had motivated me before Helena was murdered last year. And Tristan's murder was even more debilitating.

Shortly, I would walk into town to see how Dimsie was. I knew from Fliss Fairlight that despite encouraging bulletins from the police, they still weren't much further forward in the hunt for Tristan Huber's killer than the day his body had been found. Meanwhile, I sat gazing at reproductions of paintings, choosing which to include in my next anthology: *Eat, Drink and be Merry.* In one hand I held a painting by Pedro de Camprobín, *Still Life with Sweets*, and the other a picture by the same artist, another still life, this time with chestnuts, olives and wine. I loved them both. So much more relaxed and intimate than Zurbarán's work. Which would Helena have gone for? In the end, I opted for the still life of sweets, with its *tazza* of sugary cakes and *turrón.* It was more exuberant than the roasted chestnuts and prim olives. She'd been such an exuberant woman herself. It was definitely the one she would have chosen.

I went out. The sea was calm. Poison-green in patches, blue elsewhere. For once there was no wind. Flags drooped defeatedly from their poles. Seagulls hung around looking bored, or crapping on the unwary below. The High Street was somnolent except for the mix of regulars and tourists drinking half-pints under umbrellas outside the pubs.

In her showroom just off the High Street, I found Dimsie seated at a faux-neo-classical writing table placed slantwise across one corner. She was wearing a pair of over sized black-framed specs, intended to emphasize both her serious attitude to her job and her (non-existent) fragility. They were making a damn good fist of it.

She stood up and took them off when I came in. 'Find anything?' she demanded.

I explained about the police and the grass crushing. 'I don't know what you were hoping for, but the scene of crime has been trampled to shreds. There's nothing for a freelance like me to find. If there had been, the police would long ago have discovered it.'

'And your cop friends aren't feeding you information?'

'Right. Mostly because they haven't got much info to feed.'

My friend DI Fairlight had told me that there were no clues at all to be found where the body had been lying. 'Just about all we know at the moment is the fact that he – Tristan – was tortured elsewhere and . . .' I hesitated.

'And what?'

'. . . and as you already know, simply chucked out behind a hedge when they'd finished with him.' I didn't mention the pathologist's opinion that he'd still been alive at that point.

'It's been ages,' she said. 'Surely by now . . .' Tears welled up in her eyes. And mine.

'Whoever dumped him in Honeypot Lane left no traces at all for the forensics to find,' I said gently. 'And I'm also sure you're aware that it looks like he was hosed down after his chest was . . . um . . . carved up and before he was loaded into a car.'

'The man who discovered the corpse was right, wasn't he, when he said that the letters on the chest spelled out *cheat*?'

'According to the police, yes.'

'I can't imagine m-my darling brother ch-cheating on anyone.' Dimsie looked at me pitifully at me, her tiny hands clasped to her heart. 'But you'll go on looking, won't you?'

'Of course.'

If you were looking for phony, I reckoned she and the heir to the lost cotton-fields of Louisiana would be a good match for each other. Two bullshitters going head to head. I don't mean her grief over her brother wasn't real and heartfelt. Just that she had always been a bit of a poseur, too cute for her own good. What am I saying, a *bit* of a poseur? Or should that be poseuse? 'I need to know a lot more about Tristan than I actually do,' I said.

'But you've known him all your life.'

'Yeah, so he likes peanut butter sandwiches and sailing and French cuisine and New York and Rembrandt,' I said, skating over the fact that for a while there, I had known quite lot more about his likes, especially since so many of them had coincided with mine. 'That doesn't mean a thing. I've never seen him angry or depressed, but he wouldn't be human if he wasn't. I know he's terrified of your mother, but who isn't? Other than that, I know very little about him as an adult. You'll have to give me some more background. What needs to be established as soon as possible is who might have wanted to get rid of him. Who was angry enough to take the time to carve words on his chest? And why?'

'I told you, he was the sweetest, kindest . . .' Her voice cracked. 'Loved by all.'

'Not by *all*. Someone *didn't* love him so much that they killed him.' I probably sounded harsh. 'Who might that be?'

'I don't *know*.'

She looked so bereft that I wanted to hold her tight and murmur soothingly. Except I didn't entirely buy her act. Don't get me wrong. I loved Dimsie. We had had some wonderful times together over the years. But somehow I couldn't avoid noticing the gleam of calculation on her pretty face. 'If you want me to help, you're going to have to come clean about him,' I said briskly. 'The police will ask you the same questions, if they haven't already.'

She laid a slender white hand against her throat, a gesture designed to emphasize how frail and vulnerable she was. 'Not yet, they haven't,' she said faintly.

'They will. So you can look at this as a dress rehearsal. And if there's embarrassing stuff, you can rely on me to keep it to myself . . . unless it really has a bearing on his death.'

'His *murder*,' she said harshly. 'What do you want to know?'

'This word *cheat*. Who has Tristan cheated? Did he owe money? And if so, to whom?'

She shook her head. 'I don't know.'

'You must do, Dim. You ran your businesses more or less in tandem.' I turned a stern eye on her. 'Does the name Harkness mean anything to you?'

'Harkness?'

'Is he one of your suppliers? Or one of Tristan's?'

'He might have been. What does he produce?' Her violet eyes slid away from mine. 'Michael Compton, our accountant and business manager, might be able to help you better than I can.'

I leaned across her desk and took her chin in my hand, wrenched it round, forced her to look at me. 'Dim, I've known you since you were in nappies. Don't lie to me. Don't pretend you don't know what your brother was doing.'

'You make it sound as though he was up to something.'

'Quite clearly he was. Otherwise he wouldn't have ended up in a field, tortured to death. The guy or guys responsible must have been trying to make him tell them something. Any idea what it could have been?'

She started to shake her head, looking so pathetic that if I hadn't seen her two or three times in professional mode, I might have swallowed it. I reminded myself that she was Dorcas Huber-Gordon's daughter. No one could have emerged unscathed.

'Dimsie,' I said warningly. 'If there's someone out there who feels he or she's been swindled in some way, and Tristan didn't give any satisfaction, you might be next on their list.'

'What?' She sat up now, in full Iron Lady form, ready to chew iron filings as an *hors d'oeuvre* to a plateful of rusty drawing pins, all shreds of pathos suddenly consigned to the dressing-up box. '*Me*?'

'Yes, you.'

'You can't be serious.'

'Try me.'

'But what am I going to do?'

'First of all, you're going to spill all of yours and Tristan's little secrets.'

'We haven't got—' she began when saw my dead-eye stare.

'*Every*body has secrets,' I said. 'Including Tristan, it seems.'

She heaved a big sigh. 'I honestly don't know what they might have been. He was just about to fly off to Connecticut, actually. We've got several clients in that area and Tristan had been planning this trip for a while – we've been talking about opening up a branch of the business in Manhattan.'

'What exactly does "just about to" mean?'

'A few days before he was found.'

'When did you last see him?'

'Must have been a week before that.' I could see her beautiful eyes scanning their evening together to see what and what not to say. 'We had dinner at my mother's.'

'Have you spoken to her about Tristan's death?'

'I have her on the phone nearly every day. Sobbing and carrying on. Poor old bat. If she'd had to lose one of us, she'd far rather it was me.'

This, unfortunately, was true.

'Any idea what happened to that wife of his? What was her name: Coralie? Caroline?'

'Christie.'

'Right. So where is she?'

'Last seen heading to France and points south.'

'How long ago?'

'Three or four years or so.'

'And she's not been heard from since.'

Dimsie shook her head. 'Well, barely.'

Food for thought? 'What was she like?'

'She was OK.' Dimsie looked off into the middle distance. 'A bit . . . eccentric.'

'I guess that means you hated her.'

She frowned at me. 'Why are you asking me all these questions? You not trying to suggest that Christie was responsible for murdering Tristan, are you?'

'I'm not trying to suggest anything. But you might as well look at all the options. I would have heard if there'd been any children, wouldn't I?'

'Of course. You'd probably have been asked to be a godmother.'

'So what were you and Tristan currently working on?'

'He was commissioned on his own. An old school-friend with an estate near Ashford, with an American wife, a loaded one, from Texas, or Tennessee, if I remember rightly.' Which I was quite sure she did.

'Name?'

She shrugged. 'As I said, it was Tristan's project, not mine. We do sometimes work independently.'

'Presumably we can go through his records and find out what this person's called.'

'If the police let us.'

'You're family, as well as business colleagues. They can't keep you out of his offices or home for very long.' I stood. 'Come on, Dim. Let's go.'

'Go where.'

'To wherever he – or you – keep your business records.' My spirits sank at the thought of dealing with someone else's financial paperwork. I can barely keep track of my own. 'What about getting this Michael Compton person to come along too?'

'If he's free. He's a busy man.'

'Aren't we all?' I motioned towards her cell phone. 'Give him a call.'

'What, now?'

'It's as good a time as any.'

She gave a phoney little start. Slapped her forehead. Said, 'Paramore! Piper Paramore!'

I recognized delaying tactics when I saw them. 'And he, she or it is?'

'Tristan's clients. The one way over the other side of Ashford, near Tunbridge Wells. The rich person. You ought to go and interview them. See if they know anything.'

'Got an address?'

'I can find one, I'm sure. We copy most things to . . .' She stopped, stricken. '. . . *copied* most things to each other.' She busied herself at her computer for a few minutes then turned to me. 'Here we are . . . Piper Paramore. Rollins Park, near Tunbridge Wells.' She scribbled on a piece of paper and handed it to me. 'Here . . .'

'Piper . . . male, female or transgender?'

'Female.'

'I'll drive over and see if she has any insights. Anything I should know before I meet her?'

She shook her head. 'I know almost nothing about the woman. I think Tristan liked her. There's a husband. Got a title of some kind, I think.'

'I'll see if I can find out anything helpful. Though I should imagine by now that someone from the Thames Valley police will have been to see them.'

'Yes, but that's the point. That's exactly why I want you on my side. Like I said, you'll tell me what you find out, and they won't.'

'Fine.'

It didn't seem likely that the husband of the Major's next-door neighbour's cousin could be connected to Tristan, as yet, but too much information is way better than too little.

The drive across south-east Kent was reasonably traffic-free, for a change. Once off the motorway, I was in green countryside, driving past meadows and trees. Lush, as always. Pretty. But already showing faint signs of the coming autumn. And that blight which turns chestnut-tree leaves brown long before their time.

Why had Dimsie not wanted me to talk to her business manager? Were the businesses in financial trouble? Michael Compton . . . someone I would definitely pay a call on very soon. Without informing Dimsie.

I'd arranged to stay the night with a friend from my university days. Clarissa Ridgeway, queen of her year, tennis star, judo champ and acclaimed jazz singer, had received a starred First in Mediaeval History, married an engineer called Mark, travelled round the world with him for several years before she returned to a large house in the middle of nowhere to rear babies and write well-received crime novels set in the Middle Ages, featuring a travelling *jongleur* called Rondel.

As I drove up the short drive to her door, I could smell honeysuckle. Roses bloomed in beds along the front of the house. Fuchsias hung over pillared balustrades. The scent of newly-mown lawns drifted in the air. England at its most picturesque. Getting out of my car, I could hear the languid drone of a plane high above on its descent into Heathrow or Gatwick. I walked around the side of the house and found Clarissa in the back garden, looking impossibly languorous on a chaise beneath a weeping willow. There were tea things spread on a wicker table beside her, a covered silver dish of toasted teacakes and an iced walnut cake of the kind my Scottish grandmother, Lady de Cuik, used to bring down to Kent years ago when she came to stay with my parents.

'Quick!' she said, smiling. 'How lovely to see you.'

I blew a cursory kiss in her direction. 'Did you make that?' I said accusingly, pointing at the cake. 'It's my absolute favourite.'

'Which is why it's here waiting for you. And no, I didn't make it but I know the person who did.' She began to pour tea from a silver teapot. 'Or, more correctly, I know the person whose mother used to work for the late lamented Mr Fuller and who gave her the recipe on her deathbed.' She handed me a mug of tea.

'Will she share it?'

Clarissa shook her head. 'Sadly, no. I already asked.'

'And how is Rondel?' I asked.

'I'm only halfway through the new book, so naturally he's still totally flummoxed,' Clarissa said. 'Was it Fremont La Blanche, the hunchbacked chamberlain, who murdered nice Sylvan de la Mare? Or was it his rascally squire? Or was it someone else altogether? We shall see. I want to bring Eleanor of Aquitaine into the mix this time, and someone's just brought out a new biography, so I'm researching her at the moment.' She wrinkled her brow the way concerned friends do. 'And how about you, Quick? Anyone significant entered your life since the Love Rat slithered off, scaly tail up his bum?'

I swallowed a piece of my slice of layered walnut cake and shook my head. Sam Willoughby flashed across my mind. Followed – to my surprise – by Todd DuBois. 'No,' I said. Sam appeared again briefly. 'Um . . . not really.'

'*Um . . . not really* sounds promising.'

'It's not.'

'Honest?'

'Cross my heart.' I felt a twinge of guilt. Sam was a good friend, and wanted to be much more. I didn't. Was it the fact that I didn't fancy him, or something more fundamental? If I examined my attitude to him too closely, I would have to admit that there was an element of apprehension in our relationship. On my part, that is. About what? I didn't know. Nor did I want to go there, for fear of what I might uncover about myself.

'That's a shame,' Clarissa said, not believing me. 'As for your Piper Whatsit, in the house I have all the salient points about her for you to mull over. We've run across her and her husband from time to time. Drinks parties and the like. She's quite a character, I think you'll find. At least, on paper.'

We spent a convivial evening, discussing old friends and their doings, until Mark came home, when we switched to more general topics over dinner. The children were all away, except for the youngest one, who slumbered peacefully in his carry cot beside his father's place at the table until the Icelandic *au pair* bore him off to bed.

'Why are you interested in Lady Paramore?' Mark asked at one point.

I took a deep breath. 'I presume you've heard about Tristan Huber's murder,' I said. They both nodded sombrely. 'Apparently he was commissioned to do some interior design work for the woman. His most recent commission. I thought it might be useful to talk to her, see if she has anything new to add. She probably doesn't, but it's worth a try.'

'Are the police baffled?' asked Clarissa. 'Like my Rondel?'

'I don't think so,' I said. 'Not yet. It's just Dimsie – you remember Dimsie?' Again they both nodded. 'She asked me to look into it because she's afraid the police won't give her all the information that I would. If I find anything out, that is.'

'I can see her point,' said Mark. 'The fuzz like to play things very close to the chest. As,' he added hastily, remembering my former career, 'you would yourself, I'm sure.'

'And why not?' asked Clarissa. 'They're there to track down criminals, not to provide the ravening hordes with newspaper titillation over their breakfast eggs.'

The conversation continued with a discussion of why hordes always ravened, and whether, apart from a small and dwindling band of middle-class standard-bearers, anyone still ate eggs for breakfast, let alone read a newspaper while consuming them.

Clarissa handed me a see-through plastic folder before I went upstairs. I lay in a four-poster bed which smelled of woodworm and starched linen, and leafed through it. I knew that if there was any further info to find, she, a meticulous researcher, would have winkled it out.

I read that Piper Paramore was raised by her socialite mother, who'd left Piper's father and moved to New York. She'd wed again and subsequently managed to marry Piper off to a minor English aristocratic, Sir Piers Paramore, who worked at something esoteric in merchant banking. Piers brought to the marriage a shabby ancestral mansion set in some neglected acres of Kentish countryside, a pretty good income and half a dozen miners' cottages near Salford, all that was left of a considerable coal mining fortune. Piper, meanwhile, contributed money and an enormous amount of Yankee energy. In between producing four children, she had begun rehabilitating the house, doing up the cottages as holiday lets, transforming the paddocks, and setting up a thriving company offering Rollins Park as a wholesome entertainment package for families on holiday.

And in what seemed to me, lying back among Clarissa's luxurious pillows, a stroke of genius, she had invited her father over from Tennessee, where he had retired. Dad – Hank Rogers – was an established star on the rodeo circuit. His mother had been a famous barrel racing champion, whatever that was; *his* father – Elmer 'Red Tex' Rogers – was renowned for the speed in which he could rope a steer and the length of time he could stay astride a bucking bronco.

Hank's lucky break came when he was still living in Texas and they found oil in one of his back paddocks. Since then, he had done pretty much as he pleased, which had mostly involved setting up a fine stable of horses in east Tennessee, which he presented worldwide, and now, starring in a Wild West show for the delight and entertainment of the paying public in one of the Rollins Park fields. Apparently children from all over the country were dragging their parents to see the performance. There were plenty of headshots of Hank's weather-beaten face smiling from under a white ten-gallon Stetson. I stared at it for some time. Smiling, yes, but there was more than a hint of granite about the crinkled eyes and craggy jaw. Not a man you'd want to get across. There were also photos of him in thrilling encounter with mounts which definitely didn't like having him on their back and were trying their utmost to get him off it.

I looked forward to meeting him.

SEVEN

It was a weekday, and despite the number of vehicles parked in the car park, Rollins Park Amusements seemed almost deserted as I drove in through the gates and up the drive. I came to a fork and took the left-hand road, which was signposted NO ENTRY and underneath that, PRIVATE ROAD. I motored along an avenue lined on either side by well-aged lime trees. Pulled to a halt in front of a country house of no particular architectural merit but nonetheless presenting a pleasing aspect.

As I stood beside my car, admiring the tastefully repointed brickwork, someone came out of the front door and stood where two sweeping curves of stone steps met in front of it. The steps were not very high and the sweep was not exactly huge, but nonetheless, the general effect was relatively imposing.

The someone who'd emerged was now staring down at me in a distinctly unfriendly manner. She had dark hair cut like a man's short-back-and-sides. She was wearing jeans with a striped dress shirt tucked into them and a broad Western belt.

'You've come the wrong way,' she said, both her tone and her body language offensive. 'Didn't you see the sign that showed you were following a private road? Or can't you read?'

'I can indeed. And frequently do.' Unimpressed by her far from dulcet tones, I smiled up at her. 'Which is precisely why I forked left.'

'It's marked Private, so what's your reason, if any beyond idle curiosity?'

I raised my eyebrows. 'I don't know how ill-bred they are in your country, but I would have thought you'd lived in England long enough to know that on the whole we try to keep a civil tongue in our head. At least until we have good cause to be discourteous.'

There was a pause. Then she said, 'I apologize. I was rude. But if you knew how many times a day in the season we get strangers invading our privacy . . .'

'My name's Quick,' I said. 'I suppose I should have made an appointment. I was hoping to speak to Lady Paramore.'

'What about?'

'It's to do with Tristan Huber,' I said.

'The decorator?' She frowned. Looked at her watch then down again at me. 'He's not here.'

Since she had a clipped east-coast American accent, I assumed this was Piper Paramore herself. 'It's not Tristan I've come to see. It's you,' I said. I was getting heartily sick of directing my conversation to a point ten feet above my head. Besides, I was developing a hell of a crick in the neck. I started towards the nearest curve of steps.

'Hold it!' She held up her hand like a policeman, more or less forbidding me to climb any higher, so I sat down, my back to her. If this was the get-up-and-go expert, it wouldn't have hurt her to direct a portion of her energy towards acquiring some manners. She didn't speak. Neither did I. I was fairly sure which one of us would break the deadlock. It wouldn't be me. Sure enough, I heard her start to descend the stone staircase. 'What exactly do you want?' she asked, sounding somewhat less aggressive.

'Come down here and I'll tell you,' I said.

Eventually she reached the same level as me and sat down on the broad lichened steps. 'Sorry,' she said.

I stuck out my hand. 'Alexandra Quick. You obviously haven't heard the sad news.'

'*What* sad news?'

'That Tristan – Mr Huber – was killed a few days ago.'

She went pale. 'Killed? Tristan?' A sudden flush washed away the pallor. 'Tristan,' she said faintly. 'Do you mean . . . he's *dead*?'

I didn't retort that when a person reported someone had been killed, it usually meant that the someone was dead. 'I'm afraid so.'

'But he was such a . . .' she said. Tears began to flood down her face. 'He *can't* be dead.'

I said nothing. I longed to know what words she had been going to employ. Hard worker? Handsome bloke? Great lover? Old friend?

'No! I don't believe it. He *can't* be,' she said again, raising her voice as though hoping that if she denied it long and loudly enough, I would change my mind and admit that I'd only been joking and after all, he was alive and well.

I didn't. 'When did you last see him,' I asked.

'It m-must have b-been two or th-three weeks ago.' Her lower lip trembled. 'He'd taken a couple of weeks off. Not that . . .'

She stopped. She knew as well as I did that being on vacation didn't preclude getting murdered.

We sat in silence for a few moments. Then I said, 'What was Tristan working on for you?'

The use of the past tense provoked another downpour of tears. Again I waited. Finally, she got up. 'I'll show you.'

It was odd that she should have accepted the news without asking when and where, let alone how Tristan had died. Perhaps it was still sinking in. We walked across sheep-shorn turf, in the opposite direction from the amusement park. In the distance, I could hear excited screams and a voice yelling 'Yee-*haw*!' The Lariat King himself, I guessed. We were approaching a building which I mentally categorized as a gazebo or pergola, without being a hundred per cent sure what either was. It was round, its domed roof supported by slim white pillars. It was open on three sides, with views across the park in one direction and down to a broad flat river in the other. Inside, a tiny spout of water bubbled flatly in the centre of a small square pool set into the marbled floor. Beside it a metal stork stood on one leg. Unless it was a flamingo.

'We call this Lady Anne's Retreat,' explained Piper. 'After her tenth child was born, she was never in the best of health, and she liked to sit here gazing at the view, doing nothing very much.'

'I'm not surprised.' I couldn't help thinking of poor Lilian Harkness and her lack of fruitfulness.

'We normally have couches set around the walls. Small tables. House plants,' said Piper. 'A drinks cabinet. A little icebox. My husband and I like to come down here and have a martini or something, when he gets home from London. It's very peaceful. Gives him a chance to unwind.' She gestured at the wall. 'But obviously we had to take everything out while Tristan did his – his decorations in here.' She gazed at the unfinished mural. 'Beautiful pictures, aren't they? Such delicate work. He was so gifted.'

I too stared at Tristan's design. A landscape-in-the-half-round. A vista seen through mist or in a dream. I was reminded of the work of Eric Ravilious: the muted colours and slightly offbeat style complementing the real scenes outside. A distant river wound its way past woods and fields. A church with a square Norman tower lay half-hidden by cloudy trees. Another, this time with a gothic spire. There were cattle dotted about: Jersey for the most part but with a sprinkling of Fresians and big white Charolais. A flock of black-faced sheep. White weather-boarded mills. A train rattling along, old-fashioned, a plume of smoke streaming backwards above a red engine with shiny brass fitments. People stood about, singly or in small groups. All contained within a backdrop no more than six or seven feet by twelve. The scene was like a dream of lost innocence, and entirely enchanting. Especially since it was hard to say where image ceased and distant reality took over. Tears clogged the back of my throat at the remembrance that the creator of this small marvel was gone.

'So,' Piper said, turning to look forcefully at me. Her eyes were wide and fixed. To prevent further tears, I was guessing. 'What exactly do you want to know?'

I found it interesting that she didn't query what right I had to question her. *Basically, whether you could have killed Tristan Huber . . .* 'While Tristan was working on the pergola—'

'Gazebo.'

'—whatever, were there any altercations? Someone on your staff who he might have quarrelled with or annoyed in some way? Had negative dealings with of some kind or another? Did he stay here overnight or go home at the end of each day? Did anyone come to see him here that you were aware of? Did he . . . uh . . . engage in activities of which you did not approve? Did he have issues with your father or your husband?'

'Goodness, so many questions. Let me think . . .' While she thought, Ms Paramore busied herself with hiding the way her hands shook by tucking her shirt more tightly into her jeans. Smoothing down her little-boy-at-Sunday-School haircut. Picking up a stray leaf which had blown into the pergola . . . or gazebo. Straightened up, she shook her head. 'I don't think so. We could ask the Wild West personnel . . . they always seemed to be good pals with each other. Everyone liked him.' Her voice shook too.

'Fine.' I had been hoping for an excuse to talk to Mr Rodeo. I looked at my watch. 'Is your father working at the moment?'

'His next show's at eleven thirty,' she said. 'You'll have to wait until he's finished.' She nodded in the direction of the Park. 'Come on, I'll walk you over.'

Some way behind the house, what looked like an authentic-looking rodeo ground had been built, complete with sand, bleachers and rough-hewn fencing. A full complement of spectators occupied the seating.

Hank Rogers, Piper's father, was already astride a large indignant mount which been boxed into a tight space of heavy iron railings. One of the rider's hands gripped a kind of handle attached to harness round the front of the bronco, the other waved a hat in the air. The horse seemed pretty pissed-off, showing the whites of its eyes and tossing its head as it tried to shake off the man on its back. When he saw us, Hank gestured his big white hat at his daughter and, by association, me. She waved back. He was wearing a fringed buckskin shirt and leather chaps over western-cut blue-jeans, with a red spotted scarf tied round his sinewy neck. A couple of guys in jeans and checked shirts, topped with wide-brimmed cowboy hats, were standing around, looking ready for almost anything. Someone else was holding on to the top of a metal gate, penning in the bronco.

Somebody yelled something that sounded vaguely bronco-busting. The gate opened. Out bulleted the horse and its bareback rider, kicking up its heels, arching its back, while

Hank kept the arm with the hat in the air for balance. The help hovered here and there, ready at any time to turn the horse. It was a bit like a bullfight, though a lot less ceremonious. No lovely señoritas with flowers in their hair. No black sombreros and strutting suits of light. Just a bunch of overweight Brits and their pudgy children, half of them chewing sweets or chocolate bars.

'I'm so proud of my father,' Piper said, gazing fondly at him.

'He's really something,' I agreed. I wasn't quite sure what, but definitely something.

Hank clung on for grim death while the horse bucked and reared and frothed. Then suddenly, it gave up and stood docilely with its head hanging and its sides heaving. Some calves appeared in the ring, shooed in by one of Hank's assistants – I'm sure there was a more official name for them – and began running round, mooing loudly as Hank slid off the horse's sweaty back and waved his hat while the audience cheered and clapped. An assistant ran in and led off the animal while Hank twirled his lariat.

'Yee-*haw*!' he yelled, sending the rope flying and catching one of the calves by the neck. The others ran off in a group, while with a second rope, Hank expertly lassoed the calf by the back legs, bringing it to its knees, to the delight of the crowd, now fully engaged in the action. 'Come along, ya little dogies!' he shouted. 'Come along now. Come, come, come.'

He did some more lassoing while I read a poster attached to the fencing. 'What exactly is barrel racing?' I asked.

'It's a popular event at rodeos, ladies only,' Piper said. 'Basically, you race your horse in between big oil barrels arranged in a sort of clover-leaf pattern without knocking them over.'

'Sounds a bit like slalom racing.'

'I suppose it is. Sort of. It's quite exciting. I used to do it when I was a child. As a matter of fact, my grandmother was a real champion.'

'Fancy.' I tried to imagine my own grandmother, Lady de Cuik, dressed in western shirt and jeans, navigating her way through a collection of barrels. Couldn't be done.

Another guy appeared and began twirling a rope in an amazing series of artistic loops and swirls. 'Yippee ye yi ay!' he yelled, the lariat flying through the air, making complicated circles against the blue sky. Grinning, he took off his hat and waved it at them.

Well, now, I thought. Well, bugger me.

'He's good, isn't he?' Piper said admiringly.

'How long has he been part of the act?'

'He just showed up earlier this year. He had all sorts of recommendations. As it happened, we had a vacancy in the team and Dad took him on immediately, as soon as he'd demonstrated what he could do.'

'Where's he from?'

'Tennessee, I believe.' She pulled her dark brows together. 'Or was that one of the other guys? I'm not sure.'

'What's his name?' I asked.

'Jerry Baskin. Apparently his father raised horses, trained those Tennessee walking horses they have down there.' She smiled. 'And in fact, here comes one right now.'

Jerry Baskin, eh? Why did I feel so certain that someone had been eating ice cream just before being asked what his name was?

A very tall horse shuffled in and began a weird kind of trotting walk round the display ring. The front and back legs on each side moved at the same time, making its gait unlike anything I'd ever seen before, its front legs very high with each step. On its back crouched a man in a long black coat and a white shirt with a Mississippi gambler's black ribbon tie, under a stiff black hat.

The show lasted another twenty minutes and was a good one, in which Jerry Baskin more than played his part, being an obvious expert in some of the manoeuvres presented.

At the end, as the audience began to shamble out, I turned back to Lady Paramore.

'Any chance of saying hi to some of the guys?' I asked. 'I'd really like to congratulate them . . . that was a terrific display.'

'I'm sure they'd be delighted to meet you,' she said. 'Though both Dad and Jerry are going to be pretty upset when you tell them about poor Tristan. Over the past few weeks they've become good friends.' She sniffed hard. 'So have I.'

Call me a cynic, but my (unspoken) response was *I'll just bet you have*. Good as they come.

As the crowd dispersed, she led the way round to the back of the ring where a series of sheds made of weathered planks housed stables, barns and quarters for Hank Rogers and his team. The place reeked of hot animals and even hotter males, with an overlay of beer and leather. Three men stripped to the waist were standing about when we arrived, drinking beer from cans and wiping their faces with wet towels. They all turned as Piper stepped inside, with me following closely. One of them was Hank.

'Hi, Dad,' Piper said.

'Well, hiya, honey.' Hank's voice twanged like an old guitar. I thought of poor Sam, and his dreams of struttin' his stuff on the stage at the Grand Ole Opry, dressed in fancy western-style duds. Maybe he could take up rodeo as a substitute. 'And who's your friend?'

I stepped forward, hand out. 'Quick. Alexandra Quick. I really enjoyed your show, Mr Rogers.'

'Why thank you, ma'am.' He introduced the other two men: Marvin and Chuck.

'I'd love to know where you get your broncos from,' I said, 'seeing as how cattle droving isn't exactly a full-time occupation in twenty-first-century England.'

He laughed, showing a full set of ivory-white teeth. 'We ship a few over from my place in the States,' he said. 'And there's always a good supply right here of badly broken animals.'

A loo flushed somewhere, water ran, a planked door opened. The Lariat King emerged from the back, bejeaned and bechapped, his cowboy hat pushed rakishly on to the back of his head. 'Well, howdy, ma'am,' he said, when he saw Lady Paramore.

'Good show, Jerry,' said Piper. 'Meet Alex Quick.'

Jerry turned to me. He gaped stupidly, the 'Howdy, ma'am' dying on his lips. 'What the— What're you doing here?' he said.

'Why, I just came by to get me a helping of that fine old Louisiana catfish pie and collard greens I've heard so much about,' I drawled in my best down-home accent. 'Don't tell me you're fresh out.'

The others were staring at us. 'Do you two know each other?' Hank asked.

'In a manner of speaking,' I said.

'Dad,' Piper said, her voice urgent. 'We need to talk.' She jerked her head at the door leading outside.

'OK, honey. Gimme two minutes.'

I was very conscious of Jerry Baskin's fish-hook gaze on my back as we left. I won't say it sent shivers of apprehension up my spine, but it certainly wasn't a very friendly stare. We were supposed to be having dinner together in a day or two. Cooked by him. I started to wonder what access he might have to toxic substances, and whether I should cancel.

'We'll go up to the house,' said Piper. 'My husband should be back from seeing the bank manager by now. I know he'd like to meet you.'

I couldn't imagine why.

'You can save your bad news until then,' she added quickly.

Sir Piers was sitting on a terrace at the back of the house, gazing out at the artificial lake where mallards squawked and a heron looked down its beak at them. He was holding a cut-glass tumbler in which floated a hefty slice of lemon and some tonic which I could see was heavily laced with gin, since it had that give-away blue tinge to it. Ice cubes chinked as he rose to his feet. 'Darling,' he said.

'Piers, I'd like you to meet Alexandra Quick.'

He was far too well-bred to ask who the hell I was. He shook my hand. Offered me a drink, which I refused. Poured one for his wife. He was very tall, very thin, very pale, very upper class. He was wearing a beige lightweight suit over a blue-striped shirt, open at the neck. A tie was draped over the back of a chair.

'I wondered where you'd got to,' he said.

'I was showing our visitor Dad's act,' she said.

Dad himself appeared through the French windows leading out from the drawing room.

'Hank, old boy . . .' Genial as hell, Sir Piers picked up a decanter and poised it over a glass. 'The usual?'

'Thanks, son.' Hank smiled. 'Ain't nothin' like a slug of that good old sippin' sweet Tennessee bourbon,' he said, taking the glass his son-in-law held out to him. I couldn't help but note that the hokey down-home accent was coming on a good deal stronger than it had been earlier, down at the rodeo ring.

Nor could I help taking on board the look of distaste which briefly crossed the well-bred features of Sir Piers. Did I detect a slightly cool atmosphere at play between the Englishman and his father-in-law?

'Alexandra has some bad news,' Lady Paramore said soberly. She turned to me. 'Tell them.'

I explained about Tristan's murder, and that I'd been asked to work in parallel with the police. I implied that I was official. I also implied that I was some kind of professional private eye. I didn't have to be professional to take in the reactions of the two men. The colour drained from Sir Piers's already austere face. He reached for the back of a chair, his knuckles white. 'How . . . how perfectly appalling,' he said, through lips as unbending as dinner plates. 'How utterly . . . What do the police think happened?'

'At the moment they have no idea.'

'I was at school with him,' Sir Piers said, as though to excuse his evident shock. 'This is terrible.'

Meanwhile, beneath his tanned complexion, Hank Rogers had turned an unbecoming shade of red. 'What the fuck happens now?' he said. His mouth tightened over the words.

'Da-*ad*,' admonished his daughter.

Did she mean the rodeo star's language? Or the sentiments he appeared to be expressing? And what sentiment was that exactly?

Hank recovered quickly. 'That mural doodad he was painting for you . . . Not going to get finished now, is it?'

There was an awful lot going on below the surface of these civilized surroundings. I would have to delve a great deal deeper. But not now. Mainly because I couldn't think of a polite way to ask them how and why Tristan's death had affected them. Nor an impolite one, for that matter.

'I'm sorry to have been the bearer of such bad tidings.' I stood up. 'I have to get back. I imagine the police will be visiting you at some point, since Tristan was apparently working here right up until he took a break.'

I left.

On my way back to Clarissa's house, I reflected that up at the big house, they were probably going through a cat-on-hot-bricks routine, frantically trying to conceal whatever it was that they were involved in. Because that much was obvious: the three people I'd left behind at Rollins Park were up to their necks in something, whether it was criminal or otherwise.

What saddened me was the fact that Tristan Huber's life, held up to public gaze, might be about to reveal itself as much less saintly than I had thought.

EIGHT

'As I said last night,' Clarissa said, 'We've met both the Paramores from time to time but I can't say they impinge on us in the slightest.'

'She means our paths never cross,' explained Mark. 'In other words, we move in entirely different social circles.'

'Ever heard any scandal about them?'

The two of them looked at each other. 'Well,' Mark said, 'we had a couple of their personnel up before the Bench a year or so ago, on the grounds of cruelty.'

'To horses,' put in Clarissa.

Mark was the local Chairman of the Magistrates. 'What were they doing?'

'To give you a highly simplified version, they brought in a new trainer and it turned out he was using outlawed methods to exaggerate that peculiar walk the Walking Horses have. Injections, illegal weights which rubbed the fetlocks, nails inserted into the so-called pads or stacks, which build up the exaggerated gait. They walk like that because it's so darned painful for them to put their feet on the ground.'

'Mark had to bone up on all this before the guy appeared in front of him,' Clarissa supplied. 'It's quite complicated.'

'The point was that the RSPCA inspectors got on to the abuse and it was stopped. Fines were imposed and the head guy—'

'Piper Paramore's father.'

'—immediately sacked that particular trainer. And since then, there hasn't been anything untoward, as far as we know.'

'Not to do with the horses, at any rate.' Clarissa made a face involving raised eyebrows and pursed lips.

I looked from one to another. 'Gossip!' I said. 'Tell me all.'

'I yield to no one in my admiration for Piper . . . Lady Paramore,' said Mark portentously. 'And I'm well aware that she's pulled Rollins round almost singlehandedly. I'd hate idle speculation to impact badly on her.'

'*But . . .*'

'But there have been rumours here and there. Particularly in the village round the estate.'

'Rollingford,' Clarissa said helpfully.

'Rumours of what?' I said, trying not to sound impatient.

'Well, it seems that some of those rodeo riders or whatever they're called can't keep it in their pants.'

''Twas ever thus,' I said. 'Simple village maidens falling for the exotic stranger from across the seas.'

'Except that this wasn't—'

'Isn't,' put in his wife.

'—only village maidens, but village lads and, in some cases, even village children. Or so we were told.'

'Oh dear.'

'As you say,' Mark said. 'Oh dear, oh dear. But I should emphasize that this is all pure speculation.'

'Or impure,' said Clarissa, 'depending on how you look at it.'

'And where does Tristan Huber fit into all this, I ask myself?' Despite the wife, now vanished, I had from time to time wondered whether Tristan was gay, but even if he was, I couldn't imagine him indulging in anything as sordid as seducing kids. 'You're not talking about a paedophile ring, are you?'

'I'm afraid the answer to that,' said Clarissa, 'is that we don't know. And history doesn't relate. On top of that . . .' She stopped.

'Rumours,' Mark said, shaking his head at her. 'Village gossip.'

'What *about*?' I demanded.

'Anything you care to mention, really. From people-trafficking to grand larceny.'

'But nobody knows for sure. And you can't go in and search the place without a warrant.'

'And you can't get a warrant without evidence, or at least reasonable suspicion.'

'I shall have to find out more,' I said. 'It could have quite a bearing on his death. Where would I start?'

'Try Sheila, the landlady at the Rollins Arms. Halfway up the village street. Hotbed of gossip, or so I hear from one of my fellow JPs.'

When I pushed open the door, the Rollins Arms seemed to be in full late-morning somnolence.

Three elderly blokes were seated at three different tables, one reading the *Guardian*, one absorbed in the *Daily Mail*, one staring morosely at nothing in particular.

I hoicked my bum on to a stool at the bar and ordered a double tomato juice with a slug of Worcestershire sauce and two ice cubes.

'And what brings you to our neck of the woods,' the woman behind the bar – Sheila, I presumed – asked me.

'Just visiting,' I said. 'Having a look round. Casing the joint. I'm thinking of moving down from Northumberland.'

'It's a nice place to live, round here.'

'It looks it.' I sipped at my tomato juice. Got chatty. 'I went to that rodeo show yesterday. That'll be somewhere nice to take the children if we move down here.'

She pressed her lips together. Nodded several times. Said nothing.

C'mon lady, I thought, make with the tittle-tattle. I haven't got all day. 'I suppose those cowhands or whatever they're called must come in here now and then. I guess it's thirsty work, roping steers and bucking broncos.'

'Yes,' she said.

So much for the hotbed of rumour and innuendo. I was about to drain my glass and leave, when she leaned forward and opened her mouth. 'Actually,' she began.

'Now, now, Sheila, watch what you're saying.' It was the guy reading the *Guardian*.

'I haven't said anything yet, Mr Watson.'

'But you're about to. I've warned you before about unsubstantiated libel, slander and defamation.'

'I was merely going to inform this young lady of some of the other sights round here which she shouldn't miss.'

'I'm sure you were.' Mr Watson returned to his paper. I took him to be a retired solicitor. Or even a functioning one.

Sheila winked at me. She held up eight fingers and tapped her watch, which I took to mean that Mr Watson would be off in eight minutes. Sure enough, eight minutes later he folded his paper, got up and left, nodding at me and the other men, wagging a reproving finger at Sheila.

'What an old woman,' she said, when he was safely out the door.

'He's right, you know.' The kind of voice you might expect from a very elderly tortoise with laryngitis emerged from the throat of one of the other patrons. Impossible to know which one, since neither of them lifted their heads. Or even seemed aware of our presence.

'Mind you, it's not nearly as harmless as it looks,' she said.

'What isn't?'

'The village. Murder, rape, wife-beating, child-abuse, bank-robbing—'

'Incest,' came the rusty old voice again.

'—that too. You name it, we've got it.' She didn't mention paedophiles though.

'What about people-smuggling or grand larceny?'

'Ooh, no dear.' She seemed quite shocked. 'There's none of that round her.'

'But you still wouldn't recommend this as a place for me to bring up children?'

'I wouldn't go that far,' said Sheila cautiously, perhaps

sensing business being turned away. 'But we've had our share of scandals.'

'What was the murder about?'

'Peggy Mitchell . . . always was a bit odd, if you ask me. Same old boring story. Silly girl got involved with one of them Yanks up at the Park, fell pregnant, when he wouldn't marry her she threatened to kill herself. Then lo and behold, they found her in Lyden Woods. Hanged herself.'

'That's suicide, not murder.'

'Oh yes. So they all thought. Except some clever dick of a police detective came down from London, said it was impossible for her to have killed herself like that. Produced all the facts: height, weight, type of knot etc. Plus asked how she could have got the rope over the tree branch in the first place, since she was such an itty bitty little thing. Whereas her fancy man . . .' She raised an arm towards the ceiling to imply height. 'Next thing we know, this London cop and his sidekick are up at Rollins, waving warrants and demanding to see the feller she'd been with, accusing him of murder. Only by then he'd taken to his heels and gone back to his wife and kids in Oklahoma or somewhere.'

'Goodness,' I said.

'And that's not the only scandal we've had with those cowboys up there,' Sheila continued, settling comfortably into her story.

'No . . .!' I pretended shock and dismay.

'I'm telling you yes!' She leaned towards me. 'Look, this is the twenty-first century, right?'

'Indubitably.'

'I mean, we don't go in for witch-hunts and such any more . . . though there've been witches burned right outside this very door. Not all that long ago, neither. One of my own ancestors, made herbal potions and the like . . .' She paused, eyes looking back to a grimly primitive past.

'Witch-hunts,' I prompted, since she seemed to have lost the plot.

'Nothing wrong with Guy Wheatley,' she said. 'Ask me, we just weren't ready for him and his sort. Very chummy with Lady P, he was. Always up at the Park. Drinks. Dinner. Lunches and that. Him and his arty friends.'

I hardly dared asked what had happened to Guy Wheatley but I managed somehow.

'Oh, the Vicar had a word, so he packed his bags in a huff and flounced back to the city. Isn't that right, Den?' She addressed one or other of the old boys but neither of them answered. They both appeared to have fallen asleep. Or died.

'But what had the man done?'

'*You* know . . .' She sounded mildly surprised that I didn't. 'He was One Of Them.' She did one or two of those bloody silly gestures that ignorant folk go in for when describing gays. Smoothed an eyebrow. Flopped her hand forward from the wrist. I loathe bigotry. Especially against gay people. And although I've met dozens of gays, I've never seen any of them go in for eyebrow smoothing.

'What's wrong with being gay, you ignorant bigot?' I said rudely. 'As it happens, I'm gay myself.'

'Uh . . . um . . .' Sheila swallowed and backed away behind the bar, as though I might otherwise reach across and besmirch her. 'No offense meant.'

'Plenty taken.'

I knocked back my tomato juice and left. The Vicar? What the hell happened to brotherly love and all God's chillun'? But had I learned anything useful? Mainly that it would be a brave soul who stepped out of line in a village like this one. Poor Peggy Mitchell, murdered for a fuck. I wondered if the Oklahoman had ever been brought to book.

NINE

Back in Longbury, gulls swooped above the seafront. Fisherfolk flogged herring out of white polystyrene boxes. Sunshine sparkled on gentle waves.

I turned down into the High Street, past the Chinese takeaway, the pizza parlour where nobody ever came or went. Past Willoughbys Books and Vines Wines. Edward waved as I went by. I turned left, and went into Dimsie's place. For once she was there, listlessly turning the pages of a sample book of upholstery fabrics and crying. She looked utterly forlorn and defenceless.

'Oh, Dimsie,' I said. I held my arms wide and she rushed into them, burrowing against my chest like a puppy, wiping tears against my shirt. I hoped they weren't mixed with snot.

'Are you getting anywhere?' she demanded.

'Not particularly. But I have several lines of enquiry I want to follow up. If you still want me to.'

'Of *course* I do!'

'Then what I'd like from you is a list of as many of Tristan's contacts, and friends as you can remember. Especially the local ones. And if you have a contact number for his former wife, give it to me.'

'Christie? Surely you can't imagine she's had anything to do with this.'

'Not necessarily,' I said. 'But for the moment all options have to remain open. And also she may know things about him that you don't.'

'OK.'

'Any idea where she might be living now?'

'As I told you, we don't exactly keep in touch. Sometimes a card at Christmas, sometimes not. I've heard from a mutual friend that they keep a flat in London they use when they're over here. Otherwise I presume they live in Spain.' She shrugged, wiping her face. That's it, really.'

'Did you like her?'

'She was OK. But after she married again we kind of drifted apart – not that we were ever all that close.'

'Do you think she's heard that Tristan's died?'

'If she has, she certainly hasn't contacted us in any way. No condolences and so on, if that's what you mean. So perhaps she doesn't know yet.'

'Has Tristan had any fallings-out with people recently, do you know? Employees, clients, anyone who might be harbouring a grudge?'

'The Dame might be a better source of information than me.'

'Is she likely to pass anything on?'

'If it'll bring Tristan's killer to justice, she'll tell you absolutely anything you want to know.'

The pretty Georgian house where the Huber-Draytons had lived for several generations was small but rather grand. Despite a considerable amount of dilapidation, and being separated by a crumbling brick wall from a family graveyard complete with yew trees and burial vaults, the place was in much demand for photo shoots for fashion shows or period TV programmes, or even the kind of Regency films featuring Hollywood actresses who have mastered the art of speaking with impeccable English accents. Dorcas pretended to be way above the vulgarities enjoyed by *hoi polloi*, but she'd always suffered from a lack of funds and had no problem accepting their money.

I drove into the forecourt between gateposts decorated with a bracket supporting a square-shaped lantern and parked. Roses, interspersed with fecund lavender bushes and flowering sage, bloomed in beautifully tended beds, thanks to Gibson, the gardener who'd been in charge since I was about six. The gravel looked as though it had been raked just five minutes earlier. The air was fragrant with choiysa. Instead of pulling at the elaborate bell system beside the front door, I walked around the house, as I used to do in childhood, to the kitchen door. It stood open. I could see Dorcas inside, upright at the big pine table, staring rigidly at the green Aga, her hands clasped in front of her.

I had thought that Kevin Fuller's father had epitomized grief, but here was a grief more profound than any I had ever caught sight of, except possibly for an image I had once seen of a grieving Madonna. The face she turned to me as I knocked lightly and entered was a shock. She'd never been a beauty. Her eyes were too ferocious, her nose too insistent, her habitual expression too commanding. Most of the time she gave the impression of an unfriendly Komodo dragon on a bad day. Now, she looked like the rind of a dried-up melon, or a withered autumn leaf which had once been bright green. Her eyes had sunk so far into their sockets that they seemed to be no more than puddles at the back of her face.

'Dorcas.' I didn't dare attempt anything as personal as a hug. Or even a hand on her shoulder. Dorcas had never welcomed intimacies in the past and I sensed that she would not appreciate them now. 'I'm so terribly sorry.'

She moved her gaze from the Aga to stare at me for such a long time that I wondered if she had even heard me. 'Dorcas,' I began again. 'I'm so—'

'Find them!' she said. It sounded as though a harrow was ploughing its way through her chest, tearing up gobbets of flesh as it went. Normally, she spoke in the kind of voice which would stop a herd of charging hippos at twenty paces. She held out a large hand which tremored uncontrollably. 'Find them and bring them to me.'

'Dorcas, you know I can't—'

Once again she interrupted me. 'This – this cruel outrage won't go unpunished,' she said. 'And you've done it before, you've brought justice to bear. You have to do it again, for my sake. For Tri-, for Trist-, for my son's sake.'

To hear this indomitable, not terribly likeable woman reduced to a stricken falter, unable even to articulate the name of her lost child, was almost sadder than Mr Fuller's dignified grief. 'Do you have even the slightest notion of who could be behind this?' I asked.

'He was too good,' she rasped.

'In what sen—'

'Beat them all into a cocked hat. They could never keep up with him. He outstripped them all. Always did.'

I have to admit that I didn't have the foggiest idea what she was talking about. Tristan had always been an extremely able person, highly skilled in many different areas. But a saintly Leader of Men? I didn't think so. 'Are you suggesting that a rival is behind this? Someone in the same business as he was?'

She snorted unpleasantly. Her chin trembled. 'Interior Design?' she said. 'What *was* he thinking of? He had a brilliant career ahead of him in the Army. He could have been anything. Risen to the highest ranks, like his uncles.' Again she pushed her hand towards me. 'Find his murderers, Alexandra. Please.' The note of pleading in her unsteady voice was terrible to hear. 'My golden boy . . .'

'Do you have any suspicions about the identity of the person or persons responsible?' I asked.

'Not at the moment. But if I come up with anyone, you can be certain that you'll hear about it.'

It struck me that Dimsie knew as little about her mother as she did about her brother. Any chance of this poor husk of a woman, hollowed out by grief, giving me anything useful to work with was out of the question. At least for the moment. All she wanted right now was vengeance.

'One last question . . . Tristan's former wife.'

'What about her?'

'Do you know whether she or her new husband could possibly be implicated in some way?'

'No idea. Never liked the woman. And when she abandoned my son . . . it nearly broke his heart. It was unforgivable.'

I didn't like to bring up the matter of Dorcas's own marital failings.

'But no. A vulgar creature, I always thought. But not vicious. Not a murderer.' She didn't speak again. Her dislike of physical contact was so ingrained in me that I simply said that if there was anything at all I could do for her, I would be happy to do it. Then I went back to my car and drove away.

Her words had been enigmatic. *He outstripped them all* . . . What did that mean? It could have been anything, from winning a tennis match to scoring a lucrative contract from under a competitor's nose. But that must go on all the time, not just in the interior design field but in almost any commercial undertaking.

I urgently needed to see Tristan's client list. And tomorrow I would pay a call on Mr Michael Compton.

I've often wondered whether the grimy chaos in which most solicitors' firms exist is intended to create confidence in the bosoms of their clients. Whether there were obscure little companies marketing spray-on dust, dead flies and tattered files, in order to create the right impression. In such a grungy environment (the reasoning might go) and notwithstanding the holiday home in France, the yacht moored in Portofino, the legal person in question could not possibly be embezzling clients' funds. Could he? Or she? Particularly when, as so often, you added a suit which some time ago had seen better days, a ditto shirt and shabby suede Hush Puppies, one lace of which had clearly been broken at some point and had the two ends knotted back together. All of which proved bugger all.

But I wasn't here to consult a solicitor. A business manager was an entirely different kettle of fish, as I twigged as soon as I reached the building which housed, among many other enterprises, MICHAEL COMPTON, FINANCIAL CONSULTANT, followed by a string of letters. The place was in one of the choicest parts of town, halfway up the hill to the university, standing back from the road with a gravelled parking area in front of it. Which already held two Beamers, one Mercedes, and a racy little sports car in electric blue. Perhaps they were props, put away at night, intended to assure customers that this was *the* place to come for advice on money and investment. But probably not. The Huber-Draytons wouldn't be putting just any old hack in charge of their financial affairs. No, indeed.

I was shown into an office full of glass and leather. A pricey designer chair was offered. Coffee was suggested and refused. This wasn't a social call. A window looked out on to a leafy bit of garden. Above trees, I could see sunshine gilding the university bell tower. Some birds flapped busily about, the way they always do. Compton was sitting opposite me in a pale linen suit (I would have to remember to ask him how he managed to keep it so uncreased) and striped red-and-white shirt, open at the neck. Neat brown hair, expensively barbered. One of those baby's bottom chins. A pervasive scent of some bespoke aftershave permeated the air.

And he was talking. Talking mesmerically. If he'd asked me to eat a red hot chilli pepper or go out and rob a bank, I might well have done so, such was the power of his voice. Forceful, imperative, silkily superior; it hung above his wavy hair with an ungainsayable authority. Looking at him, silver spoons danced a fandango inside my head.

'So,' he said. He reached for a pair of black-framed banker's glasses lying beside the blotter on the desk in front of him and hooked them over his ears. What, hoping to make himself more impressive? Didn't work for me. 'How can I help?'

'You probably can't,' I said. 'Or more likely won't.'

'Won't?'

'Knowing people like you, I expect you'll hide behind client confidentiality.'

He gave a practised chortle. 'Oh, come now, Miss Quick. You sound extremely biased.'

'I probably am. With good reason.' I dared him to ask me what the reason was but luckily he didn't, since there wasn't one.

He straightened a file on his desk, then leaned back in his leather swivel chair. 'My client, Dimsie Drayton, has asked me to cooperate with you as far as possible. I understand you're looking into the horrible death of her brother.'

'In a purely private capacity. She felt the local homicide detectives wouldn't pass on all the details to her.'

'So, what do you want to know?' All business now, he leaned forward and put his hands flat on his desk. His elbows stuck out on either side of his body like bony wings.

'As many details as possible about Tristan's company, including his clients.'

'I can't possibly divulge—'

'Why not? It must be a matter of public record. I can find out what I need to know but it would be so much easier if you'd just tell me.'

He saw the sense of that. 'Well, as you must know, he was in great demand.'

'Yes. But where in particular? Where, for instance, were his last few projects based?'

'I don't quite follow?'

'What's not to follow? Which country? Which town? Who hired him? I know about Piper Paramore. What about the others? Over the past two, say, years?'

'I'd have to . . .' He pushed back his chair, stood up and went over to a filing cabinet by the wall. If ever a filing cabinet could be called designer, this one, clad in scarlet padded leather, could. Italian, I was guessing. Maybe even produced by my sister Meghan and her husband.

He pushed drawers in and out. I could tell he was busily trying to decide how much information to provide. 'Cooperation,' I murmured, loud enough for him to hear.

He fished out a file and brought it over to the desk. 'Right . . .' he said. He opened it. Scanned quickly through the contents in a guarded fashion as though afraid I might be adept at reading upside-down. Which, as it happens, I am. 'Well now . . .'

If ever I've seen someone uneasy, it was Mr Compton. He pulled a freshly laundered handkerchief from the pocket of his jacket and furtively wiped the palms of his hands . . . but perhaps I was misjudging him. Perhaps he just had a sweat-gland problem. 'So where or what were some of his recent commissions?' I asked firmly.

'As far as I remember, offhand, there's been one in Qatar,' he said. 'One up on the Scottish Borders. The Paramore one. One in Istanbul. One in Kuwait. Another in Vermont.'

'So he got around a bit.'

'I'll say.'

'Qatar, Kuwait . . . why would they choose an English interior designer?'

'Tristan's pretty well known in his field.'

'But even so . . .' I tried to imagine some imposing lord of the desert, a hooded falcon on his wrist, his red-and-white-checked *keffiyeh* secured by a golden *igal* band. What kind of décor would he would be looking for to embellish the interior of his icing-sugar palace under the burning sun? Fountains? Cages full of nightingales? Couches covered in gorgeous fabrics? Slow fans turning? Perhaps I'd seen too many movies. Why would you need, or even want, an Englishman to produce that kind of thing? Surely there were indigenous designers who would do just as good a job.

'Tristan was all things to all men,' Compton pronounced sententiously. 'He always worked closely with his clients, be they big or small. He provided what they asked for, made their fantasies come true.'

'Can you pass on any client names?' By now I wasn't too hopeful.

He coughed. 'I'd have to ask his sister about that.'

'She *did* request that you cooperate.'

He sighed heavily. 'I'll have my girl make a list . . .'

I could see the girl in question, cashmere cardie, string of pearls round the neck, fifty if she was a day, idly leafing through a copy of *Country Life* in the next room. I hated to disturb her. 'Surely you have them right in front of you,' I said.

'Yes, but . . .'

'Don't give me all of them. Just the names and addresses, including phone numbers, of clients over, say, the past couple of years. I don't want any further details.' Of course I did, but that would be enough to be going on with. 'And Tristan's company was doing well?' I added.

'Obviously I'm not going to divulge details of his earnings. Let's just say that there wasn't much likelihood of him being forced into panhandling outside Waterloo Station in order to supplement his income. Even given the current economic downturn.'

'There's always an economic downturn,' I said.

'That's not necessarily true.' He thrust out his jaw and removed his glasses, as though daring me to challenge him on that or any other matter. When I didn't, he added, 'Yes, My client was doing very well for himself.'

'Guided and advised by your good self.'

'Guided. Assisted. And, of course, advised. Not that he took much notice of our advice, though he was happy to accept our guidance.'

'Why would he have come to you if he wasn't going to go along with your suggestions?'

Compton shrugged. 'Who knows? I'm truly sorry about what's happened to him, but he always thought outside the box, and that, I'm sorry to say, may have been his downfall.'

'And you can't clarify your somewhat mysterious remarks any further?'

'I'm afraid not.' He stroked his grape-smooth chin. 'I've probably said too much already.'

I waited while he reluctantly wrote down my email

address. 'So all Tristan's income derived from his design company?' I said.

'Oh . . . uh . . . pretty much.'

Which meant no. Which meant he had alternative sources of income. How could I find out what they might be? Dimsie? I'd have to try and pressure her again. 'Pretty much? What else might there have been?'

'The Huber-Draytons aren't exactly scratching round to put shoes on the baby's feet,' he said.

'Is that true? I understood the Dame was always skint.'

'The house is worth a mint, but I agree, ready money has always been a problem for her.'

'So you're talking trust funds, inheritance, that sort of thing?'

He seemed relieved. Did some heavy nodding. 'Trust funds, exactly.'

He was as twisty as a tiger snake. And probably as deadly. I really wished I was able to buy his shtick.

Could I really accept that Tristan had been commissioned by clients from such disparate locations? I knew nothing about the upmarket interior designer world. It was perfectly likely that he had, though the thought of some rich guy in Istanbul or Cairo hiring the talents of a guy from the British Isles to fuss round with fabric samples and paint-charts seemed unlikely. However big the rep. And although I'd never questioned it before (why not?), for the first time it occurred to me how very unlikely Tristan's choice of post-Army career was.

All things to all men. He was too good . . . Were they talking morally or professionally? It was something I needed to explore further. And fast.

TEN

The halfwit receptionist girl was at the desk when I marched into Dimsie's showroom. Seeing me, she pushed back her chair and bolted into the rear of the premises. I can't possibly be that intimidating. Or can I?

I was saved from an uncomfortable bout of self-examination by the emergence of Dimsie from the back. She was dressed entirely in black, with a black scarf holding her golden hair away from her face. 'Samantha says you're being nasty,' she announced.

'Absolute bollocks. I didn't even open my mouth.'

'You didn't need to. She said it was your expression. Gave her the heebie-jeebies.'

'Heebie-*jee*—? What kind of an expression is that for a girl her age? My *grand*mother says things like that. Anyway, it's not really my fault if I look like an ogre.'

'I know you can't help that,' Dimsie said kindly. 'But a smile, Quick. A smile wouldn't go amiss.' As if she had other things on her mind, she opened a catalogue displaying some fine examples of bespoke furniture made by a cabinetmaker near Barnard Castle, County Durham (my upside-down reading skills coming into play). 'Anyway, what else have you discovered?'

'Almost nothing. But I've had some interesting thoughts which might lead somewhere. So I need to examine Tristan's recent bank statements, and also his passport.'

'Why?'

'Because you asked me to look into his death is why. However, if you'd prefer to leave it all to the police, that's fine by me.' I turned and headed towards the doors. 'I've got plenty of work to be getting on with.'

I pulled open the heavy glass door and, as I expected, she started squeaking. 'Come back, Quick,' she pleaded. 'I need you.'

I stopped in the doorway. 'I'll carry on for Tristan's sake,' I said. 'And if you want my advice, get rid of that airhead receptionist of yours. Not that that's a condition . . .'

'She's pretty,' Dimsie said. 'It's good for business.'

'Hmmm . . . anyway, just find me those papers I asked for. Like I said, I've got a couple of ideas I'd like to follow up, if I can get hold of the necessary information. I may say your man of affairs was on the wrong side of helpful when I went to see him.'

We went into the back, behind the showroom, where she reluctantly foraged through a filing cabinet – nothing like as fancy as Michael Compton's – and unearthed some papers, which she handed to me. 'As for his passport,' she said. 'I'm not sure he'd have kept it here. We don't share absolutely everything, you know. He has his own office.' She smiled sadly. 'Had.'

'Just have a look, will you?' Although I felt for her tragic loss, I wanted to tell her she needed to be helpful if she wanted me to go on checking things out for her. After all, I wasn't a qualified detective, only a former cop with an inquisitive nature, trying to do my best to help an old friend.

'If I can't find anything here, you can always go down to his premises and look there. It's bound to be one place or the other. Oh . . .!' She uttered a little cry of triumph. 'Got it!' She brought out a maroon passport. Held it in both tiny hands. Screwed up her face in an effort not to cry. 'It's all so horribly heartbreaking.'

'Poor little Dimsie. I know it is.' I stuck the papers and passport into my bag. 'That's why I really want to do whatever I can to find out who's responsible for this.' I blew her a kiss. 'I'll be in touch, soon as I've got something to tell you. Meanwhile, be assured the police are doing what they can.'

As I'd told Dimsie, I had work of my own to do. Having glanced through Tristan's passport, I sat at my desk, pondering while I scrutinized various picture reproductions and realized that if I wasn't careful, *Eat, Drink and Be Merry* would end up as a collection of still lifes. It required a real effort to find paintings with the bucolic feel that I was after. I thought it would be fun to include Picasso's painting called *L'Ascetique* as a kind of moral counterweight to the excesses displayed elsewhere. Nothing could be further from being merry than the misery etched on the face of the anorexic old man with his simple jug of water and his hunk of hard bread. The same was true of *The Frugal Feast*, a sort of companion piece by the same artist.

Some pictures absolutely had to be included. Diego Rivero's portrait of Cecilia Armada. *Still life with parrot*, by Frieda Kahloo. Caravaggio's *Young Bacchus* in the Uffizi, where the subject clearly has a hangover. The famous *Déjeuner sur l'herbe,* though the picnic was remarkably ascetic compared to the gargantuan *al fresco* feasts of earlier years. It wasn't the *déjeuner* which usually caught my attention so much as the breathtaking sexism of the scene . . . two fully dressed men talking across the naked body of a woman.

The phone beeped. 'Quick,' I said.

'Fliss here.'

'How's it going?'

'Slowly. We've had a couple of summing-up meetings. So far, there's darned little to sum. Your friend Tristan's turning out to be a bit of a mystery man, far as we can see.'

'Explain.'

'We've managed to extract a list of his current or recent commissions from a slimy sort of guy who appears to be his financial adviser. Compton?'

'I've met him.'

Fliss huffed for a moment. 'If ever strong drink was needed to calm me down . . .'

'I know exactly what you mean. But what's with the "we"? I thought this was Garside's call.'

'It is, but I stupidly, for old time's sake – that's you, Quick – volunteered to go round and see the guy, since one of Garside's team was off sick and another was in court.' More huffing. 'If ever I've met an arrogant sod . . .'

'Compton gives arrogant sods a good name.' I paused for a moment. 'Apart from that, did you think there was anything off about him?'

'Most definitely. I'm still trying to work out exactly what it was.'

'Someone connected to Tristan in some way is telling porkies, or at least practising evasion tactics and obfuscation, and I don't know who,' I said. 'But Compton's among them, I'm quite certain.'

'I gather that even the grieving sister is being cagey.'

'Yes, I thought that. I wonder why, when she specifically asked me to look into matters since she didn't feel the police would keep her properly informed.' I frowned. 'And when I went over to a place called Rollingford, near Folkestone, it was very clear that something not at all kosher was going on.'

'Is that the place with the rodeo show? Sir Piers Paramore?'

'Yup.'

'Hmm . . . we've been keeping an eye on them for over a year now.'

'Interesting.'

'Isn't it just?'

'Gonna tell me why?'

'No, mainly because we don't know. We have our suspicions – horses, luxury cars – but little more than that. So we have no cause – as yet – to search the place. Trouble is, the Paramores are so well connected that they'd be warned immediately if a raid on their property was imminent, which would give them ample time to hide any evidence there might be.'

'Kind of hard to hide a horse.'

'Not really. It's like a stolen car: you give it a paint job, add a sunroof or fancy hubcaps—'

'A horse with fancy hubcaps I gotta see.'

'—forge the log book, and it could be a different car. Remember that case we had at those stables near Ashford? It was the same sort of thing.'

'Whatever it is, the Paramores are in it up to the neck. And so is the Rodeo King himself, her father. And also . . .' I had suddenly remembered Jerry Baskin. 'There's a guy there who's been wandering round town here giving a spiel about his family, Louisiana aristocrats, if that's not a misuse of the word. A gifted con-artist. Kept talking about unfinished business and now it's more or less dealt with, he was going to blow town. And then, I found him right over there at Rollins Park, using an entirely different name, with an entirely different family story.' I thought back. 'Still using an American accent, though, even if it was less hokey than the last one. So maybe that's where his roots lie. So you'd have to wonder why he's hunting for prey over here, when the US is so large and it would be much easier for him to move on when or if he was rumbled.'

'Interesting!'

'Isn't it just?'

We both laughed. Conmen came in all shapes and sizes and we'd met dozens of them over the years. Charm was an essential prerequisite of the breed, together with absolute ruthlessness. What always surprised me was the gullibility of the victims. Anyone asking me to hand over my life's savings to help him through while he waited for a legacy from his hugely rich father/a cheque to clear/a house sale to be completed would, I'm afraid, be shown the door in pretty quick order. As for the ancient grandmother or adorable child needing expensive treatments to survive, complete with heart-rending hollow-eyed photos . . . Fliss and I had come across them all.

'Back to my desk,' I said. 'Keep in touch, you hear?'

Some hours later, I put away the roughs for my book and got out Tristan's papers and passport, both the stuff from Compton and the documents from Dimsie. They made interesting reading. Especially when given Tristan's pretty full order book. How did he manage to squeeze in twelve trips to Hong Kong as well as satisfy his customers?

After a while, I telephoned my parents. Edred answered. 'It's me,' I said.

'Frideswide!' he boomed. 'Darling child!'

I remained silent. 'Hello,' he said after a while. 'Hello, hello?' Another pause, then a mutter over his shoulder. 'We seem to have been cut off.'

'A Frideswide by any other name, Edred,' I said.

'Oh Christ, what's she calling herself these days? Hello?'

In the background, my mother shouted, 'It's Alex, you silly old goof.'

'Ah yes, Alex. How are you?'

'Fine,' I said. Some years ago, my sister and I had rebelled against our given names of Frideswide and Ethelburga, becoming respectively Alexandra and Meghan. I do not answer to Frideswide. My brother remained with Hereward. 'Edred, I have a question.'

'Fire away.'

'You've been friends with Dorcas the Dragon for years, haven't you?'

'Poor Dorcas. Yes, indeed. We were all up at Oxford together. I can't remember what she read, but she was definitely there. Played lacrosse, as I remember. Captain of her college team in her final year. LMH, was it? Somerville? Or was it St Hi—'

'Ask what she wants instead of waffling on,' came my mother's voice.

'What do you want?' Edred said.

'Do you remember who she married?'

'Remember? I don't think I ever—'

'Of course you do, you were their best man.' My mother wrested the phone from my father. 'He was called Padhraic Fitzgerald. Up at Magdalen. A handsome devil, full of Irish blarney, and none the worse for that. Edred and I even visited them when they were living for a while on the ancestral estates near Cork. Everything was falling to bits. A large piece of ceiling dropped on your father's head one evening as we sat with a glass of Irish whisky in the freezing cold drawing room. That probably explains a lot of things.'

'And what happened to Padhraic Fitzgerald?'

'We never knew. They lived in London for a while, and Dorcas woke one morning to find he'd disappeared, none knew whither, leaving her with no money and two small children to bring up on her own.'

'And nothing heard from him from that day to this?'

'Exactly.'

'Didn't she try to find him?'

'Not really. I think she'd realized by then that she was better off without him.'

It all seemed a little slapdash to me. 'Suppose he'd had an accident. Lost his memory. For all you know, he could still be wandering round wondering who he is.'

'I doubt it. He'd taken his passport and some clothes. Emptied their joint bank account. Obviously planned it all quite carefully.'

'French and Italian studies,' my father said in the background.

'What is?'

'That's what Fitzgerald read when he was up.'

Tristan had also read modern languages when he was up at Oxford. Was there any significance to this fact? 'I wonder where he went,' I said.

'Dorcas didn't.'

'And how come the two children were called Huber-Drayton instead of Fitzgerald?'

‘Dorcas had their names changed by deed poll the minute she could.’

‘Do they know about their father?’

‘Not as far as I know.’ Mary sighed. ‘This is horrible heart-breaking news about Tristan. I keep remembering him as a little boy. So very cute. Obstinate as hell, mind you. If he set his mind to something, he focussed on nothing else until he achieved whatever it was. Didn’t let anything or anyone get in his way. Ruthless, in many ways . . . I remember the giant radish he was going to produce when he was about eight, after Dorcas read him *James and the Giant Peach.* He was absolutely determined to go and live inside it in Hyde Park. Obsessed, he was.’

‘I remember that.’ My father spoke behind her.

‘He did end up with one the size of a turnip,’ said Mary, ‘but it wasn’t red. Another child tried to sabotage it so Tristan went round to his house one night and—’

‘Mary,’ I said. ‘Gotta go.’ This talk of giant radishes was doing my head in. I made my farewells. Promised to drive over shortly.

Call ended, I looked through the papers I’d received from Michael Compton and dialled a number. ‘I’m calling on behalf of Tristan Huber,’ I began. ‘I’m wondering if you—’

The voice on the other end burst in, raucous as a crow. ‘Look, if you’re trying to cause trouble, you’ve come to the wrong place. I know where you live and don’t you forget it.’

‘I’m quite sure you don’t,’ I said. I’m very careful about releasing my address or phone number. I even sometimes find myself copying the tactics of various criminals I’ve known, using different disposable phones depending on the kind of call I’m making and then getting rid of them in due season. I’d been tracked down by too many villains with vengeance on their minds. If minds is the right word. Most crims are as thick as two short planks, unable to make projections beyond the simple arrangements for pulling off whatever particular felony they’re about to commit and often getting those wrong.

‘Oh yes?’ demanded this guy. ‘Wanna risk it?’

‘I just wanted to confirm that the last delivery did indeed go off,’ I said, winging it. All my copper’s instincts told me that this guy was not only not on the level but was so far below it, he couldn't even see daylight. Whatever Tristan had been up to, it must have involved something being delivered from Point A to Point B, wherever either point might be.

'You saying it never arrived?' the voice at the other end of the phone said belligerently. 'Cos I'm telling you the goods left here in perfect order, as agreed. So don't you start telling me—'

'Mr Colby, calm down, will you?'

'I'm perfectly calm, as it happens. If it wasn't for some stupid cow on the other end of the line trying to insinuate that—'

'How's the redecoration going, Mr Colby?'

'Redecor— What the fuck you on about . . . oh yes, redecoration, see what you mean.' Too late, Mr Marcus Colby realized that he had almost blown his cover. 'Fine, thanks. The wife's dead chuffed, the place looks a real treat.'

'Good to hear.'

I was beginning to get a very faint glimmer of how Tristan had been organizing whatever it was he'd been up to. At least, although so far I had no facts, I felt that I might be skirting round the edge of something I didn't yet understand. One thing was clear, however: Tristan's affairs had very little to do with interior design. This guy was a case in point. One of Tristan's copy invoices had been made out to Mr Maurice Colby, with an address in Gloucestershire, for redesigning the interior of his house, The Willows, Palmerston Drive, in some village (I checked it on Google) near Cheltenham. When I telephoned, Mr Colby didn't sound the sort of man who would hire an upmarket well-known interior designer to do his renovations. Perhaps he had a rich wife. But was he or was he not being cuckolded by handsome Tristan? And if he were, was he depraved enough to murder his rival? If indeed he had a wife. Or was he – much more likely – involved in some shady deal with Tristan? It all needed to be checked out.

I inspected another headed copy invoice. Sir Nigel Inglebright of Boston, Lincs. Rang the number given at the top. 'I'm calling on behalf of Tristan Huber Associates,' I said. 'Just checking that all's going well with the restorations.'

'Are you indeed? At this time of night?' The tone was dry. 'Shows an admirable sense of responsibility, I must say.

Especially considering that the work was completed, what, two, going on three years ago?'

Too late I copped the date. But at least Sir Nigel had sounded like a genuine customer. And he was right: it *was* late to be calling, if I was pretending to represent Huber Associates. I'd have to wait until the morning to telephone anyone else.

Before I could cut the call, he added, 'Since I read in the papers that poor Mr Huber has been murdered, what is it you really want?'

'As I said, I'm from Huber Associates' follow-up department.'

'Pull the other one. Is it the Modiglianis you're after? Because let me tell you they're massively burglar-alarmed, and far too well known to be easily flogged, if you *were* to get your hands on one. Perhaps you're aware that one went for dozens of millions just the other day.'

'I wouldn't touch a Modigliani,' I said, icy as an Arctic winter. 'Not even if you were *giving* them away.' I jabbed viciously at the switch-off button.

Moments later, my phone rang. 'So if you're not from Hubers, where *are* you from?' Sir Nigel, for it was he, lowered his voice. 'The Modiglianis are m'wife's choice, not mine. Sounds as though you share my opinion of 'em. If I had my way, I *would* give them away.'

'That's nice to know. My name's Quick, Alexandra Quick, and I'm perfectly respect—'

'Are you talking anthologies? Helena Drummond, poor woman?'

'I am.'

'I have all your collections. Lovely stuff, a great reminder of galleries visited over the years. So what's next?'

I told him.

'You're a former copper aren't you? Is that why you're ringing re Tristan Huber?'

I agreed that it was.

'Interesting. If I, or we, can be of any assistance . . .'

'Thank you, I'll bear that in mind.' I liked the sound of Sir Nigel Inglebright.

I logged on to my computer and found a search engine. Looked up a couple of things. It was too late to do much more: further investigation would have to wait for the morning. Meanwhile, I delved into my picture files. I wanted something bucolic: a wedding scene, *The Marriage at Cana*. Something like that. Something cheerful.

My doorbell rang as I was about to pack up and head for bed. I spoke into the speakerphone. 'Yes?'

'Sam here.'

'How nice.' I felt myself light up like a smile.

'I've got a bottle of Edward's finest and something to show you.'

I was delighted to have his company. Soothing, undemanding, he was the perfect friend. 'Come on up.' I took two of my very best glasses out of the cupboard, and filled a small bowl with unsalted cashew nuts, another with small cubes of the most expensive cheddar cheese from our local delicatessen. Edward's wine deserved to be treated with respect. So no harsh olives, no over-flavoured and artificially-seasoned nibbles.

We drank slowly, nodding our appreciation. Then Sam took a couple of books from the leather messenger bag I'd given him the previous Christmas and opened one, found a page, turned it so I could see. 'Isn't this just perfect for your new anthology?' he said.

I looked at the beruffed figures seated round a laden table, the smug expressions on their faces, the politely concealed greed with which they waited to get stuck into their plentiful meal of fish, fowl and flesh, plus a dish of cherries. Under the reproduction was its date and title: Dutch School, *Patrician Family At The Table* ca 1610.

'Absolutely perfect, Sam,' I said. 'That's definitely going in. Thank you so much.' I leaned forward to kiss him.

He groaned deep in his throat and pulled me towards him. 'Alex,' he said.

We stared into each other's eyes. No, I thought. This must not happen. And it so easily could. I broke away.

Sam cleared his throat. He opened a second book. 'Here's another one, totally opposite. I thought it just might fit in to your concept.' He found a page and again showed it to me. A naïve painting this time, crudely executed, of people arriving to eat at a table scattered with individual pieces of food set directly on to the tablecloth: melon slices, cooked fowl, bread, while other guests held whole fish. It was in sharp contrast to the fastidiously painted detail of the Dutch one. *Bego Greeting His Guests* by the primitivist Georgian painter, Pirosmani.

'This is terrific, Sam,' I said. I wished my heart would stop beating quite so fast.

'How's the detection work going?' he asked.

'I'm not really detecting,' I said. 'That's up to the police. But of course I did know Tristan quite well, so perhaps I have a slightly different way of looking at his death. Besides, his sister more or less insisted that I did some delving as well.'

'Motives?'

'Haven't come up with anything definite yet. But there are various possibilities. Look, Sam, this is strictly confidential, but the poor man was castrated. Does that say anything to you?'

He raised his eyebrows. 'How horrible. But doesn't that lead more or less directly to a sexual motive?'

'Precisely.'

'So shouldn't you be looking for a jealous husband, or an outraged lover or something?' He poured a small amount more wine into our glasses. We didn't want to finish it too quickly. 'I didn't know him at all, though I'd seen him at Chamber of Commerce dinners and the like. Very good-looking. Woman flinging themselves at him left, right and centre, I shouldn't wonder. Men too, perhaps, though I never saw any evidence. Whichever, someone must have taken grave offense.'

'Someone who was very possessive, or who felt his or her dignity or position had been attacked.'

'One of his clients, perhaps?'

'Or someone trying to point us towards hanky-panky as a motive in order to red herring us away from looking at the truth.'

'Or,' said Sam, 'some sadist, or madman, or both, who had it in for Tristan.'

'Here's a funny thing. Not all the contacts he did work for were clients, in the normal sense of the word. Or rather, they were, but not in his capacity as an interior designer.' I explained about Maurice Colby, a villain if ever I had come across one.

'Interesting. So what do you think he was up to? Apart from possible extra-curricular bedroom activities?'

'Could be anything.' I outlined the possible scenarios I'd already come up with, then shook my head. 'Drugs, theft, money laundering, you name it. But I can't see Tristan involved in that sort of criminal enterprise.'

'Which leads us straight back to jealous husbands, and *cherchez*ing *la femme*.'

'If that's what's behind this, how would we ever find out? He was off in Dubai, Singapore, Hong Kong . . . no way I'd ever be able to suss out every hawk-eyed Prince of the Desert or his multiple wives.'

'Maybe I could go for you.' He sounded wistfully eager. 'Pretend to be a concerned employee of Huber Associates wanting to know how the renovations or redecorations were getting on. Or had got on.'

'I suppose it's a possibility.' I was doubtful. 'Anyway, I would think it far more likely that the woman in question – supposing there is one – would be in England. He couldn't go haring off to points east every time he got a hard on.' Remembering Piper, Lady Paramore, I was suddenly thoughtful. On my visit to Rollins Park, it had seemed more than possible that Tristan and she had been having it off. If so, what would that do to Piers?

'Though when you think about,' Sam said, 'why should the Not Impossible She even be a client?'

'Good question.' Tristan got around, had a full social life – in the past, I'd even accompanied him on some of it. It was just as likely to be someone he'd known for a while, or met at a dinner party or a Hunt Ball or something equally posh.

'Yes, hello, I'm calling behalf of Huber Associates, to ascertain whether you're satisfied with the work we did for you at the end of last year.' I'd carefully sorted more recent Huber Associates invoices out of the pile I had on my desk.

'Very much so, they did an excellent job for us and I've recommended you to all my friends.' The answering voice was, like the previous four calls I'd made that morning, very much from an upper-class upper-income bracket.

'I'm so glad. I'll be sure to pass that on to Mr Huber.'

'But . . .' the voice said. 'He's . . . he's *dead*. Are you an agency he employs or something? Surely you knew that.'

'Of course, I did,' I said quickly. 'I meant the company, of course, not him personally. As you can imagine, there's a great deal of winding up to be done.'

'We're all devastated by the news. My husband and I have known Tristan for absolute yonks, he was such a . . . Do you know what exactly happened?'

Same reaction as the other calls. 'We've been advised by the police not to discuss details of the case,' I said primly. I've learned over the years that primness gets you through awkward situations better than most other stances.

'Of course, yes, I completely understand. Poor, poor Tristan . . . but then of course he always did court danger, as they say.'

'Court danger?'

'Oh, you know. If there was some particularly tricky assignment to be done, Tristan was always first in the queue.'

Assignment? It had an official ring to it. This was a new slant on a man I'd considered a close friend for years. 'What kind of tricky assignment are you talking about?'

'Oh, you know,' she said again. 'A job in some danger spot, the kind the Foreign Office warns people not to visit. Tristan was always on the next plane out. When I say job,' she added hastily, 'I mean an interior design thing, obviously.'

'Well, anyway . . . thank you for your help.' Mutual goodbyes. I rang off.

I'd been speaking to a Mrs Yvonne Landis. I looked down at her address. Strathmore House, Alcombe, near Maidstone.

My next assignment would have to be to find out who or what she was. Or, possibly, had been.

TEN

I woke at three in the morning, dripping with sweat, my hands clutching the bed covers as though they were the only things which could save me from instant destruction. I'd been dreaming of Tristan being hacked to death, seeing over and over the blood and the wounds, the flies and the smashed limbs.

Staring into the darkness, I found myself yet again wondering at the ferocity of the attack. What kind of rage could induce a person to inflict such injury on another human being? Money due, love betrayed, vengeance owed? None of these seemed to justify such an attack. There was war, of course. Extraordinary rendition. Coercive grilling. Enhanced interrogation techniques . . . the Bush administration's weasel words for what was plain and simple torture. Bastards.

And, mind now fluttering like a moth, I wondered too exactly where such an execution would take place. There'd have been a stomach-churning mess to clear up, and uninterrupted time needed. And again, to transport a body in that state any distance without leaving traces would be a problem. Plastic sheeting, bin bags, cleaning materials would be needed. Plus water, in order to clean the chest and display the word carved into it. CHEAT. And, however psychotic, surely the killer wouldn't be able to conduct his grisly business in total silence. There'd be screams, moans, voices. Ergo, he'd need somewhere isolated – or possibly soundproofed.

My heart had begun to slow down but it revved up again as I considered the hundreds of places which some pervert could modify for his purposes. It was a line of enquiry I would have to follow up. I eventually fell back into an uneasy sleep.

When I awoke, a sprinkle of desiccated leaves was dancing past my windows. Always a melancholy moment, marking as it did the signs of fast approaching autumn, even though the sky was a cloudless blue and sunshine glittered across the sea.

'It's me again, Fliss,' I said. I had my phone in my hand.

'What now?'

'Yvonne Landis . . . ever heard of her?'

'Landis? Landis? A bell somewhere is ringing very, very faintly,' Fliss said. 'Can't remember in what context, though.'

'I've Googled her but got nowhere. If you get on better, let me know.'

Who was Yvonne Landis and what bearing could her newly-revealed (new to me, at least) information about

Tristan's penchant for recklessness have on his violent and cruel death? My imagination was already throwing out suggestions about her: witness protection programme, a celebrity seeking anonymity, an officer who served in the Army alongside Tristan. So where did that leave the notion that Tristan had been murdered for shagging someone else's wife? Unless *she* was the wife in question. So who was *Mr* Landis and was he an avenue worth exploring?

I made some notes for myself:

1. *Visit the Paramores again* and while there, check out the painted cupola or pagoda or whatever the hell they called it, see if there were any clues there.
2. *Check out Todd DuBois* aka Jerry Baskin.
3. *Go visit the Major again.* I had a feeling that without realizing it he knew more than he was telling.

Later, I pushed my work to one side, did a couple of Fiendish level Sudokus (and made a complete balls-up of them) by way of relaxation, and walked down to the High Street. As I'd hoped, I ran into the Major on his way to the saloon bar of the Fox and Hounds.

'Alex, my dear,' he said. 'Have you got time to join me? I'm about to indulge in a half-pint or two.'

'No alcohol for me this early in the day,' I said. 'But coffee would be good.'

'Glad we met up,' he said. 'There's something I wanted to tell you about.' We sat down at the last of the empty little tables with our drinks. He pulled at his beer. 'Remember that feller we met the other day – Brad Something, from Mississippi or somewhere similar?'

'Todd? How could I forget?'

'Well, I had a somewhat strange experience yesterday.'

I had a feeling I knew what he was going to tell me. 'Really?'

'Went over to Canterbury, wanted to buy a new sweater, you see, can't find that sort of thing here for love or money.' He stared at the pub's ancient wainscoating as though he had never seen it before, and murmured, 'Doesn't really bear thinking about.'

'And?'

'Well, I popped into one of the hotels for a small restorative—'

'As one does.'

'Indeed. Anyway, I could hardly believe my eyes, there was that Brad chappie, large as life, sitting there, dressed to the nines, chatting up some woman old enough to be his mother.'

'Nothing wrong with that.'

'Except the nines he was dressed to were sort of a caricature of the English gentleman. Striped shirt with white collar – always says something about a man, in my opinion, and none of it good – tweed jacket, Old Harrovian tie, if you please, cavalry twill trousers. He didn't notice me so I was earwigging away, as you can imagine.'

'What was he selling this time?' Outside the lead-paned windows, people passed up and down the street, normal life carrying on as it always does.

'Property, far as I could tell. Some castle he owned up north, but now that his dear mother, the Dowager, had passed into Higher Service – his phrase, not mine – he's having to sell up. Big sigh, says it's always been his favourite of the family residences, she revelled in doing the Church flowers, stalwart member of the local WI, all that sort of thing.'

'Things he knew nothing about until you mentioned them the other day. The man's as absorbent as a sponge. What was the woman doing?'

'Lapping it up. More or less drooling, not to put too fine a point on it. He had her practically whipping out her chequebook on the spot. But the weird thing is, he looked and sounded as English as you or me.'

'Did you speak to him?'

'Went over and said something along the lines of "Brad, old chap, old sport, good to see you." So he gives me this haughty stare, says he doesn't believe he knows me, and turns his back on me. Such impudence! Flabbergasted is the only word to describe how I felt. Especially when I remember that only a couple of weeks or so ago, I was all ready to set up a bistro with him in sunny France.' The Major looked downcast. 'I suppose that's not going to happen now.'

'I hope you didn't give him any money.'

The Major snorted. 'Believe me, my dear, I was near as dammit about to. Luckily, at the last moment, wiser counsel prevailed.'

'You do realize he's a gifted con-artist, don't you?'

'I do now. Sad, really. He seemed like a really genuine sort of chappie, too.'

'The successful ones always do.'

The Major wiped beer froth off his moustache. Said thoughtfully, 'Do you know, I seriously believe that beer is better now than it was when I was a young man.'

'Major, last time I spoke to you, you mentioned a warehouse near to your cottage, which belonged to the Harkness person whose wife committed suicide.'

'Oh that place. It's only a *sort* of warehouse, more like a derelict shed, and I may have got it wrong, m'dear. Maybe it wasn't him who owned it. Maybe he leased it from someone. Or maybe it was someone else entirely, my memory's not what it used to be.'

'How far away from your house is it?'

'Oh, three or four fields. No more than that. You go down Honeypot Lane towards the main road, but before you get there, you turn left. The track's pretty well overgrown, what with all the rain we've been having and the fact that nobody uses it. It's about a fifteen-minute walk from my place. Longer if you walk along the road, though the entrance is easier to find that way.'

'How can I find out who owns the place?'

'Let me put my thinking cap on. Can't be too difficult a problem. Land Registry or something similar, or there'll be somebody local who's in the picture. Why do you want to know?'

'Just covering my bases.' I wasn't going to tell him that given its proximity to Honeypot Lane, I was wondering whether Tristan had been taken there and tortured prior to his death, since this was pure speculation on my part. And if the place was abandoned, why not just leave him there to – oh God – decompose, rather than taking the trouble to transport his body to the field where the dog Marlowe had found him? 'Do you know if the police have been in to check it out?'

'Haven't seen any recent activity round there, I have to say. Walked that way several times with the dog, since the body was found, kept my eyes open, naturally, but then I always do. Army training: you never know what's going to come at you out of nowhere.'

It was one to pass on to Fliss Fairlight. But I would wait until she called me back about Yvonne Landis.

'You don't see Harkness any more, I take it.'

'Not since Lil's final visit, when the little'un died.'

'If the place was his, what do you suppose he stored in it? And where was whatever it was going? Didn't you say he was into disposable nappies, something like that?'

'Could have been anything. But as I told you earlier, I saw an ad for the company in some technical-type magazine. Got the impression they were into widgets or gadgets of some kind.' The Major frowned. 'Can't say I ever saw evidence of anything being delivered. Lorries, trucks, vans and so forth. I've occasionally seen lights in the distance, through the trees sort of thing, but not recently. Mind you, the place I'm thinking of is quite a way off the road, down a track leading into the woods. The police might not even know it's there.'

'You should tell them. I'm sure they'll be grateful for your information, if they haven't already sussed the place out.'

Having said goodbye, I went back to my car and made for Honeypot Lane where I drove down towards the main road. As far as I could see, there didn't seem to be any kind of a turning off to the left, nor any discernible break in the heavy undergrowth, and on the right-hand side of the lane were only fields. At the bottom of the lane, I did a three-point turn and drove slowly back up. Down here, in the little dip, it still seemed like high summer, although blackberries now glistened in the hedges and early hazel-nuts crackled under my wheels.

There was still no sign of a path. For the third time I drove along the lane, very, very slowly and this time made out an indentation in the undergrowth. It immediately seemed obvious that this must be a back entrance to the site where this large shed was, because if poor Tristan's body had been dragged or driven along what I now perceived to be a minimal track or footpath, indications would definitely have been left.

I drove further down to the bottom of the lane and turned left along the main road towards the town. Sure enough, I eventually found that there was another path, little more than a farm track, but more discernible. It was hard to believe that Garside's team hadn't checked the place out, since it was pretty close to where the body had been found, but it was clear that no vehicle had driven this way in the recent past.

I turned on to the track and drove slowly along it, leaves and branches slapping at the windows of the car and doing God knew what damage to my paintwork. After about half a mile, I reached an open space. A long, low building faced me, made of a course of bricks topped by breeze blocks, reinforced by iron struts. The structure was completed by a corrugated-iron roof which had once been painted green. It wasn't new. As the Major had indicated, it seemed semi-derelict. Some of the breeze blocks were crumbling and there were gaps in the brickwork. I wondered what had led anyone to build the place in such an isolated spot, surrounded by trees and unkempt undergrowth. When I got out of my car and stood listening, I couldn't even hear the sound of traffic from the nearby road.

In the footwell on the passenger side of my car, I keep a heavy wrench. Just in case. Even though I always make sure my doors are locked when I'm driving about, you just never know. Now, I picked it up and carried it with me as I walked around the building, looking for a way in. There was one door in the front, facing the open space where my car stood, but no windows. Nor were there any at either end of the building. At the back, however, I found two windows and three doors, one wide enough to admit a large van, the two others presumably intended for the passage of individuals. Or bodies? All three were painted green though the paint was faded and peeling. And sometime in the not-too-distant past, all three had been fitted with bright new locks, which looked a lot stronger than the doors themselves.

On the whole I don't go in for sixth senses or presentiments. Yet there was something about this place which was really creeping me out. I turned to scan the woods behind and on either side of me, but could see no indication of anyone hidden away and watching me. A bird suddenly cawed very loudly from a tree above my head, and I jumped, goose bumps forming along my arms, heart thumping. I tightened my grip on the wrench. Was that an avian alarm call? And if so, what was the cause of it, me or someone else moving stealthily between the trees? Blood thumped in my ears as I listened. Nothing. Not even a stray breeze ruffling the leaves. So probably just some bloody-minded crow, trying to scare the living daylights out me.

Back to the business in hand. Having pushed hard at all three doors and tried hammering the two windows – both fitted with wired glass and at least two feet higher than I could effectively reach – without any luck, I circled the building once again, trying to find a vulnerable spot. On one of the end walls, I noticed a place where several of the bricks seemed to be parting company with the breeze block which sat above them, and a couple had disintegrated and lay on the rough grass below. Was it worth trying to tunnel my way through, like some escaping prisoner, with the difference being that I wanted to get in, rather than out? Breaking and entering was a crime, I knew perfectly well . . . but murder was far more than that.

I had a go. My wrench proved very useful at making the small hole much wider. I hammered at the disintegrating concrete, watching as chunks of it fell away. Several times I had to retreat to the woods and stand with head bent and hands on my knees, drawing in deep breaths and trying not to vomit. The stink coming through the ever-widening aperture was stomach-turning. Rotting meat, for the most part, with a nauseating overlay of human waste. I knew I did not want to extend the opening to the point where it was big enough for me to squeeze through. I also knew I had no choice.

It took another thirty minutes before I had chipped away enough concrete to create a gap wide enough for me to slide through. Luckily I'm not built on massive lines. Although the hole I'd made wasn't enormous, anybody walking round the building could hardly fail to see the breach in the wall. On the other hand, it wasn't *that* big. I managed to cram my way into the warehouse, landing on the rough concrete floor inside. Once inside, the stench of the place was ten times worse, making my eyes water and my stomach heave. Involuntarily I screwed up my face to avoid having any more contact with the smell than I had to. On the force, we used to carry small tins of Vicks to smear under our noses when visiting a scene like this. I wished I had some with me now.

My heart, as they say in old-fashioned novels, failed me. Holding my breath, I ran over to the two single doors. Using the tails of my shirt, I unsnibbed the lock on one of them and flung it wide, letting in some much-needed fresh air. The space I was in stretched away to the far end, where a load of big boxes, resting on wooden pallets, was stashed against the wall. More stood piled against the wall which opened on to the front of the building. They looked fairly new. One corner of the place had been partitioned off with plasterboard walls to form a small space for tea-making or perhaps a loo.

At first sight, the empty space seemed harmless enough. Nothing more than it purported to be. A convenient place for the storage of goods. Until you took in the bloodsoaked hospital gurney which stood in the middle of the floor. Restraining bands dangled. Disgusting pieces of bloody paper towel, dried to a dark brown, had been chucked on to the blood-spattered floor. A couple of galvanized iron buckets stood on either side of the gurney, vibrating with hundreds of shiny green flies, their bodies bloated with blood. Here and there underneath were bits of dried-up matter which – mouth screwed up with disgust – I was able to identify as gobbets of raw meat. Or flesh knifed from the body of my dear friend, Tristan Huber. The floor was heavily splashed with dried blood and cigarette stubs. There were more of them in one of the buckets: could someone really have casually stood there and smoked while a man was sliced to pieces in front of him, before being carted off to be tossed into a field to die in agony? The thought of it, of Tristan's pain, made me literally sick to my stomach. I contemplated taking some of the cigarette butts as evidence, but reasoned that I had no official status and could be accused of contamination, or worse, if I did so.

I walked over and checked out the stacked boxes. Numbers and letters were stencilled on the sides in black, plus some oriental pictographs. Using my elbow and some brute force, I managed to shunt the top box of three of the piles sideways, so I could see if there was any indication of what they contained. And there was. Bags, I read. St Laurent, Valentino, Michael Kors . . . they were names I knew to be the envy of a world where people needed expensive accessories to give them validity and were willing to pay ludicrous prices to acquire them.

A second box appeared to contain watches, very expensive ones, Patek Philippe, Vacheron Constantin and the like. As I bent my head to read more of the names, I heard a noise coming from the little kitchen area. I froze. Was someone else already here? Someone with a right to be here? That didn't seem likely: they would have heard me breaking in long ago and come to investigate. Nobody could have snuck in through the open doors without me being aware. What if it was someone who shouldn't be there . . .?

The sound came again, a kind of scratching ripping chewing noise. Rats! I immediately knew it had to be rats. Oh God! I took a couple of steps nearer the kitchen area. More likely it was a bird which had somehow got in via the roof and couldn't find its way out again. I approached the room sideways, hoping to see what was causing the noise without actually having to go into it. I saw jeans, trainers, the edge of a shirt. It looked as though someone was lying on the floor. A body, or someone still alive? Wrench in one hand, I moved nearer the door so that I could peer round it more easily. No question, I was looking at the body of a young man, his head lying in a pool of coagulated blood. It looked like he'd been hit on the back of the head with some force. Above his jeans he wore a torn T-shirt with a logo for the university chess club and underneath it, an image of a white Queen and a black King and the words: MAKE THE RIGHT MOVES. As I approached, a rat burrowed its way out from under the body and ran to the corner of the room, where it disappeared. There was blood all round its evil little mouth.

Although it was clearly pointless, I nonetheless knelt carefully down beside him and laid a hand against his cheek. There is something about the chill of a dead body which is colder than frost. It's the haunting sense that not only has the heart stopped pushing blood through veins and arteries, but that there is nothing there any more, the spirit has fled, along with all the dreams and hopes, the loves and hates, the memories. There were some signs of decay, mostly a plumped-up look beneath the T-shirt and a bit of a pong, and it was clear that some predator – the rat I had seen? – had somehow got in and had chewed at the boy's right hand. The flesh had been stripped to the bones of his first two digits, and a dark hole gaped where there had once been a little finger. Even more chilling was the realization that this was the third violent death locally in less than a month.

I went back into the main space and called DCI Fairlight. Told her what I'd found and how I found it. Emphasized that I'd opened the doors, walked across the floor, inspected the boxes, but hadn't touched anything else except the poor chap's cheek, that insofar as possible, I'd kept contamination to a minimum. 'There's probably identification on him,' I said.

'Do you think this is the same perp as the one who offed Tristan Huber?'

'No idea . . . but it more or less has to be. Garside needs to get down here ASAP.'

'Is this an anonymous tip from a concerned citizen, or shall I tell him it came from you?'

'Let's go with the anonymous tip,' I said. 'He'll already be pissed off that his team hadn't looked carefully enough round the area. Much worse if he knows I did. There's cigarette butts,' I added.

'Someone obviously knew about the place,' Fliss said.

'Even if you find out who owns or leases it, it doesn't mean he or she is the one responsible for the body.'

'I imagine not.'

'Could just as easily, if not more likely, have been someone local.'

'True.'

'Has Garside got any theories yet as to how and why Tristan's body was removed from the torture scene – which I'm willing to bet a substantial sum on being the warehouse – and dumped along Honeypot Lane?'

'He may well have. But if so, he hasn't divulged the info to me.'

'By the way, what did you find out about Yvonne Landis? If anything.'

'Nothing.' There was something clenched about Fliss's voice which immediately made me suspect that she was lying.

'Not even though I gave you a name, an address and a telephone number for her?'

'Not even then, Quick.'

So there was a trail for me to follow, and quickly. I like driving, but I groaned at the thought of flogging down to Alcombe, finding South Street, and forcing my way into Ms Landis's life. She had sounded open on the phone. And nice.

I took one last look around the warehouse, imprinting it on my memory. Questions drummed in my head. Why had the boy come or been brought here? What state had he been in when he arrived? Was Tristan really tortured to death here? And if so, the same queries pertained. How had he been brought to this particular spot? And why here? Was there a connection between the warehouse or its owner and Tristan, or had the killer merely known about the shed and decided it provided the perfect torture-chamber?

I took a deep breath – and immediately wished I hadn't. I walked out of the open door and pulled it to. I ran to the edge of the woods, and threw up. It would be a long time before I'd be able to erase from my mind that improvised killing spot and its contents.

When I felt steady enough, I drove home.

TWELVE

Mrs Yvonne Landis. Strathmore House, 33 South Street, Alcombe, near Maidstone. It wasn't hard to find the place, which proved, as I'd expected, to be yet another of those pleasant houses that the well-heeled English inhabit. I walked across the graveled area in front, wondering what I was doing there. Surely the police had access to the same information that I had . . . wouldn't they have contacted the woman by now? She hadn't mentioned it when I spoke to her that morning, telling her that I would be in her area and might I drop in.

I was wondering what it was about Yvonne Landis that had made Fliss Fairlight clam up so tightly. And also why the name should initially have rung bells for her, however faintly.

As I approached the house, the front door opened and a bubbly sort of female stood on the threshold, waiting for me. Well-cut dark-blue slacks. Navy cardigan with an Hermès scarf tucked into the neck. Pearl studs at the ears. Bridge once a week, pampering at the local spa once a month, I reckoned. Plus regular visits to the beauty parlour, which accounted for the sugar-frosted effect of her hair.

'Ms Quick?' she asked.

'That's right.'

'Do come in!' Her voice added exclamation marks to everything she said. If I'd had to sum her up in a single word, it would have been 'perky'.

I followed her down a hall which appeared to bisect the house, noticing the number of locks and bolts there were on the solid front door. Added to the CCTV camera I'd glimpsed in the trimmed juniper in front of the house, and the alarm pad by the entrance, it could have meant that this was a security-conscious couple living in the kind of area often targeted by thieves, or that this was a security-conscious couple with something to hide. Or to be afraid of.

There was a glass door at the end of the passage, giving a glimpse of garden: orderly hedges, freshly-mown lawn, roses, lavender bushes heavy with purple spikes.

'I've got coffee in the garden room!' Mrs Landis said.

The garden room was basically one of those conservatory additions, like Edward Vine's, which had been slapped on to the rear of the house. It was full of comfortable-looking wicker furniture – sofas, chairs, coffee tables – with chintz-covered cushions everywhere. Plants in pots stood about on the tiled floor.

'Nice,' I said, since comment seemed to be called for.

'Thank you!' She settled us both down with cups of coffee and a plate of digestive biscuits between us. 'Now, how can I help?'

I'd decided on an approach which I thought might explain why I was there. 'As I told you on the phone, I'm a long-term employee of Huber Associates,' I said. 'This terrible murder of the boss . . . well, you can imagine we were all devastated. And as a long-standing friend of him and his family, it was suggested that, in a purely unofficial capacity, I make a few enquiries.'

'And who asked you to do this?' Yvonne reached for a brass-banded glass box containing a stash of filter-tip cigarettes, removed one, offered the box to me and closed it when I shook my head. She lit up and threw back her head then emitted a dragon-worthy plume of smoke. Gaahd! I tried not to recoil. I considered producing a hacking cough and thumping my chest a bit, but it wasn't my house and besides being rude, it would probably have the effect of alienating her.

'His sister,' I said. 'Dimsie Drayton.'

'Oh yes, I've met her! In the same line of business as her brother, isn't she?'

'Exactly.'

'And how do you think I can be of help?' Her hair looked crisp, like a wafer biscuit. When she patted the waves above her ears, it sounded like one, too. Her eyes rested on me thoughtfully, and I wasn't certain she believed a word I said. In my experience, those who don't believe the façade you present to the world are nearly always consummate liars themselves. On the other hand, although I've got as big an honesty button as the next man (or woman), I freely acknowledge that there are times when lying is the only way forward.

'Well, I was interested in what you said on the phone about Tristan taking risks. Always at the front of the queue when a risky assignment came up, or words to that effect. Would this have been during his army days?'

Her gaze swivelled from side to side. 'Army?'

'Yes, I wondered if you'd met through the service in some capacity or other.'

'*Me*?' She gave a false little laugh and blew a large amount of carcinogenic smoke at a plant unfortunate enough to be standing nearby. Then she jabbed her half-smoked fag into the glass ashtray beside her. Rattled was the word which sprang to mind. 'I'm afraid I'm just a little housewife!'

And I'm President Putin, I thought. She was as sharp as a needle, and doing an excellent job of concealing it. 'So how did you . . .?'

'It's my husband!' she explained. 'James.' She glanced at the perky little watch on her perky little wrist. 'He should be back fairly soon.'

'So this daredevil attitude of Tristan's . . . where did you two encounter it? Was it just your husband, or did *you* see examples of it too?'

'They knew each other from schooldays, I believe,' she said vaguely. 'Or after!'

'So your husband went to school with Tristan? Or served with him, did he? Same regiment, or something?'

'Something like that.' She reached for another cigarette. I flinched. And so, I swear, did the nearby plant. She gave another little laugh which didn't really work this time. 'Why are you asking, anyway? What difference does it make?' Her mouth turned down pitiably. 'He's *dead*.'

It sounded like a cry of pain. Was she another of Tristan's conquests? Was *she* the one his death had been all about? Perhaps the husband – James – had killed him in a fit of jealousy. I wished he'd get a move on and return from wherever he was.

'Obviously,' I said, 'since you two have known him for so long, you probably knew that ten years ago, when he was in his mid-twenties, he disappeared for more than two years.'

She nodded. It wasn't clear whether she did know or was just hanging in there, waiting to see where I went with this.

'Did he ever talk about that time?'

'Not to me. Maybe to James. But I just can't see the relevance!'

I just bet that she could. I really wished I could too.

I sipped daintily at my coffee. Took dainty little mouse-nibbles of my biscuit. Considered idly how much Yvonne reminded me of Dimsie. Concealing a laser-type brain beneath a fluttery sort of mindless femininity. My thoughts whirled like a Catherine Wheel, throwing out sparks of possibility. What did I really know of Tristan's life, away from Longbury? Whom did he love? What did he swear allegiance to? If I was on the wrong track, and it wasn't a woman behind all this, then had he really been tangled up in some dodgy business or other? He had tremendous linguistic abilities. He was strong and fit and clever. He could have been something majorly transgressive. And what about Maurice Colby? There was a crook if ever I heard one on the other end of the phone. I'd be willing to bet there were others. If that were the case, Tristan's cover occupation as an interior designer could not have been better chosen.

On the table beside her chair, Yvonne's mobile phone began a lunatic dance, like a demented wasp. She glanced at the caller ID window, got up, said, 'Excuse me, I won't be a moment!' She went out into the hall. I jumped up and poked about a bit. Nothing seemed out of the ordinary. Nothing that produced one of those *aha!* moments. Innocuous photos of the couple on their wedding day and on other peoples' showed how normal and ordinary their lives were. A picture of a dog whose breed I couldn't identify. Books on the shelves which rang no alarm bells, unless an obvious addiction to Martina Cole was a danger signal of some kind. I went over to the French window and scanned the garden, looking at the trees nearest the house: an apple, a fig, an ornamental cherry. Sure enough, snuggled in among the branches of the apple, I could just make out another CCTV camera. I had no doubt there were others, as well as motion sensors, possibly even outdoor alarms. I'd already clocked the fact that the Landis's were seriously afraid of being burgled. Or worse. This merely confirmed it.

Yvonne returned, vibrant as a robin. 'That was James!' she said. 'He just wanted to let me know that he's only about five minutes away!'

Sure he did. And had taken ten minutes or so to give you a message as bland as that? Much more likely that she was warning him someone was here asking questions, maybe telling him to get his story straight. Reminding him who they were now, whoever they might once have been. Though to be fair, there was absolutely no reason to suggest that they were anything other than they seemed. Or perhaps it was just the hypersensitive gut-feeling that coppers develop when something isn't quite kosher. Even though at first it might be hard to identify, when a case was finally sorted, that instinct always turned out to have been justified.

'While I'm here,' I said, 'I'd love to see the job Mr Huber did for you. Just for our records. Callous as it may seem, I'm afraid we can't put the company on hold.'

She jumped up. 'Of course! Life has to go on! Follow me!'

We made our way into a sitting room decorated in traditional style but not, I suspected, by Huber Associates. A great many watercolours hung on the walls, mainly landscapes and snow scenes, though there were some photographs, too, including one of two men in open-necked shirts, with what was unmistakably Mount Fuji in the background. One of them could have been Tristan.

The room led into another, smaller room, with a stripped-pine two-piece stable door banded with black iron hinges set into one of the walls. Yvonne lifted the old-fashioned latch and led me through into a two-storey barn conversion. Like the house, it was heavily fortified with locks on doors and windows.

'Tristan's done a fabulous job in here!' she said. 'A studio down here for me!' She gestured at the artist's paraphernalia which littered the room. Arching beams overhead framed large windows in the roof through which the sunlight slanted in long bars. The walls were rough-cast and painted white. She pointed. 'And another room up there!' Rustic steps led up to a railed platform where armchairs and a sofa bed were distributed round a glass-topped table, and low bookshelves filled with contemporary novels stood against the walls. I could see a counter with cupboards above, an electric kettle, a small sink and taps. The whole of the end wall was made of glass which overlooked a panoramic view of the countryside.

'Delightful.' I walked halfway up the stairs and looked at

the comfortable little room beyond the railings. 'An extra guest room?' I said.

'Or an extra sitting room!' My husband and I often sit up here, enjoying that breathtaking view!'

'May I?' I flourished my camera. 'For our files?'

She had to think about that one for a moment, brain mentally scanning the room above for anything which might reveal any clue as to the true identity of either her husband or herself. Then she nodded. Obviously it was harmless, gave away nothing.

I dashed off a few shots and then came down to her level, and we walked back through the house to the garden room. 'It was all entirely Tristan's conception, too!' she prattled. 'At one time, we were simply going to have the barn demolished, it was such a wreck!'

'You must be delighted with the end result.' I heard the sound of a car door slamming at the front of the house, followed by footsteps, a man calling.

'There's James!' Yvonne said.

James proved to be a short, rotund man with a spiky grey crew-cut, probably to conceal the fact that he was losing the hair battle in a big way. Is it better to keep some hair, just to show you did once have some, or to lose it all, and pretend that that's the way you like it? He had a hearty manner and globular brown eyes which constantly darted hither and yon.

'So,' he said, rubbing his hands together like a satisfied grocer, 'what do you think of the conversion?'

'Both useful *and* beautiful,' I said.

'Indeed.'

'You were at school with Tristan, is that right?'

'No, no. Definitely not.'

'Oh, I thought your wife said . . .'

'I wasn't sure, dear. It was before I met you.'

'Or was it the Army?' I asked.

'Good Lord no. Can you see me in the Army?'

I smiled ambiguously. I was having a hard time seeing him anywhere. Nor did I want to. He was one of Nature's misfits, entirely unconvincing as a human being, though with those thyroid eyes and spiky grey hair, on a dull day he might just have passed as a seal pup.

'So what do you do now? You're far too young to be retired.'

'Import, export,' he said, a bit too easily. A catch-all phrase which covered everything and said nothing.

'So your relationship with Tristan was through—'

'We were both in the same line of business.'

'This was out in Hong Kong?'

'That's right. Anyway, Miss Quick, have you got what you came for?'

'More or less. Love the barn conversion. My mission is two-fold, however, as I explained to your wife. Having been asked by the family to make enquiries about Tristan Huber, I'd just like to ask a few questions. Like where *did* you meet him? Not school, not the army . . .'

'It was on my gap year,' James said. 'I was trekking round South America – Peru, Uruguay, Brazil – with the intention of working my passage across to New Zealand and Australia and backpacking round the country when I got there. Fell in with Tris in Hawaii and we stuck together for the next three months before he took off for Bali and I went on to catch my boat.'

'Sounds like fun.' Also sounds like a well-rehearsed story. And of course, unverifiable, all these years later.

'Oh, it was. We were carefree, young, at least I was – he was a few years older than I. They were happy days. And, of course, I met my wife in New Zealand . . .' He smiled down at the little woman, who snuggled up close. 'So the two of us travelled along together after that. Joined up again with Tris in Sydney, did the whole Aussie Adventure thing together.'

'Is that when you discovered his reckless streak?' I asked.

'Reckless?' James looked at Yvonne.

'You know, darling . . . the way he was always up for anything that anyone suggested, however risky it sounded.' She looked vaguely panicked. 'Climbing inside the craters of volcanoes that were about to erupt, canoeing down some of those terrible rushing rivers, swimming around when he knew there were crocodiles or sharks, climbing vertical rock-faces without ropes. I was frightened stiff by some of his antics!'

'See what you mean,' James said. God, he was smooth. Or well-trained. 'Me too.'

'Life's a gamble, he used to say!'

One which he'd recently lost. We were silent for a heartbeat or two.

'Well . . .' I said. What I really wanted was James taped to a chair, naked, and Yvonne spread-eagled on electrified bed springs, and myself, armed with a blowtorch, a pair of pincers, torturing them mercilessly until they told me the truth (only kidding). 'Then you moved here, saw he was a name in the interior design world, hired him to come and do your barn for you?'

'Absolutely!' Yvonne said, quicker on that one than her husband. I'd already picked up on the fact that she was about eight times more on the ball than James. 'Amazing coincidence, wasn't it?'

'I'll say.' I looked around once more. 'You've got a lovely house. How long have you lived here?'

'Six years!'

'And – not that it's any of my business – where were you before that? You look as though you've been around a bit.'

'As we said, in Hong Kong! James was with the Thai Song Commercial, weren't you, darling?'

'That's right. Absolutely.'

'When we came back to the UK, he set up on his own, didn't you darling?'

'That's right. Like I said, import–export.'

I left. On the long drive home I pondered a bit. There was something fishy somewhere, and I hadn't the slightest idea where. Despite checking the place out as carefully as was doable without being observed, I could see no trace at all as to their past. Neither the manufactured one they had handed me, nor the true one.

Glass of much-needed wine in hand, I phoned Fliss Fairlight. 'No,' she said, when she answered and before I could even speak.

'How do you mean?'

'No progress, nothing to report, leads being followed up but basically none of them seem to be helping the investigation forward, and we have absolutely no clue as to motive, let alone a perp.' She paused. Said uncertainly, 'That *is* what you rang up about, isn't it?'

'No. I was going to ask you if you'd like to come on an all-expenses-paid trip to Capri with me tomorrow.'

'You so were *not*!'

'Anyway, thanks for the update. There are so many directions this could go in that I can't follow it all. But I'm not on the force any more—'

'Come back, come back, your country needs you!'

'—and the only resource I have which you lot haven't is that I've known the vic for years. Which isn't proving beneficial in any way. And basically, all I've learned over the past couple of weeks is that Tristan Huber was not what he appeared to be.'

'Covering his tracks, do you think?'

'I'd say so. He was obviously brilliant at his job, whatever that was. I'm inclined to think that Tristan Huber Associates was just camouflage.' I coughed slightly. 'Anything new on Kevin Fuller? Or that other body, with the chess pieces?'

'Poor lad turns out to be one Ned Swift. Identity left in his pockets . . . second-year history student, twenty-two, popular with the girls *and* with his mates, president of the chess club, played the cello.'

'No known enemies? No grudges held?'

'So far, none at all.'

'Any grieving girlfriends?'

'Not that we discovered from preliminary enquiries. No one can understand what he was doing in that shed in the first place.'

'Closet gay?'

'I don't think so. He's *had* girlfriends, that much we've ascertained. I believe one of them rather tragically died . . . he hasn't been on the dating scene much since then. This is all stuff we picked up from his fellow students, you understand.'

'But there must be some connection with the Tristan Huber case, surely.'

'Not that we've discovered so far.'

'If you find one, let me know.' A thought struck me. 'Was he on that committee to do with refurbishing the student common rooms?'

'Again, I don't know. Why don't you ring Garside yourself?'

'Great idea, Fliss. I can just see him opening up to me, of all people. Has he checked out all those cartons in the warehouse?'

'Ask him.'

'I know they're full of dodgy merchandise. Could this Ned Swift have gone there to meet a girl or something, and have stumbled across somebody up to no good and that somebody offed him so he couldn't give away his identity?'

'Sounds plausible. On the other hand, our perpetrator hasn't exactly been secretive about his actions. Three bodies, now.'

'If they're all connected,' I said. 'Which so far has not been established. But whether they are or not, this is becoming a bit of an epidemic.'

Phone call ended, I swallowed the last of my wine and poured another glass. 'Cheers,' I said to the empty room. I did not feel cheery in the least.

When Tristan was eventually exposed as whatever it was he had been, how would Dorcas and Dimsie, not to mention my own parents, or myself, for that matter, cope with the fact that they had loved him, nurtured him, laughed at his jokes? His murder was bad enough but to discover that he was anything but the saint we all thought him . . . what was that knowledge going to do to hearts already vulnerable, nights already sleepless?

Having removed the *H* from the word Tai, and then established that there was no Tai Song (goodness, that Yvonne was a bit of chancer!) but there *was* a Tai Sang, I put through a long-distance call to them. A helpful guy called Mr Sook, who spoke better English than I did, denied that they had ever employed a James Landis.

'Never, never,' he said, implying that no way would anyone called Landis be allowed through their doors, even as a depositor, let alone be taken on as a member of staff. 'This name is unknown to me, and I have been working here for more than two decades.'

'That's pretty decisive stuff, Mr Sook.'

'Yes, it is.'

'I wonder where I should look next.'

'This person you are seeking, is he perhaps a crook?'

'I believe he is, though so far I have no proof.'

'And you yourself are?'

'Alexandra Quick. Formerly Detective Chief Inspector Alexandra Quick.'

'I have always wanted to be a private eye,' he said. 'To catch a thief, this must be a fine and satisfying thing.'

'Very much so.'

'I will tell you what I will do for you, DCI Quick.'

'Former,' I said quickly, looking over my shoulder.' I didn't want to be done for impersonating a police officer.

'Once a policeman, always a policeman,' he said. 'It is like priests and doctors. Anyway, give me a description of this bad person and I will telephone round my colleagues at some of the local banks.'

I did so, emphasizing the protruding eyes.

'The game's afoot!' he said cheerfully, and rang off.

THIRTEEN

Thursday. Am-dram night.

I had decided to attend, if for no other reason than to take my mind off Tristan and the other bodies. We'd done some improv exercises. Read through a short play with girls reading the boys' parts and vice versa. We'd discussed the production the group was going to put on at Christmas in an attempt to stun and amaze any who showed up to watch. Which I guessed would be mostly parents or children of the cast, with the odd Senior Citizen who had nothing better to do thrown in.

'Considering how close we're getting to Christmas, have

we left ourselves enough time to meet the deadline?' someone asked.

'We've still got plenty of time,' said Milo. 'More than enough to get something worthwhile out there.'

'Not, please God, a pantomime again,' someone groaned.

'Yes,' agreed someone else. 'Puh-leeze, anything but a panto.'

Someone piped up, 'Hang about, you haven't seen my Buttons . . .', a remark which generated the conventional sort of banter.

'Not undone them yet, darlin', but I live in hope.'

'You should be so lucky.'

'Ooh, you are awful!'

When it was time to leave, Milo Stanton clapped his hands.

'OK, people, listen up,' he said. I tried not to raise my eyebrows. Where on earth do people get hold of phrases like that? Off the box, I imagine. *Listen up* . . . what's that supposed to mean? Can you listen down? Was I turning into a grammar-Nazi? I already kept Tippex in my bag in order to sneak around eliminating unnecessary apostrophes from signs outside shops. In my darker moments, I could see the horrible old bat I was going to turn into. I needed to get out more, hence the fact that not only had I joined the drama group, but was also in attendance at this very moment.

'Now . . .' Milo grinned his wolfish grin at us all, '. . . thank God I still have a few contacts in the biz . . .' Pause for faint sycophantic cheers. '. . . which means I've managed to persuade an old friend of mine to come down next week and give us some hands-on benefit by sharing his considerable expertise with us.'

We looked at each other as though searching for clues as to the identity of this friend, and came up with nothing.

'Since you won't be able to guess, I'll tell you,' said Milo. 'None other than . . . ta-dah!! . . . Chris *Kearns*!'

I frowned. Surely I knew that name. Something to do with eggs, I seemed to remember. On the telly. Around me, the other members of the group reacted with predictable delight.

'Fantastic!'

'Brilliant!'

'Well done, Milo!'

'Aren't you clever!'

Then it came back to me. Kearns. The leading light of an oh-so-hilarious award-winning series about a chicken farm. A popular sitcom called *Hen Pecked*, in which he and his termagant screen wife buy a chicken farm in a bid to restore the family fortunes. There'd been a second side-splitting series called *Flying The Coop*, in which the two of them tried to flog off the chickens to a series of naïve buyers, cue cameo roles from various well-known, if fading, thespians.

And next season he'd be starring, if that was the right word, in an entirely new series to be called *Spend A Penny,* where he and the termagant would be in charge of a seaside public convenience, with all its attendant uproarious shenigans.

Sometimes I lose the will to live.

Thanks to the tabloids and celeb magazines, we could hardly avoid knowing all about Chris's personal calamities: the divorce from his childhood sweetheart, the adolescent daughter raped and murdered, the son with HIV, his own battle with alcoholism. The message being that even though his heart was breaking, he still managed to make people laugh, in the time-honoured tradition of clowns and funny men everywhere.

Count me out, I thought. I'm not going to pander to the ego of some up-himself actor who, despite the tragedies in his life, will certainly just happen to bring along thirty copies of his book for us to buy, and at the same time be busy grooming us to tune in to the series about the public lav. I reflected that I must sometimes come across as a miserable old cow. Perhaps I really am one.

'All right, guys,' Milo said, staring directly at me. 'I want all of you to turn up next week come hell or high water. I don't want Chris to flog all the way down here from London to find that half of you haven't bothered to come to pick up on any pieces of wisdom on sitcom writing and, more importantly, sitcom acting, that he might be willing to share with us.'

'How about we try for a mock pilot sitcom for our Christmas show?' someone suggested.

'Yeah, with a parody of all our favourite sitcom actors.'

'Not a bad idea. We'll see how it goes. What do *you* think, Alex?'

'I haven't got a favourite,' I mumbled. 'I don't watch a lot of TV.'

Murmurs from the others. 'I'm not trying to be superior,' I said. 'I simply don't have time.'

'Well anyway, I want all of you to come armed with ideas,' Milo said, looking put out. 'We're really lucky to have a professional like Chris willing to listen to them and give us some pointers.'

As I was leaving, Milo beckoned me over. He sat with one half of his bum on the table at the front of the room, swinging a leg. 'Alex, a word,' he said.

I went over. 'Yes?'

'I've arranged to take Chris out for dinner after our session next week. Thought I'd ask two or three of the group to come along. Are you interested?'

I already knew I would have another engagement. Or invent one. 'Um . . .'

'It won't be the same without you.' He had very black eyelashes which lay on his ravaged cheeks like a door-mat when he blinked, softening and enhancing his wolfish good looks.

'Like I said, I don't watch television very much,' I said. And when I do, I thought, but didn't say, it's certainly not the likes of Mr Kearns and his idiotic caperings that I switch on for. 'And I'm hardly the most enthusiastic or experienced member of the group. And in any case, it's not really my—'

'Trust me, Alexandra. Chris is a great deal more worthwhile than you'd think from his antics on the small screen.'

'Hmm . . .'

'Go on.' His voice took on a note of deep sincerity. So did his eyes. 'I promise you won't regret it.'

Oh ho! Was it just me, or was he promising something more than dinner? And was I really up for it? Sam Willoughby passed rapidly through my head. 'Oh, all right,' I said. Gracious as always.

'Don't tell the others. I'm not asking the whole group to come along, just a select few,' he said. 'I'll be in touch to confirm details.'

'Fine.'

The following week was uneventful. I kept in regular touch with DCI Fairlight, but nothing further came up in the Tristan Huber murder. I'd seen this happen before. Cases often appear to stagnate, even though CID are doing their best, beavering away in the background, pursuing the little intel they have, interviewing possible witnesses, checking alibis, knocking on doors, delving into the circumstances of anyone who might be considered a suspect or, for that matter, have any connection with the deceased. Nonetheless, it was unusual that after three weeks and several leads, there was no movement on the case, let alone any kind of breakthrough.

Nor did I hear anything further from Mr Sook in Hong Kong. Nonetheless, I had a very strong sense that he was down there, ringing colleagues, checking on any bug-eyed bankers who might have been around six years ago.

I'd warned Dimsie that for the moment, I was out of the frame. I had deadlines coming up and needed to get my head down on *Eat, Drink and Be Merry.* She didn't like it much. Told me I was reneging on my responsibilities. (*'Surely Tristan's death means everything else should be put on hold?'*) I bit back the sharp retort which sprang to mind and repeated several times to myself that she was grieving family.

'Dimsie,' I pointed out, 'I'm an art historian, not a miracle worker, and I'm certainly not a detective any more. And I'm definitely not going to get in the way of an official police investigation. When they have anything relevant to tell you, they'll do so. You just have to trust them.'

'But they're obviously not doing *any*thing,' she wailed. 'Or they'd have solved the case by now.'

'Come on, girl,' I said. 'Get a grip.'

Fliss rang one afternoon. 'Your Mr Huber is proving to be a bit of a mystery man,' she said.

'In what way?'

'We know he travelled abroad quite a bit, but other than that, we can't find out much about him. And what we *have* got doesn't seem to check out.'

'What about that client list?'

'In the past three years, as you've no doubt ascertained for yourself, his company has taken on twenty-four commissions, situated all over England and the rest of the globe. And guess what . . .'

'I hate it when people say that. How can I possibly guess? And how disappointed you'd be if I did.'

She didn't take a blind bit of notice, just carried on. 'The interesting thing is that out of those twenty-four so-called clients, more than half don't even appear to exist.'

I frowned. 'How the hell does that work?'

'You ring the number given on the invoice, and discover their phone was disconnected a year ago. Or they've moved and not left a forwarding address. Or nobody's ever heard of them and the address is actually bogus. Garside is having kittens, convinced that he's stumbled across the Mr Big of the Home Counties.'

'Murdered by a rival gang boss, is that the theory?'

'Don't laugh, Quick. You could be nearer the mark than you think.'

'I don't believe this! At least, I don't think I do. I certainly don't want to.' Tristan Huber was turning out to be a whole lot more devious than I had previously given him credit for and I needed to do some serious re-evaluation of the man.

'Any insights so far? You've known him since you emerged from the womb, haven't you?'

'We used to share a nappy,' I said. 'Look, I'll have a think about him and what I know – what I *think* I know – and get back to you if anything springs to mind.'

'It's the manner of death, you see. According to Garside, only a gangster-style boss would order that kind of torture to be inflicted on a person.'

'Yeah, right, and the area is crawling with mobsters, crime lords and racketeers.'

'You'd be surprised. And don't forget your friend Tristan also has or had, commissions in Italy, the Middle and Far East, the Czech Republic, Serbia. Let alone in Russian oligarch territory. Also don't forget that it's costing me time and patience to screw all this intel out of Garside, or members of his team, since in theory I have nothing to do with them. As you know, he's mad keen on confidentiality, though he's not averse to sharing crumbs of information when he deems it appropriate. Here I am, busting a gut for you, when I have urgent cases of my own which I should be getting on with. Such as this Kevin Fuller.'

'Anything on him yet?'

'I've hardly got time, with all the energy I'm expending on you. But for the moment, I'm stymied. We've interviewed the family, of course . . .' She sighed heavily. 'Poor broken people. Got a detailed CV from them, from cradle to – as it were – grave. And just like with Huber, so far there's really almost nothing tangible to go on. But as you know, we're a dogged bunch, we'll get there in the end, as we always do. Trouble is, we literally don't know where to turn for suspects. We've combed through his archive, investigated thoroughly, interviewed known associates, talked to those who live near the scene of crime—'

'—such as Major Horrocks.'

'Exactly. But so far we haven't been able to pinpoint anyone with a motive, or anyone who was around at the time of the murder. Meanwhile, I'm expecting you to make it up to me in a big way.'

'Anyone for Capri?'

'Piss off, Quick.'

What Fliss had told me provided food for thought. So did the painting I was staring at, depicting *Vertumnus*, one of Arcimboldo's grotesqueries. It wasn't particularly to my liking but the character he'd created out of fruit and veg – a portrait of Emperor Rudolf II – was certainly edible, and looked pretty merry. While I considered it, I thought again about Tristan. What on earth had he been up to in the weeks before his death? I came up with nothing that I could pinpoint, just vague and nebulous possibilities. Basically, zip.

Fruit and veg . . . I thought of the giant radish episode to which my mother had alluded. It had sounded farcical, had briefly made me wonder if she and Edred were already skirting the foothills of dementia. But maybe she had been trying to remind me that the guy I'd always had a crush on was in fact, ruthless, and had been even as a boy. I seem to remember that, though at first they had prevented him from damaging the rival radish, he nonetheless managed to destroy it by smashing it to pieces with a spade. Of course he was eliminated at once from the competition, but that way, at least he hadn't been beaten by a better radish than his own.

The following Thursday evening came around all too quickly. Reluctantly I got into my car and drove up the hill. When I got to the theatre, everyone was on stage, clustered in irritating attitudes of awe and hero-worship round a figure seated on the throne-like chair that the group had used for a production of *The King And I,* which came from the props department. Fair enough, I suppose. If someone had offered any of them the chance to star in a TV sitcom, they would have jumped at the chance, and if by touching the hem of Chris Kearns' robe they thought they might achieve that goal, then good luck to them. Personally I found it hard to drum up much enthusiasm for a series about a brick public lavatory or its star, and in any case, Kearns' manic style of comedy acting didn't set any flags flying round me. If I wanted laughs I preferred wit and subtlety.

The guy looked pretty much as he appeared on screen, just as fleshily athletic but older and more muted, as though a light bulb had fused somewhere inside him. Milo saw me slip into the room and take a place at the back of the crowd, and raised disappointed eyebrows.

'Sorry I'm late,' I mumbled. 'The car . . .'

Chris Kearns, meantime, was giving his adoring fans the full Monty: the smile, the familiar gurning, the hands raking through what was left of his hair. But I could tell his heart wasn't in it. After all, we were just a potty little amateur group, and definitely not important enough. Nonetheless, I listened dutifully, even asked a few questions. We stopped for appalling coffee (instant) halfway through. I noticed Milo, his back to us, pouring a slug of something from a silver hip flask into both his and Chris's mug. I could have done with some of that myself.

Time passed with tedious slowness. I was about to double up with simulated pain and mutter something about a grumbling appendix when Milo called the troops to order. 'Let's focus on the Christmas show, folks,' he said. 'Chris says that he'll be in pantomime in Margate over the Christmas season – his Widow Twankey has to be seen to be believed! – otherwise he would be happy to come over and take part. Since a star of his calibre is what brings in the audience, we can't expect him to renege on his duties or contract. Nor would we! What a shame.'

Various exclamations of regret and disappointment arose from the group.

'How*ever*,' Milo continued, 'he has very kindly offered us some comps to the panto as raffle prizes, plus a drink with him after his show. It's the kind of thing which will be a big draw for us.'

There was a burst of clapping from the group. Kearns held up his hand. 'Please. It's the least I can do for my friend Milo here. I'm only sorry it can't be more. I'd also be happy to have those who're interested come over when we start technical run-throughs shortly, just to give you an idea of the mechanics of putting on a professional performance.'

'Anyway . . .' Milo rallied us. 'Now that we're all here, let's talk about the Christmas show, see what Chris thinks of the ideas you've brought, summed up in a single sentence, if you please, since we haven't got all the time in the world.'

We spent the next couple of hours talking through some of the plots people had come up with. I was impressed by the ingenuity that had been shown. Eventually, we voted for two of them, and then went through them in finer detail, Kearns critiquing as we went. He was inspiring, picking out details, showing impossibilities, pointing out places where we were likely to have difficulties with staging or plotting, suggesting ways to enhance a comic moment or introduce a ribald pun.

By the time the session came to an end, we had roughed out an entire routine for our Christmas offering. Even I, unwilling though I had been to listen to a half-assed comedy star, had to admit that I was impressed by the man's knowledge of stagecraft, what would work, what wouldn't. I even thought about buying his book, copies of which I could see sitting on one of the seats in the front row.

It took nearly half an hour for people to leave, by the time they'd bought a book, had it signed, and had gushed over Chris. That left Milo, Kearns himself, Charlotte Plimpton, Ricky Hadfield, William Marshall and me to walk along from the theatre to the nearest Indian. Since neither Charlotte nor I were major players, we were hardly representative of the group. Char was blonde and busty, and usually played the comic housekeeper or eccentric next-door neighbour type of role. And I . . . well, as a new member, I hadn't yet been asked to give my Second Spear Carrier, let alone my Cordelia or Rosalind.

I couldn't help noticing that Chris Kearns was eyeing Char appreciatively. So was Ricky Hadfield. When we were eventually seated, however, I had Kearns on one side and Milo on the other. I really couldn't imagine why I had been invited along.

Milo was in full breathless, arse-licking mode and Chris Kearns was sucking it up. I realized that if I never saw either of them again, it would be too soon. And that was despite the smouldering appeal Milo had originally presented, and the main reason for me staying with the group in the first place.

Across the table from each other, Charlotte and I wore identical expressions of tedium, although we tried to hide it, she better than me. The room was noisy, the food disgusting. Toying with a Lamb Rogan Josh, I couldn't help remembering an article I'd seen recently about an Indian restaurant kitchen where there were mice droppings everywhere, filthy pipes, rotting woodwork, raw meat stored in contaminated plastic bins, food three months out of date. My head began to pound. I felt nauseous.

Kearns asked me what I did and seemed genuinely interested when I described my anthologies. 'I shall have to buy one,' he said. 'I've got various arty friends who would love a copy. What led you into this line of work?'

Again I explained.

'Opted out of the police force?' he said. 'I'm not surprised. I imagine that becomes a bit soul-destroying after a while.'

'If you're in the CID, yes, it can. The sheer ugliness of the way people treat their fellow human beings is astonishing.'

'Especially, I would think, if children or young people are involved.'

'Precisely.'

He shook his head. 'Some of the things you read about in the paper . . . some of the stuff people get away with these days . . . complete lack of empathy for others, we're breeding monsters . . . it makes you despair. Or want to join a vigilante group. Make the punishment fit the crime, an eye for an eye, all that primitive biblical stuff.'

Despite my feelings about public lavatories, I was beginning to think he wasn't as bad as I'd anticipated.

'You've recently had a couple of rather grisly cases round here, haven't you?' he went on.

'Grisly isn't quite the word. Worse than that, in one instance.' Although I hadn't seen it, I had to shake the image of Tristan's tortured body out of my head.

'Nutters,' he said. 'The world is full of them. When I think of the number of—'

He was heading for a full-blown rant. 'What led to you becoming an actor?' I asked quickly.

'The usual sort of thing. My father was an amateur comedian, played the local pubs on Friday nights, further round the coast from here, near Brighton. My mother sang semi-professionally. I grew up with public performance as part of the norm.' He shrugged self-deprecatingly. 'I was pretty hopeless at school – pretty hopeless at everything, when it came right down to it. Not stupid, just not good at schoolwork, discipline and so on. I call it the Churchill Syndrome: the great man was useless at school, and went on to achieve in later life.'

'As you did.'

'Eventually. The Army wouldn't have me because I'm too short-sighted, the police wouldn't have me because I'm too short.' He shrugged again. 'In desperation, I embarked on one of those government-sponsored training courses in plumbing, but my wrists were too weak, apprenticed myself to the butcher (allergic to raw meat), the baker (allergic to wheat flour), the candlestick maker (tallow brought me out in hives) and opted out of them all in short order. Got taken on by a garden maintenance company but suffered from hay fever, and gave *that* up the minute I could.'

'Gosh . . .' This was beginning to sound like a practise run for one of his stand-up routines.

'Then there was the dairy farm, where I got kicked in the head by a cow and was concussed for a week, plus the chicken farm where I dropped a pallet holding a thousand eggs.' He smiled wryly. 'In the end, there didn't seem be much option really, but to go back to my roots and try to follow in my father's footsteps, the chicken farm providing a whole heap of material to work up into a routine for the pubs and clubs. And once I done a few gigs, the London lot started to come down to assess my performance and eventually one thing led to another, the way it so often does.'

'Success at last.'

'Right.' He grinned. I had to admit he was engaging. 'The abridged version of Chapters One to Ten of my autobiography! For free!'

Smiles and nods all round. After that, there didn't seem a whole lot to say. For all his screen antics it seemed obvious that he was, like so many clowns, a melancholy personality at heart. Gradually the conversation began to peter out, and we sat in uneasy semi-silence until in desperation, I stood up.

'Look, guys, I'm terribly sorry,' I lied, avoiding Milo's eye, 'but I have to get home. My mother's staying with me and I don't like leaving the poor old dear alone for too long.' Mary would have been spinning in her grave if she heard me describe her like that. Not that she was in it yet.

In an effort not to be too rude, I felt I had to ask if I could buy a copy of Kearns' book, since he had a large bag of them beside his chair.

'If you could sign it for my mother, Mary,' I said piously. Kearns signed a copy with a flourish and handed it over, then refused to accept any payment, which I thought was decent of him. Perhaps he was aware that in the normal course of events, I would never have forked out for it, especially since I'd made it clear that I didn't watch TV. He put an arm round my shoulders and planted a peck on my cheek. He smelled of whisky and stale tobacco.

I blew theatrical kisses – not my usual style! – and went away. I thought it very likely that I would bow out of the theatre group with immediate effect.

As I shut the front door of my flat behind me, my phone began to jitter inside my bag. I hoped very much it wasn't going to be Milo Stanton wanting to know what was wrong with me, walking out like that. Pretty he might be, but frankly, I was discovering, not much else. Actors always seem to be too aware of themselves, especially the male kind, which means they're not really aware of anyone else, except in the most superficial way.

'Yes?' I said off-puttingly.

'DCI Alexandra Quick—'

'Former.'

'—I have followed the trail assiduously in the search for your Mr James Landis.' It was Mr Sook.

'And what have you found?'

'Precisely nothing. I have drawn a complete blank. None of my colleagues in the various banks of Hong Kong know this name, nor do they believe this person has ever worked in their establishments.'

'That's very interesting, Mr Sook.' Was this good news or bad news? I wasn't sure. On the one hand it confirmed my feelings that the *soi-disant* Landises were lying through their teeth, for some reason as yet undefined. On the other, it meant that they had managed to cover their tracks in some way, and I, or DCI Alan Garside, would have to start all over again in trying to run them down.

'How-*ever*,' enunciated Mr Sook, leaning heavily on the last two syllables, 'when I mentioned these eyes you spoke of, thyroid was the word I believe you used, there was instant success.'

'That's great!'

'This Mr Landis is known far and wide in Hong Kong, although he operated under another name at that time, a pseudonym, if you will.'

'And what was that?'

'He was calling himself Jeremy Lockhart, and the reason he was known all round the colony was because of his gambling habit. He gambled, DCI Quick. He was an addict. Wherever bets could be placed, he placed them, until he had nothing more to gamble. He then disappeared from the gambling clubs, the gaming tables, the betting shops. People wondered whether he had died, or perhaps had returned to Europe. And then, suddenly, he reappeared at the tables with renewed funds. Of course there was only one conclusion to be drawn and we knew instantly what had happened.'

'And what was that?'

'He had fallen into the clutches of one of the many triad gangs which operate in Hong Kong.' Mr Sook spoke with relish. *Fallen into the clutches*: it was the kind of phrase one might wait a lifetime for and never find an opportunity to use. 'A colleague of mine believes it most likely that in Mr Lockhart's case, the triad in question was Wang Shing Wo. These dangerous people are involved in every possible form of criminal activity, from extortion to prostitution, from money-laundering to people-trafficking. Anything which will bring in good solid cash. And we are talking about multi-billions of dollars a year. I do not know if once recruited, you can ever get completely free of them.'

'It sounds quite a frightening business.'

'You are quite right, DCI Quick. And if you should break any of their rules, I can assure you that they will hunt you down. They are pitiless. Brutal and without mercy. These are people to stay away from.'

That would certainly explain the name change and the high security round the Landis house. 'Mr Sook,' I said. 'You are a star! You have been most helpful. I cannot thank you enough.' I noticed I was avoiding elisions, matching his brand of talk, and hoping I didn't sound like I was taking the mickey. 'I have another question.'

'Please,' he said. 'Any way I can help I should be delighted to do so.'

'Tristan Huber: does this name ring any bells with you?'

'Huber, Huber.' There was a fizz of excitement in his voice. 'I have most definitely heard the name though I could not at the moment state in which context.'

'If anything comes to mind, do please call me again,' I urged. 'It could be very important.'

'I will make enquiries and come back to you.' He paused then asked diffidently, 'Would I be asking you to breach police regulations if I enquired as to the nature of the investigation on which you are currently working?'

'It is murder, Mr Sook,' I said. 'Bloody murder.'

'Oh, goodness me. This is most distressing.'

'I could not agree with you more.'

FOURTEEN

'That's useful,' Fliss Fairlight said, when I passed on the name of Jeremy Lockhart, late of Hong Kong. I didn't mention the word Landis, after her previous reaction had resulted in a dead end. 'Lockhart, eh?' At the other end of the phone I could hear her fingers foxtrotting all over the keyboard of her computer. And then she stopped. 'Uh-oh,' she said. 'No good, I'm afraid, Quick.'

'Why not?'

'Ever heard of a firewall?'

'Of course.'

'Two, one behind the other?'

'Yeah?'

'Or even three?'

'Seriously tight security, in other words?'

'Hold that thought.'

I got the message. 'Thanks,' I said. 'How are Garside's enquiries into Tristan Huber's death going?'

'They're going like crazy. Trouble is, they're not actually getting anywhere. But you know us well enough to be aware of what a fine body of men and women we are. I'm confident that as usual, we'll get our man in the end.'

'Is he looking in any particular direction?'

'Disgruntled client was the first port of call – but you'd have to be pretty crazy to carve someone up like a Sunday roast because you didn't care for the colour scheme he'd chosen for your back bedroom.'

There was a meaningful kind of silence. 'What else?' I said.

'Quick, I know the guy was a good friend of yours, but there was something extremely dodgy about his business. And by extension, him.'

'Unfortunately, I've already figured that out.' There was a hollow feeling in my head, in the space that Tristan used to occupy. The long years of our friendship were necessarily being reshaped, reformulated. Whatever his mother might believe about her son, I would never be able to think of him in the same way again.

I was about to end the call when Fliss said, 'By the way, Garside's had the results of the autopsy.'

'I imagine they're pretty much what you'd expect, aren't they? Death by extreme rendition, as they say.'

'Yeah. Just one small detail: the forensic lab people noted that a couple of the . . . uh, if I'm going to be completely accurate and totally gross . . . *slices* cut from the body are considerably deep than others.'

'Any idea why?'

'None at all.'

'Would these deeper cuts be in places where you might find a tat of some kind?' I asked, snapping at a possibility like a trout at a fly. 'Some form of marking your affiliations. Just like any urban street gang. Especially if the killer stroke killers wished to conceal any connection to, say, a Triad.' Ever since my conversation with Mr Sook, the notion of an Asian criminal gang being responsible for Tristan's death had been fermenting in my brain like *saki*.

'It's worth considering, I must say. But you're reaching a bit, aren't you?'

'Consider it and come back to me if you reach any conclusion,' I said. 'Meanwhile, I'd say thank you for sharing, but I wish you hadn't.'

Poor Tristan . . .

A triple firewall! What was it with the Landis/Lockharts? Mr Sook had spoken of the possibility that James Landis had become involved with one of the Hong Kong triads, which I knew operated worldwide. Perhaps the husband and wife had been offered some form of protection by MI5 or 6, in exchange for betraying organization leaders, or revealing secrets they should have kept to themselves. Dangerous tactics, from what I'd heard of the Triads. And Tristan had obviously had a connection to the Landis couple which I was already certain must have been a lot more than the conversion work on their tumbledown barn. In addition, something about the two of them was itching away at me like a hornet sting. Some detail I'd noticed without taking it in. Something I'd picked up on somewhere, recently.

I looked again at the photographs, but nothing hit me, though I could not help feeling it should. From my desk, I looked out to sea, where white caps were tumbling towards shore. Three or four intrepid little crafts from the sailing club had hoisted their sails, which were now lying almost flat in the wind. Seagulls stubbornly beat their wings against it as they headed for somewhere more sheltered. Flags smacked at their poles; fallen leaves gathered in piles under the trees. It was only mid-September and already it was feeling close to wintry.

I tugged on a thick jacket and walked down to see Sam Willoughby at the bookshop. His assistant was working in the shop today, so I suggested he take ten minutes off and join me for a coffee at one of the small café tables he had installed in a corner of the shop.

He gave me a hug. 'Love to,' he said, and came over with a cappuccino for me and an espresso for himself. 'So, what's new?'

'I need to find something out and for various reasons can't do it myself. Is there any chance you could do me a favour and do some probing?' I said. I didn't add that my main reason for delegating the task to him was my intense desire not to bump into Milo Stanton. I was sure he would jump at the chance, since I knew that it had always been one of his dreams to become Longbury's answer to Sam Spade or Philip Marlowe, a man walking the mean streets who was not himself mean. Battling for truth and justice. Defending the poor and vulnerable and maidens in distress. Especially the latter. Not that I had any idea how many of those he came across in his line of work.

'Sure.' He looked eager. Ready to roll. 'Just point me at it.'

'I'd like to know more about the late Kevin Fuller, mature student working towards his PhD in Applied Mathematics. His likes and dislikes. Significant others, if such existed – probably male. Hobbies, interests, all the usual stuff. And any connection with Tristan Huber, other than the obvious one to do with refurbishing the student common rooms and bars.'

'Won't the boys in blue have already covered the same ground?'

'I should hope so, by now. But I want more, if more exists. For instance, he was into extreme sports and I can't help wondering why.'

'Do you need to have a reason? Maybe he just liked the excitement. The nail-biting possibility of something going horribly wrong. That whole macho, death-defying thing.' Sam waved his hands about. 'Some people really do have a death wish. Besides . . . an applied mathematician? Perhaps he was trying to prove something. As it stands, it's hardly dashingly masculine, is it?'

'I suppose not.' I gripped his fingers. Offered him my mega-smile. Watched him melt.

A woman was standing at the counter, waiting for her purchases to be wrapped and giving us the fish-eye.

'Friend of yours?' I asked, gesturing discreetly with my head. She produced a cold, cold smile. She certainly didn't seem like a maiden in distress. When Sam looked over at her, she lit up and gave him a warm little wave. The kind which suggested that not only had the two of them shared many an intimate moment in the past, but also that they would be sharing many more in the years to come.

'Not exactly.' He flushed slightly and smoothed back his hair.

'So inexactly, then.' I sounded censorious even to my own ears, though I was well aware I had no right to do so. 'How does *that* work?'

'It works just fine, Alexandra,' he said, cucumber-cool. 'Now, how soon do you want this information on the late Kevin Fuller?'

Uh-oh. Consider yourself snubbed, Ms Quick. And deservedly, I had to admit. 'As soon as you can get it to me.'

'Right. I'll go up the hill in the lunch hour.' He touched my hand. 'You can rely on me, ma'am.'

While he was up there, I intended to visit Major Horrocks yet again, to see what more, if anything, I could glean about Mr Harkness. Watching the customer exit the shop, with a last flirtatious glance at Sam over her shoulder, I was annoyed with myself. Sam's private life was none of my business. Which is precisely how I wanted it.

When I pulled up outside Rattrays, the Major was standing in the garden with a pair of shears in his hand, his short grey hair stirring in the wind as he stared dispiritedly at a ragged box hedge. Leaves and twigs lay untidily at its foot.

'Good afternoon, Alex,' he said. He gestured at the tree. 'What does that look like? Be honest.'

'Um . . .'

'A bird?' he prompted.

'Er . . .'

'A swan?'

'Definitely not. Unless it's a swan lying on its side and nursing a hangover with its wings furled.'

'Hopeless,' he said. 'Me, I mean. At this clipping and shaping lark. I just can't seem to get the hang of it.'

'Practice makes perfect,' I said. 'Why not try something simpler, like a ball?'

'I already did.' He waved at another untidy bush. 'Over there.'

'Ah.'

He stared at his watch and brightened. 'Looks like coffee-time. Why don't you come in? I made some chocolate chip cookies this morning – delicious!'

When we were seated in the Major's living room, and I was on my third cookie, I said, 'Last time we spoke about Tristan Huber's murder, you mentioned the possibility that the warehouse-cum-shed in the woods belonged to the husband of Mrs Roscoe's cousin Lilian.'

'Brian Harkness,' nodded the Major. 'That's right.'

'I don't think I'm breaking any confidences when I tell you that the police have definitively established that Tristan Huber was worked over in that shed.'

The Major sucked air in through his teeth like a Polish builder and shook his head. 'Terrible, terrible. What a business. Poor young man.'

'Can you tell me anything more about Harkness?'

'Not much. Everything I know about him I've already passed on to the police in the shape of a grim sort of chappie called Offside or some such.'

'Garside. And what exactly *do* you know?'

'Harkness was a surly bugger, 'scuse my French, that was for sure. Never had a smile for anyone, least of all his poor wife.'

'Did Nell Roscoe ever say anything to you about him or his business?'

'Only more or less what I just told you. Import–export, usual sort of ambiguity, if you ask me, could cover any amount of unlawful activity. I have to say I was under the impression he no longer used that warehouse thingy. Terrible what people get up to these days, I sometimes wonder what the world's coming to, really doesn't bear thinking about. Anyway, I passed what little I know on to the constabulary.'

I was thankful that there would be no point in me trekking cross-country to talk to Mr Harkness, since the police had probably already interviewed him and learned everything he had to tell them about the killing room his storage shed had been turned into.

The Major poured more tea.

'As a matter of fact, he was here just the other day,' he said. He flicked at a cookie crumb which had lodged itself in his moustache. 'Didn't come round to see me, I may say. Saw him trying Nell's front door. Damned impudence. Went out, asked what he wanted. He spun me some cock-and-bull story about something belonging to his wife being left behind. "Look here, matey," I said. "It's a bit late for you to come nosing round here, when you couldn't even be bothered to come to the old girl's funeral. And now everything, including the house itself, belongs to me. So why don't you just clear off?" That sorted him out, I can tell you.' He adopted a slightly sheepish expression. 'Didn't exactly tell him to clear off, but he got my drift.'

While I had no real reason to consider Harkness in any way involved with the actual murder of Tristan Huber, my mind was on high alert. It was equally likely that he had nothing to do with the rip-offs stored in his warehouse. But the bloodstained gurney? Perhaps I was being a little premature in dismissing him. After all, there was a definite connection, since he owned or leased the premises where my friend had been tortured. Perhaps he'd come here to try and retrieve something incriminating from Nell's Roscoe's house. 'I wonder what he really wanted.'

'Sheer nosiness, I should think.'

'Next time you see him, if ever, I wouldn't mind having a word. And now, Major, would it,' I asked diffidently, 'be possible to have a quick look at the work Huber Associates undertook for Mrs Roscoe?'

'Why not? The house is pretty much as she left it. To tell the truth, I haven't had the heart to change anything yet, clear things away, empty cupboards and wardrobes and the like. Get the charity shop people in. There's a lot of clutter to sort out, and Nell was a bit of a magpie, as far as I can tell. Never threw anything away. Only thing I've managed to organize is her fridge.' He grimaced. 'For such a methodical person it was disgusting, to be honest. Stuff going mouldy, everything well past its sell-by date, saucers full of festering God-knows-what. Really doesn't bear thinking about.'

'Does anything else come to mind? I said. 'Like when you first saw Tristan's body behind the hedge? Anything unusual about it – apart from the fact that the poor man had been badly cut about?'

'I can't say I was in particularly observant mode. The

shock . . . it's not what you expect to find when you take the dog for a walk, is it?'

'Do you always go the same way?'

'No. As a matter of fact, as I told you, I'd been away for three or four days, staying with my son and his family near Lincoln. And I see what you're trying to establish: you want to decide how long the body might have been lying there, don't you?'

'That's right. Though I'm sure the police officers on the case have already done that.'

The Major munched on one of his biscuits while he cast his mind back. 'Tell you what,' he said eventually. 'Sounds silly, but I couldn't help noticing what good quality trousers he was wearing.'

'And?' I encouraged. Tristan had always been what my father called a snappy dresser.

'Point being that there wasn't a drop of blood on them.'

'I suppose that's significant in some way, though I—'

'But don't you see? No blood, despite the removal of . . . uh . . . certain parts. How could that have happened?'

I tried to envisage it. Tristan tied to that blood-soaked gurney, pieces of his chest being cut off, the castration. Major Horrocks was right: it was strange. Or was it? 'If he had been stripped naked before they started on him . . . his chest had obviously been swabbed clean.' I tried to keep emotion off my face and out of my voice.

'But why would they bother to dress him again?' He chewed thoughtfully. 'Because, if you think about it, they would have to wait for the blood to dry, wouldn't they? Otherwise, they'd have got it all over the show.'

'True.' I hadn't told him about the third body in the warehouse, which I now knew had been Ned Swift, university student and member of the chess club. I did so now.

'But that's . . . that's absolutely . . .' He paled as he stared at me for a moment before bringing a starched white handkerchief out of his pocket and wiping the sweat from his forehead. Fleetingly it crossed my mind to wonder if these murders could possibly be laid at the Major's door. 'Anyway . . .' He stood up. 'Let's go and take a look at Nell's house, see if you can spot anything out of the ordinary.'

We walked out of the back door and through a gap in the hedge which separated Metcalfe from Rattrays. The Major let us in, using a key which he'd picked up from the mantelpiece before we left.

The next-door cottage greeted us with the mixture of alien smells which always hits you when you step into someone else's home, especially if it hasn't been occupied for a while. Faint remembrances of lavender furniture polish, dog, fusty bed sheets, something rotting, like a piece of forgotten citrus fruit, ancient stair-carpet in need of replacement. And illness. I remembered that the former owner of the house had been removed to the hospital with ulcerated legs and had never come home again.

Somewhere a tap dripped. We walked along a stone-flagged passage, our heels clicking loudly on the hard floor. Little dust-devils stirred in front of us and a couple of silverfish slid secretively away and into cracks in the skirting board. We passed a dusty dining room which contained an oak dresser on which was displayed an enviable Coalport dinner service. There was also a fine antique walnut dining table with a tarnished silver epergne in the centre, and ten chairs set round it. Relic, I imagined of happier days when the old lady had been in her prime, since I found it hard to imagine her hosting a dinner party for ten in the past few years. Beyond that was a small room which had evidently been used as a study-cum-office where Mrs Roscoe paid bills and answered correspondence. The walls were hung with photographs showing ranks of girls in school uniform, the formal shirt and tie ensemble gradually giving way to more relaxed open-necked blouses and navy sweaters as the years went by.

'And this,' the Major said, pushing open a door, 'is the room your friend did over for poor Nell.'

Given the restrictions of the space – low ceiling, heavy beams, small diamond-paned windows – Huber Associates had done a great job of letting in the light without spoiling the character or ambience. Sunshine-yellow walls, white-painted beams, linen slip-covers in various shades of yellow, from palest primrose to organic egg yolk. The walls were lined with purpose-built, white painted bookshelves, all filled with orderly rows of paperbacks. I checked them out. Mostly crime. Mostly contemporary. A shelf of what I knew were called Golden Age detective novels, featuring Dorothy L Sayers, Agatha Christie, Georgette Heyer, Ngiao Marsh, John Dickson Carr and many many others. A painting of an autumnal wood full of gold, orange and red leaves hung above the fireplace.

'This is lovely,' I said. 'So cheerful.'

'And a vast improvement on what it looked like before,' said the Major. He looked round. 'Nell and I spent many a happy hour in here over a glass or two of gin.' He sighed. 'I miss her much more than I ever thought I would.'

I patted his arm. 'By the way, I've been meaning to ask if you've seen any more of our American friend. Todd, or Jerry or whatever he's calling himself these days.'

'Not a sausage.' He sighed again. 'I must say, the chap's an obvious bad 'un, but he was rather fun, wasn't he?'

'I'm fine-tuned to take against criminals,' I said. 'But yes, he was. Still is, I'm sure.'

Not knowing what I hoped to find, I glance around the place. At the moment I could see absolutely no link at all between the retired headmistress and the interior design company, except for the work the one had produced for the other. But the fact that Harkness had been connected to both Mrs Roscoe and the warehouse where Tristan Huber had died had to have some significance.

'Come upstairs,' said the Major. 'I've cleaned it up a bit, done the dirty laundry and so forth. But I haven't had a comprehensive clear out, so it's still pretty much as it always was. Haven't dealt with the clothes in the wardrobes and the chests-of-drawers are still full of poor Nell's clutter.'

I followed behind him. There were three bedrooms, the beds all stripped and tidied.

'Linen cupboard,' said the Major, opening a door to display slatted shelves neatly piled with bed linen, as though I were a prospective buyer. Opening another, 'Bathroom.'

'I wonder what Harkness was after,' I said.

'Could have been anything. Or nothing. He could simply

have wanted to check that there was nothing of Lil's left in the house. And this was Lilian's room, when she visited Nell.' The Major led the way back along the corridor to a room with a double mattress on a mahogany bedstead, pillows covered in black-and-white striped cotton ticking and a puffy pink eiderdown rolled up against the foot. There was a small day-bed covered in faded greeny-blue linen, with several brilliant embroidered cushions piled up against the back. Framed photographs stood on the small cream-painted iron fireplace mantel. 'Feel free to have a look round. I'll be out in the garden when you're finished.'

The room gave off the same aura of innocence as the bedroom of an eight-year-old. I conducted a thorough search but found nothing that seemed significant. After Ms Roscoe's death, and coming into his inheritance, the Major had clearly maintained the place, without getting shot of much. For instance, when I opened Lilian's wardrobe, there were still a couple of her cardigans hanging up, a limp and shapeless dress, two awful old pleated skirts, a much-washed blouse. Lilian obviously didn't feel the need to dress up when she was staying with Cousin Nell. There was also a magnificent pink brocade robe, heavily embroidered in gold and red and green, with tiny oriental birds flaunting long tails, and a proliferation of peonies and mop-head chrysanthemums. It seemed at odds with the pathetically shabby rest.

The old-fashioned mahogany chest-of-drawers held a lipstick, three loose pearl beads, a tatty hairbrush. In the second drawer down, there were a couple of greying bras, some rolled-up tights, and a waist-petticoat. Sad stuff for a sad lady. I was about to close the drawer again when I noticed one of the pairs of tights. Something square and hard had been concealed in it. I unrolled it and found a blister-pack of contraceptive pills, with five already removed. Looked like the downtrodden wife had fought back against her bullying husband's unreasonable demand that she conceive yet again. Good for her!

In the drawer of the left-hand bedside table, I found a lavender sachet, a small tin of Vaseline (I really didn't want to go there), a lace-edged handkerchief, and a novel by

Raymond Chandler. On the other side of the bed, the drawer was empty.

I did another sweep of the rooms, not knowing what I was supposed to be looking out for. I turned back the edges of the carpets on the floors. Tapped the nice Victorian tiles set around the fireplace, listening for the sound of hollowness. Felt behind the bedsteads and underneath the drawers. Lifted the mattresses and shifted the sheets and pillowcases in the linen-cupboard. Came up with zip.

I forced myself to think. If Harkness had been trying to get into the house, it seemed logical to assume that he not only knew there was something in it that he wanted, he also probably knew where it was. But was it Lilian's, or something of Nell's?

I went downstairs again and started the same search in the reception rooms and kitchen. It could take forever to find something, even something specific. No wonder that intruders throw everything on to the floor: flour, sugar, buckets of coal, the contents of drawers. Boxes, suitcases, sofa cushions. No wonder they always leave such a mess.

I stood at the doorway of Ms Roscoe's study. A desk against the wall, its contents neatly pigeonholed. An old-fashioned wooden swivel chair, with polished arms, stood in front of it. On the seat lay a cushion cross-stitched with a pattern of forget-me-nots and rosebuds. I could easily picture the former headmistress stitching away of an evening, head bent beneath a one hundred-watt lamp, rimless glasses slipping down her nose until they were pushed back into place.

I sat down on the moulded seat and examined the contents of the desk. A small pile of spiral-bound notebooks lay in one pigeonhole and I pulled them out. Flipping through the pages of the top one, I could see that she had only got half way through before she was carted off to hospital. I opened it and read a neatly-written description of a robin pulling a worm out of the garden soil. It was the sort of exercise she might have set her own students (*'All right, girls, settle down. You have fifteen minutes to produce a short essay on what you saw on your way to school this morning'*). There was another: a spirited (and very funny) description of Major Horrocks's struggles to produce anything remotely resembling any object known to man from his box hedges.

I picked up the notebook below that and opened it at random. It was clear that she frequently took the dog Dashiell through the woods in order to spy on Harkness. She seemed adamantly convinced that it was Harkness himself who had deliberately run over ('*murdered*') Dashiell, Marlowe's predecessor. She detailed the comings and goings at the Harkness warehouse, after Lilian's death. (*'I feel I owe it to her to keep an eye on whatever it is he's up to*'). As far as she could make out, there were flurries of activity out there, followed by long periods when nothing happened. Boxes and crates being delivered, sometimes two or three times a week. At other times, consignments being removed. Marlowe (or Dashiell, as it might once have been) provided her with a legitimate excuse for snooping on the place. The arriving goods were stashed in the warehouse by workers who were not what Nell delicately called English people . . . not *English* English. I took this to mean they were of ethnic origin in some way. Africans? Or – here I had a light-bulb moment, only for it to flicker and die out – were they Asians? More specifically, Chinese? Employed by, or even members of, a Triad? I should have asked the Landis/Lockharts what nationality the workers on their barn conversion had been. In fact I might go over there again tomorrow and stick my nose into their business a little deeper than I had previously done.

The Major probably wouldn't even realize if I removed a few of the more recent notebooks. They could always be returned when I'd finished trawling through them. Back in his cottage, I mentioned the robe in Lilian's bedroom.

'Oh yes,' he said. 'Her husband brought it back for her from one of his business trips abroad. I understood from Nell Roscoe that she never wore it.'

'Why was that, do you think?'

'Because I believe that she couldn't stand the blasted man. Not after his selfish behaviour, treating her like a . . . like a reproductive vessel. It's an insult to womanhood, doesn't bear thinking about.'

'Did he often go abroad?'

'Often enough. Gave the poor woman a bit of a rest.'

'That robe looked Chinese or Indian.'

Major Horrocks nodded. 'Indeed . . . I know he had commercial interests out in that part of the world.'

'But you don't know which part?'

'Sorry. No.'

I headed for the door. 'By the way, Major, if you're planning to sell the books, give my friend Sam Willoughby from the bookshop first refusal.'

'He can take the lot, far as I'm concerned. I'm not much of a fiction reader, I'm afraid. Frankly, he'd be doing me a favour.'

FIFTEEN

I woke to cloudless blue skies. Gulls were peaceful on the rocking water, which was banded with colours shading from translucent green to Mediterranean blue. Summer had reinstated itself. My heart lifted, although my dreams had been confused: egg-ridden, pantomime-damed, Philip-Marlowed. Lying awake as morning gradually unfolded, I considered Tristan and his punitive death. What could he have done to deserve so violent an end?

I picked up my phone and dialled. 'Quick here,' I said, when Fliss Fairlight answered.

'What do you want now?'

God, she sounded just like my brother. 'Has Garside come up with any motive for Tristan Huber's death?'

'Not as far as I'm aware. Why?'

'Find the motive, find the man, as they say. Thing is, Fliss, I'm starting to wonder if Tristan had actually killed someone.'

'When you say "killed"—'

'I'm saying *murdered* someone.' If the possibility had suggested such a thing to me earlier, I would have maintained it wasn't possible, insisted Tristan wasn't that sort of guy, wasn't into stuff like that. Now, I couldn't be so certain.

'Do you mean deliberately?' asked Fliss.

'That's exactly what I mean.' And I didn't need to be an expert on Triads to know that if Tristan had killed one of their members, whether accidentally or on purpose, retribution would be swift and terrible.

'And if he had, where would this murder have taken place? Here in our neck of the woods. Somewhere else in the country. Out in Europe or the Far East?'

'It was a conjecture, not a statement of fact.' A conjecture which, now I'd come up with it, was rapidly taking solid shape inside my head. Because what else could have lain behind his ugly death? On the other hand, there was the castration. Perhaps he had been guilty of no more than sleeping with someone he should not have done. Which of course added the sexual element. Jealous husbands, furious fathers, vengeful brothers had killed for the violation of their women down through the ages. Could he have seduced the mother, wife or sister of a Triad member? Of course they'd have had mothers, but do they even *have* wives or sisters?

'Whatevs . . .' said Fliss. 'Like I told you, I don't think Garside's found out anything really concrete about the victim, let alone whether there's a murder in his background, or what the motive for his murder might have been.'

'Tell him to get his finger out.'

'I'll be sure to do that.'

Ending the call, I speculated on why I disliked Garside so much. He did, after all, get results. He ran a team of loyal and efficient officers. He wasn't bent. He was human, like the rest of us. I'd even seen him smile. Once. Was it because he insisted on playing by the rules at all times? (Not that I believe in breaking them. They exist for a reason.) I've never believed in hunches and conjecture, though I'll admit that there is sometimes a place for inspired guesswork based on very little beyond intuition. But Garside carried things to extremes, so damned cautious, in case he put a foot wrong, that it was amazing that any of his cases ever got solved. On top of that was his friendship with Jack Martin.

I made coffee and sat down at my desk with the notebooks I'd nicked from Nell Roscoe's cottage. They were written in that childishly clear hand, somewhere between copperplate and traditional cursive, which seems to belong specifically to teachers. They were very far from diaries. More a record of things seen, done, witnessed, speculated upon. People she had met, places she'd visited. Pupils or teachers who'd done something particularly good or outstandingly bad. Observations on her garden during the changing seasons. A couple more hilarious descriptions of the Major and his topiarial efforts. I pictured her hunched over the lined page of her current notebook. Was this to be my fate too? Living bleakly alone, no family of my own, my life virtually over and only a few artistic compilations to show for it? I shuddered. Please God, no.

At first reading, I found nothing that seemed in the slightest bit germane, apart from a short entry in the first few pages of the most recent notebook – at least, I assumed it was because it had been the topmost one in Nell Roscoe's desk – which read as follows: *I don't know why, but these days, Harkness is looking fraught and anxious. Good. Serves him right, after all he's put Lilian through.*

So Harkness was worried about something. I'd like to have known what. Was it simply the fact that he was becoming nervous at the possibility that his warehouse was being used for criminal enterprises? I needed to ring Fliss again to find out whether he had been interviewed by the police, and if he had, what, if anything, did they learn from him?

Perhaps he'd been aware of what was taking place on his premises but been powerless to prevent it. Perhaps he had been plumb ignorant and the news had come as a nasty shock. Or maybe he had known in advance – blackmailed or strong-armed into agreement what was going to take place – hence the fraught and anxious bit. I could easily get his phone number from the Major and call him direct to ask, but from what I'd heard, I had a feeling that if I did, I'd get a bloody rude response.

Still too restless to concentrate on work, and with the sun blazing down outside, I decided I needed to go in search of a coffee and some information.

The air along the front was salty and glittering. I filled my lungs, savouring it as I walked. I turned down towards the High Street and through the open door of the bookshop. Sam was at his desk, reading, the sun catching his hair, and I was struck again by the fact that for a bloke who wore specs, he was pretty much of a hunk. One of the pleasures I'd forfeited by abandoning the gym was the sight of Sam Willoughby keeping himself fit, in readiness for the day his country came calling.

He didn't realize I was there until I snapped my fingers under his nose. He jumped back, gasping. 'Don't *do* that,' he said, his voice higher than usual.

'Just testing your reflexes, Willoughby,' I said. 'And I'm not terribly impressed, if truth be told. As a possible MI5 agent, you're supposed to be on the alert at all times, not shrieking like a girl encountering a mouse every time someone approaches you.'

He picked up his book, which had fallen to the floor. 'I was deep into the story,' he said. 'And for once, the characters are empathetic. There seems to be a growing trend these days for thrillers and crime novels which are full of people whom I intensely dislike, even if they're the main protagonists. Anyway, can I get you a coffee?'

'Yes, please. And then come and tell me what you discovered when you went up the hill.'

He appeared three minutes later with two mugs of coffee. 'Loved by all,' he said, when I questioned him further with regard to Kevin Fuller. 'Popular, clever, fearless and kind. A thoroughly nice guy.'

'A saint, in other words.' Which was pretty much how Dorcas Huber-Drayton had described her son, Tristan. But then she would, wouldn't she?

'No, just a good human being.'

'And everyone agreed? No dissenting voices?'

'None whatsoever. Everyone I spoke to seemed completely shocked that anyone could have murdered the guy. One person suggested that given his known sexual orientation, it could have been a homophobic thing that got out of hand, some Christian fundamentalist nutter or someone.'

'Presumably there are groups of them up at the uni.'

'Yes, but I asked and everyone was adamant that they were harmless and inoffensive.'

'Whatever your religious beliefs, murder does seem a bit extreme.'

'Come on, Alex. That has to be one of the more brainless remarks ever made.'

'I meant at college level, not at a biblical or even global level.'

'Whatever . . .' Sam unfolded a sheet of paper and smoothed it out on the table in front of him. 'As well as all his sporting prowess, he was also active in student life, heading up various committees and so on. Especially when it was party time, like the Graduation Party, the Freshers' Bash, the Founders Day Celebration etcetera, etcetera.'

'I know about the redecoration of the student common rooms. Anything else?'

'There's a thriving international exchange programme. Both students and lecturers take part. You know the sort of thing . . . you send someone out to the University of Adelaide, and the Adelaide people send someone over here. Our man was involved in that, choosing who would get to go and where to, organizing grants and so on. And then there's the—'

'Which countries were there exchanges with?'

Sam looked down at his notes again. 'Australia, USA, Russia, China, India. Five every year.'

'And did Kevin go himself?'

'According to the department secretary, he went once to Russia and once to China.'

'How long for?'

'Russia for three semesters, China for two, at HKU, as we old China hands call it.'

'HKU being the University of Hong Kong?'

'Correct.'

'Yay! I'll just bet he was in Hong Kong at the same time as Tristan Huber.'

'And if he was, what would that prove?'

'I'm not a hundred per cent sure at the moment. But I just know it's significant in some important way. Gotta be. Stands to reason.'

Sam produced another sheet of paper. A4, this time, not torn out of a lined notepad. 'I also found this . . .' He saw my raised eyebrows. 'Summer's not my busiest season, as far as selling books is concerned. People check out the second-hand and charity shops, since they know they're going to be leaving the book behind once they've finished it. No point paying money for a new one.' He grinned. 'Which is why I have plenty of time for trawling the Internet, thank you.'

'Did I say anything?'

'Didn't have to. I knew what you were thinking. Anyway, look at this . . .'

I took the page from his hand. It said:

> *A typical initiation ceremony takes place at a dedicated altar with incense and an animal sacrifice, usually a chicken, pig or goat. After drinking a mixture of wine and blood of the animal or the candidate, the member will pass beneath an arch of swords while reciting the triad's oaths. The paper on which the oaths are written will be burnt on the altar to confirm the member's obligation to perform his duties to the gods.*

'Sounds revolting,' I said. 'Any ideas what these oaths are?'

'This is where we might be getting somewhere. There are about twenty of them,' explained Sam. 'I printed out what I considered to be the most interesting, when you look at the penalties to be inflicted if the member breaks the oath.'

I read some more.

> *I shall never embezzle cash or property from my sworn brothers. If I break this oath I will be killed by myriads of swords.*
>
> *I will always acknowledge my sworn brothers when they identify themselves. If I ignore them I will be killed by myriads of swords.*
>
> *I shall not disclose the secrets of the Triad family, not even to my parents, brothers, or wife. I shall never disclose the secrets for money. I will be killed by myriads of swords if I do so.*

'*Myriads of swords*.' I frowned. 'That sounds pretty much like what happened to Tristan.' I swallowed, trying not to think about the knives and the cutting.

'If the oaths and his death are connected, which oath do you think he broke?' Sam asked.

'The first seems most likely. Embezzlement, or theft, from someone in the Triad organization. He's hardly likely to be divulging Triad secrets to his mother or sister, as if they'd be interested. And there'd be absolutely no reason at all for him to be dissing any of his sworn brothers if they showed up in Longbury.'

'Except that from what you told me, his commissions came from all over the globe.'

'Yes but think about it. He's in Dubai or San Francisco and encounters some guy who makes with the funny handshake or whatever . . . why wouldn't he just say, "Oh, hi there, let me buy you a drink"?'

'Mind you, this is all guesswork,' Sam said.

'But pretty informed guesswork. At least, I think so. I'll bet you those deeper cuts which my friend Fliss Fairlight mentioned were to make sure there was no identifying mark left on the body.'

'Except we have absolutely no evidence which even suggests he's been allowed to become a member of a Triad. Let alone be tattooed.'

My mobile rang. When I answered, a voice whispered hoarsely, 'He's here.'

'What?'

'He's *here*,' insisted the voice.

'Hello? Who is this?'

'Horrocks here. Just trying to say that Harkness is at his storage facility. Better get down here so you don't miss him.'

'I'm on it.' Flipping the phone shut, I got up. 'Gotta go, Sam. Right now.' Before Sam could react, someone walked into the shop. The same damn woman as I'd seen last time I was in here. 'Thanks for all your help,' I added, 'and have fun with your customer.'

* * *

'He's down there,' the Major said, *sotto voce*, as though afraid he could be overheard if he spoke above a whisper. We were standing in the rustic little porch of Rattrays. He jerked his chin at the woods. 'Don't know what he's up to, don't want to, either.'

'Thanks for letting me know. I'll walk down and see what I can find out.'

'Want me to come along? Provide back-up for you?'

'Well . . .' I had no idea whether Harkness was a giant or a dwarf. I'd have guessed the former. Friendly or aggressive? I'd have guessed the latter.

'Or I could just stay in the background, ready to pitch in if needed,' whispered the Major.

'That would be a good idea. But keep out of sight unless it proves necessary to show yourself.'

'Roger wilco, over and out,' said the Major. There was a warm flush to his cheeks. His moustache was eager. I guessed he was reliving his glory days in the Army. He moved carefully after me, dodging from tree trunk to tree trunk as I set off towards the shelter of the woodland.

I looked back once and could have sworn he had an oriental dagger clenched between his teeth. But I'd be the first to admit that I have an overactive imagination. I trod along the mossy track. I could see the walls of the warehouse between tree trunks, a grey smudge which could have been mistaken for a lowering sky hanging above the town beyond. Nell Roscoe must have come here on a regular basis, keeping an eye on her niece's challenging husband when he appeared. Had she stood at the edge of the trees, or had she crept in closer to peer through the door which today was open? What did she suspect him of, other than being a domestic tyrant?

I paused to consider strategy. Should I march straight in, beard Harkness, announce who I was and what my interest might be? Or did I pretend to be an innocent passer-by, taking what I hoped was a shortcut to the shops? Or should I just play it by ear, taking my cue from whatever front Harkness presented? After all, I knew very little about the man . . . I'd adopted Major Horrocks's probably prejudiced view of him without having a chance to form my own opinion. For all I knew, the man was a pussycat.

Either way, giving Harkness some warning of my approach seemed like a good idea. I didn't want him to realize someone was there and come racing out with a gun or a knife in his hand so I kicked at stones along the path, coughed loudly, even managed a fake sneeze, while swishing the undergrowth about as noisily as possible.

Harkness must have heard me, for he appeared at the door. Only a tattered piece of police tape, still wrapped round a couple of tree trunks and flapping dismally when the breeze stirred, indicated that just a short time ago, this had been a crime scene. The SOCOs had obviously been and gone. 'Can I help you?' His tone was not exactly welcoming, but at least there were no visible knives or guns. He was a big man, his shirt straining across a prize-fighter's torso, with florid cheeks and a belt hidden beneath the overhang of his belly.

'Oh, Mr Har—it *is* Mr Harkness, isn't it?' I said. Ingenuous as hell.

'Yes.' His agreement was grudging, as though he wasn't going to give up his name without a fight.

My brain felt jammed, as though a tube of superglue had been emptied into it. I could think of nothing plausible to say, either about why I knew his name or what I'd come for.

'You're not a reporter, are you?' He took a step forward, clenching his fists. 'Better not be.' His burgundy cheeks swelled. If this guy was a pussycat, I wouldn't be stroking him any time soon.

'Absolutely not. No way.' I stepped back and opted for the partial truth. 'I'm sorry about what happened here recently. The murder.'

'So am I.'

'It's just, the victim was a good friend of mine. I can't help wondering how and why he was brought here, of all places, and who might have been responsible.'

'I hope you're not looking at me,' he said savagely. 'As I already told the police, I have no idea why this place should have been chosen by whichever murderous brute was to blame.'

'You'd almost think it was someone local, wouldn't you? I mean, who else would know about it? It's pretty damned isolated.'

'From what I understand, the . . . uh . . . victim lived around here. I'd imagine his killer would have scouted the location before abducting him, wouldn't you? Cased the joint and so on, then broken into my premises. It wouldn't be difficult. In fact . . .' He beckoned me to follow him as he led the way round the side of his building, '. . . look at that!' He pointed out the place where I had pushed my way inside some days earlier.

'Goodness,' I said.

'That's obviously where they got in. Man squeezes in, goes and opens the door, they drag the poor sod inside and set about hacking him to pieces.'

'I wonder why *now*?' It was a question I'd failed to consider before.

He shrugged. 'No idea.'

'It must have been a shock for you to discover what had happened. Especially since you knew Tristan Huber.'

'Knew him? What're you talking about?'

I looked puzzled. 'Oh. That's odd. I was told that you two were friends, out in Hong Kong.'

His face grew dark. 'Who told you that?'

'Um . . .' I snapped my fingers. 'Gosh, my memory . . .'

'Whoever it was, they were mistaken. I've never been to Hong Kong.'

Surely that wasn't true. Especially given that silk wrap hanging in Lilian's wardrobe. 'Strange,' I murmured. 'I could have sworn . . .'

'You'd have been perjuring yourself. I had a stopover there once, on the way to Perth, that's all. Didn't even leave the airport.' Too much information, I thought. As soon as they start weaselling round with unnecessary detail, you know they're lying. 'In any case . . .' He squared up to me, '. . . who the hell *are* you?'

'Oh sorry . . . I should have introduced myself. Quick, Alex Quick. Like I said, I knew Tristan too.'

He drew in an exasperated breath. 'I already told you, I didn't know the man. Not here, not in Hong Kong, not anywhere. Anyway, what right do you have to come poking around here, asking questions which are none of your business?'

None at all, obviously. I inched round so I could see into the interior of the building. The place had been cleaned up since my last visit. There was no sign of the bloodstained gurney, which I assumed the police must have removed as evidence. Nor of the pallets loaded with counterfeit goods. Had they been shipped on, or simply taken away to another location? Or even seized by the police? 'Shall you keep this place on? I mean, after what happened?'

'Of course!' he snapped. 'Why wouldn't I?'

'Painful memories and so on . . .'

'Look, I feel sorry for the guy who was killed, but I had absolutely nothing to do with it.'

I was inclined to believe him. I half-turned away, as though about to leave, then turned back. 'Funny about you never meeting Tristan Huber. My informant seemed quite definite on the point.'

'Sorry, but he – or she – was wrong. Thinking of someone else entirely.'

'Well, thank you anyway.' From the corner of my eye I could just see the Major, lurking in a thicket of elder bushes.

Harkness waited at the door of the building as I left, thick arms folded across his chest. Poor Lilian, I thought, having to submit to the man's embraces when she had no wish to do so. How soul-destroying, to be desired only for procreational purposes. Love-making reduced to nothing more than some loutish man forcing his way inside your body without tenderness or feeling, in order to plant his seed in your unreceptive womb. It didn't bear thinking about, as the Major so often said.

When I was back in my flat, I checked Harkness out on the Internet again, in greater detail. It was something I should have done earlier. It didn't take long to find a website for W. J. Harkness & Sons, established 1894, currently conducting business from an industrial estate outside Bedford. Their main business seemed to consist of manufacturing bicycles of various kinds and their complicated components. Bottom brackets, derailleur hangers, shifters, headsets, freewheels, chains, dozens and dozens of elaborate items of equipment. Widgets, in other words, as the Major had said. Not to mention gadgets.

It seemed that the company had been handed down from father to son for over a hundred years. No wonder Harkness was so desperate for an heir. I wondered if he had found a new woman who would give him the son he wanted so much. Or, indeed, had already done so.

Glancing out of the window as I got up to pour a glass of a new Shiraz I'd bought from Edward Vine's shop, I saw a racing green Jaguar parked along the seafront. It had been there a couple of days ago, too. Nice car, if a bit showy. I sighed. I didn't suppose I would ever aspire to a car costing anything like that – or looking anything like that.

Maybe I should start charging Dimsie Drayton for the time I was spending on looking into her brother's murder.

SIXTEEN

Just occasionally, providence plays into your hands. Without me having to go out and find her, or track her down by phone, Dimsie showed up at my front door two days later, and rang the bell, keeping her finger pressed down until I opened up. Grim-faced and emitting stale wafts of yesterday's scent (most un-Dimsie-like), she marched in and plonked herself down on the sofa.

'She's here,' she announced. She picked my glass dolphin up from the coffee table and tried to balance it on its tail. Couldn't be done. I'd tried many times.

'Is she?' I said, itching to take the dolphin away. If it tipped over, it would break in two.

'Right here in town.'

'Ah . . .'

'Are you going to speak to her?' demanded Dimsie. Mercifully she put down the dolphin and lifted the triangular leather box banded with copper wire, which one of Meghan's handsome Italian craftsmen had made especially for me ('*la tua bella sorella*'). She couldn't break that.

'What about?'

'Tristan's murder, of course. The police don't seem to be getting anywhere.'

'I possibly would, if—'

'Not that I expect she has anything useful to tell you. But you might just pick something up from her. A clue or something.'

'Dimsie, who the hell are we talking about here?'

She stared at me as though I had started speaking in tongues. 'Christie, of course,' she said impatiently. 'Who did you think?'

Christie. Tristan's former wife. Here in Longbury? 'Why do you think she's come?'

'I imagine she heard about Tristan, wanted to establish a presence. Maybe hoping for something in his will.'

Oooh, bitchy. 'Or maybe to offer condolences to your mother, or you? Or something?'

Dimsie snorted. 'She'd be on a hiding to nothing if she tried that with my mother. Dorcas is unlikely to accept commiserations from the woman who dared to reject her son.'

'What about you? If she dropped round to see you, would you be nice?'

Dimsie considered. 'I'd be polite,' she said. 'Icy, but polite. But then she hasn't contacted me, so the matter doesn't actually arise, does it?'

'Why can't you talk to her? If she's got anything useful to say, she'd be more likely to open up to you than to a total stranger.'

'Only problem there is that she hates my guts – probably with good reason. I wasn't very nice to her. She'd just clam up if she saw me.'

'Or make an excuse and leave.'

'That too. Oh Alex, you aren't going to let me down, are you?'

I sighed. Loudly. Heavily. Just so Dimsie would realize what a time-wasting hassle this was. 'Any idea where I'd find this woman?'

'I was told that she was staying at the Admiral.'

The Admiral is the best hotel in the area, situated on the seafront on the other side of town, many of its rooms possessing extensive sea views, with balconies from which to enjoy them, plus a chef constantly hailed as one of the best in southern England. 'I'll mosey on down there, see if I can catch her,' I said. A thought struck me. 'Have you informed the police that she's here? They might want to ask her some questions.'

'I haven't yet. Besides, like I said, I don't suppose she knows anything at all that would be helpful. I only told you because you asked about her.'

'What's her story these days?'

'I haven't particularly kept up. I've got better ways to spend my time than keeping tabs on my brother's ex-wife.'

'So have I, Dim.'

'Oh Alex . . . I'm sorry.'

Suck it up, Alex . . . 'When's the best time to catch her?'

'Five thirty onwards, in the bar, I should think,' Dimsie said promptly, her pretty mouth forming itself into a semi-sneer. 'She likes a drink or two, does our Christie. Or even three.'

'That's got to be her,' Sam said. I'd roped him in to coming with me to the saloon bar of the Admiral Hotel. The woman he had indicated was at a table, talking to a couple of the retired nautical, navy-blue blazered, yachting-capped types who lived in the town, still dreaming of their days before the mast and happy to tell you all about them. At great length. She was unmistakably Christie. I'd seen her before, but only in photos. She'd put on quite a bit of weight since then.

At first glance she seemed immediately likable, *très sympathique*. She was a large lady, with masses of golden hair arranged in the kind of complicated chignon that she couldn't possibly have done herself. So either she travelled with a lady's maid or, much more likely, had paid an afternoon visit to the beauty parlour. She wore white linen trousers, a loose tunic of dark green linen, heavy statement necklaces of jade and beaten silver round her neck, the ensemble completed by expensive high-heeled boots which must have cost a bomb. Draped over the back of her chair was a flowered jacket which I'd seen featured on an emaciated model in the most recent issue of *Vogue* at a price which had made my hair bleed just thinking about it. At her feet was a gorgeous green leather bag.

She laughed at something one of the old tars had said, an attractive, full-bodied laugh, loud and slightly coarse, and spread her hands, which were covered in large emerald and diamond rings, so big I almost doubted if they could be real. But she didn't look like the sort of woman who wore fake jewellery. So she was either loaded, or else shacked up with someone pretty affluent.

Seated at another table, I trained my demonic powers on her, willing her to look my way. Which she finally did. I waved encouragingly and indicated the empty third chair between me and Sam. She looked puzzled, but after a while, she made gracious signs of withdrawal, went to the bar and ordered drinks for the two guys, twinkled her fingers at them and came over to join us.

Sam stood up and pulled the spare chair out for her. 'I'm Quick. Alexandra Quick,' I said.

'I recognize the name.' She gave us both a big smile.

'I'm a friend of Dimsie Drayton's.' Too late I realized this was hardly a recommendation, given the hostility between the two of them.

'Dimsie . . .' Her forehead wrinkled. 'Didn't I see that poor woman on eBay not long ago, trying to pick up a second-hand brain cell?'

You didn't have to be seated within half a mile of her to pick up the vibes. 'Um . . .' I said, wondering what the best way to deal with her sudden change in attitude was.

'So if you're a friend of dear Dim's, you must also have been a friend of my former husband's.' She raised her chin confrontationally. All signs of amiability had vanished. 'In fact, thinking back, I know you were.'

'This is true.'

'And what exactly is your role in this, Ms Quick? I assume you're not with the police.'

'Not any more,' I said. 'It's just that Dimsie asked me to look into Tristan's death—'

'Tristan's *murder*, Ms Quick. Tell it like it is.'

'— independently of the police, since she thought they might not keep her in the groove.'

'No reason why they should.' Christie stared at us both for a moment, then rummaged in her beautiful bag and pulled out a paper tissue. 'Please don't think that I wasn't desperately sorry to learn of Tristan's death,' she said. 'It was a particularly unpleasant way to go, to put it mildly. But our divorce was pretty damned nasty, not to say antagonistic.' She sighed. 'Of course, the whole break-up was cleverly manipulated by his mother and his sister, neither of whom thought I was anywhere good enough for him. Poor old Tris just didn't know which way was up when those two bitches had finished with him. By which time, I was pretty much eager to get away before blood was drawn.'

'Do you have the slightest idea why he was killed, or who might have been responsible?' Sam asked.

'None at all. Mind you, he moved in some fairly strange circles. Both here and in Hong Kong.'

'I hadn't realized that Tristan was married when he was out there,' I said.

'He wasn't. He and I first met in the MO Bar. I was working for one of the multi-nationals at the time. The job meant I had to take visiting clients and prospective customers out and about, show them a good time – and indicate where they could get an even better one, if they wanted to.'

'You said strange circles,' Sam said.

'I'd often run across him in different bars, huddled over a table at the back of the room, in deep conversation with various dodgy-looking characters. I just assumed that drug deals were going down, as they so often did out there.'

'A bit public for that sort of thing, wasn't it?'

She shrugged. 'I brought it up a couple of times, after we were married, but Tris maintained it was just normal legitimate business meetings, that people out there like to conduct business over refreshment or entertainment of some kind. I had no reason not to believe him. Why would I? First flush of love and all that.' There was sadness in her eyes.

'But that changed?' Sam asked.

'I'll say. I quickly learned never to enquire too closely into his business affairs. But I'm not a total moron. I knew perfectly well that he was involved in some pretty dodgy deals. Worse than dodgy.' She frowned. 'Think of some of the very worst rackets you can, and Tristan was part of them, if not instigating them. I fell madly in love with him the first moment I clapped eyes on him, but I gradually realized that he was utterly ruthless, quite merciless, didn't give a toss what filthy business he dirtied his hands with, as long as there was money in it. *Big* money. He would do anything for money, and absolutely nothing and nobody was allowed to stand in his way.'

'And may I ask why you've returned to Longbury now?'

She looked away, twirled the stem of her glass, then lifted it and drained the contents in a single swallow. 'Wouldn't you, if it was your husband, divorced or not, who'd just been murdered?'

Would I? If my in-laws were hostile, and my divorce had been a nasty one? And the husband himself had been a right bastard? I tried to imagine Jack Martin the Love Rat found dead in ugly circumstances, and what I would do. 'Do you have connections here?' I asked.

'Not really. There are people I know here, from when we were still together, but none of them very well.'

'Will you be staying long?' Sam asked.

Again she shrugged. Looked down at the table top. Twisted round in her seat and gestured to the guy behind the bar for refills. 'I . . . I'm not sure.'

She was stalling. I glanced at Sam and could tell he was thinking the same. I couldn't think of anything else to ask her. Nor was I clear in my own mind as to whether meeting up with her had achieved anything but a muddying of already murky waters.

The bartender brought our fresh drinks over. I liked a drink, but I couldn't get them down at the rate that Christie was managing. I decorously lifted mine and put it down without tasting it. 'I have no official role here,' I said, 'but there's one last question: do you know some people called Landis?'

She was good, but she couldn't disguise an involuntary jerk of surprise, though she tried, fussing with the tissue which had been tucked just inside her sleeve, dabbing at her nose as though she'd suppressed an abortive sneeze.

She shook her head. Made a face by throwing her lips forwards. 'Landis? Never heard of them.'

Is that so?

But why would she lie?

She leaned towards me. 'If you're looking for a motive for Tris's death, I'll tell you this for nothing. As I'm sure you're aware, he was a hard man. Very much a tooth-for-a-toother was our Tris. You do him wrong, he'd do you a worse wrong right back. Maybe someone resented it. Maybe he overdid the score-settling.' She spread her hands. 'I know nothing . . . have no suspicions. It's just a possibility, is all I'm saying.'

'Someone bore him a grudge?' Sam said.

'It's more than likely.'

Why would she bring this up so soon after I mentioned the name Landis? Was she trying to tell us something?

I checked out the clock on the wall above the bar. It was time to leave. 'Well, enjoy the rest of your time here,' I said. 'I assume you'll drop in at the cop-shop at some point. They'll be interested in what you can tell them.'

As we left the room, I glanced back. Christie had already reached across the table and was swallowing my untouched drink.

Sam was having dinner with some friends, so I had a long bath, washed my hair and wrapped myself in my dressing-gown. Made cheese on toast and quartered an apple. Sat down in the corner of the sofa and switched on the TV. As usual the fare on offer made me want to cut my own head off with a blunt nail file, or else pull all my teeth out with an eyebrow tweezer. I went into rant mode. Dumbing down. Mindless pap. Pandering to the lowest common denominator. If I didn't enjoy watching Wimbledon Fortnight in the summer, and rugby during the winter, I wouldn't have a set at all.

I knew I ought to get on with *Eat, Drink and Be Merry*. I'd received a cheery email from my publishers only the day before, informing me that they were so much looking forward to receiving the manuscript when it was ready and hoping that everything was going well. Which in publisher-speak meant: don't forget your looming deadline. I was well aware. I had all the illustrations ready: I just needed to complete the final accompanying texts.

It was proving much harder than it ought to. Tristan's death weighed heavily on me. Unsettled, melancholy, I knew I wouldn't be able to concentrate on my work. In front of me was the brand-new book of Japanese prints which had arrived that morning. Delicate and charming, each picture triggering ideas for another anthology, I intended to go through the pages slowly, making notes. I was about to reach for it, but leaning forward, I caught sight of Chris Kearns' book lying beside it. I could see that three sections of black-and-white photographs interspersed the pages of the volume.

I love looking at the photos in biographies. Often they're the most interesting part. I flipped through this one. Here were the Kearns grandparents, the Kearns parents. Here were big moustaches, hats like flower stalls, terrible teeth. Striped bathing dresses and straw boaters. The piers at Margate and Clacton. Chris in a pram. Chris as a boy in a school cap and tie. He wrote well. Even engagingly, his text spiced with amusing anecdotes and references. Despite myself, I found I was drawn into his disaster-strewn story.

He had a happy childhood – or was that simply emotion recollected in tranquillity? I often wonder where truth lies in memoirs. Was childhood indeed as idyllic as brilliant memoirists like Laurie Lee or Dirk Bogarde portrayed it? Truth is always subjective and rarely absolute. Apart from the misery-memoirs – and how truthful are they? – in retrospect, the golden sun of yesteryear seems to shine continually, far brighter than any contemporary real life sun. On the other hand, were I to write my own record of childhood, I'd be hard put to it to find anything negative or traumatic to record. The death of a pet, a teacher's caustic comments . . . hardly the stuff of bestsellerdom. Especially if not followed by a noteworthy later life.

Kearns married the girl who lived next door. Moved into a flat. Undertook various menial jobs, none of which he was very good at. I realized I'd already been given a potted version of this over the Indian dinner, when he'd come over to talk to the am-dram group. He worked the men's clubs, the comedy workshops, made promotional videos for anyone who asked, contributed material to other more successful comedians' TV shows, his name one of those in the lines which whizzed past at the end of the programme. He voiced a disagreeable beetle in a Pixar production. He had an ability to make his life sound like a series of comic sketches, which in a way it was.

He began to get better known on the circuits and in panto. He played the nervous fiancé in a popular radio series, and did the voiceover for a series of ads. An old mate gave him a chance. Success beckoned. Children arrived. The youngest died of cot death at ten days old. His wife began to drink. He started—

Hang about . . . what was I thinking? I'd been reading this rubbish for over an hour now.

Except, much as I hated to admit it, it wasn't rubbish.

There were more photos. Kearns' wedding day. His children: Damian and Zoe. A publicity release of him horsing around on a Morecambe and Wise Christmas Special. I read more of the narrative, but it became increasingly beset by heartbreak. I decided to leave the rest for another day.

I was tucked up in bed with Bertie Wooster when the phone rang. 'Quick,' I said.

'Fliss here. Tell me, does this sound familiar to you, seeing as how you know the Huber-Draytons so well?'

There was silence. 'Does what?' I said, after a moment.

'Oh sorry. It's just we've had that woman, Tristan Huber's mother, down here at the station, or telephoning, complaining that someone's trying to spook her. Sending notes or making phone calls, saying "this is what it feels like".'

'What is?'

'*This . . .*'

'Wonder what that means.'

'Exactly.'

'Presumably it has something to do with Tristan's murder.'

'Just what I thought. So I wondered if – unless it's unconnected to her son – it might be some childhood catchphrase you used in the days of your youth. Or a game you all used to play together.'

'Not that I remember,' I said. 'Though even if it was, I can't see what it would have to do with Dorcas. She wasn't exactly the kind of mother you sat down to play Monopoly with. Have you asked Dimsie Drayton? She'd be more likely to know than I would.'

'It was her who suggested we call you, since it meant bugger all to her.'

'"This is what it feels like"?'

'That's right.'

I shook my head. 'No, doesn't mean a thing.'

Having ended the call, I lay back on my pillows, P. G. Wodehouse abandoned on the duvet. I'd denied any remembrance of the phrase . . . and yet the more I considered it, the more it had a faint ring of familiarity about it.

Don't sweat it. Go to sleep. The memory would come back to me eventually, I was sure.

Some berk on a motorbike whose exhaust pipe was in serious need of attention – like its bloody owner – woke me at half-past four. I lay fuming. It was too early to get up, too late to go back to sleep. Why are people so inconsiderate? Restless, I turned over, bashed my pillows, cursed all owners of motorcycles. And felt my mind clear . . .

This is what it feels like . . . I was immediately twelve years old again. Sitting by a lake or pond somewhere, with Dimsie and Tristan and the Chinese boy for whom Dorcas acted as guardian during term-time, while he was at boarding school. What was his real name? Cheng or Wing, I think, but bizarrely, he preferred to be called Albert. None of us liked him. He was a big lad, eyes like raisins in the suet of his face, and a real bully.

Dimsie was screaming as Albert, laughing, inflicted what we called a Chinese burn on her, gripping her wrist with both hands then rotating them painfully in opposite directions. Suddenly Tristan jumped up and grabbed Albert's own arm. Thin-lipped and ferocious, he twisted the boy's wrist until he howled and struggled.

'This is what it feels like,' he kept saying, through gritted teeth. 'OK? Like this. It hurts, doesn't it? Doesn't it?'

'I'll get you for this,' Albert said, when Tristan finally released his arm. 'Just you wait, you bastard. You'll be sorry.'

'So will you, if you don't leave my sister alone.'

Was it possible that this Chang or Wing, aka Albert, was involved in Tristan's murder? Could he be a member of a Triad? I knew all about revenge being a dish best served cold, but twenty-five years or more was a heck of a long time to wait for anger or hurt to cool. You'd think the dish had gone off by now. Been chucked in the garbage long ago.

Nonetheless, I would have to pass this on to Fliss, see if she could make anything of it, whether indeed it even had any bearing on the case.

SEVENTEEN

The man in the green Jag was parked on the seafront again. This was the fourth time I'd seen him out there. He sat in his car, gazing out of the window at my apartment block, occasionally speaking into a phone or lighting up a fag. The sight of him annoyed me. What the hell did he want? Normally I tried to ignore his irritating presence in front of my windows. Today, I went downstairs, crossed the road and rapped sharply on the half-closed window.

He jumped, then wound it down fully. Stale cigarette smoke drooled from the car's interior, together with an unpleasant smell like male underpants well overdue for a wash. He looked at me from heavy-lidded eyes.

'Yeah?' It wasn't just the lids: everything about him was heavy, from his jowly face to his bookmaker-check jacket and denim-covered thighs. Plus what I could see of all the bits in between.

'Can I help you?' My tone was not exactly friendly.

He looked me up and down. He was at a definite disadvantage, since he was sitting down inside a car and had to squint up and sideways, just to see my face. No way did I intend to squat down to his level.

'Maybe.' He sounded stroppy, twice as unfriendly as me. 'And maybe not. What's it to you, anyway?'

'I've noticed you parked out here a lot. Not doing anything, just staring out to sea.'

'How d' you know I'm not a creative artist, replenishing my . . . uh . . . aesthetic impulses?'

'Oh pleeeze . . .' A more unlikely creative artist of any sort would be hard to find. Unless he was an accountant.

'How do you know, eh? Or a man simply hoping against hope that his ship will come in?'

'Mostly because you don't look like it. In fact, to tell the truth, you look as if you're up to no good.'

'If you really wanna know, I'm keeping an eye on someone who lives in that block of flats.'

'Staking the place out, you mean.'

'Since you just came out of there, maybe you know her. Name of Quick,' he said. He stared at me truculently, fiddling with the handle of the car door in an effort to open it and climb out. He wasn't going to be able to unless he pushed really hard, or I stepped back a bit.

'Why not go over and check out the mailboxes?' I said. 'Ring the woman's doorbell? How're you going to identify her if you just sit on your tod all day? And why do you want to catch up with her, anyway?'

'Got a few questions to ask, that's all. I'm not trying to cause trouble, if that's what you're thinking.'

'Oh, no?' The voice had been teasingly familiar from the moment he first opened his mouth. Now I recognized those faintly whiny accents. 'It's Mr Maurice Colby, isn't it?' I said, chirpy as a chipmunk. 'We spoke on the phone not long ago.'

'What the . . .' His face flushed red with fury. 'You fucking bitch. You're the bloody cow I'm trying to get hold of, aren't you?' Pressing down the handle, he slammed against the door as hard as he could. Once and then again. The third time, I moved away and he tumbled out on to the pavement in an undignified sprawl.

I looked both ways along the seafront. Plenty of people were walking up and down. I needn't fear sudden death unless he pulled out an AK-47, gunned me down and sped off down the road before anyone could react. Bending over him, I said, 'Come on, Mr Colby. What do you really want?'

He got himself on to his hands and knees, hooked his fingers over the door of his car and clumsily climbed to his feet. 'What's your bleeding game?' he demanded. 'Ringing me up under false pretences. Assaulting me. I could have you for that.'

'I doubt it. Meanwhile, maybe I should be asking you what *your* game is. Because it's obviously nothing to do with interior design. Probably more,' I added, taking a shot at random, 'to do with expensive watch rip-offs and the like.'

His oystery eyes stared into mine, while the skin crinkled around them. 'What you on about?' he demanded indignantly, though even to himself his righteous anger sounded as phoney as the Patek-Philippes back in the murder-scene warehouse.

Keeping an eye on him, I gazed out across the restlessly heaving water. A tanker drifted along the horizon. Nearer to shore, little sailboats flocked like marine sheep. 'Know this area, do you?' I asked. Direct questions often take people unawares.

'As it happens – though I can't see what business it is of yours.'

'So that's a yes?'

'My Gran used to have a smallholding . . .' He waved vaguely behind us. 'Somewhere out in the country. Used to come down with my mum and brothers in the school holidays. Explore. Make camps in the woods. Little boy stuff.'

Which made it quite likely that he knew all about that warehouse which had been stacked with rip-off luxury goods. Probably even stashed them there himself. 'And why were you trying to trace me?'

'Wanted to know why you gave me a bell the other day.' He lifted his shoulders. 'Perfectly natural thing to want to find out.'

A suspicion struck me. 'You have *heard* about Tristan Huber, haven't you?'

'Heard what about him?'

'That he's dead?'

'Dead?'

'Murdered.'

'*What*?' He went pale, the blood draining dramatically from his face, leaving it a waxy beige. '*Murdered*?'

I explained the circumstances. Watched as the meanings and options of this news computed in his head. I could almost deduce the permutations he was evaluating. If this had happened to Tristan, might it happen to him too? Was he next in line? What should or could he do about it? Did he have time to get out of whatever shady business it was that he was engaged in?

'I'm sorry to be the bearer of such bad news,' I said. 'You and he were obviously close.' God, I could be nasty. On the other hand, I was fairly sure that Maurice Colby wasn't above some fairly despicable behaviour himself, though not so despicable that he could have murdered Tristan. If for no other reason than that nobody could fake the way he had gone pale at hearing of the murder. A crook, yes, but a relatively civilized one.

'No,' he said forcefully. 'No, we weren't.' He turned away from me, distancing himself from the news he had just heard and everything connected with it. 'Not close at all. Just . . . just former business colleagues.' He bent his arm at the elbow and gazed at his knock-off watch then edged towards his car. 'Look, I have to be going.'

'And there's nothing more you want from me?'

'Nah. Tell the truth, I thought you were Crime Squad or something similar.'

He opened his car door and hoisted himself into the driver's seat. Turned on the ignition. Gunned the motor.

'An easy misunderstanding,' I said. 'But if you haven't already done so, I'd shift the merchandise PDQ, if I were you.' As parting shot, I asked, 'Do you know the Landises?' and watched his knuckles whiten as he gripped the steering wheel. He didn't answer, just drove off. Watching his tail lights fade away into the distance, I took that as an affirmative.

After that, I telephoned DCI Fliss Fairlight and learned that there had been little or no movement on the murder of Tristan Huber, though the police were actively pursuing a number of significant lines of enquiry.

Oh yeah?

And incidentally, that my friends the Landises were being questioned by the locals.

Huh . . .

And after *that*, I walked into the High Street, turned left halfway down and pushed open the door of Dimsie's show-room. The girl behind the faux Louis VI writing desk tried to get up when she saw me come in but I was on her before she could push back her chair. 'I just want to speak to Dimsie,' I said soothingly, pressing her down in her seat. 'No need to panic.'

'She's upstairs, looking at some new fabrics.' Looking round for the nearest exit, she rolled her eyes, showing the whites, like a startled mare. 'Why don't you just, like, go on up?'

I did, and found Dimsie, in a yellow cotton dress with her hair piled into an overflowing top-knot, sitting surrounded by spreads of luxurious upholstery materials. She seemed pensive as she held up a swatch of gold-infused red silk brocade and compared it with a gorgeous strip of grey-patterned damask. I was strongly reminded of Watteau's *The Pleasures of Love*.

She brightened when she saw me. 'Alex! Any news?'

''Fraid not.'

'But why *not*? It's ages since . . . since Tristan was . . . since he died.'

'I know.'

'Surely somebody, somewhere, must be able to find out what happened and who's responsible.'

'You'd think so. But so far they've found no traces at the scene of the crime – that warehouse-cum-storage shed in the woods round Honeypot Lane – and no evidence of anything that could prove to be an identifier. Normally you can pick up all kinds of trace . . . skin particles, hair, soil from shoe-soles, minute bits or this and that . . . which could be significant. But according to my police contact there's nothing. It seems that the perpetrator was very, very careful.'

'I don't know what to say.' Tears filled her beautiful eyes as she spread her hands in a dramatic gesture of despair.

'Nor do I, Dim. Which is why I've come to tell you that for the moment I have to quit any involvement.'

'But you *can't*! You were Tris's *friend. Close* friend.' She nodded meaningfully.

So she knew about that, did she? Tristan and I had tried to keep it quiet. 'Sorry,' I said, 'but I'm not a police officer any more. And I'm finding the investigation very distressing. And on top of that, I've got work to finish, Dim. Perhaps the cops will do better than I can. Best to leave it to them. To be honest, I don't believe I'm being given all the facts and I'm not sure who is holding out on me.'

I wasn't certain that she herself wasn't one of the holder-outers. I gave her my death-ray look but she didn't flinch. Proof in itself, I'd say. I had seen her gazing in this same steadfast manner in the past, to prove that she was innocent of whatever sin she was being accused of, from stealing money from her mother's handbag to stealing other women's boyfriends. In fact, now I thought about it, she was a bit of a hard case herself, just like her brother, as I had belatedly been discovering.

'Have you seen my poor mother recently?' she demanded.

'Not in the past few—'

'She looks like a ghost, poor old cow. She's lost a huge amount of weight. She's not sleeping. Not eating. And now some nutter is tormenting her, telephoning all the time.'

'Threats?'

'No. Just this voice, sounding like the person's speaking from the bottom of a mineshaft, saying "it's like this".'

'What is?'

'I don't know. Nor does she. It's a nightmare. You know as well as I do, Alex, that she and I haven't always got on, but losing her adored son was enough torture for the poor old girl, without having to endure this kind of harassment on top. Why are people so *cruel*?'

'Is it a man or a woman making these calls?'

'A woman, she thinks. But could possibly be a man disguising his voice. The police are on to it, and the telephone company. But as soon as they installed a device to try and record him, he stopped. Texts her, instead. It's truly horrendous.'

'I'm sorry to hear this. Can't they trace texts?'

'No idea. But you'll stay on the case, yeah?'

'It's pointless, Dim. I'm not achieving anything. Much better at this stage to leave it to the cops.'

'No, Alex. Please. Promise me you won't give up, please.'

'But I'm not—'

'*Please*, Alex.'

I flatter myself that I am firm, cynical, able to hold my own, not taking any shit from anyone. But Dimsie, with her violet eyes, her peaches-and-cream complexion, could beat me at my own game any time she chose. I mentally cursed and sort of nodded. What a sucker I was, when it came right down to it. 'Oh all right, I guess.' If she heard the reluctance in my voice, she ignored it.

'Thank you, Alex. I *knew* you wouldn't let me – us – down.'

'By the way, I met your former sister-in-law the other day.'

'What did you think of her?'

'I liked her.'

'Did she have anything useful to say?'

'Not really. Just some confirmation of a couple of points. But she did make me wonder about your former spouse.'

'Mine?'

'Yes, yours, Dim. I've known you all these years, and I know absolutely nothing about your husband.'

'Which is exactly how I want it,' she said sharply.

'Which is exactly why I don't to be involved any more. You're withholding what could be crucial evidence. How do you expect me to operate when I'm not in full possession of the facts? And how do you know that he isn't the person responsible for Tristan's death?'

She jutted her chin. 'He isn't. I can assure you he isn't.'

'How do you *know*?'

'Because he's not the violent sort. He just isn't. You'll have to trust me on this one, Alex.'

'You have absolutely no proof.'

'That's right. Only my gut-instinct after living with him.'

'It's not good enough.'

'It'll have to do.'

Dimsie looked and sounded just like her mother. I always found it disorientating when the Komodo Dragon revealed itself beneath her normal porcelain surface.

Stand-off time. 'Well,' I said eventually. Feebly. 'I may have to reconsider my position.'

And left before she could apply any more of her particular brand of persuasion.

Walking back to my flat along the seafront, warm breezes ruffled my hair. The air was pure, the water like glass. I might be some distance from London, without immediate access to galleries, museums, theatres, but I was also some distance from major pollution, noise, traffic, a capital city that was gradually losing its identity.

Later, errands run, email answered, work over for the day, I poured myself a glass of red, heated the slice of homemade pizza I'd bought earlier from our very own Italian bakery, and for want of anything better to do, plus (having met the guy) a tad's hair of curiosity, settled down on the sofa to dip once more into Chris Kearns' book.

I grew more and more impressed as I read on. He was a powerful and unflinching writer and I found myself in tears as he recounted the loss of his sixteen-year-old daughter, (named Eunice for the purposes of the autobiography, don't ask me why), his wife's descent into acute alcoholism and the difficult struggle the two of them went through to get her sober. He detailed with unsparing honesty the vomiting, the abuse both verbal and physical, the self-soiling, the rows, the relapses, the domestic destruction, the drunken rages. It was horrendous and, I'm almost ashamed to admit, gripping stuff.

I could only thank whatever powers there be that I had not made a similar journey to the brink of hell. There had been many a lonely evening after Jack Martin had left, and I'd lost the child I was carrying, when I'd got outside most of a bottle of wine followed by a whisky or two.

Common sense and a strong dislike of not being in control

eventually took over. Forced me to take stock and realize how close I was to becoming dependent. That, plus the sight of my bleary puffy face in the mirror.

The following morning, I rolled out of bed, cursing Dimsie. I really didn't want to be driving halfway across south-east England on what could be nothing more than a wild goose chase. At least I would have a chance to visit with Clarissa and Mark Ridgeway – I had indeed already invited myself for lunch, prior to visiting Rollins Hall again.

Clarissa was looking radiant. 'I'm two-thirds of the way through my book,' she enthused. 'And Rondel is beginning to piece the puzzle together before nailing the villain.'

'So will it be the hunchbacked chamberlain?' I said. 'Or his wicked squire?'

'Neither, of course.' She clasped my arm and smiled at me. 'But far more important than that . . . I'm expecting. Again!'

'Fantastic! Congratulations to you both.'

She lifted an apologetic hand to her mouth. 'Oh, Alex. I'm so sorry. I forgot.'

'Just because I had a miscarriage doesn't mean nobody else is ever allowed to have a baby.'

'No, but . . . I don't need to flaunt my fecundity.'

'You're not. At least, not yet. And I'm truly delighted.' My body ached. Would I ever be pregnant again? Sometimes my longing for a normal family life was almost overwhelming. And, as I often reminded myself, the tick-tock of my internal rhythms was getting louder, sounding through my dreams like the call of a bugle.

Over lunch I asked if there had been news from Rollins Park. 'I believe Lady Paramore's father had to return to the States,' Mark said. 'And there've been more visits from the RSPCA, re those Tennessee Walking Horses.'

'In fact,' said Clarissa, 'I think I read in the local paper that they're planning to put the whole rodeo show on hold for the moment. At least until Hank Rogers gets back.'

'I wonder if they'll put something else on instead.'

'If so, what?'

'An historical pageant or something.'

'Actually . . .' Clarissa smirked a bit. '*Ackshully*, they've already talked to me about producing a script. For instance, at least one of their ancestors was beheaded.'

'Cue Tudor or Stuart with his head tucked underneath his arm,' I said.

'Exactly. The kids would love that. And there was also someone back in the eighteenth century who was accused of witchcraft, and someone else burned at the stake . . .'

'Not exactly wholesome family entertainment,' I said.

'We'd have to skirt over that a bit. Plus there're masses of gorgeous authentic costumes stowed away in the attics, longing for a twenty-first-century airing. It could be a winner.'

I kind of hoped that Todd DuBois, aka Jerry Baskin, was still hanging around. I'd like to get down and dirty with him, push him a bit, find out what exactly he was doing here, what his unfinished business was, or had been. I already knew he was eel-like in his ability to slither away from any direct questions, but if I came across him, this time I'd do my damnedest to pin him down.

When I arrived at Rollins Park, I turned in at the gates and, ignoring the private road leading to the house, headed directly for the designated parking for visitors, which was already half-full of cars. As I walked towards the showground, I could hear distant cheers and a 'Yee-haw!' or two, which would indicate that the rodeo had not yet been put on ice. Great! The chances of catching up with Jerry Baskin were looking good.

But he didn't seem to be performing that morning. Perhaps it was his day off. When the final lariat had been twirled, and the last cowboy had ridden off the ground, the last family group had dropped its ice-cream wrappers and paper cups on the floor, the way a dog might pee against a lamp post to indicate it had passed that way, I stepped down the bleachers and made my way across the sanded showground to the Western-style log houses at the far side. I could hear voices, a shower running, someone singing 'Streets of Laredo', the clink of an empty beer can being tossed at a waste bin and landing on the concrete floor instead.

I rapped at the door, and heard the place go quiet. Someone approached and lifted the latch. A good-looking hombre in a towel and a Western hat stood there. Tats snaked down his arms. An inked spider lurked on his neck, just below his left ear.

'Well, hi there,' he said. 'Can I help?'

'I was looking for Jerry Baskin,' I said. There was a belch, a guffaw, a voice saying, *sotto voce,* 'Aren't they all?'

'Baskin took off,' Tattoo Man said.

'Where did he go?'

He shrugged, nearly dislodging the towel and offering an unwelcome glimpse of a shiny pink testicle. 'Who the fuck knows?'

'Who the fuck cares?' came the voice in the background. There was a prolonged burp.

I was getting the impression that Jerry Baskin hadn't been the most popular man in the show. 'When did he leave?'

'About eight days ago now.'

'Without leaving a forwarding address, I should imagine,' I said. 'Why'd he leave?'

Tattoo Man stood back from the door. 'Hey, why don't you come on in, set for a while?'

'Thank you.' I stepped into an almost visible reek of sweat, stale beer, damp towels and aftershave. Fringed suede jackets hung from pegs, spurred cowboy boots lay untidily around on the floor. More pegs held twines of rope, leather chaps, a couple of western saddles. Beneath the pegs were benches set all round the walls, rather like changing rooms at football or rugby stadia.

'It was more like nearly a couple of weeks ago that Baskin vamoosed.' Another semi-naked guy – the Greek chorus, I assumed – showed up and smiled an all-American smile. He lifted a hand to his wet hair in a sort of salute. 'Howdy, ma'am.'

I nodded. Neither of them was the Marvin or Chuck I'd been introduced to on my last visit here.

'So what do you want with Brother Baskin?' one of them asked.

'I'm not a wronged girlfriend, if that's what you're wondering,' I said. 'Just wanted to ask him a few questions. Perhaps you could help.'

'What sort of questions?'

'For a start, where did he come from?'

They looked at each other. 'Well, now,' one of them said. 'Depends who he was talking to.'

'That's right. Never knew *where* he was from. He'd tell you something one day, and the next you'd hear him say the exact opposite to someone else.'

'Yup. And if you took him up on it, he'd either say you must've misheard him, or he'd flat out deny it.'

'So basically, you haven't the faintest idea.'

'You got it. He just showed up here one day, looking for work, and Hank took him on.'

'Have to say he certainly seemed to know his way round horses and rodeo.'

One of them reached for a can of beer, dragged at the ring-pull which he tossed over his shoulder, and offered it to me. 'Thanks but no thanks,' I said. 'Where are you guys from?'

'I'm from Louisville, Kentucky.'

'Gainesville, Florida.'

'And despite the whoppers, where would you say the so-called Jerry Baskin actually came from?'

'*So-called* . . . you spotted that too, did you?' He held out his land. 'I'm Luke, by the way. And he's Duke.'

'You'd have to be blind and deaf to miss it,' I said. 'Even if you'd never bought a tub of ice cream from the supermarket.'

The two of them fell about. 'Ben & Jerry's!' they chortled. 'Baskin Robbins!'

'So if you had to choose a home state for him, what would you opt for?'

They looked at each other and shrugged. 'Ask me, I'd say probably California.'

'Definitely from the States,' agreed his friend, 'but I wouldn't be able to say where.'

'But not from a plantation in Louisiana?'

Both of them laughed again. 'Louisiana . . . fuckin' A,' said one.

'He was good, I'll give him that,' said the other.

'Darkies crooning the blues, Ol' Man River . . .'

'All that crap.'

'But you only had to spend, like, half an hour with him to see he was a real three dollar bill.' Duke cracked open another beer.

'Easy enough dude to get on with, under all the sweet talking, but I wouldn't trust him further than I could throw him.'

'Him nor his Lord and Ladyship, ask me.' Duke nodded wisely. I couldn't help wishing the towel round his waist was larger. Or his balls were smaller.

'Not to mention old Hanky Panky.'

I made my eyes round. 'What?'

'Plus that decorator guy – Christian or whatever.'

'Tristan? You think he was involved too?'

The guys nodded at each other. 'Matter of fact, I'd guess the Tristan guy was the big cheese.'

'Are you saying you think the Paramores are crooks?'

'All of them're in it up to the neck.'

'Wow!' I said. 'And what do you reckon "it" is?'

'We thought drugs, at first, didn't we, Duke?'

'Sure did. It's the obvious thing. But then we caught on to the fact they was always going off with them big horse boxes without any particular reason—'

'Not races, or them point-to-points you have over here, or attending other rodeos—'

'They'd have needed us for that.'

'Right. So we reckon they's dealing in maybe horses, or stolen autos, something biggish like that.'

'Even wondered about people trafficking, girls and stuff. Pick 'em up at Southampton or wherever, drive 'em up to the big city, sell the poor gals on.' Duke spat into the litter of straw which wisped about the floor.

'Lotta money to be made out of hookers,' Luke informed me. 'East Europeans and like that. Not saying I approve, natch.'

'Quite the opposite.'

'But you've never seen anything suspicious?'

'What, like chicks screaming for help in a barn or something? Definitely not.'

'On the other hand . . .' The other guy's face grew sombre.

'Now I think about it, they's been a helluva lotta cars coming in through the back way recently.'

'Where's the back way?' I asked keenly.

He indicated the landscape behind us.

'What's there?'

'Oh, you know . . . the usual shit. Barns and sheds and outbuildings, like that.'

I hoped the implication wasn't that the Paramores were running a brothel of some kind in the grounds of Rollins Park. 'Can I access the back way from the . . . uh . . . back?'

'Sure can, ma'am. They's a road . . .'

'Wanna know something?' said Luke. 'I'm about ready to split, know what I mean? This place is beginning to seriously gross me out.'

'You 'n me both, dude.'

'Any reason in particular?' I asked.

The two of them laughed. 'Where to start, man.'

'Supposed to be these high-class dudes. Ask me, they's nothing but a bunch of weirdos.'

'Crooks, too.'

Somewhere nearby a horse gave a high-pitched long-drawn-out whinny. Harness jangled. I could hear childrens' voices. Must be getting on for show time. The second house.

'I'd better leave you two to get ready for the next performance.' I stood up.

'Look, don't know if it's any help . . .' Duke said, '. . . but if you're really trying to track down this Baskin guy, I know he had connections somewhere near Canterbury. Heard him on his cell phone several times.'

'How would you know where he was phoning?'

'I asked him. As in, "Who the hell you calling, dude?" Said it was some woman he knew, someone from the good old days.'

'Ah . . . the good old days,' repeated Luke. 'I often wonder what they was.'

'Or when.'

'Thank you for that,' I said. 'And for the other info. You've been very helpful.'

'You gonna have a word with his or her Lordship? 'Cause if so, watch your back.'

'They've both got tempers on 'em that would frighten an alligator out of its skin.'

This shed further light on the Paramores. 'I'll be careful.'

Though as I walked towards my car, I felt as though I had a boxful of jigsaw pieces. All I had to do now was fit them together. It was a pity there was no helpful picture on the lid.

How exactly was I going to tackle the Paramores? I didn't have any kind of relevant lead-in. On the other hand, I was right here, on the premises, as it were, and it would be daft not to take the opportunity to talk to them again. Which I would do. Definitely. Just as soon as I had worked out an opening sentence. And another to follow it. Couldn't be all that difficult, could it?

EIGHTEEN

I'm not a big fan of hunches and intuitions, either in real life or in crime fiction. In my opinion, those moronic girls beloved of Women In Jeopardy writers, who pursue baddies into draughty cellars with only a guttering candle for illumination, deserve everything they get. Solid facts, hard evidence, irrefutable proof: those are the verifications I operate by in my art anthologies, and the same goes for the kind of amateur detection I've recently found myself embroiled in. Not that I'm not reasonably sensitive to atmosphere. And boy, was there a lot of that flying round the Paramore residence!

I didn't have to be psychic to realize that since my last visit, the domestic situation had changed very much for the worse. Waiting for Piper or her husband, to join me in the small sitting room into which I'd been shown, I was chilled by a feeling that things were falling apart, the centre was having a hard time holding. It wasn't so much the particularly English shabbiness of the room – faded chair covers, sagging curtains, threadbare rugs, smelly spaniels (although I'd previously been given to understand that Piper had spent a fortune doing the place up) – it was also a pervading impression of just-slammed doors, chilly hatred, plates thrown in a rage, angry voices speaking through gritted teeth just out of earshot. Family photos stood about, mostly of Sir Piers in various pugilistic poses, holding a gun or an archery bow or even stripped to the waist in boxing gloves and satin shorts.

So unpleasant, even menacing, did the house feel, that if the housekeeper person who'd parked me in the room had reappeared to report that unfortunately she had found one (or even both) of the Paramores in the Blue Drawing Room or the Yellow Parlour or wherever, with a knife through the heart or a bullet to the head, I don't think I would have turned a hair. After all, it would have been part and parcel of what was already a violent family history – the ancestress drowned as a witch, the forebear beheaded on Tower Green, the pregnant parlourmaid turned away after being raped by the son of the house, the vengeful uncle stabbing his brother for a swindled inheritance. Like Clarissa Ridgeway, I'd done some research on the Paramores and knew that was just for openers.

However, nothing as dramatic as that took place. Piper showed up looking business-like, wearing a padded hunting-green *gilet* over a checked shirt with the sleeves rolled up to the elbow, and greeted me with a distinct lack of enthusiasm. She seemed strained and pale, much thinner than at our last encounter. Her Eton crop had lost its vitality. There were deep vertical lines between her eyebrows which I didn't remember seeing on my former visit.

She shook my hand briskly. 'How can I help?'

'I don't know if you can. Basically, I'm still checking out various aspects of Tristan Huber's death.'

At the sound of his name, she flinched as though someone had just stuck a red-hot fork into the back of her hand. Her fingers toyed nervously with the antique gold locket round her throat. She recovered enough to raise patronizing eyebrows. 'As far as we're concerned, nothing new has occurred since we last met,' she said.

'You mean to do with Tristan?'

'Of course. What else?'

I shrugged. 'I don't know . . .'

She put a hand on my arm. 'My dear,' she said, sounding

like my Scottish grandmother. 'Nothing has changed, I assure you. Nothing.'

Too much protestation. Cue instant scepticism. 'Is that true?'

She nodded.

'What about you closing down the rodeo show, for instance?'

'That hasn't happened yet.'

'But hasn't your father gone back to the States?'

'He had some urgent business matters to attend to.' Very *de haut en bas.*

'Ah . . .'

'And in any case, I can't see that his temporary absence has anything to do with Mr Huber's unfortunate death.'

To be honest, neither could I.

Frown lines paralleled across her forehead. 'Where did you get this information, anyway?'

'I have local friends who heard about it.'

'Oh.'

Not a friendly monosyllable. 'Have you talked to the police yet?' I asked.

'Naturally. They came here, asking questions, but we couldn't tell them anything useful. As far we were concerned, Mr Huber had been employed to decorate Lady Anne's Retreat and that was the extent of our relationship with the man.' She said that as though she not only genuinely believed it, but also expected me to. 'We certainly didn't know anything about his private life, or what he got up to elsewhere.'

'I see.' I tried to look nonchalant. 'And how long has your father gone away for?'

'I can't see that it has anything whatsoever to do with you, Miss . . . um . . . Quick.' If I'd been asked to produce an identikit picture of a vicious homicidal maniac, it would have come out looking a lot like Piper did at that moment. Especially round the eyes. 'I suppose your friends *heard* about that too,' she added.

'Actually not.'

'So who told you?'

There was no way I was about rat out my new best friends, Luke and Duke. 'I honestly can't remember,' I said. Lying through my teeth.

If Piper realized, she didn't let on. 'Well, I'm sorry, it's good to see you again, but I don't think we can be of any further help.' She began herding me towards the door of the room in a sweep which any sheepdog would have been proud of. I had no choice but to allow myself to be shepherded into the hall – just as Sir Piers appeared, loping down the stairs, one hand in the pocket of his red chinos, his shirt open at the throat. He stopped halfway down.

'Oh,' he said. 'You again.' Breeding had won out over inclination last time. It didn't now. 'How can we help?'

'As I've just explained to your wife, I was just checking up on whether there had been any further developments in the Tristan Huber case.' I was ad-libbing at speed, to no great effect. Judging by the jut of his jaw and the bunch of his fists, this was a man who had undoubtedly been a bully at school and was one still. I didn't want to find myself being used for target practice.

'Isn't that the question we should be asking you?' he said coldly. The glance he shot sideways at Piper was very far from friendly. I hoped she wouldn't find herself in the way if he happened to aim a lunge at someone. He came several steps further down the stairs. 'What are you really after?'

'Simply checking up.'

'For a second time? We told you all we know when you were here before.'

I spread my hands. 'I'm only—'

'It's not as if we had a lot to do with the fellow, Tristan Huber, though I believe my wife invited him in for a drink a couple of times to discuss the progress of his work,' he said. 'To be quite honest, we don't normally hobnob with the tradespeople.'

Maybe you don't, buster. But I bet your wife did. 'I thought you went to school with him.'

He looked a trifle embarrassed. 'I did. But . . . painting and decorating? I mean, really. Besides, people move on, choose different paths, lose any common interests they might once have shared.'

I was damn sure he didn't normally refer to Tristan as a tradesperson. Wouldn't dare. 'So how come you chose him to decorate Lady Hilda's Haven or whatever?' I asked.

'We were given a personal recommendation by some local friends,' he said coldly. 'Not that it can possibly have any bearing on his death.'

'I agree. By the way, now that I'm here,' I said, 'is there any chance I could take a stroll round your park before I leave?'

He stared at me, his features heavy with disdain and disbelief. 'What? Of course you can't. How the hell would you feel if I turned up at your place uninvited and demanded to walk round your garden?'

Scared, was the answer. 'I'm something of an arborealist,' I said. 'I've heard you have some really rare species of trees and shrubs.'

'This lady seems to hear a lot of things,' Piper said.

'Well, whoever told her we had rare trees growing here was talking out of his backside. Giving you a lot of bull,' Paramore said. His face assumed a sneery Lord Lucan expression as he added: 'And I'd prefer it if you did not trespass any further on either my property or my time!' He came down the rest of the stairs to the hall. To Piper, he said frostily, 'I'll be in my office if you need me.' He gave me the briefest of nods and turned towards the rear of the house.

'You must forgive us if my husband appears to be acting rather brusquely. He has a lot on his mind right now.' Piper moved me onwards to the front door, which stood open as though expecting me.

About to step outside, I turned. 'How long exactly did you and your husband spend in Hong Kong?' I asked.

She did that flinching thing again. Feigned deafness. 'Sorry?'

'Your husband worked for HKSB back in the day, didn't he?'

'And where did you discover *that* fact?' She produced one of those unconvincing laughs which are laced with menace. 'Sounds as though you've been prying into our private affairs.'

'Come on, Lady P, you're a celebrity in these parts. Naturally people tittle-tattle about you and your family, and naturally one picks up gossip here and there.'

'Does one indeed?' She stepped firmly towards me so that I had no option except to move outside. 'Anyway, thank you so much for dropping by. I do hope the police manage to solve the mystery of poor Mr Huber's death.'

It wasn't until I was inserting the key into the ignition that I realized she had neatly sidestepped my question. The one about the length of time they'd spent abroad. Not that it mattered, since I already knew the answer. Sixteen months in total, to be exact. The Internet is a lovesome thing, God wot. Anyway, it no longer had any real significance since I had by now more or less abandoned my foolish Triads theory.

Driving down the long avenue to the road beyond the grounds, I shivered. A riot of questions rampaged round my head. Had Luke and Duke been right? Was Rollins Park really mixed up in some kind of vile trade in women's bodies? Had Tristan been part of it? Could there truly be abandoned sheds or empty barns dotted about the estate where helpless women were kept prisoner before being shipped off to the larger metropolises like London or Bradford or Glasgow? And if so, how old were they? What was their nationality?

I was fully aware of the obscene statistics concerning prepubertal girls whose immature bodies were highly sought after by sexual deviants and perverts. I'd seen too many of the squalid houses and conditions in which these poor women were kept. Many of them had been lured to the UK with promises of work as waitresses or hotel chambermaids, earning far more money than they would get in their own countries, then forced into prostitution once they got here. I had even busted a couple of the brothels or holding-houses during my days on the force, though unfortunately the bastard traffickers got away before we could identify and detain them. The remembrance of those powerless little girls, huddling together in sordid backrooms and basements, the memory of their desperate, pleading faces, was so sickening even now, that I had to stop my car and take some deep breaths.

Trafficking. A big money spinner for organized crime networks. And Tristan Huber, my friend, was obviously heavily involved, along with the Paramores, Hank Rogers . . . and others. Including Maurice Colby and the Landises? I felt sick at heart, as well as stomach. How would I ever find out if what I was beginning to suspect about Rollins Park was true? I couldn't go to the police unless I could produce some kind of evidence. And it would be hard for me to search the grounds single-handedly without being spotted and immediately kicked off the estate. Especially after specifically being told I couldn't. At least I could alert DCI Fairlight.

I drove away from the house and down to the entrance gates. Turned right, instead of left, then right again when the road finally reached a T-junction. One more right turn, and the road ran parallel to a six-foot high brick wall all along the back of what I judged to be the grounds of Rollins Park. It was impossible for me to see anything over it without the aid of a ladder. I drove on until I came to a tall wrought-iron gate, elaborately curlicued and heavily padlocked. I pulled up. This side of the estate was wooded, mainly beech and birch and heavily shrubbed. The unmade road on the other side curved off into the distance between deep stands of rhododendron. There was no sight of any buildings. I was about to switch off my engine and try to see if I could climb over the gate when a Land Rover appeared from between the bushes and drove towards me. Sir Piers was at the wheel. Two German Shepherds leaped out of the rear when he pulled to a juddering stop, just yards away from me, and started barking and snarling at the tops of their voices. Pointed teeth were bared. Drool dripped. A black paw scratched at the gate. A suggestion of rabies hovered in the air.

I was out of there.

I pulled to a stop outside Strathmore House, in Alcombe. As I rang the bell, the door opened. Yvonne Landis was standing there, wearing a beige linen jacket, a sky-blue T-shirt and dark linen trousers. One of those must-have, to-die-for handbags, worth several thousand pounds, was hanging from one arm. Another stood on the table just inside the door.

'Miss – um – Quick,' she said. The exclamation points had vanished.

'Yes. I wondered if—'

She took a step forward. 'I'm afraid I'm just on my way out.'

'I see,' I said. Behind her, in the hall, I could see suitcases piled up. 'Going away?'

'We're taking a cruise along the Norwegian fjords. Leaving this afternoon, as a matter of fact. As soon as James gets back.'

'I hope you enjoy it.'

'I'm sure we will.' Seeing that I wasn't about to jam my foot in the doorway and force her back into the house, she relaxed slightly. 'Did you want anything in particular?'

Only a few answers. Like why you have a triple firewall protecting your identity on the Internet. What you did, whose secrets you betrayed, what necessitated your current name change, along with all the security whistles and bells?

'I happened to be passing,' I said. 'Just wondered if you might have thought of anything further which could help the police in their enquiries into Tristan Huber's death.'

She shook her head from side to side. The rigid cap of her hair stayed in place. 'I'm afraid not. After you left, James and I went over everything we knew about Tristan and couldn't think of anything at all that might be of use to you.'

'That's a pity.'

'Isn't it, though?' She gave me a kind smile. 'I'm sure there'll be a breakthrough in the case sooner or later.'

'Me, too.' I moved back towards my car. 'Thank you anyway, Mrs Lockhart . . . sorry, I mean Landis.' And made a dash for the driver's seat before she could say anything further. I have to say that I regretted being so callous when I looked out of the window and saw the stricken look on her face, the hand stretched beseechingly towards me. Her cover blown . . . did I have to do that? Especially when I was pretty sure that the husband and wife were not responsible for Tristan's death.

Yvonne on her own I might have been able to make a case for, if forced. But Thyroid Jim? Nah, I didn't think so. They had been fairly up front about knowing Tristan, both when they were all in Hong Kong, and when they'd returned to the UK. Nor did I think that it was Tristan they were afraid of. They would never have asked him to organize their barn conversion, otherwise. What was remarkable about Tristan's murder was the amount of time it must have taken. I couldn't see the Landis/Lockharts using such a long-drawn out method of slaughter. Much more likely the quick shot from the rear window of a car, or the sudden bludgeoning on a deserted street, followed by a quick getaway and back home, miles from the scene of the crime. Mission accomplished.

But what would have been their motive? Blackmail? Exposure of some kind, such as a threat to reveal their true identities, thus bringing the vengeance of the Triads down upon them? Not a pleasant prospect. If that had been the case, I could well imagine that they might want to eliminate Tristan one way or another.

But hadn't I abandoned the Triad possibility? Perhaps – as far as Tristan was concerned. But Mr Sook had been fairly explicit when it came to James Lockhart. Unfortunately, from what I now knew of Tristan, I could believe him capable of almost anything, including murder. But the Landises? I don't think so.

Since I was already on the road, I decided I might as well keep going. I found myself eventually parking a few doors up from the dry-cleaning establishment belonging to Kevin Fuller's father. There were several people inside waiting at the counter to collect or deposit items. One woman came out with a duvet shrink-wrapped into a plastic bag, reminding me that I ought to check my own bedding, as we began the summer wind down into autumn and on to winter.

When the place was finally clear, I got out of my car and walked across the pavement to push open the door. Mr Fuller was piling winter coats into one machine and at the same time yanking at the door of another one. The chemical smell was strong, and as I always did when picking up my dry-cleaning, I found it hard to believe that Health & Safety procedure permitted a worker to spend eight or more hours a day inhaling those fumes.

'Mr Fuller,' I said.

He looked up. Sad tired eyes set above shrunken cheeks. Visible weight loss. 'You came before,' he said.

'That's right.' I hated to bring his son's death up again, even though it was very clear that the trauma of Kevin's murder never left him.

'They still don't have a clue as to who killed him,' he said. His eyes watered.

'That's why I'm here. I wanted to ask if you can remember anything at all that might have some bearing on his death. Anything odd. Unusual. Even the smallest detail can sometimes provide a breakthrough in a case.'

He looked blank, then went into the back part of the shop and lifted the kettle. 'You'll have a cuppa, now you're here, won't you?'

'Thank you. That'd be great.'

Tea made, we sat down on either side of the table. He clasped his hands round his mug. 'You asked about anything unusual . . . the only really odd thing – apart from him not being here, of course . . .' He gulped, and stared down at his tea. '. . . we've been getting these phone calls. Late at night, or very early in the morning. A voice, always saying the same thing. Don't know if it's a man or a woman, could be either, but—'

Interesting. '"This is what it feels like",' I hazarded.

He stared as thought I'd produced a stoat from my pocket. 'How did you know?'

'Someone – probably the same person – has been making similar calls to the mother of Tristan Huber.' If anything was guaranteed to link Tristan and Kevin's murders, it was this. It might be interesting to check up on the family of Ned Swift.

'I don't understand what whoever it is means, or why they're doing this,' said Mr Fuller. 'It's not as if we aren't suffering enough already.'

'You should go to the police. They might find the information useful.'

'It doesn't really bother us,' he said. 'Now we've lost our Kev, I don't think anything will ever bother us again.'

Oh dear.

'And apart from that, you can't think of any link between your son and Tristan Huber?'

'Nothing. Apart from that committee to do with the redecoration. And I seem to remember there was some kind of end-of-term shenanigans they were both concerned with – a couple of years ago, now – though I'm not sure why that decorator fellow would have been involved, it was a university occasion, after all.'

'Designing the streamers, or something,' I said. 'Or perhaps the party was themed in some way. I should think Tristan would be a good man to have aboard if you wanted to decorate a gym hall for a party or something.'

'You're probably right. Not that I ever met the man.'

'By the way, does the name Ned Swift ring any bells?'

Frowning, he pondered. 'It does, but for the life of me I couldn't tell you why.'

'Was it through some connection that you know of with Kevin?'

He shook his head. 'Sorry. Can't remember.'

'Didn't you tell me that your son was involved with the university chess club?'

'I can't remember doing so, but yes he was. President for a while, I believe. Had the T-shirts made for club members, printed with MAKE THE RIGHT MOVES. His mother and I thought that was . . . was . . .' He gulped again and bowed his head over the table. '. . . clever.'

Another definite link between two of the victims. I put my hand over his and squeezed. There was nothing anyone could do for the man to alleviate the agony he was feeling. There never would be.

I finished my tea. 'Thank you, Mr Fuller. And of course, if we hear anything . . .'

He nodded. I let myself out.

Once in my car, I called Fliss Fairlight. 'Quick here,' I said. 'Have you had complaints about anonymous calls from Ned Swift's family?'

'Funny you should ask,' she said. 'Dr Swift is on the phone every day, complaining about it, telling us we need to get our collective finger out. Having fielded two or three of his calls, I can tell you he has a wide and extensive knowledge of ripe language.'

'And was the message he's getting the same one as Dame Dorcas was moaning about?'

'Indeed it was.'

'Sounds like our perp is emerging more and more out into the open.'

'Just what Garside said this morning.'

'What do you know about Swift *fils*?'

Most of what she told me I already knew via Mr Fuller. 'The father was going on about some hussy who'd targeted his son last year, said she thought she was on to a good thing, since Ned wasn't short of a bob or two, liked to throw it around. Dad seemed to think it might have had something to do with his murder.'

'What do you think?'

'The man's talking through his hat. Funny thing about him, and his wife. Quick . . . neither of them seemed to be that concerned.'

It had been a long busy day. Time to go home and collapse.

NINETEEN

Driving home, I asked myself if I'd turned up anything useful. I had a feeling that I'd been told something vaguely new, maybe even helpful, but like a splinter in the thumb, since I couldn't bring it to mind, I was going to have to wait until it had worked its way out, rather than trying to probe for it in the recesses of my brain. Or was I? As I drove along the familiar roads, through the residential districts into the shopping area, down Castle Street and into the by now almost deserted High Street, I grew increasingly irked at not being able to recall what it was that might prove to be a lead worth pursuing.

Once home, I sank into the comfort of my sofa, then lifted the phone to dial Sam Willoughby and ask him if wanted a nightcap.

He did. When he arrived, I laid all the information I had in front of him.

'Hmm . . .' he said, sipping whisky. 'What do we know about this Ned Swift? Poor bloke.'

'At least his death was quick,' I said.

'That's some compensation for being dead, I suppose.' He slipped a dram or two more into our glasses. 'You know, you'd think someone would have noticed our murderer, wouldn't you? He'd have to have been covered in blood.'

'I don't know. You do your dirty work, you exit the warehouse, pulling the door to behind you, you stow your victim into your boot – possibly having covered it with a plastic sheet beforehand – you drive to your previously chosen dumping ground, dispose of your body and take off, none knows whither.'

'And he wouldn't necessarily be someone who lives locally,' Sam said thoughtfully. 'But it would more or less have to be someone who knew the area, however superficially, because otherwise—'

'–how would the killer have known about the warehouse?'

'Exactly.'

'How do you feel about organized crime in general, the Chinese Triads in particular?' I asked.

'Pretty negative.'

'If it was them, surely we'd have noticed them hanging about the place.' I picked up the whisky bottle and poured us each a second wee dram of single malt. I was beginning to feel a pleasant buzz, composed of exhaustion allied to alcohol.

'Why would we? For a start, they wouldn't be hanging about. They'd come discreetly, do what they have to do, and depart equally discreetly. And I can tell you that from my vantage point in the middle of Longbury High Street, for pretty well eight hours a day, I've never seen any oriental gentlemen wandering up and down, except for the occasional guided party of Japanese tourists, come to take selfies of themselves on the ramparts of the Castle.'

'Let me put this another way,' I said. 'Do you think I'm barking up the wrong tree, attributing Tristan's death – and Ned Swift's, because he must have died by the same hand or hands – to Triads or people like them?'

'Honest answer? Yes.'

'But, Sam, there are so many links to Tristan's time in Hong Kong.'

'They could all be purely coincidental.'

'The way he was killed . . . all those cuts to his body. It was *you* who gave me the info in the first place . . . Triad rituals and so on. *Killed by myriads of sword* . . . it seems to be one of their classic methods of dispatching a traitor.'

'There could be other explanations for his death, *and* the killer who might have carried it out, is all I'm saying. And you've had your mind so fixed on some kind of Asian connection that you haven't bothered to look elsewhere.'

'You're absolutely right.' I groaned. 'Oh God, I just can't start all over again.'

'Then don't. Leave it to the rozzers. Your mate Inspector Garside, for instance. That's what they're paid for.'

'You don't know Dimsie Drayton the way I do,' I said. 'But the hell with it. I'm not going to think about it at the moment, I'm too tired.'

Sam moved closer. Put his arm round my shoulders. Pushed my hair back from my face, pulled me against him. I heard the beat of his heart, the pulse of blood in his veins. Breathed him in. 'Dear Sam,' I murmured, 'you always smell so good.'

'So do you.' He nuzzled my face. His lips touched my cheek.

'I'm whacked.' I closed my eyes. Drifted. 'Know what? I'm going to go to sleep right here.'

'Not really a good idea.' He shifted. 'I'd better go.'

'No, Sam. Don't go. Not just yet.'

'Then let's get you into bed.'

When I woke the next morning, it was still early, the sky outside the window only a shade or two brighter than dark. There was no sign of Sam. I was wearing a nightdress. I still had my knickers on. Getting up to deal with an overfull bladder, I saw that he had washed last night's glasses and left them to drain. Along with the dirty dishes I had embarrassingly left in the sink two days ago. He'd think I was a real slut.

Back in bed, I wondered if 'anything' had taken place. Or if Sam had spent some of the night in my bed. Was I misremembering warm arms, a hand on my breast, breath against my cheek? But Sam wasn't the sort of man to take advantage of a tired and slightly pissed woman. I was glad. If 'anything' was ever to take place between us – not that it was likely to – I wanted to be fully aware.

In that mad swirling way that one's thought processes have in the early morning, before the affairs of the day start crowding in, I reflected how nice Sam was, how very much I wanted to stop looking into Tristan's death, Dimsie or no Dimsie, what the Norwegian fjords would be like at this time of year. I thought of the am-dram group, of the toothsome Milo Stanton, chess pieces, bungee jumping, Chris Kearns, puppets, Sam playing rugby. And it struck me that, however deeply Tristan might be involved in matters oriental or criminal, the likelihood of Kevin Fuller being similarly embroiled had to be just about non-existent. So why had he too been tortured and killed? What was the justification for his death?

I had fallen back to sleep when the phone rang. 'Quick,' I mumbled, barely awake.

'It's Milo here,' a voice said.

'Milo! Hi! How are you?' I came to fast. I knew I was sounding over-bright, all exclamation marks, like Yvonne Landis. What would have happened last night if it had been Milo who'd undressed me, undone my bra, eased off my jeans, surveyed my underwear. Oddly, I didn't find the prospect remotely erotic.

'Long time no see and all that crap,' he said. 'How are you?'

'Just fine, thanks.'

'Sorry to ring so early, but I got an email from Chris Kearns inviting me over to see a one-off rehearsal of his pantomime, along with some of the theatre group. How about it?'

'When?'

'Like today.'

'Kind of early to be starting to rehearse for Christmas panto, isn't it? It's only September.'

'Long lead time,' he said.

'Well, I'm not a panto buff.'

'Oh, come on, it'll be fun,' he said.

'Hmm . . .' Why didn't I come right out with it and say I didn't want to traipse over to some sleazy seaside resort or wherever to see some cross-dressing thesp prancing about the stage and flaunting his huge frilly knickers or enormous knockers?

'I'll pick you up this evening at six,' he said firmly, and put down the receiver before I could protest.

There were six of us in the people-carrier. Milo was driving, with a vapid new recruit beside him in the front passenger seat. Dolly, she was called; long blonde hair cascading loosely over her shoulders, a sensuous mouth, a frequent and irritating giggle. She was born to play the young ingénue. In the back were Charlotte Plimpton, Ricky Hadfield, me, and a bearded bloke whose chief attributes were a stomach of Falstaffian size and a Father Christmas laugh, known far and wide as Fred, although his parents had named him Timothy Timm. Which might have been why he preferred to be called Fred.

'Can't say I'm particularly looking forward to this evening,' Char muttered. The two of us were in the back seat, behind Fred and Ricky.

'Nuts and bolts time, dear,' rumbled Fred. 'We all need to know what goes on backstage.'

'Why?' I asked. We were all keeping our voices down in the hope that Milo wouldn't hear us.

'Yeah, why? It's a bit pointless for me,' said Char. 'I have no ambitions whatsoever to run the show.'

'Suppose the entire management team dropped dead at the beginning of Act Two,' said Ricky. 'What would you do?'

'I'd cancel the show.'

'Or they all went down with virulent food-poisoning?'

'I'd still cancel.'

'Whatever happened to the idea that the Show Must Go On?' wondered Fred.

'We're not professionals,' said Ricky, loudly enough to be heard from the front seats.

'Speak for yourself,' said Milo.

Oh yes, and when did *you* last appear in legitimate theatre? I thought. Then also thought *No! Stop! I must not be catty.* Yes, I'd voluntarily joined the group, giving in to urgings from Char Plimpton on the grounds that I ought to get out more. But that didn't mean I enjoyed being dragooned into this kind of senseless outing.

‘Looking forward to the evening?’ Milo asked.

‘Yay!’ we chorused.

‘It’s good of Chris to invite us, don’t you agree?’

Muffled agreement from the back. There was a silence, during which Dolly giggled. Perhaps it was a nervous tic.

‘Well, I can tell you that he really is as genial as he looks,’ said Milo from the front. Dolly giggled again. ‘He’s had a hard life in many ways but he seems to have things on an even keel now.’

‘Good.’

‘Have any of you managed to read his book?’

‘I have,’ I said. I did wish Milo would concentrate on the road ahead, rather than twisting around in the driver’s seat to talk to those of us in the back.

‘And?’

‘I found it very interesting. *And* well-written. He’s certainly had a few knocks over the years, so more power to him for managing to get himself back on track. And he doesn’t seem in the least bit self-pitying, which is a plus.’

‘Hear, hear,’ agreed Milo.

‘Ever wish it was you, Milo?’ asked Ricky. ‘Starring in your own sitcom, giving your Widow Twankey or Ugly Sister?’

‘Do you mind? I’m aiming a lot higher than *that*, thank you.’

‘Lear? Hamlet? Macbeth?’

‘All or any. Whatever. And believe me, guys. I don’t *wish*. I *know*. One of these days, there I’ll be. Red carpets, fans flocking, name up in lights, beautiful women throwing themselves at me. It’ll happen, trust me.’ He seemed deadly serious.

Not happening yet, I thought, so simmer down, Olivier.

Beside him, Dolly giggled. As well she might.

Chris Kearns was on hand to greet us when we eventually straggled into the theatre. ‘So pleased you could come, darlings,’ he said, jittering about like a Mexican jumping bean. ‘Now, sit yourselves down in the third row of the stalls, and take notes. All got pen and paper? Good. If you get bored, creep out . . . there’s a pub just round the corner. Otherwise, come backstage after, and we’ll have a quick one before you leave. And by quick one, in case anyone thinks

I've fallen off the wagon, mine's a vodka and tonic without the vodka!'

He slapped Milo on the back and spun away, while we settled into our seats. I was expecting one of the more boring evenings of my life, and by God, I was right. The whole occasion was even worse than I had anticipated it would be. To start with, thanks to work commitments, only three-quarters of the cast was present, which robbed the occasion of any animation or glamour it might have had. There were some flat jokes, some uninspired backchat, and plenty of displays of temperament. Dear, oh dear. And this was only a familiarisation pre-pre-pre technical run-through, intended as no more than a way to get the cast into a receptive frame of mind. What it'd be like when they began to rehearse for real three or four weeks from now, I didn't like to contemplate.

I made a firm resolution that if I stuck with the uni drama group, it would be in make-up or wardrobe. I'd hate to find myself part of this kind of egotistical one-upmanship on a regular basis. Or to be thought of as someone who was. I was definitely not an actor – though given the fact that I was no longer one, I flattered myself my Police Inspector On the Case performance had been pretty convincing.

The evening rolled slowly on. There were long periods when absolutely nothing was going on, while people clustered round other people, some holding scripts, others with bits of chalk. Every now and then, Chris Kearns came to the front of the stage, shielded his eyes from the half-lit footlights and asked if we were all right. To which Milo replied enthusiastically that yes thanks, we were. I longed to shout out that, speaking personally, I wasn't, that I was suicidally bored, that I wanted to go home and curl up with a good book. But of course I was much too well brought up to do any such thing. Besides, Milo had the transport.

When Char leaned towards me and murmured that she couldn't take much more of this, was heading for the pub and did I want to . . .?, before she'd even finished speaking I had assumed that crouching stance that people employ when shuffling along a row of theatre seats, even though there was nobody sitting behind us.

'I don't want to hurt dear Milo,' Char said, when we were sitting with drinks in front of us, round the corner from the theatre. 'But honestly . . .'

'Sigh,' I said.

'I have no ambitions to be a thesp,' said Char. 'And in any case, even if I were to become the star attraction in of the group's productions, I would only be a big fish in a little pond.'

'In my case, I'd be a little fish in a tiny pond. I only joined because you more or less forced me to.'

'In my case, it was my mother. She's desperate to get me married off again. Bridge or drama, she said firmly – she's a very firm person – and I'll babysit. So I chose what I thought would be the lesser of two evils.' She sank half the contents of her lime shandy. 'No, it's quite fun, really, but life's too short to spend an evening like the one we're in the middle of. Apart from this bit of it.' She smiled at me.

'What do you think of Chris?' I asked.

'What do *you*?'

We looked at each other. Shrugged. Made that turned-down-lower-lip pout that usually goes with a shrug. Didn't want to be negative, even if we felt it, because the man was Milo's chum.

'As an actor, or as a person?' asked Char eventually.

'Either. Both. Seems OK to me,' I said. 'If you like that sort of thing.'

'On the whole, I do. Mind you, I wouldn't want to get on the wrong side of him.'

'Why not?'

'He reminds me very much of my former husband. As nice as pie, everybody's best friend, until somebody gets across him. Then pow! Watch out for fireworks!'

'Short fuse, eh?'

'It's much deeper than that – with my ex, at least. Obviously I've no idea about Kearns.'

'Interesting,' I said. Or was it?

TWENTY

The following few days passed without murder-related incident. I finished my final texts. Put the anthology together. Picked out – as instructed by my publisher – three paintings, one of which would be chosen to grace the front cover. Drove over to ArtWorld Books to discuss things with Cliff Nichols and his assistant Elaine.

The outcomes were extremely positive. On the downside, I intensely missed Helena Drummond, my former collaborator, who had been murdered last year. Her knowledge, her humour, her warmth. I wanted to have a simple dedication on the copyright page: *For Helena*, and Nichols was happy to go along with it. There were a couple of niggles about three of the paintings I'd chosen but I had anticipated their objections and brought along alternatives which we all found acceptable.

So a good week, overall.

Until the phone call.

I was dragged out of sleep by the insistent beeping of my mobile on the table beside my bed. Only half awake, I squinted at the green glow of the digital display. It was well after one o'clock. What the f . . .? I snatched up the phone, pressed the right buttons, lifted it to my ear.

'Quick.'

'Fliss here, Alex.'

She only called me Alex in times of significant stress. 'What is it?' I said, alarmed. Anxiety swelled inside me like a toxic fungus.

'Joy's just got back from work.'

'At this hour? They certainly make sure she earns her crust of bread, don't they?'

'It wasn't the department, it was the police who kept her.'

'My God, Fliss, what on earth has she done?' I was wide awake now. Fliss's partner, Joy, was aptly named, one of the world's life enhancers. Happy, witty, clever, stunning in every way. To think of her being questioned by the police for some crime or other was—

'Not *her*, for Christ's sake, Alex. But someone.'

'What's this someone done then?'

'There's been another murder.'

'Another? But that's four in the past month, Fliss. What the hell is going on?'

'That's what we're trying to find out. But the thing is—'

'Do you think they're related? Or is it still too early to—'

'Stop gabbling, Quick!'

I was silent. Whatever she was trying to tell me, I didn't want to know. 'The thing is, it's someone you know.'

'Who?' My heart plunged like a high-speed lift. 'Not one of my parents.'

'No!' She paused.

'Nor . . .' The lift crashed through the ground floor into the basement. What would I do if— '. . . Sam Willoughby.'

'Not him, either.'

'Who, then, for God's sake?' I braced myself.

'Remember when you came round for a drink with us, what, a couple of months ago? You were raving and drooling about some hunk with black hair who ran a drama group that you'd joined?'

'You can't possibly be talking about Milo Stanton, can you?'

'I can.'

'Milo murdered?'

'I'm afraid so.'

'Tell me—' I swallowed. Once. And again. 'Tell me what happened.'

'The police were called because some motorist nearly ran over his body which was lying in the middle of the road. He'd been tortured, just like your friend Huber, and tossed into a ditch along the verge of Borton Road. The awful thing was that he was still alive when he was dumped, and he somehow managed to find enough strength to crawl to the tarmac, where he collapsed and died. He had all his ID in one of his pockets, so we had no problem identifying him – but we already know that's part of the killer's MO.'

'That's . . . *terrible*.' To think of Milo dead – so handsome, so energetic, so avid, so certain the future was bright – was too dreadful. And dying in such a manner.

'Quick?'

I coughed, trying to clear my air passages. I couldn't squeeze any words past the back of my throat.

'I'm really sorry, Quick. I know you fancied him.'

I made some kind of grunt. Truth was, my fancying had been short-lived; Milo was fancied too much by Milo for anyone else to matter. Nonetheless, foibles and all, he was a fellow human. Why would anyone want to kill him?

'Of course the driver who found him was questioned, but he obviously had nothing to do with it.'

'Are you linking his death to the others?' I managed to croak.

'Not yet. For a start, the MOs weren't the same. And of course the sites were in different places.'

'Linked or not, when this murdering bastard's finished with them, they've all been removed from the original kill-site. Which is something I've been wondering about . . . with these other three murders – and now Milo – why would a killer want to take the bodies of his victims and dump them somewhere else? Somewhere where they'd be bound to be discovered.'

'Cocking a snook at us, the cops? Because we know the villains always think they're smarter than we are.'

'A desire for attention, wanting the world to take note of his handiwork?'

'Or simply *hoping* to be caught?'

'Quite likely. Because if he'd left Tristan Huber's body in that warehouse, it could have been weeks before anyone found him. And that,' I added sombrely, 'would negate the point. And think of the risks he'd take, the trace he'd be scattering all over the place, by moving him.'

'Hang on a minute, Quick. I thought you were fingering some Chinese crime organization for the Huber death. Now you're referring to a single perp.'

'Only in a manner of speaking. Incidentally, good as you and your colleagues are at crime solving—'

'You used to be one and I wish you still were.'

'—if one of the Triads is responsible, they could thumb their noses at British law enforcement, just close ranks and you'd never get anywhere near an arrest, let alone a conviction. Remember that case in Borton? We knew exactly who was responsible, but hadn't a hope in hell of pinning it on anyone.'

'I remember it well.' She yawned loudly. 'Anyway, *ma chère*, I'm going to bed.'

'Sleep well.' I very much doubted that *I* would.

After I'd switched of the lamp, the bedroom was dark. Very occasionally the lights of some late home-goer swivelled across the ceiling and were gone. I thought of poor Milo, his dreams of seeing his name up in lights in some West End theatre now forever extinguished, his Lear cancelled, his Hamlet still-born, his Macbeth aborted.

Despite myself, I fell asleep. At eight o'clock, I awoke again and staggered downstairs. I'd just made a pot of coffee when the doorbell rang. I lifted the speaker phone. 'Who is it?'

'CID,' replied a voice I recognized from my days on the force, despite the phone's tinny resonance. 'We'd like to have a word.'

'Come on up.'

I had time to pull on some clothes before they were knocking at my door. 'Inspector Richards,' I said, throwing open the door. 'Do come in.'

The burly man in front of me frowned. 'DCI Quick?'

'Ex.'

He was puzzled. 'What are we . . .' He turned to the female DS behind him. 'Is there some mistake, Lindsay?'

'No, sir.' Lindsay Griffiths winked at me. 'Is that coffee I can smell?'

'Sure is.' I led them both into my kitchen and filled three mugs. 'How can I help you?'

'We're investigating the death of Milo Stanton,' Richards said. 'We believe you knew him quite well.'

'I knew him. But not well.'

'You don't seem surprised to hear that he's dead,' Richards said.

'That's because I already knew.'

'How come?'

'I was informed late last night.' Before either of them could ask by whom, and not wanting to land Fliss in it, I added, 'They'd just heard, I don't know how. The point was that the last time I saw him I was with some other people from the drama group he ran up on the hill. I expect you'll be talking to them.'

'Quite right.' Griffiths pulled an iPad from her bag and turned it on. 'Charlotte Plimpton, Richard Hadfield, Timothy—' She produced a kind of snort. '—Timm, Dorothy Overdene.'

'They're the ones. But there are others in the group. Fifteen or twenty of us in all.'

'As an ex-copper, you might be considered more likely than others to have noticed anything out of the way in the dynamics of the group,' said Richards.

'Absolutely nothing, I'm afraid.'

'What was this Milo guy like?'

'Handsome, vibrant. A bit up himself. But then as far as I can see, most actors are. It seems to come with the territory.'

'Any idea at all who might have it in for him?'

'None at all.' I thought back to the people who'd travelled with him to the technical run-through for the panto Kearns was going to be in at Christmas. And the rest of the am-dram group. 'I only recently joined. I barely knew any of the other members. They'd be much more helpful than I would.'

'It was worth a try,' DS Griffiths said. 'Which is why we came to you first.'

'Sorry, I didn't anticipate seeing *you* when you opened the door,' said Richards. As though the town was rife with people called Quick. 'No wonder DS Griffiths insisted we come here before we went anywhere else.' He gave her an approving smile.

As they left, I murmured to Lesley, 'You'll *love* Timothy Timm.'

'Can't wait.'

'He's a huge bloke, calls himself Fred.'

She grinned. 'I'm not surprised.'

Later, I dialled Sam's mobile. 'Are you at home, or in the shop?' I asked, when he answered.

'The shop. What's u—'

'I'll come down,' I said, and disconnected.

He was waiting for me when I pushed open the door. He said nothing, just spread his arms wide. I leaned against his chest. 'Oh, Sam,' I said. 'I seem to spend half my time leaning on you.'

'I love it,' he said. 'Feel free.'

I dropped a few tears on the front of his shirt. Straightened up. Explained what had happened.

We sat down at one of the café tables in a corner of the shop I sipped at the cappuccino he brought me. We stared at each other. 'I didn't really know him,' I said. 'But . . .'

'Any man's death diminishes me?'

'Donne and – sadly – dusted.'

He put hand over mine. 'Looks like we've got a serial killer on the loose.'

I shook my head. 'Someone else suggested that but I don't agree.'

'You can't believe there're four separate murderers in town all at the same time. Or do you still . . .' He groaned. 'Not your pet theory again. Chinese gang members swarming all over Longbury. Come on, Alex. The victims can't all have been involved with Triads.'

'It doesn't really hold water, does it? Although I should point out that you were the one who came up with the intel re death by a thousand cuts or myriad swords or whatever.' I frowned. 'If the same guy killed all of them, and assuming it's not just random murder, what we have to find out is why *these* people, and why *now*? What do they have in common? How did he snatch them or overpower them?'

'Pen and paper time.' Sam produced a lined notebook and a couple of fine-tipped pens. 'OK, let's write down what we know and see if the four victims can be linked in any way.'

'And having done that, try to work out who might have been responsible.'

'Right.'

We wrote them down: Tristan Huber, Kevin Fuller, Ned

Swift, Milo Stanton. I wondered if DCI Fliss would be generous in sharing any information the police had uncovered. After all, any questions needing to be asked, or information Sam and I unearthed, the cops would surely have already latched on to. Longbury wasn't a big metropolis, as well as being a town of which the sea occupied 180 degrees of the available space. Four murders in just a few weeks was verging on an epidemic. But it didn't necessarily imply a serial killer.

'So,' said Sam. 'What did the victims have in common?'

We made a list.

1. *They're all men.*
2. *At least two of them had spent time out East (as had the Landis/Lockharts).*
3. *Three of them were connected to the university. Tristan, too, though only peripherally.*
4. *All had interests outside their main fields of expertise: extreme sports, chess, theatre, though apart from the fact that two of them belonged to the chess club, none in common, unless you considered marionettes as theatre. Or playing in a band, like Swift.*
5. *Kevin Fuller had been on the redecoration of the junior common room committee, which brought him into contact with Tristan, and possibly Swift and Milo.*

'Did Milo Stanton or Tristan Huber play chess?' Sam asked.

'Not that I'm aware of. But I didn't know Milo very well – and thinking back, I do believe I've played chess with Tris in the past. And lost.'

'Apart from Tristan, were any of them into interior design? Or were artists?'

'Don't know. It looks like one of us is going to have to go up to the uni and poke around a bit,' I said. I gazed at him, my expression full of significance.

Sam picked up on it. 'You mean me, don't you?' he said.

'God, you're quick! Yes. Because you're so good at winkling the gen out of people,' I said. 'Look what you found out about Kevin Fuller.' A sudden thought struck me. 'Hey, we know he was gay. Do we know anything about any partner, or long-term relationship he might have had?'

'If there was one, it wasn't volunteered when I was pursuing my enquiries earlier,' said Sam. 'Why are you asking?'

'Knowledge is power. And if you don't ask questions, you'll never get the answers.'

'Gnomically put.'

'Just call me Dopey,' I said.

'Tomorrow's Sunday,' said Sam. 'I'll pursue the trail of truth and justice on Monday, since most people will be gone for the weekend. But only on one condition.'

'And that is?'

'That you cook lunch for me on Sunday. And I mean lunch with all the trimmings: roast lamb, mint sauce, redcurrant jelly, roast spuds, sprouts, lashings of gravy. Even Yorkshire pud, though I know that's supposed to go with beef rather than lamb.' He smiled at me. 'Deal? Or no deal?'

'Deal.' I enjoyed cooking, was good at it. A necessary defence against my mother's culinary shortcomings.

On the way back to my flat, I did the requisite shopping. As I pushed open the door of my building, I found Char Plimpton standing in the lobby. 'Alex!' she exclaimed. She looked terrible, face ashen and blotchy, eyes red and swollen, hair all over the place. 'Have you heard this frightful news about Milo?' She broke down, great sobs shaking her body, mouth unattractively open as she wailed.

'Unfortunately, yes,' I said. 'Look, come on up and I'll fix you a coffee – or something stronger.'

She followed me up the stairs and into the flat, still weeping loudly. I set my bags down on the kitchen counter. 'What would you like, Char?'

'Something stronger,' she gulped.

'Go and sit down in the sitting room and I'll bring it in.'

A swig or two of brandy later, she'd calmed down a bit. 'It's so awful,' she said. 'So unbelievable. I mean, who would want to kill Milo, of all people?'

Nil nisi bonum and all that, but I was willing to bet that there was a quite a cast-list ready to audition for the part, if not of First Murderer, certainly of Grievous Bodily Harmer.

Then chided myself for unkind and inappropriate thinking. 'I know,' I agreed. 'It's terribly sad.'

'Oh, Milo, why?' she mourned. 'Why, oh why?' She was beginning to sound like a B-list tragedienne. Any minute now I feared she was going to start beating her bosom or plucking out her hair.

'Is there a Mrs Milo?' I asked.

'Not so's you'd notice. At least, not so anyone who knew Milo would notice.' She sat up a bit and sipped again at her brandy balloon, looking considerably pinker of cheek. 'I don't normally drink in the middle of the day but . . .'

'So there *is* one?'

'Plus two little Milos.' She raised a hand to her forehead. 'Oh Lord, those poor people . . . losing their husband and father. And *why*?'

'I didn't really know him,' I said. I poured a little more brandy into her glass.

She produced a short barking laugh. 'In my opinion, there wasn't a whole lot *to* know. What you saw was what you got. Poor man, he was so determined to make it big.'

'Did he have any aptitude for the stage?'

'Oh yes, some. But nothing like he thought he had. It was the wife who's got the talent. I believe there was quite a bit of domestic friction about the fact that she was always getting parts in TV sitcoms and BBC drama – you must have seen her in that last historical series they produced . . . what was it called? About some French queen? She played the title role, got pretty good notices, too. And she's always on quiz shows and the like.'

'Milo must have been proud of her,' I said, though it seemed unlikely.

'You'd think so, wouldn't you? Trouble was, she's much more successful than he was ever likely to be.'

'So jealous rather than proud?'

'You'd think he'd have to be, wouldn't you? He certainly never asked her to take part in any of the group's shows. Or maybe he did, and she refused.' Char grimaced, then hiccupped. 'Oh, 'scuse me! I often thought that was why he chased women all the time, to prove to himself that he could at least do something, that at least he was still able to pull the chicks. Sad, really.'

'Was his self-esteem that low? I know he always seemed to be brimming over with self-confidence, but that's so often nothing more than a defense mechanism.'

'Nonetheless,' said Char, hiccupping again. 'I was very . . . fond of him. Actually, I loved him, in a quiet sort of way, I mean I'm a happily married woman etcetera and so on, but I'm . . . well, I'm devastated to hear of his death. Totally devastated.' Tears began to flow once more.

'Should we try to carry on with the Christmas show, as a kind of homage to him?' I asked.

She looked shocked at such levity. Then her face lightened. 'That's a brilliant suggestion! And it would give us all a focus, help us to come to terms with what's happened. And if the others don't think it's practical, without Milo, we could always hold our own little memorial service for him.' She got up. 'Alex, m'dear, thank you so much for allowing me to let off steam. I'll get in touch with the rest of them, and see how they feel about the idea. Both ideas.'

'And then let me know.'

'Of course.'

'By the way, where do the wife and children live?' I asked.

'In Dovebridge.'

'Really?'

So did Edred and Mary Quick, my parents. I would have to make a quick trip over there, invite myself for lunch with them. On second thoughts, since Mary was so gastronomically challenged, make that for tea. And I'd provide the cheese scones. I'd cracked a tooth on the last batch she'd whipped up.

It would give me a chance to call on Mrs Milo Stanton and offer my condolences. Maybe learn something more, though I knew it showed a horrible degree of insensitivity on my part. But no more than the investigating officers would. It was always difficult to walk the line between information-collecting and intrusiveness.

At the door, I put my hand on Charlotte's arm. 'A few more questions: do you have any suspicion of who could have been responsible for his death? Did he ever get across anyone enough – as far as you know – to generate hatred or violence? Was he universally liked or disliked? Was he currently living with his wife or kids?'

She laughed nervously. 'Goodness, you sound like a policeman or something.'

'Funny, that,' I said.

'As for suspicions, I really haven't a clue. I didn't see him outside the group – at least, not really.' I deduced that she and Milo had at some point enjoyed a passage of arms. 'And as far as I'm aware, he hadn't split up with Tamasin. Not yet, anyway. As for who might have . . . might have *killed* him, I absolutely have no idea.'

'So no enemies?'

'No.' She shook her head violently from side to side. '*No!* There were muttering in the ranks sometimes, when he got a bit uppity. High-handed. But it was never serious.'

'Any names you'd care to pass on?'

'Well – gosh, I feel like a Judas – I know Ricky and he had a major row about something – don't ask me what. And Bill Marshall – the guy who always plays the aristocratic uncle or gentlemanly father – they had a real knock-down drag-out earlier this year. I'd never seen Bill so upset. Or so bloody crude, for that matter.'

'Any idea what the row was about?'

'Something to do with Milo coming on to Bill's wife, I believe. Actually, if it turned out to be Bill Marshall who killed him, I wouldn't start back in horrified surprise.'

'So you think he's capable of murdering Milo?'

'I'm not saying that at all, Alex. Not at *all*.'

When she'd gone I sat for a while considering the dynamics of the group. I had enlisted in their number too recently to be able to assess most of the members for potentially murderous inclinations. I also wondered whether Mrs William Marshall had responded to Milo's overtures. I'd questioned earlier, when Tristan was murdered, whether the killer could have been a cuckolded husband. The death by a thousand cuts aspect had put me on to Triads and the like. Perhaps I'd allowed myself to be overly side-tracked. Sam certainly thought so. In any case, I was really only concerned with Tristan's death, and then only because he was an old friend.

Call me irresponsible, but I had had enough. I was moving on. I know I'd said it before, but this time I meant it. From now on, it was up to the police, not to me.

TWENTY-ONE

A car I didn't recognize was parked in front of Edred and Mary's house. I rang the doorbell, rapped the brass lion's head knocker – as always, verdigrised and in dire need of a polish – and let myself in.

'Yoo-hoo,' I called, just to let them know their youngest child had come to visit. I found them sitting in their favourite places, round the kitchen table. Behind them, a kettle was madly dancing on the Aga.

'Hello,' Mary said. She'd gone so far as to put out some mugs, a jug of milk and a bowl full of sugar lumps, along with a pair of tarnished silver sugar tongs. But neither they nor their visitor were drinking tea. There was a one-quarter full bottle of wine on the table, and three smeary glasses, each with a low level of wine in them.

The visitor was Dorcas Huber-Drayton. Grey hair, grey face, grey cardigan pulled tightly across her chest.

'Lovely to see you, darling,' my father said. He held up the depleted bottle. 'Want some?'

'No thanks. I'm driving.' I plonked a lump of good Cheshire cheese from Hanscombes ('*Hanscombes on the High Street, est. 1923*') on the table, together with some of the shop's superior oatcakes.

'Oooh, lovely,' said Edred. He reached some plates down from the china-crammed pine dresser which took up one wall of the room and fished some knives out of the cutlery drawer.

'How are you doing, Dorcas?' I asked.

'Guess,' she snapped.

'Has there been any further news?'

'None at all. It's disgraceful. I don't know what your lot are playing at. Why isn't anyone in custody yet?'

'Alex hasn't been on the police force for several years now, Dorcas,' Mary said, 'so you can't really blame her for the lack of progress.'

'I can and I do. Pshaw! The whole lot of you are tarred with the same brush.' She turned the blowtorch of her gaze on me. 'But in any case, weren't you supposed to be looking into the matter of my son's murder on behalf of his sister?'

'I said I would do my best.' I was determined not to let the bloody woman rile me. I reminded myself of her agonising bereavement. 'Whoever's responsible has done a darned good job of keeping an extremely low profile. My contact on the local CID unit seems to have no more information than I do.'

'How *is* the dear girl?' my mother said.

'Which one?'

'Felicity, of course. You must bring her round – it's ages since we last saw her.'

'I'll ask her when she's likely to be free.'

'While you three are busy arranging your social calendar,' barked Dorcas, her voice like acid, 'I'm more interested in bringing a killer to justice. And I want to know why nothing seems to have been done.'

'You'll have to take that up with the local CID,' I said. 'Meanwhile, do any of you know someone called Tamasin Stanton? Lives in the village?'

My parents looked at one another. 'It's that actress woman. On Pensfield Avenue,' Mary said. 'We saw her in that television series, Edred. Remember?'

'No.'

'A French queen. Mother of Richard the Lionheart.'

'And Bad King John,' Dorcas added sourly.

'Eleanor of Aquitaine,' I supplied.

'Oh, of *course*,' my parents chorused.

'Or was it Isabella of Angoulême?' said Edred. His gold-rimmed spectacles fell off his nose and hit his wine glass which by now was fortunately empty. 'I can't remember which.'

'Eleanor,' said my mother.

'No, Isabella,' said my father firmly.

'And she's often on other programmes.'

'I read about her being in something at the Almeida or the Royal Court, can't remember which.'

'Nonsense, woman, how could she be? She died four centuries ago.'

'Not Eleanor, you silly old goof. I'm talking about that woman in the village – Tamasin Stanton.'

Dorcas gave vent to a windily exasperated sigh. 'For God's sake, does it matter?'

'Thing is, whether it's the Royal Court or Almeida, the poor woman's husband . . .' I glanced sideways at Dorcas. Her fingers trembled on the stem of her glass. There was a nervous tic winking under the skin below her left eye. 'While I'm here I thought I'd pop in and see her. Make myself known. I'm in her husband's amateur dramatics group at the university.'

'Good heavens!' Edred exclaimed. He rattled his newspaper to capture our attention. 'Listen to this! Seems that Arthur Dibdin is dead.'

'Dibdin . . . I've always liked that name,' Mary said. 'So . . . salty.'

'Who's Arthur Dibdin?' I asked, spooning Edred's home-made marmalade on to my toast.

'One of our local taxi-drivers. Bad-tempered old bugger, very disobliging man. We didn't use him if we could avoid it, did we, Mary?'

'Who's he insulted now?' my mother said.

'I just told you . . . he's died.'

'We've all got to go some time,' said Mary.

'Yes, but not the same way as poor old Dibdin, I hope. Seems he was run over by his own taxi.' Edred stared into the middle-distance. 'I wonder how he managed that.'

'Some disgruntled passenger fed up with his rudeness probably set it up, I shouldn't be surprised,' said Mary callously. She looked over at me. 'Dibdin spent his time ferrying children to and from school, and after school hours took bookings from people going out to dinner or parties or whatever. Picking people up after office or university functions. He may have been a grumpy old sod but he'll be a loss to the local community.'

'Oh, and look, Mary,' Edred went on. 'There's a performance of *The Creation* at the Longbury Assembly Rooms on September twentieth.'

'I know.'

'Should we get tickets?'

'We're both *singing* in it, for God's sake.'

'Of course we are.' My father opened his mouth and burst into song. '*The heavens are telling the glo-ory of God,*' he sang. '*The-e wonder of his work—*'

'Stop it, Edred!' shrieked Dorcas. She had a voice that could zap angry hornets at twenty paces. She used it now, as she banged a meaty fist on the table. 'All this chit-chat about concerts and taxi-drivers is not going any way towards solving the death of my son.' She stared accusingly at me. 'Why are the police dragging their heels?'

'I don't think they are,' I said. 'It's just that they have so little to go on.'

'It's been days now,' she said. '*Weeks.*'

'I know. But the person responsible has been very, very careful. As far as I can gather from my friend on the force, they haven't got much to go on. But I know for certain,' I added hastily, as she opened her mouth, 'that enquiries are being energetically pursued.'

'Not energetically enough, if you want my opinion.'

Which I didn't.

'Will you come back for supper?' asked my father, as I prepared to leave. 'Now you're here you could even stay the night. Your room's always ready.'

'And I've made a casserole,' Mary added.

Cripes . . . my mother's casseroles were things to avoid if humanly possible. Any old rubbish she'd found at the back of the fridge, stuff in the freezer well past its sell-by date, once even, I swear, roadkill. A rabbit found by the roadside and inexpertly skinned by Edred. God only knew how long it had been lying there. 'Thank you both,' I said. 'I'll play it by ear, if you don't mind.'

'*Play it by ear*.' My mother settled her elbows on the table. 'A curious phrase for not committing yourself.'

'I'll wing it, then,' I said.

'Even more curious.'

I left them to it.

I knocked at the door of 1 Pensfield Avenue, a leafy suburban street on the edge of the village, completely separate from the mediaeval alleys and twittens which made Dovebridge such a charming place to live.

'Could you tell me which is Mrs Stanton's house?' I asked.

'You don't look like a stalker. Or an assassin,' the very old boy who opened the door told me, clacking his dentures around.

'That's because I'm neither.'

'She's at number 27. The woman's a bit of a celebrity round here. She was in that telly programme about Eleanor of Aquitaine. Or was it Isabella of Angoulême? I get confused, sometimes. Whichever it was, I thought she was pretty good and historically the programme was very accurate.'

'I haven't seen it,' I said. 'Not yet.'

'You shouldn't miss it. You can get a boxed set, you know.'

'I might just do that. Thank you.'

Number 27, when I got there, didn't appear to be inhabited, though there was a pink tricycle lying on its side under a bush in the front garden, and a doll's pram in the porch. Property of the little Milo orphans, obviously. I rang the doorbell several times, but there was no response from inside the house.

'She's gorn away,' a well-spoken voice behind me said.

I turned to find a woman in a battered felt hat and a grubby fawn raincoat, who had stopped on the pavement in front of the house. She looked like she was understudying Maggie Smith in *The Lady in the Van*. She had a Welsh corgi on a lead.

'I see,' I said.

'Just lost her husband, poor lass. Not that he was much cop, spouse-wise.'

I walked down the path to join her, while she hoisted one

hip to rest it on the low brick wall which separated the house from the road.

'Not much cop?'

'Never here, was he? Poor Tammy had to raise those girls more or less on her own, as well as be the family breadwinner. Luckily her mother lived with them, did most of the childcare, took the children to school and so forth.'

'They'll miss him,' I said.

The woman grimaced. 'I don't want to sound callous, but what's to miss, quite honestly? Good riddance really, not that one would want the man dead, of course, but I expect it's something of a relief all round, when you come right down to it.'

'That's a bit harsh.'

'It is, isn't it?' she said. The corgi moaned. Or possibly groaned. It was hard to tell which. She got down from the wall. 'I'd better be on my way. Llewellyn's desperate for a pee.' She yanked at the dog and set off towards the park at the end of the road.

Driving back to my parents' house, I realized I knew no more about Milo Stanton now than when I arrived. Certainly nothing that might lead to his being murdered. I would have to contact Char Plimpton again . . . she'd been too upset when we met earlier for me to start asking probing questions about the row between William Marshall and Milo. Or the one involving Ricky Hadfield. Not that I supposed either of them to have any hand in Milo's death. But they might widen the field of suspects, or point the enquiry in other directions.

Meanwhile, there was my mother's casserole to be endured.

The following morning, after discovering, against all the odds, that I hadn't gone down with food poisoning or the plague, I joined my parents for breakfast before setting off home. As always, the two of them were deeply immersed in the papers, both local and national. I poured myself a mug of tea, stuck a couple of slices of bread into the toaster, and wondered, as so many times before, how two such educated and discerning people could allow themselves to eat sliced bread. It wasn't just the diminished taste, it was also the chemicals added to preserve it on the shelves, plus the fact that once opened, it went mouldy before you were halfway through the loaf. I concede that it's useful if you have to get kids breakfasted and off to school, or packed lunches to prepare, but practicality is not a constituent of flavour.

Driving back to my flat, I accepted that Milo could not possibly have been embroiled in some Triad organization. That was far too big a stretch.

So, I had to assume that all this time, as Sam had pointed out with varying degrees of acerbity, I had been way off the mark, and Triads were not after all involved. I felt stupid. And embarrassed. Like my friend Clarissa Ridgeway's mediaeval *jongleur* protagonist, Rondel, I was baffled. Sam was right (darn it!), there had to be some other link between the three/four of them. The only thing they seemed to possess was a connection to the university. Tristan was only peripherally involved, through the Junior Common Room redecoration scheme, but the other three were definitely part of the uni system. Kevin, because he was working towards his PhD, Ned Swift as a student, and Milo because of the theatre group. And I had no idea where Mr Dibdin fitted in, if indeed he had anything to do with the other victims.

Was it worth my while talking to someone there? Frankly, I thought not. Leave it to the force. Especially considering that even if someone came up with a solid twenty-four-carat gold motive, along with means and opportunity, to murder one of the dead, it was highly unlikely to be applicable to the others. Improbable though it seemed, any one of them might have been a stand-alone murder.

I telephoned DCI Fairlight. 'How's Garside's investigation going?' I asked.

'Stalled for the moment, as far as I know. As always, Alan's playing his cards pretty close to his chest. I'm fairly sure he suspects that you and I are exchanging information. He certainly doesn't seem to want to give anything away. Even in the team's daily briefings.' She dropped her voice. 'On the other hand, Quick, I understand from DS Griffiths that he's close to bringing someone in for questioning.'

'Who, for gosh sakes?'

'I don't know. Griffiths was being very circumspect.'

'Tell me, Fliss, is he linking all four murders?'

'He'd have to be. Or three of them, anyway. He's far from stupid, and he can't possibly imagine that they're all separate incidents, with four different perps.'

'Has he taken on board the possibility of the organized crime element I was talking about when Tristan Huber was found?'

'It's up on the wall of the Incident Room.'

I coughed. 'I think I may have been a little wide of the mark with that theory.'

'A little?' She laughed. 'You're not the only one who thought so, darlin'.'

'It had legs,' I said defensively.

'On crutches, Quick. And for your information, Alan did take it seriously enough to contact the Met, and they've been checking round their contacts in the Chinese communities, who were naturally *outraged* at the very notion that one of their lot might have gone round killing innocent British citizens.'

'Has someone been to interview the Landises?'

'Yup. And those people at Rollins Park. Garside may be a misogynistic old prick, but he's an extremely competent officer.'

'You've mentioned the Paramores before . . . I suggest that you urgently set up a further enquiry into them. Like you told me earlier, I think they're heavily into people-smuggling, trafficking, thefts of expensive cars, whatever.' I outlined why I thought so.

'That's a lot of skulduggery,' Fliss said.

'Oh, and add in missing horses.'

'How do you mean, horses?'

'You know, Fliss. Four-legged creatures, capable of amazing turns of speed.'

'Thank you, so helpful. But come to think of it . . . yeah, I have a feeling . . . just a mo . . .' I heard her riffling through some documents, then tapping her computer keys. 'Yes, there've been several recent reports of horses going missing in the area. Why, what do you know?'

'Only what I just told you. And it might not be all the things

I mentioned. But you should definitely get involved. Or at least call the locals, who'll have to include you.'

Conversation ended, I mulled over the facts as I knew them. Four murders, four crime scenes . . . how many killers? Very slowly, my head began to spin. Too many facts, too much supposition, too little solid ground.

I wanted to get back to my own work.

I spent some time at my computer, then walked to the High Street. Went into the florists shop, bought a single pink rose, asked them to tie a matching ribbon round it. Then I carried it further along the street and round the corner to Dimsie's studio.

'This is for you, my dear,' I said kindly, handing the rose to the girl behind the desk, who'd jumped like a frog when I came in. There wasn't a lot she could say after that. She kind of smiled. Rictussed would be nearer the mark, if there is such a word. Silently, she pointed towards the floor above.

I clomped up the stairs where Dim was dealing with paperwork. I set out my table, as they say. And pretty plain pickings it was.

'I'm finished,' I said. 'I've spent far too much time investigating poor Tristan's death. I'm not doing anything more than work in parallel with the police, finding out very little more than they have so far, and with absolutely no idea of who might be the guilty party.'

She tried to interrupt, but I held up my hand. 'I've printed out everything I know and here it is . . .' I laid several pages down in front of her. 'Now I'm out of it.'

'B-but Alex . . .' Quivering chin, filling eyes, trembling lip.

I felt a pang for both her and Dorcas, but really, what more could I do? I seem to have spent the past weeks driving aimlessly around south-east Kent to almost no avail. Certainly very little that was of any use. It was time to move on. The truth was, I needed to shut down. I'd had my fill of murder and cruelty and sadistic killers.

I had about five days of peace. Went up to London with Sam Willoughby to see a play. And again to see an exhibition at the National Gallery. Went to dinner at Charlotte Plimpton's house along with some others from the am-dram group. Spent a day browsing through my extensive collection of art books, looking for inspiration, jotting down ideas. Then Fliss Fairlight rang.

'Thought you might be interested, Quick.'

'I probably would be if I knew why I should be.'

'We've finally had reports back from forensics,' she said. 'They drew our attention to something a bit quirky. With two of the victims – Huber and Stanton – they found faint traces of salt water on the bodies.'

'So the perp lives by the sea? Or even on it? Aboard some boat in one of the harbours round here?'

'Not seawater, Quick. Tears. Looks like the killer might have been crying while he offed his victims.'

I thought about that. 'Wouldn't it be much more likely that the vics were doing the crying?'

'DNA says otherwise. As I'm sure you know, tears only contain traces of DNA if they've rolled down the face and picked up some epithelial cells that contain DNA. Anyway, the concentration of salt in seawater is much higher than in tears.'

'Quirky, all right.' I sighed. Against my will, I'd been plunged back into the hideous underworld of sudden and violent death. I didn't want to be there. 'What does Garside make of it?'

'Not much. At the briefing this morning we were told to give the matter our close attention, while we went about our other jobs, and report our thoughts back by the end of the day.'

'I'll have a think too,' I said.

TWENTY-TWO

There are many theories as to the purpose of dreams. We know that they help to explain and store away recent events for future reference. Most dreams deal with everyday experiences which, in my opinion, suggests that they're messages from the subconscious, attempting to analyze our recent activities. In other words, they're trying to convey something to us.

I just wished I could work out what my current dreams were telling me. Because I'd begun to spend my sleeping hours wreathed in paper chains, bombarded by balloons, festooned in rainbow-coloured garlands. Or dressed in outfits ranging from pirate chiefs to mermaids, from tea-seeking tigers to hungry caterpillars, throwbacks to my childhood.

My parents were never going to achieve five stars in the Good Parent Guide, but they came into their inventive own where parties were concerned, particularly fancy dress ones, which they threw at the least excuse, both for their friends and ours. But that was a long time ago. So why was the remembrance of parties past invading my sleep? Was it something to do with my latest anthology of paintings, *Eat, Drink & Be Merry*? Or was it because I recently had been given a snippet of information and was failing to recognize its importance?

Needing some fresh air, I set off along the seafront. Way off, on top of one of the headlands, I could see the university, its buildings converted by pale sunshine into a mystical otherworldly prospect. Out at sea, tankers were moored. A cross-Channel ferry moved in stately fashion across the water to France. The wind was brisk. Leaves were already beginning to drift down from the trees.

As I walked, I recalled the supper-party I had recently attended at Char Plimpton's house. The guests were all members of the theatre group, in sombre mood. Milo's violent death had saddened and shocked us, but we all felt that the right and proper thing to do would be to arrange a memorial of some kind for him, even though the body was unlikely to be released for a while.

'One way or another we should show our appreciation for the poor chap,' Ricky Hadfield had said.

Char shuddered. 'I absolutely hate to think what his last moments must have been like.'

'We could all bring along something to read, a poem or piece of prose, something pertinent,' suggested Bill Marshall.

'Excellent idea.'

'And a bottle,' someone said. 'Raise a glass to the bloke.'

'Hear, hear,' Bill agreed. 'He and I had had our ups and downs – as most of you know – but nobody could possibly wish him dead.'

While he spoke, we had all done our level best not to look at Helen Marshall. Dressed in some kind of grey wool outfit and sensible (i.e. frump's) shoes, she didn't seem like the sort of woman that two guys would come to blows over.

'How about inviting Chris Kearns to say a few words?' someone else said. 'He was a friend of Milo's. He wouldn't have to stay long or anything. But it would show solidarity, wouldn't it?'

We all agreed that it would. What with, wasn't clear.

'What about his wife?' I'd asked. 'Stanton's, I mean. Tamasin.'

'Good question.' They'd looked at one another and nodded.

'I envisage this as a purely private occasion,' said Char, who had assumed a leadership role. 'Just us am-drams. Otherwise Tamasin might feel we're trespassing on her private territory.'

'Belittling her grief sort of thing.'

'Who's going to contact Kearns?' asked Ricky.

'I'll do it, if you like.' Bill Marshall had looked from one to another of us. 'I appeared in a play with him once, years ago, one of those one-line, the-carriage-awaits-my-Lord parts, up in Darlington. Me, obviously, not him, although it was still a while before he'd made it big.'

'Has anyone read his book?' Helen Marshall asked. 'I enjoyed it, though, dear me, what a terrible life he's had.'

'I have.' I said. 'I thought it was pretty good. Very well written.'

'Hard to believe one man could have suffered so many tragedies,' Helen had said. 'Wife, son, daughter . . . what next?'

'I remember Milo telling me something about the daughter,' said Char. 'A drug overdose, as far as I remember.'

'Terrible,' repeated Helen.

In the High Street, I waved at Edward Vine as he shifted bottles and labels around in his shop window. Exchanged a few words about lemon cookies with Major Horrocks, who was just coming out of the Fox and Hounds, and received with thanks the paper bag of almond ones ('*made 'em myself,*') he pressed on me. I walked into the bookshop, where I found

Sam Willoughby pouring himself a coffee from the pot which was perpetually on the go.

'Make that two,' I said. 'And cream in mine, if you please.'

'Yes, madam.'

I sat down at one of his little café tables. 'If you have tears, prepare to shed them now,' I said, when he joined me. I handed him an almond cookie. 'At least – don't. But tell me in what circumstances you *might* shed them.'

'If someone I loved – you, for instance – died. I'd definitely shed them then.'

I ignored the subtext. 'What about if you were in the middle of murdering someone?'

'Tears and murder don't seem to go together. Not if it's the murderer shedding them.'

I explained about the tear-traces that had been found on the bodies of Milo Stanton and Tristan Huber. 'I've been trying to imagine why someone with a sharp knife, wired up enough to be slicing pieces of flesh from a body, let alone smashing his broken knees with a sledgehammer, would be weeping as he did so. What possible reason could there be?' It had seemed an important piece of information when DCI Fairlight passed it on. It still did. It still told me nothing.

'Very strange,' commented Sam. 'Perhaps he felt guilty about it. Or sorry for what he was doing.'

'Could the killer have been forced to do the deed by a third party?' I suggested.

Sam looked at me sideways. 'In that case, might it have been a woman?'

'Why do you say that?'

'Because – and present company excepted, of *course* – a) women are more easily coerced than men, and b) having been coerced, they're more likely to weep. Especially if they're being compelled into some bizarre or barbaric misdeed.'

'That's an interesting thought.' Had Alan Garside considered that one?

'On the other hand, why would a killer want to get someone else to do his dirty work?'

'I can think of various reasons. As a punishment, for a start. Or something as simple as voyeurism.'

'Or perhaps they were making a snuff movie.'

'That's a bit improbable.'

'No more so than any other suggestion. How about he somehow induces the actual killer to do his dirty work for him because he doesn't want to leave evidence which would point to him/her? Because obviously he/she would know that the police would eventually be investigating it.'

'Or can't use his own hands for some reason?' I tried to remember if I knew anyone even remotely connected to the case who had lost the use of a hand.

'Or for some kind of bizarre revenge on the knife-wielder rather than on the victim himself?'

'Exactly. But it all seems pretty far-fetched to me,' I said. 'And if you think about it, the third person would surely then have to kill the actual perpetrator if he didn't want to blow his own cover.'

'Could the third person also be a woman? For instance, say Tristan had remarried after the departure of Christie, and the new wife discovered he'd been having an affair with someone, so she forced the lover to kill him. Sounds like a convenient way to kill two birds, don't you think?'

'Why not?' I shrugged. 'Anything's possible.'

But I think we both knew this scenario was too fantastical to be true. Like most of the others we'd come up with.

My phone buzzed. I took it out of my bag, click it open and listened. It was Fliss Fairlight. 'Quick, get this . . . There's been another murder!'

'Oh, no,' I groaned. 'Who this time?'

'Some old geezer, lives on the Dovebridge Road, in that little group of cottages on the left as you drive into Fonthill. Used to run a one-man taxi service.'

'Dibdin,' I said.

'How the hell did you know that?'

'I have my sources.'

'Poor old boy was apparently shot in his own car. Someone had clearly waited for him to come out of his house and get in his car to go to work, before opening the door and shooting him. Or so forensics says, and we have no reason not to trust their judgement.'

'Golly. Didn't anyone hear him? He must have shouted for help.'

'His neighbours are all blind or deaf or both. So nobody came to help him. Poor old boy.'

'From what I heard, he was a pretty nasty old boy as well. So a wide field of suspects, I suppose.'

'As so often, Quick, you suppose right.' I didn't contradict her, despite the whole Triad fiasco. 'Yup,' she continued. 'We've a whole long list of people he'd pissed off.'

'Any of them connected to the murders round here?'

'Can't see the slightest connection. At least, at the moment.'

'Did anything come out of that think-fest Garside organized?'

'Zilch. A few wildly improbable ideas but nothing remotely useful.'

'So after all this time, you're no further forward?'

'More or less. But you didn't hear it from me. By the way, Garside's holding a press conference later today.'

'At this stage in the proceedings, any particular reason?' I asked.

'The Press've been all over him, demanding to know what's going on, we can't sleep safe in our beds until this lunatic has been brought to book murders are more important than speeding tickets, yada yada yada. Maybe you should drop by, sneak in at the back.'

'And maybe not,' I said. 'Unless I'm in deep disguise. If he sees me, there'd be hell to pay. For both of us.'

'Hmmm . . . I'll keep you posted.'

The rest of the day drifted by. Desultorily, I put together more work-notes. Truth to tell, much as I loved working on my art compilations, I was beginning to feel there wasn't enough action in my life. I wanted to be back in the thick of crime investigating, alongside my still-friendly colleagues. The Love Rat had left town, along with his ever-increasing family *('I'm not ready to be a father.'* Huh!), and there was no reason why I shouldn't return to the force – if they'd have me.

Later, having bought two terrific cheeses from *Fromage*, our local cheese vendor, plus a walnut and olive loaf, I discovered – as I'd anticipated – that they went wonderfully together with a glass or two of the Merlot I got from the new wine shop Edward Vine had mentioned.

Expecting nothing, I turned on the TV. And nothing was exactly what I got. I flipped through a dozen channels or so, and then hit one which gave me a repeat of an episode from last season's Chris Kearns hit. I watched for six minutes, while he gurned away, scampered about, side-splittingly extricated himself from the most improbable scrapes. Trouble was, my sides remained resolutely unsplit.

Life's too short . . . I switched off. His book lay on the table in front of me. On a piece of bread I spread a thick layer of absolutely *á point* Chaourse, melting out of its crust and on to the plate, swallowed a swig of my wine. Oh, bliss! Little things really do mean a lot. The ghastly programme had reminded me that I still had a good quarter of Kearns's book to finish. I picked it up and turned to where I had left off. The chapter was entitled 'Eunice', and was about his dead druggie daughter. Most of the coppers I know are like me: not hugely sympathetic to the users, and even less so to the dealers, who to a large extent manage to keep themselves hidden in the shadows. So I wasn't expecting to feel warm and fuzzy about the girl.

According to her father, she'd never taken drugs before (but he would say that, wouldn't he?) and that night, it was only because one bastard at a party she attended had given her a tab of Ecstasy. For those reading his tale who didn't know, he obligingly detailed some of the symptoms related to taking MDMA.

-A euphoric state of being.
-A distorted perception of time.
-Increased levels of sexual arousal.
-A heightening of mental awareness.

Classic stuff. I'd seen many of them displayed in my days on the force. I'd also seen the bodies of some of those who succumbed to the negative effects of the drug.

As far as the police could work out from witness statements given by some of those who had attended the party, Eunice had swallowed the pill her boyfriend had given it to her, and almost immediately began displaying the euphoria connected with introducing MDMA into the system. Again, Kearns quoted some of them.

'Floating round the room as though she was sitting on a cloud,' said one person.

'Told me she was a balloon . . .'

'Started kissing me, pushed her hand down my trousers.'

'Kept saying embarrassing stuff like "stick it in me, baby."'

'Swaying about, knocking into things.'

'Pulled down her top so we could all see her boobies.'

'Embarrassing.'

'Humiliating.'

'Honestly didn't know where to put myself.'

My daughter was my entire life, Kearns had written. *The fairy on my Christmas tree, the candle on my cake, the apple of my eye. She gave meaning to everything I had achieved. She enhanced me.*

He went on to say that he couldn't blame anyone but Eunice herself. Apparently she'd had an argument with the boyfriend, had stumbled out into the cold air in high-heeled sandals and skimpy clothes, had thrown up all over herself and been found in an alley near to the small hotel where she was planning to stay the night. She'd been raped and half-strangled.

I put the book down. It made painful reading. And right on cue, the phone rang.

Char Plimpton said, 'I've just been reading Chris Kearns's book.'

'So have I.'

'Have you got to the chapter about his daughter?'

'That's exactly where I was up to. Not an easy read.'

'I'll say. But had you cottoned on to the fact that the college she went to the party at, the Christmas do, was *here*? Up on the hill?'

'*What*?'

'Yes.'

'He doesn't say so.'

'But it's true. One of the students who was there at the time told me.'

I thought rapidly. 'Come to think of it, he doesn't really mention names or places, does he?'

'Perhaps he's afraid of a libel action.'

'I wonder why nobody ever talks about it. It doesn't reflect too well on the college authorities, does it?'

'Nor the student body.'

'Do you think poor Milo was involved?'

'I should think he'd more or less have to be since he was one of the chief organizers of the party where it happened. Him and that Kevin Fuller guy. Fuller and Milo were pretty close, from what I've been told.'

'Are we any further on this memorial meeting for Milo?'

'Yes, indeed. And the good news is that Chris Kearns has agreed to come. So since he'll be down in this part of the world on Tuesday next, we'll have it then. Chris can only stay for an hour or so, so Bill Marshall will organize things round that.'

'I'll be there.'

TWENTY-THREE

Fifteen of us were grouped round a table in the middle of the room. Charlotte had taken charge of the evening and organized us into making an effort to produce something of a festive occasion ('*Celebrating Milo's life rather than mourning his death.*'). A red tablecloth covered the table, with a vase of red roses standing on it, next to a framed headshot of Milo. There were stemmed glasses and bottles of wine. Char had arrived with some upmarket nibbles: tiny squares of home-made pizza, miniature smoked-salmon blinis. I'd brought a block of excellent Double Gloucester, another of Caerphilly, plus oatmeal cakes, knives and a board to cut the cheese on. Others had contributed generously. The result was that it looked as though we were having a slap-up party, instead joining together for a sorrowful occasion.

But . . . 'It's what Milo would have wished,' we kept on assuring each other as we refilled our glasses and toasted his photograph again and again. I was glad I had arranged for Sam to pick me up at the end of the evening.

Nearly an hour passed with the noise in the room increasing. 'Is Chris Kearns coming?' Ricky asked Bill Marshall. 'Or should we start our readings without him?'

'He said he was. Said he might be a bit late, though.'

'How late is a bit?'

'Your guess is as good as mine.'

We heard a door slam and echo in the halls below the room we were in. Footsteps came running up the stairs. Then silence. Char went across and opened the door, stuck out her head, said, 'We're in here!'

'So sorry I'm late, guys. Signal failure outside Faversham.' Kearns came into the room, shaking his shoulders like a dog who'd just emerged from the sea. Rain drops flew off his jacket.

'Here, have this.' Bill Marshall handed him a glass of red.

'Thanks.' Kearns looked round at us. 'Just what the doctor ordered.' He hoicked a couple of blinis off a plate and stuffed them into his mouth. 'Mmm, lovely,' he said, when he could talk.

There was more chat, until Bill Marshall clapped his hands. 'Since Chris can't stay for too long, we'd better get on with the next part of the proceedings. Tributes to our friend Milo would be good. Just a few words . . . anyone want to start?'

A man I hadn't noticed previously put up his hand. 'I'd like to say something.'

'Go ahead, Don.'

'I joined this group more or less as therapy,' Don said earnestly. 'Not because I had any particular wish to tread the boards sort of thing, but to try to get over depression after my mother died. Milo was wonderful, so encouraging, so kind, everything a mentor should be. A real help.' He looked up at the ceiling. 'Milo, I wish you the best of everything, wherever you may be.'

Someone else chimed in. 'I'm never going to be any kind of a thesp . . . I'm too awkward, too self-conscious . . . but Milo was such an inspirational leader that sometimes I just thought I might.'

More tributes followed. Marshall looked at me, but I shook my head. I hadn't been part of the group long enough to have anything meaningful to say.

Chris Kearns raised his hand. 'If I might . . .' Everyone nodded vigorously.

He took a deep breath. 'I've known Milo for many years. He was just a broth of a boy – no more than fourteen or fifteen – when he came round to the stage door at the theatre where I was playing Tony Lumpkin in *She Stoops To Conquer*. Wanted to know if I could help him get work in the theatre, said he'd do anything, make the tea, clean the loos, didn't mind how menial the jobs were. I asked him to show me what he could do, and he launched into something from the Scottish play. Frankly, he was terrible – but you could see that he had promise and, better than that, he was absolutely focussed and determined. Naturally, I advised trying to get into one of the drama schools, but he didn't want to do that, said he wanted hands-on experience. The roar of the greasepaint, the smell of the crowd – that's what he was after, authenticity, the real thing.

'Well, I did what I could for him, gave him a few tips, but it wasn't much. Time drifted by. After a while, we lost whatever touch we had. And then years later, he came round to another stage door at another theatre where I was playing, wanting to buy me a drink. Over a couple of pints he told me what he was doing, that he was still focussed on the dream, and that the advice I'd given him was invaluable. I couldn't even remember what I told him all that time ago, but the point was that we became friends, saw quite a bit of each other, kept in touch. I liked him, people. I'd go so far as to say I loved him like a – like a son.'

Everyone in the room was silently aware of the tragedy of his true son. 'He hadn't yet achieved what he wanted to, but I was sure that one day he would.' There was a dramatic and well-timed pause. His voice broke. He raised a knuckle to his eye. 'But now he never will.'

Behind me, someone was snivelling quietly. 'So,' Kearns said, 'let's raise our glasses to a man who never gave up. A man with talent and courage. A man who would surely one day have realized his dream.' He sniffed a bit, laid a hand on his heart, and added, 'Milo Stanton, we salute you.'

We all applauded this performance, delivered without notes, as though Kearns had memorized it in advance, just as he would have done a theatrical piece. Which I suppose in a way it was. Tears were standing in his eyes.

'That was lovely, Chris.' Charlotte Plimpton led a round of applause. 'Now, most of us have brought something to read that was appropriate to the circumstances, and that we thought Milo might appreciate.' She looked across the table at Chris Kearns and clasped her hands together. 'Please don't judge us too harshly.'

'As if I would,' he said, giving her a warm smile.

Someone read *Do Not Stand at My Grave and Weep.* Char chose Emily Dickinson's *Because I could not stop for Death.* In sonorous tones, Bill Marshall read *Fear no more the heat o' the sun.*

There were more offerings: A Burial Vault poem, Dylan Thomas's *Do Not Go Gentle Into That Good Night, When I have Fears that I may Cease to Be,* a prose piece, a charming description of a Northumberland country churchyard from a Victorian travel guide. I'd opted for something short and expressive, by Rainer Maria Rilke.

Before us great Death stands
Our fate held close within his quiet hands.
When with proud joy we lift Life's red wine
To drink deep of the mystic shining cup
And ecstasy through all our being leaps—
Death bows his head and weeps.

Concise and apposite, I thought smugly. And definitely not over the top. I lifted my mystic shining cup of Life's red wine to my mouth, and noticed that it was empty. Shame . . . but I would refill it shortly.

While we were mingling, before finally bringing the evening to a close and setting off back to our various homes, Chris Kearns came over to me. 'Nice to see you again, Alex,' he said. 'How's it going?'

'Just fine. You?' I tried not to wrinkle my nose at the whiff of old cigarettes which accompanied him.

His expressive clown's mouth turned down. 'About as well as could be expected,' he said. 'And that was never very high.'

'I've been reading your book,' I said. 'You write extremely well.'

'Why, thank you. That's very kind of you.'

'You've really taken some hard knocks.'

'I'll say.'

I plunged in with a question I had been dying to ask. 'Someone told me that your daughter's death occurred after a Christmas party right here at the college.'

He tensed, tight as a hangman's rope after the trap has opened. He looked round then lowered his voice. 'Where did you hear that?'

'As an ex-copper, I never reveal my sources,' I told him, smiling firmly to show I meant it.

'I deliberately didn't mention it in the book. I didn't want to upset the college, or let them think I was implying that they were somehow to blame for Zoe's death. Nor did I want to deal with a libel suit or something of the kind.'

'Zoe?'

'My daughter. I call her Eunice in the book.' His mouth twisted with sad irony. 'It means "joyous victory" or "she conquers". Unfortunately, my poor Zoe didn't.'

'I'm so sorry, Chris.'

'Thank you. So you're a copper?'

'Ex.'

He clapped his hand to his forehead. 'God, my memory! It's all coming back . . . and now you concentrate on art appreciation and anthologies and things like that, is that right?'

'It is.'

'I apologize for not remembering . . . I meet so many people. So you've put your sleuthing days behind you?'

'More or less. I do still look into criminal matters from time to time. I mean, if someone particularly asks me to.'

He laughed. 'In a town the size of this one, that can't happen a lot.'

'You'd be surprised. We've had a spate of brutal murders

in the area over the past few weeks. One of them being the brother of a friend of mine.'

'But that's horrible!' He touched my sleeve. 'I'm sorry . . . how awful.'

'I know. My friend is devastated, as you can imagine.' Remembering his lost daughter, I wished I hadn't mentioned Tristan's death. 'She asked me if I'd monitor the progress the police are making because she feels they won't keep her in the picture as regards their enquiries.'

'Don't they have liaison officers and so on to deal with that sort of thing?'

'They do . . . but I can well imagine that my friend – and the victim's mother – would spurn that kind of comfort.' I could so easily visualize Dorcas, her face screwed up in dragon mode, spilling 'Pshaws' all over the place, and demanding to know why the police weren't getting on with the job of catching murderers, instead of wasting their time providing spurious aid and reassurance to people who didn't want or need it.

'Well . . . I'm sorry on your friend's behalf. I know what it feels like.'

'Of course you do.'

We exchanged rueful expressions and went our separate ways.

I know what it feels like . . . an innocuous enough phrase. Anyone might have used it. I wished it hadn't so closely resembled the phrase that Ned Swift's and Kevin Fuller's families, and Dorcas herself, had heard whispered down the phone.

The next day, I waited until I knew the morning briefing would have taken place at the cop-shop. Then I called Fliss Fairlight. 'Any news on Tristan Huber's death?' I asked. 'Or any of the others we've been discussing?'

'Still pursuing enquiries. Garside is not best pleased at the lack of progress. And before you ask, the Landises were let go, but on police bail, suspicion of fraud and theft. And the locals are preparing a raid on Rollins Park even as we speak.'

'Just as I suggested ages ago.'

'That would be "ages" as in eleven days or so.'

'So still no suspects for the murders?'

'Whoever's doing this seems to know exactly how to conceal all traces. We've got DNA from the fags in those disgusting buckets where your friend was killed, but with no one to test it on. Trouble is, so many lowlifes smoke, despite the Government warnings. Could be anyone.'

'Most lowlifes are as thick as a McDonald's triple whopper with half the IQ, whereas our perp clearly isn't,' I said. 'Anyway, thanks, Fliss, for keeping me up to speed. I owe you.'

Brooding over a mug of coffee, I pondered what kind of perpetrator could commit four murders and manage to exit the scenes of crime without leaving a single usable piece of evidence. An experienced one? A practised one? Had there been spates of similar crimes elsewhere which hadn't yet been connected to our local ones? Equally, starting from a different tack, what motive could he have? Four – or possibly five, if Dibdin was somehow connected, though it didn't seem likely – different deaths, with nothing more than a tenuous connection to the university to link them.

I found the piece of paper on which Sam and I had written down what little we knew. There was nothing much to add. Nonetheless, I wrote down the name of Eunice/Zoe Kearns, Chris's daughter. I got out my mobile and pressed in Char Plimpton's number. 'Quick here,' I said, when she answered.

'Hi! That was a good send-off we gave Milo, wasn't it? I thought we—'

'Sorry to interrupt you, Char. You told me that Eunice, or perhaps I should say Zoe, Kearns was at the Christmas party up on the hill.'

'Yeah . . .' she said guardedly.

'She'd taken an Ecstasy tab . . . had words with her boyfriend and run off into the night?'

'That's right.'

I was pretty sure I already knew the answer to my next question. 'Any idea who he was?'

'Of course. He was that poor kid who was killed not long ago. Name of Swift. Ned Swift.'

'What was the quarrel about?'

'From what I've heard on the college grapevine – student

gossip and so on, because I wasn't there, obviously – she was more or less out of her head on E. She tried to insist that the two of them leave. He said he couldn't just walk out, because he was one of the organizers. So she flounced off . . . and we all know what happened next. Poor Chris . . .'

We chatted some more, then I ended the call. The phone immediately buzzed. Fliss Fairlight again. 'You were asking for news, Quick.'

'Yup. What've you got?'

'The case seems to be breaking at last. The Landises have come clean.'

'In what sense?'

'They've revealed all. And believe me, there's quite a lot of all to reveal.'

'Shoot.'

'Your friend Tristan seems to have been one hell of an entrepreneur. The *capo dei capi*, though not as lethal. He had his fingers in dozens of pies. He'd do anything, according to Yvonne and James, that would turn a profit. And most of his enterprises did. Not, oddly enough, that you'd ever know it. Reasonably modest quarters – a rather choice little house in a village near Canterbury – nicely appointed, as they say, but nothing splashy or over the top. Bank balance healthy but nothing more than that. No designer clothes in the wardrobes. No fancy cars in the garage. Good lifestyle, according to his friends and associates, but that was all. No wife or mistress, or children. So what was he spending his dosh on? If the Landises are to be believed – and I think they are, because they're terrified of being handed a sentence – there was plenty of that coming in. *Plenty*. So where the fuck is it?'

'Bank accounts under another name?'

'Naturally that's the first thing we thought of. But we couldn't find any, despite the best efforts of our financial guys. And another thing, James and Yvonne said he liked to deal as far as possible in cash. But thousands and thousands of pounds worth of the stuff, which is what they say he was pulling in . . . where did it go?'

'I take it you've examined his socks? Looked under his mattresses?'

'Real *and* metaphorical. Apparently he didn't trust banks further than he could throw one. So where would he keep it?'

'That much cash, he must have spread it around a bit. It can't all have been in once place.'

'And if you think about it, whatever his prejudices, he must have kept at least some of it in banks or building societies, whatever he may have said.'

'And there'd always be the danger of fire or flood. Or someone either breaking in to wherever it is and lifting the lot, or doing exactly what they . . .' An idea hit me. 'Hey, Fliss, could that be what whoever's responsible was doing; trying to torture him into telling them where he kept his stash?'

'It would explain a lot. But not all the other victims.'

I remembered something else. 'I told you that Tristan employed a sleazeball – in my view – financial manager. Name of Michael Compton.'

'We already talked to him.'

'Talk some more. I bet you could lean on him pretty hard.'

'We'll do that. But, Quick . . .'

'What?'

'The money aspect doesn't explain the other deaths we're dealing with. If we go on assuming that there's a link somewhere.'

'If there *is* one, between us we'll find it.' I sounded a lot more confident than I felt. And in any case, it was really nothing to do with me. I was only on the scene as a participating observer, rather than the other way round, my obligation to Dimsie long since over.

A couple of days went by while I looked at pictures and thought about money. Lots of it. But Tristan didn't trust banks. What did he want it for? Where was it? Was he laundering the stuff? Spreading his assets, buying up property in various parts of the world? What did he want it all for? What did he do with it all? He must have opened accounts in different names and banked at least some of it. These days, you couldn't just board a plane with suitcases stuffed with greasy fivers. Even so, he must have had plenty left to transfer hither and yon, if the Landis/Lockharts were to be believed. And like Fliss, I was inclined to think they were.

Garside was getting somewhere, but without any real lead to the killer of Kevin Fuller, Ned Swift, Tristan or Milo. By now Fliss had filled me in on what the DCI and his team believed had happened. As king-pin of the organization, Tristan was dealing in all the usual crime-syndicate business, drugs, prostitution, trafficking. Plus the rip-off luxury goods, the horses, any other profitable enterprise he could get into.

Marcus Colby had been hauled in. Likewise the Paramores. Turned out that Colby and the Landises handled the luxury items. Tristan himself dealt with the drugs, everything from cannabis to legal highs to crack cocaine, inventing ever more ingenious ways to import, manufacture and distribute them. The Paramores were responsible – as I had guessed – mainly for the poor women tricked into believing they were leaving their home countries for a better life in England, providing a halfway house on the estate. And the Lariat King himself, ol' Hank Rogers, was responsible for the horses. Well, yee-*haw*!

The odd thing was that Tristan seemed not to have faced opposition from other criminal mobs. Until now. The manner of his death had echoes of the punishments inflicted on their victims by the Kray brothers and other East End gangs.

I felt we were (that's me and the police!) near to a final breakthrough in the case. Just one more step, and we'd have the perpetrator. It wouldn't help to keep on mulling all the facts over and over. I thought again of the wake organized for Milo. A good send off, taken all in all. The pieces read, touching on death and churchyards, yew trees and coffins, were mostly standard offerings on similar occasions. It was difficult to come up with a new take on someone dying. I was tired. A hot bath, a wee dram, a good book, an early night, and I'd be dead to the world within fifteen minutes.

Later, nearly asleep, eyes glazing over, I picked up the book beside my bed and attempted to read it. I managed about a paragraph before falling at last into dream-filled slumber.

Which is where the usefulness of dreams came in. I woke the next morning with a clear vision in my head of a small stone vault, roofed with lichened tiles of slate, decorated with carved panelling. There was an area in front of blueish gravel, and round pots on either side of the entrance containing small evergreen shrubs. And I knew exactly where it was.

I felt around the gutter above the door and found the key. I'd been there on a couple of occasions with Tristan, wondering at the time at his display of family piety. I'd stepped inside, ducking my head beneath the stone lintel. Smelled the dust of ages, sensed the presence of ancient bones, of lives long ago ended. Felt the rising queasiness of claustrophobia and stumbled out into the free air, while Tristan remained inside for another ten or fifteen minutes. What had he been doing? I hoped to find at least part of the puzzle.

The edifice was about the size of a small garden shed. I pushed at the little door which led down three or four steps to a larger area where small rectangular plaques were set into the walls. Some were metal, some stone, some even in wood. The only light came from the space above, but I could see each plaque was inscribed with the name of long-ago Huber-Drayton ancestors. I looked round the space. Then walked round all four walls, tapping at the plaques as I went. Several of them were slightly loose. With some difficulty, I prised one halfway open. Inside was a metal box containing God knew what relics of a once-human body. And a large black plastic sack. I reached in, tore at the plastic, caught a glimpse of thick packs of paper money.

'What the hell do you think you're doing?'

I whirled round, slamming the plaque shut. Dorcas stood there, snorting like a wild boar, not quite pawing the ground, but pretty close. 'I'm . . . uh . . .'

'Get out!' She gestured at the steps. 'Get out! How dare you trespass on private property like this!'

'It's me, Dorcas,' I said, fairly sure she couldn't actually make out who I was. 'Alexandra Quick.'

'Alexan . . . What are you doing here?' she demanded. 'What are you looking for?'

'Nothing. It was a trip down memory lane, that's all.' I

wished I'd had time to inspect a couple more of the loosened memorial tablets.

'I must ask you to leave immediately,' Dorcas growled.

Which I did.

From my car, I called Fliss, told her what I'd discovered. 'I'm betting there's masses more cash hidden in that vault. Possibly millions. It might be worth taking a look for yourselves,' I said.

'I can't see how it would help much. How we'd pin it on your Mr Huber, how we'd connect it to our other suspects.' She paused. 'It's an ingenious hiding place, though. Unlikely to burn down. Not subject to wind or weather.'

'Precisely. The loot could stay undisturbed for decades.' I shuddered. 'Oh boy, if ever there was dirty money . . .'

'I'm not sure what grounds we'd have for inspecting the place. I'll put it to Garside.'

As soon as I got home, I ran up the stairs of my flat to the bedroom and picked up Chris Kearns' book. I'd fallen asleep over it last night, but now I read the relevant page a great deal more closely.

The night the police came to inform me of Eunice's death, Kearns had written, *was, without any question, the bitterest and bleakest moment of my life. I had fallen into a pit so black that I could see no way out. If you have never lost a child – and pray God you never do – you cannot begin to understand what it feels like. My heart was nothing but a shrivelled prune caught in the harsh mesh of my pain. My beloved daughter, my adored child, gone for ever, because of a small round pill. The knowledge that if she had been rushed to hospital, she could have been saved, might be living the happy, useful life that was intended for her, has been part of the horror. How can you adequately describe the pain of a child's death? How can you say to people: 'This is what it feels like' and expect them to understand?*

I wept. I screamed. I pounded my hands raw against the walls. I vowed revenge on someone, anyone. The need to avenge her blazed like a white hot flame inside me, searing my soul. But whatever I did, nothing was going to bring

Eunice back. And besides, who could I blame except Eunice herself?

Was he telling the reader something more than merely a description of his agonized feelings at learning of his daughter's death?

I went round to the bookshop. Ordered a coffee. Laid out my suspicions in some detail. 'What do you think?' I said finally.

'I think you've made a very convincing case against the man,' Sam said. 'And it's a lot more sound than those damned Triads.'

TWENTY-FOUR

At his trial, Kearns pleaded guilty to five counts of murder. He was quite open about it, pleading guilty, showing no remorse for the lives eliminated. He had planned it very carefully, taking his time, getting to know his victims first, their habits and routines, then waylaying them, overpowering them and killing them. He blamed Tristan first and foremost for supplying the Class A drugs at the college's Christmas party where his daughter Zoe died, although evidence at her inquest revealed that despite his insistence that she had not touched a drug before, she had been a regular user for several years.

'I took my time over Huber,' he told the courtroom in a final statement, 'as I held him particularly responsible not only for my daughter's death but for the ruin of many other young people. He was a liar and a cheat. I felt very strongly that with his upbringing, and all the social and financial advantages he enjoyed, he should be punished as severely as possible.' He cleared his throat.

'Kevin Fuller was different. He had assured the university authorities that, as one of the principal party organizers, he would be keeping a careful eye on the students attending. The threat of drugs at this kind of gathering is always going to be a matter of concern. The same went for Milo Stanton.'

He had looked around the court. It was very obvious that he saw this as a final appearance in front of his public. 'I was sorry,' he said. 'From all reports, Fuller was a good man. But he reneged on his promises when he not only tolerated drugs on the premises in the first place but also allowed my daughter to consume the Ecstasy tablet which eventually was the cause of her death. As for Milo . . . I loved the man. So did Zoe. She would have trusted him to see that she came to no harm. And with what result?'

The spectators in the gallery listened to his testimony with disbelief. The man had clearly been driven out of his mind by grief, and seemed unable to see how irrational his arguments were.

'As for the boyfriend, Swift, I had no prior knowledge of him, but how could he have let a girl who was clearly suffering from the effects of an illegal substance just leave, late on a dark winter night in December? How could he do that?'

The judge pointed out at this juncture that the court had heard that Ned Swift and Zoe Kearns had only been out together a couple of times and that in the opinion of other students, it was only because kind-hearted Ned had felt sorry for her, had referred to her as a serious oddball without any friends.

'Nonsense,' Kearns had replied. 'Zoe was a warm and loveable girl, with many friends and a great future ahead.'

His fifth and last victim had been Dibdin, the taxi-driver. In the course of his research, he had noticed that the old boy would come out on cold mornings and start his taxi up, leave it in front of his house to warm up the engine before driving off to start his day's work. Zoe had climbed into his cab after running out of the party venue and as far as the police could conjecture, had thrown up on the back seat, at which point the cantankerous old fellow had turned her out into the street, not caring how she would get home. When he'd driven off, some scumbag had emerged from the shadows, dragged her into an alleyway, raped her and then strangled her. In revenge, Kearns had simply waited one morning until Dibdin came out of his house and climbed into his taxi, then shot him, and made a quick getaway. It might have remained an unsolved killing if Kearns hadn't eventually confessed.

'You almost felt sorry for Kearns,' I told Sam later.

'Not really,' Sam said. 'He was playing to the gallery – quite literally.'

'I know, but even so . . .'

'I thought he was an arrogant, narcissistic sod with a pronounced God-complex, who felt that the world owed him,' Sam said firmly. He cut me another slice of the walnut-and-Stilton quiche he had brought with him. 'I can't say your friend Tristan will be much missed, but four other more or less innocent people died for his daughter, three at least of them with far more potential than she would ever have. I hope he doesn't forget that when they lock him up for good.'

Which they never did. Kearns evaded justice by hanging himself in his cell, knotting together his shirt-sleeves to produce a makeshift noose. He hadn't been put on suicide watch, mostly because of his cocky attitude. He seemed to be convinced that he had the sympathy of the court, that the judge and jury would find his actions no more than any reasonable parent might have committed.

A week later, my parents telephoned to say that Dorcas Huber-Drayton was in hospital and not expected to survive. Apparently she had suffered a heart attack and fallen into the blazing bonfire she was tending in her garden, ending up with third-degree burns over half her body.

'I didn't even know she had a heart,' Dimsie commented. 'Poor old girl.'

Sam and I were sitting with her in Dorcas's drawing room, drinking a glass of white wine. It was a gloomy day, with the sun bursting through scudding cloud to illumine the garden and the churchyard next to it.

'The revelations about Tristan can't have made her very happy.'

'Well, they wouldn't, would they?' Dimsie stared gloomily round the room. 'I suppose all this is mine now. And I *so* don't want it.'

'I'm still not clear why she had lit a bonfire in the first place,' I said. 'I'd have thought that was Gibson's job.'

'Yes. Except it wasn't garden rubbish that she was disposing of.' Dimsie held out her glass with something – actually, a lot – of her mother's imperiousness, and waited while Sam refilled it for her.

'It was money, wasn't it?' I said.

'How the hell did you know that?'

'Just a lucky guess.' I was fairly sure that having seen me in the Huber-Drayton vault, Dorcas had gone back into it as soon as I'd left, and discovered – if she hadn't already been aware – the huge amounts of money stashed there by her son. She'd removed it, before the police could do so, and then burned it when the revelations about Tristan had begun to emerge.

Now Sam and I sat close together on my own sofa. 'Are you really going to go to New Zealand?' I said. There was a crumb of Stilton on the edge of his mouth and I reached up to dab it away.

'Would you miss me if I did?' he asked.

I thought about it. 'Actually, yes,' I said eventually.

He put an arm round my shoulders. 'Is that all?'

Curved in his embrace, I looked up at him. He was a lovely man. 'I'd miss you more than I can possibly say,' I said. And I meant it.

Lightning Source UK Ltd.
Milton Keynes UK
UKOW04f0340200118
316484UK00001B/4/P